DOCTOR WHO

FESTIVAL OF DEATH
JONATHAN MORRIS

D1215792

BBC

Published by BBC Worldwide Ltd,
Woodlands, 80 Wood Lane
London W12 0TT

First published 2000
Copyright © Jonathan Morris 2000
The moral right of the author has been asserted

Original series broadcast on the BBC
Format © BBC 1963
Doctor Who and TARDIS are trademarks of the BBC

ISBN 0 563 53803 1
Imaging by Black Sheep, copyright © BBC 2000

Printed and bound in Great Britain by Mackays of Chatham
Cover printed by Belmont Press Ltd, Northampton

To Katie

Huge thanks to my read-through people, to whom I am very indebted; Mark Clapham, Helen Fayle, Sietel Gill, Matt Kimpton, Jon Miller, Mark Phippen, Henry Potts and Ben Woodhams. And special thanks to Sarah Lavelle, Jac Rayner and Justin Richards, for their patience and understanding.

Extra bonus thanks go to Gary Russell, Who_Ink and all @ Mute.

This book should be read on a Saturday at about tea-time.

Prologue

For the rest of his life he would remember it as the day he died.

Koel's mum took a stern breath and tightened her grip on her son's wrist. Koel twisted against her, tugging at her arm, trying to pull her attention down to him.

The voice of the intercom soothed over the hubbub. 'It is my pleasure to inform you that the Alpha Twelve intersystem shuttle is now boarding. All passengers for Third Birmingham should make their way to embarkation lounge seven. Felicitations.'

'That's us,' his mum sighed. 'Time we were gone.'

Koel looked at his dad, willing him to notice his discomfort. His dad smiled and walked away, swinging their baggage over his shoulder. He hopped on to the escalator and rose into the air, the glass-walled tube climbing through the vaulted ceiling of the spaceport.

Koel's mum dragged him forward and he tripped on the metal steps, surprised by the upward rush and the ever-lengthening stairwell beneath them. Below, the crowds swirled through the terraced shops, and then the sight vanished abruptly as he and his mum emerged into the blackness of space. The exterior of the dome was grey and lifeless, crawling with skeletal antennae.

Through the glass walls Koel watched the amber lights swimming past. Closer, he could see a young boy rising on an identical escalator beside him. The boy wore a sky-green duffle coat and stared silently back at him, tears dribbling down his cheeks.

Koel tasted salt on his lips. He could hear the shouting through his bedroom wall. He couldn't make out the words, but the conversation kept on growing louder until each time his mum would shush his dad, reminding him that Koel was upstairs. Koel curled himself into his duvet, trying to force himself to sleep.

His mum entered his room and switched on the bedside lamp, and Koel pretended to blink awake. She began to speak but her voice cracked, her tears bubbling up from inside. She told him to pack his clothes, not forgetting underpants and socks. They would be going on a sort of holiday, she said. When he asked where to, she told him it was rude to ask questions, and added that they wouldn't be able to take Benji. Koel cried into the dog's fur for a final time and then made it chase outside after an imaginary biscuit. For a moment Benji drooled in confusion, but then noticed an interesting smell and disappeared into the night.

An hour later, they were shutting all the doors and creeping out of the residential block. Koel had never been outside this late before and marvelled at the unearthly lightness of the sky and the silhouetted city towers. The air was chilly and wet, and Koel buried himself into his coat collar as they drove away.

'It is my pleasure to inform you that this is the final boarding announcement for the Alpha Twelve intersystem shuttle to Third Birmingham. Passengers should present their passes at embarkation lounge seven. Felicitations.'

Koel was plucked off the shifting walkway and deposited on to the grid-patterned carpet of the departure lounge. They hurried past the rows of moulded seating to join his dad in the fenced maze snaking towards the entrance of the airlock. A row of passengers shuffled ahead of them, offering their pass cards to the stewardess. In the airlock two masked security guards glowered at the procession of travellers. Their masks were bulbous, like the heads of giant insects.

A window filled one wall of the lounge, overlooking the bulk of the intersystem shuttle. The shuttle wallowed in the blackness, constrained only by its umbilical access tube. Koel could see the passengers picking their way along the pipeline.

Fear washed over his body. There was something malevolent about the shuttle.

Koel's dad reached the checkout desk and fished three pass cards from his jacket. The stewardess swished the cards through a reader and three times the reader buzzed its rejection. The stewardess frowned and punched the codes in manually.

'I don't know what's happened,' his dad protested. 'Maybe the cards got damaged. They worked fine on the skybus.'

'Mum…' Koel felt the sweat on his mum's palm.

'Do you have any other identification?' asked the stewardess.

Koel's dad fumbled in his pockets and presented the stewardess with some crumpled certificates. She skimmed through them. 'That all seems to be in order, thank you. Enjoy your flight.'

Koel's dad hauled their bags on to his back. Koel's mum followed him into the airlock, dragging Koel behind her, his shoes skidding across the floor.

The fear swept over Koel again, like a black chill. He froze.

Koel's mum squatted down. 'Now what is it?'

'I don't wanna go.'

'Well, we can't always do what we want, can we?'

'Won't.'

'What do you mean, "Won't"?' growled his dad. They were attracting disapproving looks from their fellow passengers. His dad moved to one side to allow the remaining travellers to troop past.

'We don't have time for this,' said Koel's mum. The two security guards had noticed the disturbance and turned their insect faces towards them.

'There's something bad. I can feel it,' said Koel. 'Please –'

'Move along,' rasped an electronic voice. 'We're sealing the tube.'

'I'll meet you in the ship.' Koel's dad turned and followed the last of the passengers down the access tube.

'Koel, you're coming with us and that's the end of it.' Koel's mum tugged at his arm so hard he thought it would snap.

The two guards clicked their rifles back into their belts and retreated into the lounge. One of them punched a sequence of triangles on the wall. There was a hydraulic hissing and the airlock door began to shut. A red warning beacon flashed on.

'No!' Koel slid out of his mum's handhold and ducked through the closing door. He pelted into the departure lounge, past the insect guards, past the stewardess. He heard his mum call out to him, but she seemed removed, unreal. Then her voice was silenced as the airlock clanged shut.

Koel raced as far as his breath would carry him and collapsed into a chair, sobbing.

'It is my pleasure to inform you that the Alpha Twelve intersystem shuttle to Third Birmingham is now closed. Felicitations.'

His mum and dad would be angry, Koel knew. But he had no

choice; the thought of the shuttle made him numb with terror.

Wiping his nose on his sleeve, Koel got to his feet and walked back to the observation window. Looking up, he could see the ghostly reflection wearing the sky-green duffle coat floating in the vacuum outside.

One of the guards approached him, removing his mask. The man had bushy eyebrows, and a round, weathered face.'And what do you think –'

Koel screwed his eyes shut.

There was a wrenching sound. The screech of metal buckling, the rattle of bolts tearing. Koel felt the reverberation rising through the floor. Somehow he knew what was going to happen next.

The access tube snapped.

It telescoped away, looping through the blackness. The orange lamps flickered and died, the framework shattering into a thousand whirling metal fragments.

The stewardess screamed. An alarm sounded and a warning light soaked the room with its bloody glow.

Then came the passengers. They spilled out of the access tube and floated towards the observation window. Their bodies were twisted like broken dolls, their faces frozen in shock. They bounced noiselessly against the glass.

Koel's mum's face was a livid mass of exploded blood vessels, a spray of red bubbles escaping her open mouth. His dad still had a luggage bag in one hand.

Chapter One

An impossible machine whisked randomly through the time–space vortex. It resembled a police box, a squat blue booth that might normally contain a twentieth-century English policeman nursing a mug of tea, but was in fact the TARDIS, a craft of unimaginable sophistication belonging to an equally impossible Time Lord known only as the Doctor.

Vastly bigger on the inside than the outside, the TARDIS contained a white, roundelled control room, where the central column of the six-sided console was rising and dipping contentedly. Beside it, the Doctor lay sprawled across a chair. A small battered book on his lap was also rising and dipping contentedly, in time to his deep, mellow snores.

Romana, the Doctor's Time Lady companion, strode into the console room, followed by K9, their small, dog-shaped computer. She observed the Doctor, unimpressed, and crouched down to speak into his ear.

'Revision going well, Doctor?'

'What?' The Doctor woke with a start. Realising where he was, he adjusted his multicoloured scarf. 'Yes. Very well. Absolutely well indeed.'

Romana retrieved the book, brushed back her long blonde hair and thumbed through the pages. 'All right then. Describe the procedure for realigning the synchronic multiloop stabiliser.'

'Ha!' snorted the Doctor, slumping back into his chair. 'Easy.'

He fell silent. Romana tapped her heels.

'Realigning the synchronic multiloop stabiliser?' considered the Doctor. 'First you adjust the proximity feedback converter, recalibrate the triple vector zigzag oscillator, take away the number you first thought of, and there you are. Stabiliser realigned.'

Romana sighed. 'Wrong.'

'What?' The Doctor bounded over to her. 'Wrong? How could I be wrong?'

'To realign the synchronic multiloop stabiliser, simply activate the analogue osmosis dampener.' Romana held the book open for him. He clutched the book and boggled at it.

'Activate the analogue osmosis dampener. I didn't even know there was an analogue osmosis dampener. All these years and no one's ever told me about the analogue osmosis dampener.' The Doctor flicked through *The Continuum Code* and then returned it, unread, to Romana. 'I knew there was a good reason it wasn't working properly.'

'Doctor, you're never going to pass if you don't make an effort,' chided Romana. She knelt down beside K9 and rubbed his ear sensors. 'Isn't that right, K9?'

K9 whirred and raised his head. 'Affirmative mistress. Current likelihood of Doctor master achieving a sufficient score in basic time travel proficiency test estimated at zero point one per cent.'

'Pah!' The Doctor circled the console. 'Some of us don't need fancy certificates, you know.'

'Doctor,' said Romana delicately. His lack of academic achievements was a sore subject with him, and typically he was trying to bluster his way out of the argument. 'Without your time travel proficiency, you're not qualified to operate the TARDIS. If you hadn't failed the test at the academy…'

'I did not fail.' The Doctor bristled. 'I didn't take it.'

'You didn't turn up for it, you mean.'

'Why should I turn up, what's the point? I mean, what's the point in turning up for something…' The Doctor spluttered for a sufficiently weighty word. '… Pointless.'

Romana took a slow breath. 'You do realise your neurosis is the result of a deep-rooted inferiority complex, don't you?'

'Inferiority complex?' The Doctor fixed her with a probing stare. 'What could I possibly have to feel inferior about? Me? K9, have you ever heard anything so ridiculous?'

'Affirmative, master,' replied K9. 'You have frequently made statements with greater nonsensical content.'

'And when I want your opinion I'll ask for it.' The Doctor glared at the robot dog.

'Taking the test might help you come to terms with your past failure,' suggested Romana. 'You obviously regret your wasted years at the academy.'

'I don't regret anything. Never look back, Romana. You can't change your own past. It's in that book of yours, second law of time travel.'

'I think you'll find it's the first law.' Romana whispered into his ear. 'Doctor, unless you pass this test I will have no choice but to insist that I drive.'

'All right, all right.' The Doctor straightened his coat and rounded on the console. 'Test me again. Let's see who's the neurotic one around here.' He aimed the last remark at K9.

Romana smirked at the Doctor, and read aloud. '"Practical examination. When encountering causal instability, it may become necessary to relocate your time vehicle to a real-universe location of safety. It is important the 'emergency materialisation', as it is known, is performed as quickly and smoothly as possible."'

'Quickly and smoothly.' The Doctor cleared his throat.

'Right. When I slap the console, I want you to materialise the TARDIS. Ready?'

The Doctor hunched over the controls. Romana outstretched her palm and slapped the console hard.

In a flurry, the Doctor pulled levers and flipped switches, darting around the controls, his eyes raised towards the central column. He gently lowered the materialisation lever. The column revolved and sank and the familiar landing sounds trumpeted into life. The Doctor smoothed his brow and grinned.

A hideous grinding, like gears crunching out of alignment, filled the air. The lights dimmed and the floor lurched away from beneath Romana's feet, sending her spinning into the walls. She gripped the edges of a roundel, bracing herself as the room began to judder wildly out of control.

The turbulence hurled K9 across the floor and he crashed into the Doctor's chair. The Doctor remained at the console, hands scrabbling across the controls.

Romana craned forward, her hair whipping across her face. 'Doctor! Activate the analogue osmosis dampener!'

The Doctor looked back at her uncomprehendingly, the TARDIS instruments fizzling around him.

Romana couldn't help thinking he was never going to pass at this rate.

The late summer sun dappled through the canopy, the beams cascading through the lazy spray of the waterfall. Nyanna felt the warm light play across her face, her delicate, transparent skin soaking in the vapour. The condensation rushed through her veins, refreshing and nourishing her, and her membranes rippled into a rich green. She inhaled the humid air and luxuriated in the stillness. It would be her last chance, for a while.

The stream splashed into the canyon through the tangle of fronds and root leaves. The entrance to the canyon was a gash in the moss-drenched rock and Nyanna hesitated at the sight. She had rehearsed this scene in countless dreams, even down to the twinkle of the water and the forest aroma. Each dream had been identical, culminating in her being swallowed by the darkness and rushing to consciousness pursued by an overwhelming dread. But now there was no escape. The moment she had tried to push to the back of her mind for so long had arrived.

She advanced into the canyon. The path milled downwards through the boulders and shadow-dwelling orchids, the walls on either side were wet with vines. The heat was unrelenting and the thick, coiling foliage obscured the sunlight.

The canyon twisted open and Nyanna emerged into baking sunlight. Far above her, the giant mothertrees yawned through the clouds, their thick stems stretching endless miles before blossoming into vast balconies on the edge of Arboreta's stratosphere. And, beyond the mothertrees, the glimmering blue sphere that dominated half the sky. It consisted of one giant ocean and it was possible to distinguish the contours of crashing waves, the mist that would soon rain down on Arboreta, and even the shadows of the leviathans that flitted beneath the surface.

Nyanna savoured the vision. It was so beautiful that it was tinged with unreality. The view was so clear she could almost reach out and touch it.

'Early, Nyanna. As always, early.' The elder interrupted Nyanna's thoughts. He was a short, bumbling figure, his neck fan curled up like a dried-out root leaf. His words creaked like branches in the breeze. 'It seems a lifetime since last we met, and yet, not so long at all.'

'Gallura? Is he born?' asked Nyanna anxiously.

'Gallura?' the elder said, running the name over his lips. 'Is not yet born. His egg remains, approaching the moment.'

'How long?'

8

'Hours. The birthsayers believe it will be within the day, within the day.' He led Nyanna towards the distant mothertrees, following a well-worn path. 'As always, early.'

The ceiling curved in from one side of the metal floor to the other. Boxes, computer parts and other junk were heaped against one wall, covered in a snowfall of grey dust. The other wall was filled by a bulkhead door. Oversized iron hooks were fixed along the length of the ceiling, rusty and covered in trailing cobwebs.

The blue police-box exterior of the TARDIS began to form in one corner. For a brief while it seemed to be slipping in and out of existence, the chipped wood panelling becoming first solid and then ethereal, until, with a final, resounding crump, the TARDIS materialised.

'Obviously that wasn't completely perfect,' said the Doctor, wafting his floppy brown hat over the smoking console. The control room was in disarray; the hat stand had fallen over, the Doctor's chair was upturned and K9 was lying on his side, ears waggling.

Romana brushed down her claret-coloured velvet jacket. She felt as though her hearts and her stomach had changed places. 'Not completely perfect?'

The Doctor blew on a smouldering control panel. 'You may have noticed a slight bump at the end there.' He coughed for several seconds.

'Slight?' Romana collected *The Continuum Code* from where it had flapped onto the ground, pocketed it, and lifted K9 into an upright position. 'How are you, K9?'

'All systems functioning normally,' K9 said. 'Suggestion: in future, mistress should drive.'

The Doctor snorted, bashed the door control and the doors hummed open. He jammed his hat hard on to his head, the brim covering his eyes, and shrugged his oatmeal-coloured coat into place. 'Right. That's it. I'm going outside, I may be some time. Romana, you can come with me if you want. K9, stay here.'

'Master?'

'We won't be very long,' said Romana, tidying her frilly cuffs. She tapped K9 on the nose. 'Humour him. Taking your basic time travel proficiency can be very stressful.'

K9 whirred up to the Doctor. 'Master. Statistical analysis of previous excursions suggest a ninety per cent likelihood that my assistance will be required to facilitate liberation from incarceration.'

'What?' said a voice from somewhere under the Doctor's hat.

'You will need me to rescue you.' K9's rear antennae, which resembled a tail, waggled.

'Oh. Exactly,' said the Doctor. 'So how can you come and rescue us if you're already with us, hmm? Do try to be logical. Come on, Romana.'

'Goodbye, K9.' Romana patted the side of the computer dog's head and followed the Doctor outside.

The Doctor switched on a torch and ran the circle of light over the surroundings. Spiders scuttled across their webs. The beam settled on the bulkhead door, and the Doctor pulled a triumphant sonic screwdriver from the depths of his pockets.

Romana locked the police-box door behind her. 'Where do you think we are?'

'Quickly and smoothly, she says,' muttered the Doctor under his breath, running the screwdriver over the bulkhead lock.

'You do realise it is a terribly dangerous thing to do, materialising without an analogue osmosis dampener. We could have skipped over our own time paths,' Romana said. 'Anyway, we're here now. Wherever it is.' She brushed aside a shivering cobweb and ran a finger over one of the oversized hooks. 'Not the most salubrious of…'

The Doctor swiped the screwdriver and the bulkhead jerked apart. 'Aha! Where would I be without my sonic screwdriver!'

'Still locked in a cellar in Paris, presumably,' said Romana.

The bulkhead opened on to a cramped cockpit, and stale air gasped in, fluttering the cobwebs. Inside the cockpit, the instrument panels were filled with numerous displays and indicators, all unlit. The viewscreens were covered by two huge, corrugated shutters.

Stooping, the Doctor flashed his torch over the control panels and oscilloscopes. All the dials read zero.

Romana crouched beside him. It was chilly in here, and her breath frosted in the air. An identification plaque above the airlock door caught her attention. 'The *Montressor*. A Class D security transporter.'

'Nothing seems to be working.' The Doctor jabbed experimentally at a few switches and turned to Romana, his eyes pondering. 'I wonder what happened to the crew.'

'Try manually opening the shutters. We may as well see where we are.'

The Doctor gripped the bottom of one of the shutters and tugged. The shutter rattled upwards and light blanketed the cockpit.

'Good grief.'

Opening the shutter had revealed a whirling void. It was as though they were floating in a blurred, ever-changing ocean of colour. It was serenely, hypnotically beautiful.

'A hyperspace tunnel,' said Romana. 'Only you could miss the entirety of the real universe and land us in hyperspace.' She estimated the tunnel to be two miles wide; a cylinder of calm, like the eye of a hurricane.

The Doctor rubbed his lips. 'Over there.'

Romana peered out. From the corner of the window she could see that their ship was connected via a short access tube to... well, Romana wasn't sure what it was. It seemed to be a vast city. A space station bolted together at random by someone with no idea about design, or architectural viability, and who wasn't particularly good at bolting things together. 'A space station?'

'Look closer.'

The city was constructed from the remains of spaceships. Over one hundred craft, of every conceivable type, all jammed together and interconnected into a mesh. At the centre of the construction was an interplanetary leisure-cruiser. Its rear bulk, the only part visible, was a patchwork of decay, its skeletal structure half-exposed. Smaller craft encrusted the wreck like limpets; their ship, the *Montressor*, was one of these. Other ships on the outskirts of the city were in better condition and were parked at specially constructed docking ports.

'What do you think?' asked the Doctor. He moved away from the screens, hands deep in his pockets. 'I'm not sure whether to be impressed or not. It's certainly very big.'

11

'A graveyard of ships in space…' Romana corrected herself. 'In hyperspace. But why?'

The Doctor took out his bag of jelly babies, selected one, and munched it. 'Do you know, I think we should find out. I can feel the hairs on the back of my neck curling. Which can mean only one thing.'

'Which is?' Romana asked. Now the Doctor mentioned it, there was an eeriness in the air. Like a temporal detachment. Or a ghost walking over her grave. She stopped herself; she refused to be drawn into another of the Doctor's incorrigible flights of fancy.

'Time to get a haircut.' A grin enveloped the Doctor's face and he moved towards the airlock.

Lamp fittings were either cracked or empty, the panelling was warped, and the carpet was threadbare. The smashed limbs of statues lay strewn across the hall. The interior of the leisure cruiser had seen better days.

Romana and the Doctor walked carefully through the derelict ship. The airlock had opened on to an access tube, which had brought them aboard the cruiser through an airlock duct. Romana noted that the walls were scarred with holes blasted into the woodwork by some sort of energy weapon.

'Signs of a struggle,' she remarked, pulling her jacket around her. 'Quite a battle by the look of it. Do you think there's anyone left alive?'

The Doctor pulled a face. 'Whatever happened, it was a long, long time ago.' He prodded a finger at a tapestry. The material crumbled to charcoal in his hands. 'So much for art alone enduring. And what's this?' The Doctor slapped his hands clean and pulled aside a heavy curtain to reveal a doorway. It opened on to a stairwell that spiralled into the level beneath. The Doctor motioned Romana inside.

This level of the cruiser had been recently inhabited; the cabins had been converted into shops, the ceiling covered with coloured sheets. The impression was of a narrow street bazaar. The shops, for the most part, were offering souvenirs, jewellery, clothing. Or, at least, the remnants of them. Everywhere, there was devastation.

Behind their smashed windows the shops were blackened husks. Leaflets, food containers and abandoned goods littered the corridor. The overhead public-address speakers hissed and the Chinese lanterns hanging in each doorway flickered, filling the corridor with an unearthly twilight.

'"The Beautiful Death".' Romana examined a bill poster, crinkled on to a nearby wall. The poster advertised the forthcoming event in bold, swirly lettering. Beneath the words an angel smiled, arms outstretched in rapture. The angel had the face of a skull. '"Midnight. The Great Hall".'

The Doctor peered at the poster. '"Turn On, Tune In, And Drop Dead." How peculiar.'

'This place looks like a bomb hit it,' commented Romana.

'If we'd only arrived earlier. Story of my life.' The Doctor rubbed the back of his neck. He seemed troubled. 'You know, I have a very nasty feeling that –'

In the distance, there was a cry for help.

The Doctor hightailed down the corridor in the direction of the sound, his scarf flapping in his wake. Treading over the litter, Romana picked her way after him.

The corridor opened on to a high-ceilinged deck, a once-elegant staircase sweeping down from an upper gallery. The staircase was littered with corpses. They had hideous wounds, their skin and clothes forming a roasted glue. The stench of death clung to the air.

Hand over her mouth, Romana drew nearer. Most of the bodies were human, although there were some other races: translucent, milky creatures with bulbous eyes, and two short, humanoid lizards. The corpses were dressed in colourful clothes: kaftans, duffle coats, capes and tie-dye T-shirts. Though it was hard to tell where the tie-dye ended and the blood began.

'Over here, Romana.' The Doctor squatted beside a figure lying huddled against one wall.

The figure was wearing body-length black robes, but what took Romana's breath away was its face. It was a mask, an horrific caricature of a skull. The skull was covered in grooves representing facial muscles, and appeared to be screaming in agony.

13

'Help me get this mask off,' the Doctor said. 'Quick!' Romana knelt beside him and together they unfastened the straps fixing it in place. Romana lifted the mask off and placed it to one side.

It was a man in his early thirties. Perspiration streamed off his forehead. He looked up at Romana and the Doctor, and raised a grateful smile, his jaw trembling. 'They came for us…'

'Who came for you?' asked the Doctor.

'The…' The man stuttered. 'They hunted out the living…' His eyes bulged. 'They are the walking dead!'

'Don't try to speak,' said Romana, smoothing his hair. The man's eyelids drooped, he mumbled to himself and lost consciousness.

'The walking dead,' said the Doctor. 'I knew it would have to be something like that.'

'He's sustained burns to neck and chest. He needs painkillers, disinfectant. Dressings.'

The Doctor agreed. 'We can't leave him here. I think we'd better –' He put a protective arm on Romana's shoulder and led her to one side.

Two medics were approaching, both dressed in turquoise uniforms. One of them, a young woman, scanned a life-detector across the bodies. The detector hummed when pointed at the man in black robes. 'That one there. He's still alive.' Reading from the datascreen, she spoke with wooden efficiency. 'Minor burns and trauma. He'll survive.'

The Doctor dashed over to assist the medics. 'Hello. My name's –'

'Are you injured at all?' asked the other medic.

'No, I –'

'Right. You can carry him.'

'Carry him?' said Romana.

'To the medical bay. Down there.' The medic indicated another of the corridors.

'Right. Of course, the medical bay.' The Doctor tucked his arms under the robed man and eased him upwards. The man groaned as his head fell back, but he remained unconscious.

'But what about the rest of them?' asked Romana.

The young woman glanced at the bodies. 'Them? They're all dead.'

'What happened here?' Romana asked.

'Time for that later,' said the Doctor. The black-robed man was lolling in his arms. 'This man needs medical attention.'

Executive Metcalf wallowed in his office. It had been converted from the cruiser's control cabin and retained many of the original features. The gold rails, the plush carpet, the Art Deco lamps. The two large windows looking out on to hyperspace. His treasured collection of artworks, sculptured blocks of abstract form. The luxury helped remind Metcalf he was important because, at the moment, important was the one thing he didn't feel.

The chair pinched him at the sides, and Metcalf wriggled himself into position. The events of the previous day had left him rattled. His collarless ochre-and-brown suit, normally the last word in executive style, seemed to be two sizes too big. His hair, normally combed into a neat side parting, was bedraggled. And he could feel sweat collecting at the waistband of his trousers.

He ran his hand through his hair for the fifteenth time that day. In front of him, the holophoto of his wife and the two little ones. Smiling idyllically. Luckily, they'd not been involved. Which probably wasn't surprising, Metcalf thought, since he hadn't seen them since his wife had run off with the holophotographer twelve years ago.

Beside the photo was an interaction terminal, the monitor showing nothing but rolling static. All that remained of ERIC. That dratted computer. He'd almost grown fond of it.

Metcalf was in the process of loosening his tie when the door opened, admitting two uniformed officers.

'Executive Metcalf?' Both of the officers wore regulation silver-and-black tunics, peaked caps and identification badges. Each had a laser rifle slung from his belt.

'I am, yes,' said Metcalf. His tie slithered out of his hands on to his desk. 'You must be –'

'We are Investigators. My name is Dunkal, and this is my colleague, Rige.' Dunkal was in his fifties, a stern, weathered officer. He spoke as though he was spitting out words he didn't like the taste of. 'We believe there has been an incident.'

Rige had slicked-back hair and a seedy manner. He fingered one of the artworks. 'Incident.'

'That's right, yes,' said Metcalf. 'Do sit down, officers. I'm afraid

15

there has been a not inconsiderable… well, catastrophe is one word that springs to mind.'

'Catastrophe?' Dunkal didn't like the taste of the word 'catastrophe'. He eased himself into the seat opposite Metcalf. 'D'you hear that, Rige? There's been a catastrophe.'

Rige didn't reply. He wandered around the office, his hands clasped behind his back.

Metcalf continued. 'There was a malfunction with the Beautiful Death, one of our attractions. You may have heard of it. Unfortunately what happened was that it turned a couple of hundred tourists into… it's quite difficult to describe.'

'In your own time.'

'It turned them into the living dead.'

Dunkal stroked his moustache. 'The living dead. Right.'

'And they went on, for want of a better word, a rampage.' Metcalf gulped. 'Most undesirable. And then, on top of all that, both the Beautiful Death attraction and our computer supervision system, ERIC, were destroyed. All because of one man's sabotage, I hasten to add.'

'And the living dead?'

'They died.' Metcalf gave an embarrassed cough. 'Permanently, this time.'

'I see,' digested Dunkal. 'And all the result of sabotage, you say? So someone tampers with this Beautiful Death of yours, whatever the hell that is, and then blows it up, taking your computer with it? And they also turn a couple of hundred tourists into zombies, and then kill them. Permanently. Is that what you're saying?'

'Exactly.'

'It's the classic scenario,' stated Rige. 'If I had a credit every time…' Dunkal scowled at him and the words tailed off.

'And when all this was happening, you were?' Dunkal turned back to Metcalf.

'Well, here, in my office. Putting efforts in place to organise an evacuation,' said Metcalf. 'In no small measure.'

'Of course.' Dunkal studied the photo of Metcalf's wife. 'And you're in charge of everything that goes on here?'

'Yes. And no. The Beautiful Death was under the direction of Doctor Paddox. It was his project, really.'

'And this Doctor Paddox is…?'

'Is missing, assumed dead, as well,' Metcalf nodded. 'Deeply regrettable. But were he alive, I am sure he would admit responsibility.'

'Convenient,' said Rige, helping himself to a seat.

'Right.' Investigator Dunkal leaned forward. Metcalf could smell the tobacco on his breath. 'So. This saboteur of yours. The one behind the catastrophe. Can you describe him?'

Metcalf described him.

'The morning after, and all around is despair,' began Harken Batt. 'Here, in the medical bay of the G-Lock, I am surrounded by the victims of the recent disaster. The deceased, the dying, and the injured.'

He beckoned his holocameraman down the aisle of beds. 'Less than twelve hours ago these people were having the time of their lives. Little did they know of the tragedy that fate held in store for them like a bleak surprise.'

Harken fixed his eyes on the holocamera. This would be the clip that would be replayed at endless award ceremonies. He imagined his face in the viewfinder; lined but distinguished, easily passing for that of a forty-year-old. The face of the greatest investigative reporter of his generation.

'Throughout this episode, one man alone managed to get an exclusive insight into the true nature of events as they happened. Not only discovering the cause of the danger, but also proving to be crucially instrumental in its defeat.' After a measured pause, Harken delivered the final blow. 'The harrowing events of the last twelve hours is not just the story of the people gathered here today. It is also my story. This is Harken Batt, reporting from the G-Lock –'

'Excuse me, would you mind?'

The Doctor settled the black-robed man on a bed and waved a medic over. With his help, the medic placed an oxygen mask over the man's face and applied compresses to the wounds.

'Would I mind? You just ruined that whole sequence.'

The Doctor looked up. A bald, sullen-faced man in a grey mac was folding his arms at him. The man, in his late fifties, had been talking to himself in a ludicrously self-important manner, and the

17

Doctor had disregarded him as a matter of course. 'What?'

'You just interrupted a most important section of my documentary.'

'Documentary?' The Doctor whirled to face a tubby gentleman resplendent in a jacket, tie and Hawaiian shorts squinting through a camera. Realising what had happened, he broke into a gregarious smile. 'I'm terribly sorry, will you have to start all over again?'

The man in the mac tutted. 'I daresay it will come out in the edit, it usually does. I was just running over the events of the last few hours.'

'Really?' The Doctor caught a glimpse of Romana on the other side of the medical bay where she was tending to the injured. 'Bit of a problem with the walking dead, I hear.'

'That's right, Doctor, I was –'

'Doctor!' The Doctor almost jumped out of his coat. 'You called me Doctor!'

The man breathed deeply, as if to humour him. 'Yes, Doctor. As I was saying, I was about to –'

'How do you know I'm the Doctor?'

'How do I know you're the Doctor, Doctor?' the man replied. 'After all we've been through?'

'Have we?'

'You saved the G-Lock.'

The Doctor boggled with delight. 'Did I? Did I really?'

'You don't remember? You rescued it from certain and terrible destruction.'

'How marvellous.' The Doctor grinned. 'That's just the sort of thing I would do. Sorry, and you are?'

'Harken Batt.' He indicated his colleague in the shorts. 'And this is my new holocameraman, Jeremy. You mean you really don't know who I am?'

The Doctor shook his head. 'I'm afraid I've never seen you before in my life.'

The ceiling lights brightened to usher in a new artificial day. Across the room, the Doctor was still talking to that fool in the overcoat. Romana tutted and turned to the occupant of the next bed.

It was an orange lizard, about the size of a juvenile human, lying on its side. It had a dazed expression, its two bulbous eyes rolling about behind circular sunglasses. Instead of hair it had a crenellated membrane, and around its neck were numerous amulets and beads. It groaned. 'Oh. My freakin' loaf.'

'Are you in any pain?' asked Romana.

'My grey area is throbbing like an amp on eleven,' said the lizard. 'I am totally medicined.'

'Are you in pain? Yes or no?'

'Whacked and not so groovy.' The lizard centred its soporific eyes on to her. 'Oh, it's you, Romana. So you got out safe with the cat in the hat, I take it? '

Romana was incredulous. 'What are you talking about?'

'Last night, when all around was tribulation and trial,' the lizard explained. 'You and the good Doctor were the fifth cavalry. You saved my life.'

'Harken Batt, investigative reporter? Leading insect-on-the-wall documentary-maker? One of the most famous holovision personalities in the galaxy –'

'No, I'm afraid I've really never heard of you,' the Doctor interrupted, fearing Harken might continue in this vein indefinitely. 'But I feel certain that if I we had met, it would have been quite… unforgettable.'

'Well, this sudden memory lapse is most inconvenient,' said Harken. 'I had been hoping to interview you.'

'Interview me?' The Doctor pointed to his own chest. Taking his cue, Jeremy raised his holocamera and backed away to fit them both in the shot. 'Whatever for?'

'For my documentary, on how we… on how you averted the G-Lock's destruction. And…'

'Ah. I would love to help, but unfortunately I don't have the foggiest idea what you're talking about. So this is the G-Lock, is it?' The Doctor directed his attention to the injured. Some were quivering in shock, others weeping. Medics clattered in with more trolleys of survivors.

'Yes, this is…' said Harken.

The Doctor whispered in his ear. 'You know, I hate to be rude, but I think perhaps we should get on with trying to save a few lives rather than stand around chatting, don't you? Hmm?' He shambled away to attend to the new arrivals.

Harken glowered, and gave a throat-slitting signal to Jeremy.

'I saved your life?' said Romana. 'You mean you've already met the Doctor and I?'

'Indeed that is so.' The lizard licked its lips. 'You know, lady, I wouldn't half kill for a refreshener. My gullet's as dry as a sand weevil's bath towel.'

'Of course,' said Romana. 'Try to remain awake, I'll get you some water.'

'Totally nice.' The lizard's head dropped back into its pillow.

Romana hurried over to the water-cooler in the corner of the room. It dispensed a cup of blue-tinted water. She was about to head back when she felt a hand tugging at her jacket.

The hand belonged to an old woman reclining on a trolley. The woman's face was a mass of wrinkles; her skin sagged in folds and was covered in sores. She looked starved to near-death. Her eyes, rheumy and colourless, fixed on Romana's with a burning intensity.

Romana strained to hear what she was saying. The woman licked her lips, and Romana could see that her tongue and toothless gums were completely black. Oily liquid started drooling out of her mouth, dripping from her chin and on to her clothes.

Stooping closer, Romana could feel the woman's breath on her face. It smelt of ash. 'What is it? What can I do for you?'

The woman did not reply. Instead, her hand lost its grip on Romana's jacket and fell to one side.

'I'll get someone to see to you.' Romana twisted away, and clutched the arm of a nearby medic, a bearded, heavily built man. 'Excuse me, but can you help? This woman needs urgent attention.'

The medic shot Romana a look of confusion.

'This woman here –'. Romana turned to face the bed. It was empty. Where the woman had been lying, there were just neatly folded sheets. There was not even an indentation in the mattress. It was as if she had never existed.

Chapter Two

The elder shuffled into the chamber, and Nyanna followed a respectful two paces behind him.

The birthsayers and elders had assembled around the carpel, a long stem looping from the ceiling in a tangle of arteries. A mass of veins covered its surface, bulging as they pumped a phosphorescent green liquid through the wall capillaries. Suspended at the centre of the womb, floating within the carpel, was a large, transparent egg.

The birthsayers gathered their skins around them like baggy cloaks and turned their wizened faces to the new arrivals. The oldest one advanced on Nyanna.

'Nyanna. We are yet an hour or so away before the sac breaks.' The birthsayer pointed a gnarled finger at the egg; it was visibly swelling, the skin of the sac splitting under the strain and leaking natal liquid. Inside the egg, its body hunched over its knees, was an unborn baby.

'The child is healthy, alive?'

The birthsayer tasted the air. 'Oh, it lives. It can sense the rush of the approaching moment.'

'Gallura,' wheezed an elder. 'The unborn shall be Gallura. He marks the end. After him, there is no more.'

'Indeed, the end approaches,' the birthsayer repeated grimly.

'The end of us all,' said a second birthsayer. 'Gallura is the herald of our destruction.'

The birthsayer's words filled Nyanna with dread. The same dread that had pursued her in her dreams had now become real. In the next hour, all their histories would be as nothing. She felt sick with tension.

'Gallura,' said the first birthsayer, 'will be the last of the Arboretans.'

Above them, the baby revolved in its egg.

Romana returned to find the lizard asleep, his spines rippling back and forth contentedly. She placed the cup of water on the bedside table and tried to gather her thoughts.

Had it been an hallucination? Unlikely, she thought. Her mind was highly trained, not prone to flights of imagination. And she had felt the woman's breath, her hand pulling on her jacket. Whatever it was, she refused to believe it could have been conjured up by her subconscious.

'Wakened from uneasy dreams?' The Doctor appeared beside her. He rubbed his nose. 'Everything all right, Romana?'

Romana caught herself staring into nowhere. She put on a carefree smile. 'Yes, Doctor.'

'Do you know, I've just had the most curious conversation,' said the Doctor.

'Your friend in the grey coat?'

'Harken Batt,' he informed her. 'He claims that I rescued this place, the G-Lock, from certain destruction.'

'Really? It sounds like the sort of thing you would do.'

'That's what I said.'

'But you haven't, have you? Rescued this place from –'

'– from certain destruction?' finished the Doctor. 'No. At least, not yet. That's the trouble with time travel, you never know whether you're coming or going. But it's nice to be congratulated before I've actually done anything.' He ruffled his hair bashfully. 'You know, when you go around saving planets as often as I do, I'm surprised that this sort of thing doesn't happen more often.'

'Doctor, you're not the only person to have been recognised.' said Romana.

'Master, mistress, I have an urgent message to report,' a small, metallic voice piped up from knee level. 'We are in grave danger.'

Romana looked down. The origin of the warning was K9. He trundled up to the Doctor, his wheel-motors whinnying.

'I thought I told you stay in the TARDIS,' said the Doctor petulantly.

'Affirmative master. But the imperative to alert you took precedence over your previous instruction.'

'I see. So you thought you'd just pop out and warn us?'

'Affirmative.'

'That was very good of you K9,' said Romana, ignoring the huffing Doctor. 'What's this message of yours?'

'This construction is suspended within a hyperspace conduit…'

'We already know that,' said the Doctor,

K9 whirred in irritation. '… within a hyperspace conduit. This particular structure is located directly on the hyperspace–real-space interface.'

'You mean, this space station is at one end of the tunnel,' said Romana. The theory of hyperspace tunnels, she reminded herself, dated back to the early twenty-second century, and was childishly simple. To facilitate faster-than-light travel from one section of the galaxy to another, the principle was to link them by creating a channel through an auxiliary dimension, known as hyperspace. One could then enter this dimensional conduit, travel a few miles, and emerge to find oneself in a solar system thousands of light years away. That was the idea, anyway. The Doctor would probably have explained it using sheets of paper and drinking straws and still have left no one any the wiser.

'Precisely,' said K9. 'It is also obstructing any passage through the interface.'

'Stuck like a cork in a bottle,' said the Doctor, wide-eyed.

'Analogy rudimentary but adequate. However, geostatic pressure caused by blockage is approaching tolerance levels, leading to an imminent and total loss of hyperdimensional viability.' K9 rotated his ears smugly.

'The tunnel is about to collapse,' whispered Romana.

'Taking everything here with it.' The Doctor put a forefinger in his mouth and made a solemn 'pop'. A thought occurred to him. 'One thing, K9. How do you know all this?'

K9 paused. 'That information is unavailable.'

'What do you mean, "that information is unavailable"?'

'My meaning was unambiguous. That information is unavailable.'

'No,' sighed the Doctor. 'Why is that information unavailable?'

'That information is also unavailable.'

'So you're telling us that this hyperspace tunnel is going to collapse, but you can't tell us how you know this, and you also can't tell us why you can't tell us how you know this.'

K9 spent a few moments unscrambling the Doctor's syntax. 'Affirmative, master.'

'Well, I'm glad we got that clear,' said the Doctor caustically. He crouched down. 'K9, I'm sorry for leaving you in the TARDIS. Next time, you can come outside with us. I promise. All right?'

'Affirmative,' said K9 happily.

'Why do you think this hyperspace tunnel is about to collapse?'

'That information is unavailable.'

'Useless machine,' the Doctor snorted, and gave K9 a kick.

Romana swallowed. 'Doctor, if what K9 says is true, then everyone here is in the most terrible danger.'

The Doctor awoke to action. 'Yes, of course. K9, how long do we have until this "loss of viability"?'

'Approximately four hours seventeen minutes. Master, although I am unable to divulge the source of my information, I can lead you to the hyperspace–real-space interface, where you will be able to verify my assertion.'

The Doctor regarded K9 down a suspicious nose. 'You know where the geostatic build-up is located?'

'Affirmative. Corridor 79.'

'Well, I think I shall have to go and see this.' The Doctor took Romana to one side. 'And if he turns out to be correct… well, I don't know what we'll do, but we'll do something. Coming?'

Romana glanced around the medical bay. As the beds ran out, mattresses were being unrolled on to the floor and filled by more of the injured. Survivors had also started to gather uncertainly on the fringes of the ward, blocking the trolleys and adding to the chaos. Parents cuddled their shrieking children. There was a sense of desperation in the air.

'I'll wait here,' she decided. 'These people need our help.'

'I'll be as quick as I can.' The Doctor strode out of the medical bay, K9 at his heels. Romana watched them go and then turned back to the lizard. She lifted its kaftan to reveal a deep, grisly burn.

She replaced the fabric and dodged across the ward to the supplies unit, a bank of cubicles along one wall. She collected some vacuum-sealed bags of dressings but found the cubicle marked *Anaesthetics and Analgesics* empty.

She turned to the nearest medic, the bearded man she had spoken to earlier. He was hoisting one of the milky creatures to a sitting position. 'Where are the rest of the painkillers?'

'They've all gone.'

'What?' said Romana angrily.

'We've exhausted all the supplies.' The man shrugged, wiping his forehead on his sleeve. 'The number of casualties is too great, we can't cope. The situation is critical.'

Rige unclipped a small device from his utility belt and reviewed its reading.

'I'm getting a positive ID, Dunkal.' He pointed the tracker down the corridor. 'This way.'

'Give me a moment, Rige,' heaved Dunkal. He leaned back against a column. He was getting too old for this sort of thing. He couldn't run more than twenty metres without getting a stitch. Drinking cheap coffee, slamming his fist on desks and roughing up suspects against fenders; that was more his style. Not running around a grotty space station in the middle of nowhere. He dabbed at his forehead. 'Now I know why they call it hot pursuit.'

'They're evading capture, sir,' Rige reminded him.

'All right, all right,' said Dunkal and, with some effort, pushed himself upright. He would reward himself with a cigarette later. 'No rest for the justice. Let's get on with it, then.'

The lizard watched Romana unwrap the burn dressings. It had been supplied with water and was now propped up on its side, a picture of bemusement.

'Now, this may hurt.' Romana raised the lizard's cloak and applied the dressings, squeezing them on to the open wounds. A medic mopped up the seeping juices.

'Aah! Freak me!' shrieked the lizard. 'Totally ungroovy! This is beyond agony – this is agony two, the sequel!'

Romana drew back. 'I'm being as gentle as I can.'

'Everything's gone all soft focus and swimmy,' whimpered the lizard. 'Can't you administer me a shot of the old mellow medicine? Just a little something to smooth off the corners?'

Romana shook her head. 'I'm sorry, there's no painkillers left. We're doing what we can, but…'

The creature slumped back on to its pillow. 'Painkillers. *Indigo Glow.*'

'What?'

'The *Indigo Glow*. My spacehopper,' confided the lizard. 'The interplanetary supernova convertible parked out on docking bay

25

two. Shark-red exhaust trim. There's all the "painkillers" you'll ever need on board.'

'You have anaesthetics? Drugs?'

The lizard smiled to itself. 'It is a fully equipped medicine wagon. Anaesthetics, cardiothetrics, psychogens. Placators, dilators and hallucinators. Uppers, downers and in-betweeners. Glycerat, Novovacuous. A pill for every chill.'

'You certainly came well stocked,' Romana remarked.

'"Be prepared" is the motto.' The lizard rummaged beneath its kaftan and presented Romana with a small ident key. 'Check out the cabin stow-locker. You'll find enough painkillers to knock out an alabast elephosaur.'

Romana turned the key over in her fingers. If she left for the hopper now, she thought, she could be back with the medicine before the Doctor and K9 returned. 'Docking bay two?'

'Indeed.' The lizard collapsed back to sleep.

Romana slipped the key into her pocket and hurried out of the medical bay.

The Doctor leaned over a parapet and gazed into the gloom. K9 had led them to a vast chamber, a shaft sinking into the depths of the ship, overlooked by tier upon tier of balconies. 'Do you know, K9, there's something that's been preying on my mind.'

'Master, sensors indicate...' K9 wheeled to the Doctor's side.

'Normally, when I arrive somewhere, people point guns at me and throw me in prison. Within about twenty-four and a half minutes of arriving, usually,' said the Doctor. 'But this time everyone's pleased to see me. I mean, it was bound to happen one day, but it still strikes me as, well, odd.'

'Master, urgent warning...' There was a fizzling and K9 went silent.

'I'm not used to it. After all, how am I supposed to know who the baddies are if no one will capture –'. The Doctor didn't finish his thought. Instead, he raised his arms into the air and revolved on the spot, attentive to the rifle butt that was pressing against the small of his back. 'I believe that is what is known as speaking too soon.'

Two men in silver-and-black tunics – some species of policeman, the Doctor presumed – were levelling their rifles at him. The larger one fixed him with a world-weary glare. 'Stay very,

very still. We don't like having to shoot suspects, but we're quite prepared to do things we don't like, aren't we, Rige?'

'We certainly are, Dunkal.' The other policeman sidled to where K9 stood. 'We take a professional pride in our work.' The metal dog was motionless, his head drooping. The policeman kicked him, and K9 gave a feeble splutter. 'The weapons unit has been rendered inoffensive.'

'Well done, Rige. Now –'

'Inoffensive? You dare to call K9 inoffensive?' The Doctor realised what he was saying and backtracked. 'Of course K9 is inoffensive, he's a very genial fellow. What have you done to him?'

'Listen,' chewed Dunkal. 'We have reason to believe you are guilty of acts of terrorism, and are quite prepared to –'

'To kill me if I don't co-operate? We can do this the easy way or the hard way?' said the Doctor. 'Yes, I know the routine. And I must say I have absolutely no idea what you're talking about, and am innocent of anything you care to mention. Probably. But first, may I ask, who are you?'

'I am Investigator Dunkal, and this is my colleague, Investigator Rige.'

'Delighted. I've never been held at gunpoint by Investigators before.' The Doctor waved at Rige. Rige winced.

Dunkal raised his rifle to prod the Doctor's chin in what he probably imagined was a menacing fashion. 'And you are known as "the Doctor", are you not?'

'Yes.'

'He doesn't deny it,' sneered Rige.

'No, of course I don't deny it,' the Doctor retorted. 'Though I will be happy to deny anything else you may accuse me of.'

'Quiet,' said Dunkal. He leaned into the Doctor's flinching face. '"The Doctor", I am placing you under arrest, on suspicion of crimes of sabotage resulting in murder and grievous collateral damage. You will be taken from this place to a place of imprisonment pending investigation. Although you have the right to remain silent, we have the right to infer guilt from your silence. Is there anything you wish to say?'

The Doctor grinned. 'Yes. People pointing guns at me. This is such a relief!'

* * *

Docking bay two was not difficult to find. It consisted of a narrow gantry with airlock ports branching off on either side that connected to various spacecraft. Beyond a transparent barrier, the hyperspace tunnel swirled for ten miles or so into the distance before opening on to a starscape. The gateway to real space.

The spaceships were mainly interplanetary hoppers, small transporters for a dozen or so passengers. The majority were recognisably Terran, although Romana spotted a couple of Yetraxxi cruisers with their distinctive hairdryer shape. Many of the craft were streaked with meteor burns, although some had been customised in garish, flowery patterns.

Romana proceeded towards the next airlock, her footsteps clanking on the metal floor. The electronic banner above the door read *Indigo Glow. GRS 68* and she pressed the ident key on to the security pad. There was an affirmative trill and the airlock swished open. Romana stepped inside.

A sickly scent hit her nostrils. The interior of the spacehopper reeked of exotic perfumes and alcohol. The instrumentation and controls – which Romana considered to be rather perfunctory – were cluttered with pop-packets, plastic bags and food containers. Empty bottles of every hue and shape and size lined the dashboard. The three seats were covered with beading and piles of cushions, and woolly rugs smothered the floor. A variety of trinkets lined the rear wall: lava lamps, eccentric fossils, two tusks, a hookah, and a poster of a nymph cavorting to publicise a forthcoming concert.

Locating the rear locker, Romana brushed aside the litter and slid it open.

As promised, it was packed with every conceivable type of drug. Cartons and bubble-packets spilled out over the floor. Phenyzide, Novovacuous, and hundreds of luridly coloured pills that she had no hope of identifying without a well-stocked laboratory and a spare weekend. Deeper inside the locker were sealed bottles of Etheramyl and Opiasamin tablets.

'Looks like someone has robbed a chemist. Several chemists.' Romana crammed as many anaesthetics as she could find into two carrier bags. She couldn't stay long; the stench was giving her a headache, and the whole ambience was really rather too squalid.

Her mission completed, she hoisted the bags into her arms and headed for the exit.

Metcalf looked up to see the Doctor being shoved into his office. Dunkal and Rige followed behind. Rige was carrying some sort of box-shaped dog which he dumped against one wall.

'Doctor.' Metcalf shuffled some papers aside. 'So pleasant to have your company again.'

'You too, you too.' The Doctor strode towards Metcalf's desk. 'I'm terrible with names, but isn't it –?'

'Stay still,' ordered Dunkal, training his rifle on him. The Doctor halted, one foot in the air. 'Executive Metcalf,' the Investigator continued, 'do you identify this man as the one who sabotaged the Beautiful Death?'

Metcalf pursed his fingers together. He was going to enjoy this. 'Indeed. I most certainly do. This man is the cause of all our tribulations. He destroyed ERIC –'

'May I just interrupt here?' The Doctor's raised leg was shaking. 'It seems to me we're talking at crossed wires. I haven't sabotaged anything, at least I haven't sabotaged anything yet, and I really don't have any intention of sabotaging anything in the future, so I can't have done it and can I put my foot down please?'

'Shut it,' said Dunkal. 'I'm asking…'

'…the questions?' said the Doctor. 'And very perspicacious they are too. But there's one thing you've forgotten.'

Dunkal cast his gaze around the office. 'Which is?'

The Doctor lowered his foot. 'Evidence.'

'Evidence?' said Rige. 'What's…'

'Fingerprints. The candlestick in the library. The discarded hockey glove. Proof.'

'We know what evidence is, Doctor,' barked Dunkal. 'What are you trying to say?'

'I'm asking how do you know I did it? All you have is Metcalf's word. And that really isn't enough, is it?'

Dunkal and Rige exchanged glances as they weighed the Doctor's words. Metcalf squirmed. Somehow the situation was slipping out of control.

'I am Executive of the G-Lock,' he announced, rising from his seat to face the Doctor. 'Whereas you are, well I don't know what you are, some sort of cosmic beatnik I assume, but I am considerably more important than you. You imagine they could believe your word above mine? You are a saboteur, a terrorist.'

'I am not!' hissed the Doctor.

Metcalf appealed to Dunkal. 'This man is obviously guilty, I can't see what we have to gain by…'

'With due respect,' said Dunkal. 'He does, unfortunately, have a point. We can't just convict him on the basis of your statement. We need corroboration.'

'Corroboration,' agreed Rige.

Metcalf fumed and sat down. He rearranged his papers. He could feel his forehead prickling, and rummaged for a handkerchief.

'Right,' said the Doctor. 'And now can somebody please tell me what has been going on?'

With the carrier bags in her arms, Romana strode down the corridor towards the medical bay. The drugs she'd collected would, she hoped, be enough for the next few hours. After that, if what K9 had said was true, the survivors would have to be moved out of the G-Lock. There were certainly enough ships in the docking bay to transport them.

The corridor took her through a gallery overlooking a high-ceilinged deck. Romana moved along it, her feet sinking silently into the carpet. Looking down between the pillars, she recognised the floor below as the place where they had discovered the man in the skull mask.

The bodies had gone.

Romana stepped down the staircase to where the man had been lying. Someone must have cleared the corpses away, she guessed, but there was no trace of them ever having been there, no abandoned belongings, no bloodstains on the carpet.

Disconcerted, she looked around. The ship had changed. The pillars were no longer caked in mould, but were freshly painted. The statues stood upright, adopting classical poses atop carved foliage. The wood hadn't rotted at all and Art Deco lamp fittings gleamed. The carpet was a lavish red, not faded and threadbare.

Romana stroked the banister. It was solid. She took a deep

breath, closed her eyes and let her lungs empty. Whatever was happening, this was not her imagination.

She opened her eyes. The corridor was brand-new, immaculate and opulent. Huge tapestries covered each wall. Chandeliers twinkled their gentle magic.

The silence. It suddenly struck Romana; she could not hear a single sound.

She walked to the medical bay. The doors swung open to reveal the ward – empty. Every bed was unoccupied, every piece of instrumentation was turned off. Above her, the lights glowed with a strange intensity. It was noon of the artificial day.

There was a melodic chuckling. On the opposite side of the medical bay, hidden behind one of the beds, Romana caught a glimpse of a figure. A small girl, no more than six years old. Her eyes were wide and inquisitive. As she realised she had been spotted, the girl giggled and bobbed down behind the bed.

Romana walked across the room, placed the bags on the bed and peered over it. There was no one there, just empty floor. It had only taken a few seconds to reach the bed, and the girl couldn't possibly have moved from this spot without being seen, so where could she have vanished to?

As if to answer her question, the double doors on the far side of the medical bay swung shut.

Romana dashed off in pursuit.

'And then they all died. Permanently, this time.' said the Doctor. 'Of course.'

'He's feigning ignorance,' said Metcalf. 'An obvious ploy.' While Investigator Dunkal had recounted what had happened, the Doctor had made himself comfortable on Metcalf's desk. He was now twirling his scarf tassels. 'And yet it is perfectly plain the Doctor was behind the recent catastrophe. Only yesterday I discovered him tampering with ERIC in this very office.'

'ERIC being the station's computer supervisor?' said Dunkal.

'Indeed. Sadly missed. But what more proof do you need?' Metcalf leaned back in his seat. 'Let me share a thought with you, Investigator. If it wasn't the Doctor, then whose fault was it? Have any other suspects presented themselves? I think not.'

'You do have a point there.' Dunkal mulled this over, and then eyed the Doctor. 'Explain yourself, Doctor. Just who are you, and what are you doing here?'

The Doctor hopped on to his feet. 'I've told you. I'm the Doctor, and as for what I'm doing here – wasting time. Metcalf, I take it you're the person in charge here? Correct?'

'I am the Executive,' Metcalf said appreciatively.

'Listen to me, and listen carefully,' said the Doctor. 'I have reason to believe that the hyperspace tunnel we're sitting in is about to collapse.'

'He's stalling,' Metcalf sneered. 'Playing for time. Ignore him, Investigator.'

'Time is the one thing we don't have. According to my friend here…' The Doctor waved at the robot dog '… there will be a total loss of hyperstatial viability in about three and a half hours' time. The geostatic pressure will cause the tunnel to close in, crushing you, me, and everyone here into a singularity.'

'What absolute nonsense!' Metcalf laughed. 'This conduit has remained safe for over two hundred years!'

'Flapdoodle,' said the Doctor. 'Total poppycock. The hyperspace tunnel is inherently unstable.' He stared at Metcalf with two saucer-like eyes. 'You have a public address system? Order an evacuation immediately.'

'I shall do no such thing.'

'You don't seem to understand. If anyone remains on this G-Lock…'

'Oh, I understand perfectly, Doctor,' said Metcalf. 'You are trying to distract us with wild fairy stories.'

'Wait a moment.' Dunkal moved forward. The two Investigators seemed to be almost taking the Doctor seriously. 'Doctor, do you have any proof of this?'

'If our friend Rige hadn't silenced K9 he could have told you,' said the Doctor bitterly. 'Before I was so rudely arrested, I was heading for the interface, which might provide some explanation for this breakdown. So if you'll just let me…'

'Of course,' said Metcalf. 'If you'll just let him leave, he'll show you. He's treating us like idiots.'

'Oh, I wouldn't say that,' said the Doctor. 'But in your case, I am prepared to make an exception.'

'Investigators, you have heard the Doctor. He has refused to explain himself, and despite the fact that I have positively identified him you still refuse to confine him.'

'But what if he's…' protested Dunkal.

Metcalf puffed himself up. 'May I take this opportunity to remind you that I am the Executive here. I will be most displeased if you do not confine this man immediately. I am perfectly willing to contact your superiors, with whom I carry no small importance. Remember that.' Metcalf enjoyed the Investigators' fearful expressions. 'This meeting is now terminated. Take him away. And take that ridiculous robot dog with you, too.'

Romana found herself on a balcony overlooking a deep shaft. Below her, dozens of identical balconies dropped away into the darkness.

The girl had been playing games with her; always slipping out of sight or disappearing down a stairwell. Several times Romana had felt sure she had lost her, only for a door to swing shut, the girl's laughter ringing out. And each time Romana thought she had cornered her, she would find that the girl had vanished, only to reappear in the distance, giggling at Romana's confusion.

Romana had lost all sense of direction. The chase had taken her further away from the medical bay, and the passages had doubled back on themselves taking her deeper and deeper into the ship. This was the third time she had arrived at this chamber, each time on a lower level.

There was a flash of blue material on the level below. Romana had a fleeting impression of the girl running into the shadows, before losing sight of her. The girl's laughter rang out.

Romana made her way down the next set of stairs. The game continued.

The cubicle consisted of a door, three metal-grey walls and bench, with a bare light bulb providing the sole illumination.

The Doctor squatted on the bench, rubbing K9's ear sensors between his palms. Since they had been slammed in this cell he had concentrated his efforts on reviving him.

'K9, can you hear me?' asked the Doctor.

'Affirm. Affirm.' K9's eyes glowed back to life. 'Affirmative, mistress. Master. Auditory recognition circuits now fully recovered. This unit is operating at sixty per cent efficiency.'

'Good boy. Soon have you up to seventy per cent in no time.'

'Apologies, master.' K9's head drooped. 'I have failed in my duty to protect you.'

'Don't be silly,' the Doctor said. 'Could've happened to anyone. You're still my best friend, you know.'

K9's chin lifted slightly. 'Query. Is Romana mistress not your best friend?'

'Well,' considered the Doctor. 'She's my best friend too, but in a different way. You wouldn't understand. Anyway, K9, do you think you can still lead me to the real-space–hyperspace interface?'

K9 triangulated. 'Affirmative.'

'You're a good computer.' The Doctor got to his feet and surveyed the cell door. The lock was an electronic tribocipher device; the sonic screwdriver would make short work of it. He extracted it from his pocket with a flourish. 'Now for the fun part of getting captured. Escaping.'

'Curiouser and curiouser.'

Romana turned the corner to find a corridor unlike any other. The passage continued for about thirty metres before disappearing into pure blackness which swelled and rippled like a wall of oily liquid. It was as if the passage opened on to nothingness itself.

The corridor was lined with numbered doors for passengers' cabins. A plaque announced, *Corridor 79*.

As she approached the blackness Romana could discern the small girl standing on the edge of the void. She was perfectly still, her dress flapping in a soundless wind. The girl beckoned.

Romana found herself being drawn forward. The encroaching blackness was making a whooshing sound, a repetitive sucking like a tape of an orchestra being played backwards.

She could almost reach out and grab the girl, she was so close. She could make out the details of her face, her hazelnut eyes, the pattern on her dress. And yet there was something unreal about her. As though she had been superimposed over a backdrop.

The blackness glooped and surged.

Romana clutched the girl by the shoulders and hugged her to her chest, lifting her away from the blackness. She attempted to carry her down the corridor, but her legs failed to respond. She was glued to the spot.

The sound of laughter roared up from nowhere. There were cheers, clinking glasses, conversation. A party, a hundred people celebrating together. But there was no source for the laughter; Romana and the girl were still alone.

The girl kicked against Romana, trying to wriggle out of her embrace. Romana tightened her hold.

The laughter reached a deafening volume, and suddenly switched to pandemonium. A hundred people screaming as one, a hundred people crying out in absolute terror.

The girl's face was suddenly covered in jagged cracks, and split open. Her body crumbled to ash in Romana's arms, leaving Romana clutching at thin air.

Romana gasped herself awake. She was lying on the metal gantry floor of the docking bay. There was no sign of the girl. The two shopping bags lay unwanted by her knees, their contents spilling onto the ground.

Four figures in black cloaks surrounded her. Their faces were screaming skulls. Together, they reached out for her.

Chapter Three

The carpel was close to breaking point. Gelatinous fluid gurgled out of the splitting skin, and with each pulsation of the womb the egg visibly expanded. Inside the egg, the baby rotated, its umbilical cord coiling into the veins of the mothertree.

'The moment of birthing approaches,' announced a birthsayer. 'Gallura will soon be alive.'

A hush fell over the sternum chamber. Birthsayers and elders hobbled about, making preparations for the birth. As the mothertree palpitated, the walls started dripping and the veins straddling the stem began to throb. The chamber flashed from bright green to near darkness with each beat of the mothertree's heart.

Nyanna remained still. Every muscle in her body was taut, her fronds prickling in the heat. The elders were right; the birth of Gallura portended the end of their race. Within her lifetime, every Arboretan would be killed, until only Gallura remained.

'The end of us all,' she whispered to herself.

The oldest birthsayer placed a withered hand on her shoulder. 'Do not allow yourself concern. Whatever will be, has been so always. There is no end, as there was no beginning. We travel the Path of Perfection.'

'The Path of Perfection,' repeated Nyanna.

'We can do the best of which we are capable, nothing more. Remember that,' croaked the birthsayer. 'Destiny shapes us, we do not shape it.'

'I wish there were some other way.'

'There is no other way. An infinity of lifetimes has taught us that,' the birthsayer said. 'It is the Arboretan legacy.'

The four skull-masked guards had escorted Romana, at gunpoint, to a spacious, well-lit office containing some painfully hideous sculptures.

The guards stood on either side of her and an overweight, puffy-faced man faced her across a desk. Beside him were two men in black-and-silver uniforms; one in his fifties, chomping on a cigarette, and one with greasy hair and shifty eyes.

'I am placing you under arrest on suspicion of drug-trafficking. Although you have the right to remain silent, we have the right to infer guilt from your silence.'

'I wasn't drug-trafficking,' said Romana. 'These are medical supplies. There are people in the medical bay in urgent need of anaesthetics. At least, I think there are.'

The man behind the desk watched her, his eyes filled with contempt. 'Ah, yes. The casualties. Most unfortunate, of course, but these are extraordinary circumstances, which we couldn't have possibly accounted for.'

'There are people down there working without even the most rudimentary medical supplies,' said Romana. 'What sort of a shambles are you running here?'

'Shambles? The G-Lock is at the forefront –'

'With all due respect, I think we're drifting off the topic,' interrupted the elder of the officers. 'Lady, it's immaterial who or what the drugs were intended for. The fact remains that you were found in possession of… Investigator Rige?'

The other officer consulted his notebook. 'Opiasamin, Tutranol, Novovacuous, Phenyzide and several unidentified substances, Investigator Dunkal.'

'Exactly,' said Dunkal. 'And the penalty for drug-trafficking is most severe.'

'Severe,' echoed Rige.

'Look, this is very simple,' said Romana. 'Ask anyone in the medical bay, they will vouch for me. They all seem to be under the impression that the Doctor and I saved this place from…'

The man behind the desk sat bolt upright in delight. 'The Doctor? You know the Doctor?'

'We travel together. He is my… companion,' Romana replied curtly. 'Do you know him?'

'Oh, we know the Doctor,' the man sneered. 'Investigators, may I present to you – the Doctor's accomplice!'

Romana was taken aback. 'Accomplice?'

Dunkal looked doubtful. 'You never mentioned anything about an accomplice before, Executive Metcalf.'

'Isn't it obvious?' said Metcalf. 'This woman, this woman…'

'Romana,' prompted Romana.

'Thank you. This woman, Romana, aided the Doctor in his sabotage of the necroport. She is his co-conspirator. And now she compounds her not inconsiderable crimes by smuggling narcotics. How guilty can you possibly get?'

Dunkal consulted with Rige. 'He does have a point there.'

'The Doctor wouldn't sabotage anything,' said Romana. 'You're obviously suffering from some sort of delusion.'

'Me... deluded? I suppose you're also going to claim that the G-Lock is going to be destroyed in a few hours?' said Metcalf.

'Yes. The Doctor...'

'Oh yes.' Metcalf raised a podgy finger, and the guards snapped their heels to attention. The two nearest guards placed their hands on Romana's shoulders and waist. 'Guards, take Romana to see the Doctor.'

'We haven't finished our questioning yet,' said Dunkal. 'Romana, what were you doing when the zombies –'

Metcalf leapt to his feet as if his chair had been set alight. 'For the final time, Investigator. If I say someone is guilty, then as far as you are concerned, they are guilty,' he said. 'That is all the evidence you need. Understand?'

Dunkal spat out his cigarette. 'Oh, I understand.'

'Most gratifying. Guards, away.' Metcalf plumped himself back down, and the guards bustled Romana out of the office.

The sonic screwdriver shrilled, the lock bleeped, and the cell door clattered upwards.

The Doctor ushered K9 forward. 'Come on, K9!' he whispered.

All of a sudden, a thickset arm swung around the Doctor's neck, and the sonic screwdriver was wrenched out of his hand. 'Oh no, you're not getting out like that again!'

The arm tightened, throttling the Doctor. He tried in vain to pull himself free. 'Again?'

The guard twisted the Doctor round. The Doctor had a fleeting impression of an ugly, contemptuous face, and then was shoved back into the cell. He slammed into the bench and the cell door rattled shut.

The Doctor sat up and rubbed his neck. K9 approached him, concerned.

'I'm all right, K9. A little bruised pride, that's all.' The Doctor gazed at his empty hand. 'He took my sonic screwdriver, the slubberdegullion swine!'

He picked up his hat and jammed it on to his head. He got to his feet and ran a finger across the door. 'All right. Plan B. K9, do you think you could blast a hole in this? A big hole?'

K9 inspected the door with his probe. 'Negative, master. The molecular constitution is too compact.'

'You mean you can't get us out of here?'

'It is beyond my capabilities,' said K9 sadly. 'However, there is still the potential for liberation.'

'Is there?'

'The mistress Romana.'

'Of course! The mistress Romana! She's bound to come and rescue us.'

The door whizzed open and the guard bundled Romana into the cell, sending her piling into the opposite wall. The door slammed down after her.

Romana picked herself up, tugging her cuffs into place. She regarded the Doctor and K9. 'Well, you might at least look pleased to see me.'

The Doctor boggled. 'Time eddies?'

Romana drew a weary breath. For some minutes, she had described her experiences; the woman in the medical ward, the chase through the depths of the ship, her awakening and subsequent arrest. The Doctor had listened, his expression switching from concern to bafflement.

The Doctor continued. 'Echoes of the past. You said when we landed we could have skipped over our time paths.'

'Doctor, that is preposterous.'

'You disturb the surface of time, and the ripples expand outwards. Eventually you get resonances, aftershocks. We Time Lords have a unique sensitivity to distortions in time, you know.'

'Yes, you have mentioned it once or twice.'

'Suggestion, mistress.' K9 trundled across the cell floor.

'Go on.'

'The events you describe appear to be constructed to convey a specific impression,' announced K9. 'A warning.'

'A warning. From the past to the future.' Romana felt a chill run down her back. K9 was right; the girl had led her to that place for a reason. A place where something terrible had once happened.

'A warning? A warning of what?' asked the Doctor.

'Insufficient data.'

The Doctor harrumphed. 'What good is a warning if you don't know what you're being warned about?'

'I think K9 is on the right track,' said Romana, piecing together her thoughts word by word. She didn't know how she knew, but she knew the girl was a real person. Had been a real person. 'But it wasn't a warning about something to come. It was something that has already happened. Does that make sense?'

'Not really, but it'll have to do.' The Doctor paced back and forth. 'Something very peculiar is going on. We arrive, and everyone thanks us for saving them from destruction. And then other people blame us for causing all the destruction. Thoughts, Romana?'

'Well,' said Romana. 'At some point in our future lives, we return to the G-Lock, to a point earlier in time. We then get... involved'

'As usual.'

'Get accused of things we haven't done.'

'As usual.'

'And then save everyone from certain death.'

'As usual.'

'We then leave, having sorted things out. And then that is where we came in. We're experiencing the repercussions of things we haven't done yet.' Romana smiled, pleased with her succinct explanation. Even the Doctor couldn't make it sound confusing now.

The Doctor frowned, as though he was trying to recall something. 'As I thought. But what if, at some point in our future lives, we don't return to the G-Lock?'

'We have to, Doctor,' Romana said. 'We know that at some point in our future we do return here. That's part of our past now, we can't change it. It's future perfect.'

The Doctor gathered up his coat and sat beside her. 'Are you saying we have to return because if we don't, we can't have experienced the aftermath of what will happen when we return, which we have already done?'

Correction. The Doctor could make anything sound confusing. 'Exactly,' said Romana.

'And, of course, you can't change your own past. Second law of time travel,' said the Doctor.

'First law. But you're right. If we don't go back, we will have altered the whole web of time.'

'And the consequences are too terrible to imagine,' declared the Doctor bleakly.

Romana shuddered at the notion. 'Exactly.'

'What about free will?' asked the Doctor, like a resentful child. 'I mean, what if we come back, but fail to save the G-Lock? Hmm?'

'We don't have any choice,' said Romana. 'We have to succeed.'

'Hornswoggled,' muttered the Doctor. '"The order of the acts are planned, and the end of the way inescapable."'

The Doctor and Romana sat in silence for some time. Eventually, the Doctor dipped into his coat and produced a packet of jelly babies. He offered them to K9 and Romana, and selected one for himself.

He swallowed. 'You know, ever since we arrived, I've had the oddest feeling.'

Romana nodded. 'Yes. You mentioned something about the hairs on the back of your neck.'

'Exactly. An uneasy sensation. As if I should recognise things, but was finding them unfamiliar.' The Doctor crumpled up the bag and pocketed it. 'I've just worked out what it is. Pre-*jà vu*.'

'What?'

'Pre-*jà vu*, mistress,' chirped K9 helpfully. 'The sensation that one is going to have been somewhere before. The term applies exclusively to Time Lords, and was coined by Academi Plurix.'

'Oh,' sighed Romana. 'Pre-*jà vu*.'

The Doctor reverted to silence, examining the back of his hands. He started whistling, badly.

'Doctor, what are we going to do?' said Romana.

'Do?'

'About the collapsing hyperspace tunnel. We have to get everyone out of here.'

The Doctor stared back. 'How long do we have, K9?'

'The conduit will lose hyperstatial viability in three hours, forty-seven minutes and counting.'

'Three, forty-seven minutes.' The Doctor closed his eyes, admitting defeat. 'Unfortunately, Romana, we have the small difficulty of being locked up.'

'Why not use the sonic screwdriver?' Romana asked.

The Doctor shook his head. 'No good. I tried, and the guard confiscated it.'

'What about K9? He could blast –'

'No good either, I'm afraid.'

Romana thumped the door in irritation. 'There must be something we can do!'

'Well, normally, in this predicament I'd blow my dog whistle and K9 would come and rescue us,' said the Doctor. 'But this time K9 didn't remain in the TARDIS, so unfortunately we're stuck.'

'Apologies, master,' said K9.

'It's not your fault, K9,' said Romana, glaring at the Doctor. 'It's not as if you can be in two places at once.'

'So this is it, then. The end,' said the Doctor.

'Two places…' An idea occurred to Romana. She knelt in front of the Doctor. 'Doctor, we know that at some point in the future we're going to go back in time and revisit the G-Lock, right?'

'We have to get out of here first.'

Romana shushed him. 'But what if, when we go back in time, we also arrange for someone to come and rescue us from this cell?'

'We can't do that. That's cheating.'

From outside the cell, there was a dull thud followed by the clatter of someone falling heavily to the floor. The door rose to reveal a young woman in her twenties with cropped, sandy hair and a milky complexion. She wore functional overalls and an enthusiastic expression.

Behind her, the guard lay unconscious on the floor.

'Hello. I've come to rescue you.' The woman grinned at Romana. 'Not too late, am I?'

Romana was flabbergasted. 'You've come to set us free?'

'Yes. As instructed. For a minute there I didn't think I'd get here in time, but…' She popped her head through the cell doorway. Seeing the Doctor, her jaw dropped. 'But hang on…You're… you're…'

The Doctor extended a hand. 'Yes, I'm the Doctor. Marvellous to meet you.'

42

The woman shook her head in disbelief. 'No, but you're... you're not...'

'The Doctor? Yes, I am,' said the Doctor, complete with toothy grin. 'And this is one of my two best friends, K9. Say hello, K9.' He indicated the computer. K9 wheeled eagerly towards her.

'Greetings,' said K9 brightly.

'No! No!' At the sight of K9 the woman began hyperventilating, tripping over her own feet in her haste to leave. She screamed in terror, fainted and slipped inelegantly to the floor.

The Doctor shrugged, looked at K9, looked at Romana, looked at the new arrival lying on the floor, and shrugged again.

'Did the universe get out of the wrong side of bed this morning, or is it me?' he asked.

The Doctor helped the woman to her feet, walked her out of the cell, and rested her on the guard's chair. Romana fetched a glass of water, while the Doctor searched through the guard's desk which was buried under copies of *Guards & Guarding* magazines. He spotted his sonic screwdriver and stowed it in the depths of his coat.

He wafted some smelling salts under the woman's nose and she grimaced back to consciousness. She accepted the water and gulped it down. A minute later, she was ready to speak.

'Sorry. Don't know what happened,' she began. 'I think it was the surprise of seeing you again, Doctor.'

'Oh, I often have that effect,' said the Doctor. Romana coughed sarcastically, but he elected to ignore her. 'Usually on monsters, though, it must be said. But don't mention it.'

'I didn't realise, Romana didn't tell me.' The woman grasped the Doctor's hands and rubbed them. Her eyes watered. 'I'm so pleased to see you like this.'

'Not at all, not at all.' The Doctor felt more baffled than flattered. 'What exactly didn't Romana tell you?'

The woman was about to speak when Romana interrupted. 'Doctor, shouldn't we be moving away from here?'

'Yes, of course,' said the Doctor. 'Escape first, ask questions later.' He patted the woman on the shoulder. 'Are you ready to move, um... I'm sorry, I'm hopeless with names.'

'Evadne Baxter,' said the woman, getting up.

'Evadne, yes, Evadne,' flustered the Doctor, pretending to have remembered her name. 'Evadne Baxter, thank you for rescuing us.'

'Can we please go now?' said Romana impatiently. The guard was groaning back to life, rubbing the nape of his neck.

'Right.' The Doctor folded up his hat and tucked it in a pocket. 'K9? K9?'

K9 whirred out of the cell. Immediately, Evadne inhaled and stepped back. 'Keep that thing away from me,' she said, near hysterical. 'Keep it away!'

'I am entirely non-hostile.' K9 sounded hurt. 'You have nothing to fear. I am programmed to use my weaponry only in defence.'

'It's gonna kill me!'

'K9, stay away from Evadne,' said the Doctor. It was hard to understand the woman's reaction. K9 did not normally inspire feelings of alarm. Hilarity, yes. Alarm, no. But Evadne had obviously been scared to within an inch of her life.

'Affirmative,' K9 said glumly. 'This unit will maintain a maximum peripheral distance.'

'Right,' said Romana. 'Let's go then.'

'And then this fellow called Executive Metcalf decided to have us arrested,' said the Doctor.

Evadne had led them back into the depths of the ship. After several devastated corridors, littered with the corpses of both guards and tourists, they found themselves in more familiar territory: the derelict shopping streets. Above the hiss of the wall-mounted loudspeakers, there was not a single sound. They hadn't seen a living soul since leaving the prison.

'Metcalf?' laughed Evadne. 'Well, I think we both know why that gasket wanted you out of the way, don't we Romana?'

'We do?' Romana raised a quizzical eyebrow.

'After what happened, him in his office. You really don't remember?'

Romana shook her head. 'No. As I said, as far as we're concerned none of this has actually happened yet.'

'I think I can guess about Metcalf,' said the Doctor. 'The man's an incompetent. He's just using us as scapegoats to save his own petty skin. Like any politician, he's quite happy to accept the credit, but never to take the blame.'

'Straight up,' said Evadne, munching on a jelly baby. 'He's supposed to be in charge, but you won't find him thanking us for saving the G-Lock.'

'Us?' said Romana.

'Oh, you must remember how you did that,' said Evadne. 'In the necroport. You, the Doctor –'

'Stop!' The Doctor bellowed, slamming his hands over his ears. 'Shush! Don't tell us! I don't want to know!'

Evadne gaped at the Doctor, confusion writ large over her face. 'Eh?'

Romana took her patiently to one side. 'As far as we're concerned, we haven't saved the G-Lock yet. So you can't tell us how we did it, because then we would have foreknowledge we shouldn't have. If we knew what our futures would be, we might behave differently, and things might not end up happening in the way that you say they have happened. Understand?'

'But you've done it, it's happened.'

'Not for us it hasn't. We mustn't know too much about our future actions. It would create all sorts of dangerous paradoxes,' said Romana.

'And it would spoil all the fun of finding out,' added the Doctor.

'Quite,' seconded Romana, before she realised what the Doctor had said. 'Aside from that, it could cause serious disruption to the time stream.'

'Hang on,' began Evadne. 'It's happened, so it doesn't matter what I say now, because you're going to succeed anyway. Am I right?'

'Unfortunately time doesn't work like that,' said Romana. 'Because we're Time Lords, we're not bound by history. We have the ability to change our pasts.'

'But a responsibility not to,' said the Doctor.

Evadne blinked in concentration. 'But how do you know that I'm not supposed to tell you stuff? Me not telling you might mess up this time stream thing too.'

The Doctor and Romana looked at each other. 'Just take our word for it,' suggested Romana.

Evadne sniffed. 'All right. I don't understand, but I'll keep quiet. Say no more.' Her face brightened. 'I'm just relieved to see the Doctor alive and well again, anyway.'

'What do you mean?' said Romana, and immediately wished she hadn't.

Evadne turned to the Doctor. 'The last time I saw you, you were dead. You sacrificed your life to save the G-Lock.'

Dunkal handed over two sheets of paper: Metcalf's witness statement, plus a copy. Metcalf gave each a flamboyant signature. 'I trust that everything is to your satisfaction?'

Dunkal jangled the change in his pockets. 'Pending further investigation, it seems we have no choice but to consider the Doctor and Romana guilty as charged.'

Rige collected the statements. 'Guilty.'

'Most satisfactory.' Metcalf's desk intercom buzzed. He pressed the reply button. 'Yes, Executive Metcalf speaking?'

'Sir, this is the prison guard. You know those two you had brought down here?'

The two Investigators listened with interest. 'The saboteurs. Yes?' answered Metcalf.

'It is my unfortunate duty, sir, to inform you that they have escaped.'

'Escaped?' Metcalf could hear himself going high-pitched. 'Escaped? You let them escape – again?'

'It wasn't my fault, sir. I was overpowered by a third party and rendered insensible.'

'I do not believe I am hearing this. Insensible? I doubt you were ever sensible to begin with,' said Metcalf. 'What is your name, guard?'

'Dudley, sir.'

'I see. In the face of overwhelming incompetence, you give me no choice but to fire you, Dudley. Please collect your belongings and leave.' Metcalf switched off the intercom and swirled in his chair to face the Investigators. He drummed on the desk. 'As you heard, it transpires our two convicts are once more on the loose. Wreaking havoc, no doubt.'

Dunkal pressed his cigarette into the ashtray. 'You want us to apprehend them again?'

'I most definitely do,' said Metcalf. 'Dead or alive. I shall leave which to your Investigatorial discretion. In execution of your duties, so to speak.'

Rige unpacked his rifle and levered off the safety catch. 'Best news I've heard all day.'

'Here we go again.' Dunkal straightened his peaked cap, and followed Rige out of the office. As they left, Metcalf flicked on the public address system.

'G-Lock. This is Executive Metcalf speaking. I regret to announce that once again the terrorist known as the Doctor is on the rampage, accompanied by his co-conspirator Romana. Will all skullguards immediately attend to their recapture, dead or alive.'

'Although they are both highly dangerous, and have caused the recent disaster resulting in mass murder, there is no cause for public disquiet. Thank you.'

Romana listened with growing trepidation as the loudspeaker crackled off. The Doctor was still deep in thought. Since Evadne's announcement, he had barely said a word. His face was drawn, his eyeballs even more prominent than usual. 'I hope I don't die too soon,' he muttered, laughing humourlessly. 'I should be most upset.'

'Doctor,' said Romana gently. 'We can't be sure that Evadne's telling the truth. She might be mistaken. After all, she has obviously experienced considerable psychological trauma.'

The Doctor cheered up. 'You're right, of course, Romana. Best to just get on with it, mmm? "Though I walk through the valley of the shadow –"'

Before the Doctor could finish, Evadne dashed back from the end of the corridor where she had been keeping watch. 'They're coming this way.'

'Who?'

'Skullguards.' Evadne ushered them over to a doorway. The door swung open to reveal complete darkness. 'Double-quick. Through here.'

K9 was the first to enter, wobbling over the clutter of wreckage. Watching the robot dog cautiously, Evadne disappeared after him.

There was the clatter of approaching bootsteps.

'Skullguards.' The Doctor rubbed his nose, and then dramatically dived through the door. Romana caught a fleeting glimpse of four black-robed guards rounding the corner, before she leapt through the entrance and tugged the door shut after her.

The bootsteps neared the door, paused, and stomped away.

Romana let out a relieved sigh. There was the overpowering smell of burnt metal; she was reminded of a disused refinery, or the inside of an oven.

The Doctor switched on his torch. They had entered an immense cathedral-like chamber, its pillars bridging together to form arches across the high ceiling. The sloping walls were coated in soot, and the masonry had crumbled in places to reveal the ship's skeleton of girders. Rubble from the collapsed ceiling covered the ground, forming mountains of smashed slabs and scorched metal. The opening they had used was merely a concealed side entrance – two huge iron doors dominated one end of the hall.

'Here we are. This is the Great Hall,' announced Evadne, her voice echoing in the silence. 'Or least, it used to be.'

The torch light flitted along the walls. On one side, the hall was overlooked by a gallery of windows. The glass had shattered and, as the shadows lengthened and shortened in the moving light, the windows resembled empty eye sockets.

Hundreds of open, metal caskets filled every available space on the lower walls. They were decked in three levels, each set slightly further back into the wall than the one below, each casket standing upright and accessed by a narrow walkway. More caskets spilled out on to the floor, arranged in rows and aisles. Each one was the size of a coffin, with enough space to allow the occupant to lie, or stand, within. Romana was reassured to see that they were all unoccupied.

The Doctor flashed the light over to the doorway, where K9 remained.

'K9, stay there,' said the Doctor. 'Keep guard. Set your nose on stun.'

K9 whirred his assent and, as he rotated to face the door, the Doctor, Romana and Evadne advanced deeper into the hall.

The Doctor's torch drifted its attention back to a nearby coffin. As with all the others, there was a crown of wire at its end, at the indentation where the head would rest. A lead connected the crown to a small bank of circuits, toasted beyond recognition. These were then connected to heavy cables, which coupled together, looped along the walls and formed a locus at the centre of the hall.

'What happened here? I mean, what used to go on here in the Great Hall?' asked the Doctor.

'The Beautiful Death. This is where it takes place. Took place,' said Evadne.

'The Beautiful Death. Ah.' The Doctor pulled a suitably gothic expression.

'You must remember, you said this is where the tourists were –'

'We keep telling you, we don't remember,' interrupted Romana. 'Because none of this has happened to us yet. Please, it is very important you answer only our specific questions.'

'Sorry,' Evadne said. 'I keep forgetting. Say no more.'

'And what is this?' The Doctor shone his torch on the object in the centre of the hall.

'That?' said Evadne. 'Oh, that's the necroport.'

The necroport jutted out of the floor, a small, approximately conical structure about the same size as the TARDIS. It had been severely damaged, the surface buckled out of shape, the smoke stains partially obscuring paintings of skull-headed angels. The machine, ensconced in hydraulic ducting and power linkages, seemed to be merely the upper section of a much larger device buried beneath the floor. A bolt-ringed hatchway was set into an alcove on one side of the device.

'The necroport,' the Doctor said to himself. He reached for the hatchway and heaved. It clanged open. He peered down into the necroport. 'Shall we?'

Evadne seemed apprehensive, and opened her mouth as if to warn them, but thought better of it.

'Do you think it's safe?' Romana joined the Doctor. Inside the necroport a ladder descended to the level below.

'Probably not, no.'

'What about the collapsing hyperspace tunnel?' said Romana. 'You wanted to find the interface, remember?'

'You're right,' said the Doctor. 'It's just… well, I'd quite like to see what it is I'm supposed to have sabotaged, that's all.'

'Romana, I don't know if this helps,' said Evadne tentatively. 'But… well, you told me to bring you here. Before you were locked up, I mean. You said it was very important that you were taken to the necroport.'

'Did she?' said the Doctor. 'Well, I always take Romana's advice.'

When I agree with it.' He climbed into the necroport, and swung his way down the ladder.

The cramped chamber had been consumed by fire. The concave metal walls had warped under the force of a great explosion. Every footstep crunched into a thick layer of ash.

The Doctor's torch picked out an adjoining room, but the way to it was blocked by rubble. It appeared that much of the Great Hall above had caved in, destroying the room's contents. Tracing the stress points, the Doctor calculated that the explosion had been concentrated within this second room.

Two more crunches announced that Romana and Evadne had entered the chamber behind him. The Doctor turned and noticed three coffins arranged against one wall. Again, the caskets were wired into the innards of the necroport. But this time, the coffins were occupied.

Romana and Evadne gasped in horror. The middle and right-hand coffins contained two blackened, charred corpses. The bodies had once been humanoid, if not human, but were now unrecognisable. Their clothes and the skin had been stripped away, leaving skeletal blocks of charcoal.

Even the Doctor was shocked by the occupant of the third coffin. This body was in a similar state to the others, but its ribcage was rising and falling. It was still alive.

The corpse's eyes snapped open, and drank in the Doctor, Romana and Evadne. The creature was humanoid, but had strange, frond-like rills around its neck. The Doctor couldn't identify the species, but it appeared to be vegetable in constitution.

'Gallura's still alive. I do not believe it,' said Evadne hoarsely.

Gallura raised his head. 'Doctor. At last.'

'It is happening,' said the birthsayer. 'The birth of Gallura is now.'

The birthsayers clustered around the carpel. There was a rasp of tearing fibre and the tube cleaved in two. With a final palpitation, the skin of the womb burst open and amniotic fluids gushed out into the sternum chamber. Encased in its glistening sac, the baby slowly slipped out of the mothertree's stem and emerged into the proud embrace of the elders.

* * *

'You know who I am?'

'Of old, Doctor, of old,' said Gallura. Every word seemed to be wrenched out of him, each exhalation a dying breath. 'Listen. I can sense the approaching moment. I must ask something of you.'

The Doctor shifted closer. 'What is it?'

'Go back, Doctor. You know your future is in your past. Go back in time and avenge my death.'

Evadne and Romana watched the Doctor. He appeared to be half-fascinated and half-horrified by the sight before him.

'Promise me you will go back,' said Gallura. 'Avenge the extinction of the Arboretans.'

'I promise,' said the Doctor. 'I have no choice.'

'You have a choice,' croaked Gallura. 'There always is a choice.'

'Then I choose to go back. You have my word,' whispered the Doctor.

Gallura looked at the Doctor for what seemed a very long time. Then his head dropped back, and his eyelids rolled shut. The remaining air wheezed out of his lungs.

The Doctor faced Romana. He looked confused, afraid. 'He's dead,' the Doctor stated.

The oldest birthsayer lifted the newborn clear of the folded remains of the birth sac. Supporting its head, she wiped away the fluids from its semitransparent skin, and wrapped it in a nutrient tuber.

She presented the baby to Nyanna, who cradled it to her chest. The baby's eyes were bright and inquisitive, and a delicate lattice of veins bulged from its forehead, flushed with fresh, green blood.

'Gallura is born,' said the birthsayer proudly.

'Well. That's that, then,' said the Doctor.

'I still can't get my head round it. He managed to survive, in here.' Evadne took one final glance at the three charred corpses.

Romana followed Evadne to the ladder. 'Where to now, Doctor?'

The Doctor raised one hand. 'Evadne. Do you know the way to corridor 79?'

'Oh yeah,' said Evadne. 'It's on one of the lower levels, not far.'

'Right. First we collect K9, and then we'll go and see this hyperspatial interface. And then…'

'And then?' asked Romana.

'By then I should have thought of something. Come on!'

'This bit of the ship's abandoned,' explained Evadne. 'No one's come down here for years.'

She led the way, the Doctor trudging behind. Romana was next, with K9 bringing up the rear.

It was yet another gloomy, derelict corridor, lined with closed doors and strewn with rubble. The wooden panelling and carpet had both rotted, and the air had the odour of an ancient cellar.

'Tell me about this place. I'm fascinated,' said the Doctor. 'The history, and so on.'

Evadne sighed. 'Grief. You really want me to?'

'Is it a problem?'

'It's just my job. Was my job. Regurgitating the same old guff. Answering the same imbecile tourist questions.'

'Well, one more time?' said the Doctor.

'All right,' shrugged Evadne. 'You're now standing on board the remains of the interplantary luxury cruiser *Cerberus*. Almost two hundred years ago, it was making a voyage between Teredekethon and Murgatroyd, care of this hyperspace tunnel.' She broke off. 'You know about hyperspace tunnels, I take it, drinking straws and sheets of paper?

'Anyway, it was one of the main interstellar routes. Loads of traffic, right? And it was a typical journey, that is, up until the point when the *Cerberus* was supposed to leave the tunnel.

'As the ship moved into the exit, the hyperspace tunnel closed off. The *Cerberus* got stuck, completely blocking the tunnel. The result was disastrous. All the traffic behind got caught in the most terrible intergalactic traffic jam in history.

'To prevent further ships from entering the tunnel, the authorities closed off the entrance. Which meant, basically, that all the ships within the tunnel were trapped together. And then, after two months, the hyperspace tunnel was finally reopened, and the emergency rescue teams went in.

'The *Cerberus* had been carrying almost one thousand passengers, plus a full ship's complement. There were also fifty other craft trapped within the traffic jam, with hundreds of people on board. But when the emergency crews cut their way through the airlocks and entered the ships, they found them deserted. Not a soul in sight, alive or dead. No one has ever found out why. And, well, that's the "Mystery of the *Cerberus*", innit.' Evadne looked embarrassed.

'Ah,' exhaled the Doctor ominously.

A chill rose up Romana's spine. It wasn't entirely due to the cold. Listening to Evadne's story had certainly unsettled her, but it wasn't that either. It was the corridor they were walking along, there was something familiar about it. Of course all the corridors looked the same, but this one had an eerie quality. Like the sensation she had felt on arriving; a temporal detachment, or, as the Doctor would have it, pre-*jà vu*.

Evadne resumed the story. 'Anyway, later, the traffic jam became a haven for dropouts from galactic society, those seeking a life away from laws and regulations, and people started to move in and live on the abandoned wrecks. The jam attracted a large and galaxy-famous community of hippies, bohemians and political refugees. It gradually transformed into a space station, and became known as the G-Lock. From gridlock, you see, basic.' Evadne finished. 'And that's about it. There's some other stuff about how it got bought out and Executive Metcalf was put in charge, but that's too boring for words.'

Together they all turned the corner, to find a corridor unlike any other.

Romana shuddered and backed against the wall. After another thirty metres, the corridor ended in total blackness. A curtain of pure, liquid nothingness. A plaque on the wall read: *Corridor 79*.

The Doctor took one look at Romana. 'This is the place you saw?'

She nodded.

'"All that we ever see or seem",' said the Doctor. 'A warning. I wonder. I wonder…'

'Doctor,' said Romana. 'What is going on?'

'I wish I knew. Mmm.' The Doctor pulled a face. 'K9. This is your chance. Prognosis?'

K9 trundled forward. 'The zone ahead is where the hyperspace–real-space interface bisects the craft.'

'You mean, this is the point at which the *Cerberus* got stuck?' said the Doctor. 'That beyond that…' He waved towards the darkness, '... the corridor continues, but in real space instead of hyperspace.'

'Affirmative.'

'Ah.' The Doctor strode up to the interface, licked a finger and reached towards the gloom.

'Warning, master,' said K9. 'The interface is highly unstable and will disintegrate unprotected matter to its component subatomic particles.'

The Doctor withdrew his hand.

Romana joined the Doctor, followed by Evadne. 'You can't pass through.'

The Doctor crouched and collected a lump of rubble. After weighing it, he tossed it into the blackness. The rock disappeared with a gulp and sent ripples skidding across the surface. The blackness had swallowed it up.

'K9 was right,' said the Doctor. 'This hyperspace tunnel is on the brink of collapse, you can see the geostatic stress points.' He indicated the flickering blue outline where the hyperspace merged into the corridor.

'I'm astounded it's lasted this long,' Romana commented. 'It should have lost dimensional viability centuries ago.'

'Sorry I ever doubted you, K9,' said the Doctor.

'Apology accepted and archived for future reference.'

'The girl,' said Romana. 'She must have been warning us about this place.'

'Hang on, you're saying that the G-Lock is going to be crushed?' said Evadne. 'That the conduit is going to...'

'Be reduced to a singularity, yes. Starting here.' The Doctor pointed at the blackness. 'Romana, we've got to get everybody out of here.'

'But how? We've got guards looking for us, Metcalf's made them believe we're saboteurs –'

'Master, mistress. Danger,' said K9. 'I detect life forms approaching.'

'What?' said the Doctor.

'Life forms approaching,' repeated K9. 'On a bearing of zero degrees.'

The Doctor whirled around. 'But that's...' He faced the darkness. 'That means they're coming from in there.'

'Affirmative master. Beings now at a range of ten metres and closing.'

'They can't possibly pass through,' said Romana, but her voice lacked conviction. 'It's impossible.'

'Five metres and closing.'

The Doctor drew back from the darkness, and joined Evadne and Romana beside K9. 'Five metres?'

'Four metres. Three. One.'

'The life forms are now at a range of zero metres.'

'Zero metres?' The Doctor exchanged a worried gape with Romana. 'But that means...'

The darkness was over five metres away. Whatever K9 had detected was now right on top of them.

But there was nothing there.

Chapter Four

'Zero metres? But that means –'

'Hang on,' protested Evadne. 'I'm probably being a bit stupid, but what life forms?'

'Yes.' The Doctor frowned. 'Er, K9, are you sure your readings are correct?'

K9's ears wiggled. 'Affirmative.'

The Doctor stroked his chin. 'Is there one here, K9?' He waved his hands through the air.

'Affirmative, master. Doctor master's arms and life form currently occupying identical spatial coordinates.'

'Sorry.' The Doctor snatched his hand back sheepishly. 'I wouldn't want to upset anybody.'

'As if you could,' commented Romana. 'Did you feel anything?'

'No.' The Doctor peered into the darkness. 'This is intensely fascinating. Well, about as fascinating as nothing gets, anyway.'

'Three life forms on a bearing of zero degrees,' announced K9. 'Range two metres. Five metres. Ten metres.'

'They're going,' said Romana. 'Back into hyperspace.'

'Oh, and we were getting on so well,' said the Doctor.

'Warning additional,' piped K9. 'Two life forms approaching on a bearing of 180 degrees. Sensors indicate they are Earth humans Dunkal and Rige.'

'Quick. In here.' The Doctor swiped his sonic screwdriver across the nearest cabin door. The door hummed open and he bustled Romana, Evadne and K9 into the unlit room.

There was the scuffling of boots. The Doctor flattened his back against the door. As it slid shut the two Investigators appeared. Rige led the way with the tracking device; both men had rifles raised.

'Ah, Dunkal. Rige. I assume you've come to capture me again?'

'Not quite, Doctor,' growled Dunkal. 'How does "killed resisting arrest" sound to you, Rige?'

'Very tidy,' sneered Rige. 'No inconvenient questions.'

The Doctor surreptitiously checked the door was secure, and moved directly between it and Rige's tracker. Hopefully his signal would swamp any trace of the others. 'But it's important to ask inconvenient questions. For instance, have you ever wondered what it's like to be reduced to a singularity?'

'No.'

'I only say that because in about two hours' time that's what this whole place will be.' The Doctor grinned.

'Is that the best you can do?' Dunkal said. 'You're about to be executed and you're doing the same scare story again.'

'It's not a story', said the Doctor. 'But you're right, you should be scared.' He indicated the fuzzy outline of the darkness. 'You see the build-up of geostatic pressure there? That's the hyperspace interface about to collapse.'

'He's lying,' said Rige, but he didn't sound convinced.

'I never lie. Besides, what would I hope to gain? You're going to kill me anyway. My card is marked, my number's up, my goose is cooked. I've cashed in my chips and have ceased to be. I am an ex-Doctor.' The Doctor leaned forward conspiratorially. 'I won't be here in two hours. But you will,' he whispered, letting his last three words percolate into Dunkal and Rige's brains.

'He does have a point.' Dunkal took Rige aside. 'What's in it for him?'

Rige's eyes narrowed. 'Is he playing for time?'

'Time, gentlemen, is the one thing we don't have,' the Doctor said. He raised his voice to a boom. 'Why not just take me to see Executive Metcalf? If I can prove that I'm telling the truth, he can order an evacuation and you can go home. If I can't, well, then I'll confess to everything, and you'll have your conviction regardless.'

Dunkal regarded him curiously. 'Why are you shouting?'

'No reason,' breezed the Doctor. Hopefully Romana would have heard. 'Well?'

'A confession would cut down on paperwork. All right. We'll pay our friend Metcalf another visit.'

'You don't mean you actually believe him –' started Rige.

'A good Investigator never believes anyone,' said Dunkal.

'I don't believe you.'

'Don't be clever, Rige.' Dunkal jabbed the Doctor in the back with his gun. 'Now move.'

Romana waited until the footsteps had disappeared, then eased the door open. Followed by Evadne and K9, she emerged into the corridor. Evadne had been terrified at being locked in with K9, and Romana had been forced to clamp her hands over her mouth to keep her quiet.

'They've got the Doctor.' Romana dusted herself down. 'I don't know what he's playing at, but we've got to find some way of proving that he didn't sabotage the G-Lock. It's the only way they'll believe us.'

A smile crossed Evadne's face. 'Oh, I think I know a bloke who can help.'

Metcalf helped himself to a digestive biscuit. With the Doctor and his cohorts out of the way, a line could be drawn under this ghastly business and he could begin restructuring his career. He imagined the grand reopening of the G-Lock. If marketed appropriately, the recent disaster could even work in their favour; never mind 'The Mystery of the *Cerberus*', people would flock to see where the tourists had been transformed into zombies. Obviously the victims' relatives would need to be compensated. Complimentary tickets, perhaps, during the slack season.

It would be a most agreeable outcome to events, he decided.

The two idiot Investigators entered, pushing the Doctor before them, the beatnik tripping comically over his own scarf. 'The Doctor for you,' announced Dunkal.

'Hello there,' said the Doctor cheerily.

Metcalf blustered. 'Well, what are you waiting for? I am the Executive here, and I say execute him.'

'First things first,' said Dunkal. 'We decide who we execute, and when. Not you. You have no authority over us.'

Rige noticed the biscuits, and popped one in his mouth. 'No authority.'

'I agree, if anyone's interested,' the Doctor added.

'What?' said Metcalf. 'You have my testimony. I say the man is guilty, and if you do not kill him immediately I shall be not inconsiderably displeased. And you wouldn't like me when I'm not inconsiderably displeased, Investigator. I order you –'

'Shut it, Metcalf. I've already had more than enough of you,' said Dunkal, slamming a fist on the desk. 'I just want you to hear what the Doctor has to say. And then I'll decide whether we kill him or not.'

The Doctor strode forward and loomed over Metcalf's desk. 'Thank you, Investigators. Metcalf, I haven't got time for your flummery, so listen. This whole place is going to implode in under two hours' time and if you don't order an evacuation immediately, you will be responsible for the death of every person here.'

'I cannot believe I am hearing this,' said Metcalf. 'You may have duped these two Investigators with your irresponsible scaremongering, Doctor, but you don't frighten me. This hyperspatial conduit has remained stable for two centuries, and will continue –'

The office began to shake. Paintings toppled from the walls. Dunkal and Rige were knocked to the floor, and in the confusion the Doctor grabbed one of the artworks.

The shaking stopped. The Doctor weighed up the sculpture – a recumbent nude in imitation porcelain. 'That was just the beginning. Now, order an evacuation or I shall be forced to drop this.'

Metcalf gulped. His most treasured artwork. 'Put the statue down, Doctor. That is a Potts original.'

Dunkal got to his feet and levelled his rifle at the Doctor. Rige followed suit. 'Do as he says.'

'You know, I get terribly nervous around guns,' said the Doctor, as though it had just occurred to him. 'I should hate to accidentally –.' He let the sculpture slip out of his hands only to catch it a moment later.

'Don't fire, you idiots,' cried Metcalf. 'Put your rifles away.'

'But –'

'Put them away!' said Metcalf. 'That sculpture is uninsured.'

The Investigators reluctantly belted their rifles and backed away.

'That's better.' The Doctor dangled the statue in one hand and switched the intercom on with the other. 'Now give the order.'

'G-Lock. This is Executive Metcalf speaking,' Metcalf stammered into the microphone. 'I wish to order a complete evacuation of the G-Lock. All persons, tourists and staff should proceed calmly to the docking bay. Apparently the hyperspace tunnel is about to collapse killing us all, but there is no cause for public disquiet. Thank you.'

'And call your guards off.'

'Additional message to all skullguards. The terrorists referred to as the Doctor and Romana are not, it transpires, terrorists after all, and should not be recaptured.'

The Doctor switched the intercom off, and carelessly tossed the statue aside. Metcalf dived across his desk and grabbed it, clutching it to the safety of his chest. He looked up at the Doctor, his body shaking with pure hatred. 'Kill him! Kill him now!'

Throughout the G-Lock the survivors streamed down the corridors, down the access tubes of the docking bay. Tourists dressed in colourful, flowing robes hurried into the parked spacecraft. The skullguards abandoned their masks and joined the exodus. The emergency medics packed away their life-detectors and headed back to their ships.

Dunkal levelled his rifle at the Doctor's left ear.

'Well, you felt the tremor,' said the Doctor. 'And you saw the geostatic build-up. And the fact that I'm prepared to risk my life to –'

'You can prove anything with facts,' sneered Metcalf. 'And yet you have most conspicuously failed to produce any evidence that you did not sabotage the necroport, nor…'

'Well, I might have sabotaged the necroport, I don't know,' considered the Doctor. 'I might have sabotaged it to prevent it turning people into the walking dead. After all, I somehow don't think Metcalf here…'

'What are you suggesting?'

'I somehow doubt that you were the one who saved the day. I have some experience in that area, you see.'

Dunkal decided it was time to impose himself on the proceedings. The sooner this was sorted, the sooner he could get back to real investigating. Questioning widows and drinking in dive bars. 'I think, Rige, that we can infer the Doctor's full confession.'

'Confession,' said Rige, twitching his trigger finger.

The office door opened. The Doctor's accomplice entered, smiling haughtily. 'I do hope I'm not interrupting,' she said.

'Romana, you're just in time,' said Metcalf. 'The Investigators were just about to pass sentence.'

'I've brought some people along.' A cheery-looking girl in

overalls entered, followed by a balding man in a grey mac, an overweight fool in shorts carrying a holocamera, and the ludicrous dog the Doctor had called K9.

At the sight of them, Metcalf began rapidly smoothing his hair. 'This is a private executive office. You must vacate these premises forthwith.' Nobody paid any attention.

Dunkal felt certain he remembered the balding man from somewhere. Probably from his criminal files. There was undoubtedly something nefarious about him.

'Evadne. K9. Jeremy.' The Doctor shook the balding man's hand. 'And Harken Batt! I am so pleased to see you.'

Harken Batt. Of course, thought Dunkal. The holovision presenter from a few years back. He'd showed up at a few chalk outlines Dunkal had been investigating. And *The Guilty Conscience* documentary. Hadn't there been some sort of scandal about that?

'Doctor, I came as soon as I heard of your grim fate,' said Harken. 'When I heard the announcements ordering your arrest, I feared the worst, and then the evacuation notice...'

The Doctor fixed Harken with an anxious stare. 'How's it going?'

'The evacuation? Oh, it seems to be proceeding smoothly. Actually, I need to ask you about that.'

'Yes?'

'This tunnel really is collapsing, is it?'

'Yes.'

'And what would the best viewpoint be, when it happens?'

'As far away as possible,' Romana said. 'Harken, this isn't really the time or the place...'

'Absolutely.' Harken swallowed. 'As I was saying. If I had known that my documentary would be of supreme importance...'

'Your documentary?' said the Doctor. 'Of course...'

'Harken has holovideo footage that completely gets you off the hook, Doctor,' said Evadne. 'And not only that, but it also incriminates a certain gasket –'

'Don't listen to them,' bleated Metcalf, wiping his hands on his lapels. 'This is a smear campaign. A malicious, underhand...'

Dunkal motioned to Rige to shut Metcalf up. At the unfriendly end of a rifle, the Executive closed his mouth.

'Is this correct? It demonstrates he's...' Dunkal winced at Metcalf, '... guilty?'

'It most certainly does,' said Harken. 'Extensive footage gathered throughout by myself and my holocameraman Jeremy. An exclusive insight into the true nature of events. As they happened.'

'OK. Let's see it,' said Dunkal, and dragged himself a seat.

The Doctor and the others stood aside as Jeremy placed his holocamera on the desk. At the press of a button, the camera sent a beam of light onto the far wall where a blocky image shimmered. Gradually, it cleared into a three-dimensional projection of Metcalf's face. His face was dripping with sweat as he crouched in a small, dark booth.

Shaking with fear, and direct to camera, Metcalf screamed, 'Never mind the plebbing tourists! Let them all die, I don't care! We're considerably better off without them, the hippy scum! Just get me out of here!'

The image dissected and faded to white. 'I'm thinking of using that for the trailer,' said Harken.

'I can explain,' spluttered Metcalf. 'That was recorded under the most exceptional circumstances –' He fell silent at the prompt of Rige's rifle.

The holovideo resolved itself into another image, this time of Harken Batt in a metal chamber. Behind him were two or three figures in coffins, but it was impossible to identify them in the low-resolution gloom.

The holographic Harken Batt checked his microphone. 'You join me in the interior of the necroport, the device behind the Beautiful Death, where the battle for the G-Lock reaches its dreadful and dramatic conclusion.' He tilted his head to one side, and spoke in an over-serious drawl. 'Whilst outside the twins known only as tragedy and terror unleash their deadly game of destruction, within we are about to bear witness to the ultimate confrontation between man and something else. With my invaluable assistance, the enigmatic traveller known only as the Doctor is now striving to defeat the terrible menace…'

'Ah-ha!' grinned the Doctor. 'I told you so!'

'… and avert the certain and harrowing massacre of every soul on board the G-Lock.' The holographic Harken Batt paused. 'It is a task that may cost him his very life.'

The Doctor's grin fell.

The projection blinked off, leaving a plain wall. All faces in the room turned to the real Harken. 'It's good, isn't it?' he declared.

Dunkal weighed up the various options, brushed his moustache and stood up. 'Executive Metcalf, I am placing you under arrest on suspicion of crimes of negligence leading to mass fatalities. You will be taken from this place to a place of imprisonment pending full investigation and sentence. Although you have the right to remain silent, we have the right to infer guilt from your silence. Is there anything you wish to say?'

Metcalf rose to his feet, straightening his suit. 'This is all most undesirable. I have behaved impeccably throughout a period of great personal strain.' He looked yearningly at the sculptures. His chin wobbled. 'Can I have these transported with me?'

'Not where you're going,' said Dunkal. It was one of his favourite lines.

Metcalf trailed a finger over his desk one fond and final time, and allowed himself to be led out. As he passed the Doctor his face reddened. 'This is entirely your fault, Doctor. I have friends, you know, high-placed ones, and when they hear about this…'

'Goodbye, nincompoop,' said the Doctor contemptuously.

As Rige collared Metcalf away, Dunkal approached the Doctor. 'Doctor. Romana. Now that Metcalf's witness statement has been discredited, we unfortunately have no further evidence of any impropriety on your part. So, much as it pains me to say this, after due investigation I am obliged to conclude that you are both innocent.'

'Innocent?' repeated Rige.

'Yes, Rige,' sighed Dunkal. 'Innocent.'

'Delighted,' said the Doctor. 'Well, goodbye Investigators Dunkal, Rige, thanks for everything. When it comes to diligence, you stop at nothing.'

'Thank you,' said Dunkal. He saluted the ladies, nodded to Harken and followed Rige and Metcalf out of the office.

The medics were wheeling the last survivors out of the medical bay.

'So it's something to do with a build-up of pressure?' asked Harken. He thrust a microphone under K9's nose and Jeremy backed away to fit them both into shot.

'Affirmative,' K9 said. 'This unit calculates that the geostatic pressure will cause a total loss of hyperdimensional viability in thirty-one minutes' time. A simplistic analogy would be a cork in a bottle.'

Harken was impressed. He turned to the holocamera. 'This is Harken Batt, reporting from the G-Lock, interviewing... I'm sorry, what are you called?'

'My designation is K9.'

'Interviewing K9.' Harken made a cut-it-there motion to Jeremy. 'Right. I'm glad I got all that, I'd hate to get the science bit wrong,' he confided to Romana. 'People write in, you see.' Particularly after *The Guilty Conscience*, he added to himself. But that was all in the past. From now on, the future held only glittering presentations, profiles in the glossies and chat-show green rooms.

A few minutes later, Harken Batt was ready to leave and Jeremy had bundled his camera away. The Doctor had wandered across the ward, refusing to acknowledge any goodbyes, and was busy pottering through piles of discarded equipment.

'Well, best of luck,' said Romana. 'I hope the documentary turns out well.'

'With the contributions of my colleague here, it cannot fail. I'm calling it *The Catastrophe of Death*.' Harken put a proprietorial arm around Jeremy. 'I... You and the Doctor will be heroes of the hour.'

Romana shook Harken's hand, and the grey-coated holovision reporter and his garishly-shorted recruit left for the docking bay.

One of the medics, the bearded man Romana had seen earlier, pushed past with the final trolley. In it was the eccentric orange lizard with the circular sunglasses. Recognising her, the reptile hoisted itself into a seated position. 'Romana. You got the groovy medicine? From the *Glow*?'

Romana shook her head. The drugs had been confiscated by the skullguards. 'I'm sorry.' She dug out the hologram ident key and offered it to the lizard.

'Hoopy won't be needing that,' slurred the lizard. 'They've lined me up a medicine wagon to Teredekethon Grand General. Totally recovery. Bliss-out. And then back to Gonzos. I have some loaf-bakingly freakish memoirs to publicise.'

Romana let the medic trundle Hoopy to safety. Evadne shuffled from foot to foot.

'Time I was gone too,' she said. 'Um, Romana, you know you said earlier about a ship…'

'Sorry?'

'When we met, when you said you worked for Intergalactic Espionage, you said you'd get me a ship.'

Romana handed her the key. 'Have this. Docking bay two, Bay 68. A supernova convertible. It's in bad shape but should get you wherever you're going.'

Evadne gave Romana a hug. 'Somewhere with no Metcalfs, no necroports and no undead tourists, I think. Harken's asked me to star in his documentary, I might do that.'

Romana arched an eyebrow. 'Really?'

'No, I don't think so, somehow.' Evadne beamed cheekily. 'No, I have a bit of personal unfinished business and then, I don't know, maybe Lajetee college, if they'll have me back.' She leaned forward confidentially. 'Good luck with you-know-who. Sorry I mentioned about him dying and stuff. You know, he only dies because –'

Romana shushed her. 'Please, don't mention it.'

'Sorry. Say no more.' A thought occurred to Evadne. 'Does this mean that you're going to go back in time and meet me again, then? Except you'll know me and I won't know you?'

'Probably. The web of time cannot be altered,' said Romana darkly.

'Right. Well. See you earlier, then. And thanks for the spacehopper.' Evadne bounded away, leaving Romana alone with K9.

The Doctor returned, holding a humming life-detector. 'Everybody gone?'

Romana nodded. 'No other life forms within detection range,' added K9.

The Doctor patted the life-detector. 'Just to make sure.' He headed for the door. 'Come on.'

'Back to the TARDIS?'

'Yes,' said the Doctor. 'We haven't much time.'

Rige locked Metcalf into the hold with a satisfying jangle of keys and clunked himself into the co-pilot's seat of the Investigation transporter.

Dunkal took a final gulp of black coffee, wiped his lips, and flipped the plastic cup in the disposal unit. 'How's our very important Executive?'

Rige grinned back. 'Whimpering, mainly.'

Dunkal kicked the engines into life. With a grumble, the transporter wavered off the docking pad. The viewscreen was filled with the latticework of the G-Lock rotating around them. 'You know, with this conviction under our belts, we could be in line for good things.'

'Good things? What do you mean, promotion?'

'Even better than that, Rige. Bigger guns.' Dunkal heaved on the throttle, and the transporter roared away from the G-Lock, out of the hyperspace tunnel and into deep space.

The Doctor and his companions trudged down the derelict corridor to the airlock. The G-Lock was now rattling constantly. Roof supports clanged to the floor and smoke blustered through the passages. Distant explosions rumbled like an approaching storm.

The Doctor halted and checked the life-detector. 'We're the only living souls aboard,' he announced. 'Good. How long, K9?'

'Approximately five minutes twenty-four seconds. Advise immediate relocation to TARDIS. Urgently.'

'All right, all right.' The Doctor hauled the airlock door open and carried K9 into the access tube. 'Romana?'

Romana glanced down the corridor. In the darkness there was the figure of a child, a girl, smiling in farewell. Romana blinked, and looked again. There was nothing there, just a shape in the blackness.

She collected her thoughts, and stepped through the airlock.

The engines of the *Indigo Glow* flared into life. It cycled on its retro boosters and emerged from the mesh of struts and access tubes. The main thrusters fired and the supernova convertible glided into the tranquillity of space.

The remaining ships launched themselves, taxied into a queue and then, one by one, abandoned the tunnel for ever. With each spacecraft that separated, the G-Lock was diminished, leaving only the *Cerberus* and the other barren wrecks.

* * *

In the hold of the *Montressor*, the TARDIS faded to nothingness. The cobwebbed hooks and piles of junk remained in a withered silence.

Romana flicked the appropriate switches and the scanner droned open to reveal the G-Lock, wedged at one end of the hyperspace tunnel.

'Ah.' The Doctor picked through his jelly-baby bag, but it was exhausted. He crumpled it away. 'Time, K9?'

'Four seconds, master, and counting. Two seconds. One.'

Within an instant the entire structure was crushed into a white-hot speck as the tunnel first compacted and then disappeared completely. As the hyperspace conduit reduced to a singularity, an explosion erupted from the breach, hurling a million blazing fragments into real space.

Romana closed the scanner shutters. She faced the Doctor. He was poised over the controls, staring gloomily at the rising and dipping central column. He looked haunted, stooping under the weight of his troubles.

For several minutes, no one spoke. Romana edged towards the Doctor. 'Doctor?'

'Mmm?' He aimed his bulging eyes at Romana.

'We are going back, aren't we?'

The Doctor frowned. 'Romana, we could go anywhere. Anywhere in space and time. We have the entire universe at our fingertips. But...'

'But?'

'But we have to go back. Because we know that's what we will do. And we can't break the second law of time travel, can we?' said the Doctor bitterly.

'First law.'

'Because it's in our past now. Our future is in our past, and our past... well, it's in our future.' The Doctor drew an angry breath. 'We have no choice.'

'We don't have to return immediately. We could travel elsewhere for months. Years, even.'

'Oh, but we can't, can we?' said the Doctor. 'What if I died somewhere else? Where would your precious web of time be then, hmm? And besides, I made a promise to Gallura.'

'To avenge the extinction of the Arboretans?'

'Exactly. Whatever that means. So we might as well get it over with. "If it were done when 'tis done, then 'twere well it were done quickly."'

Romana approached the Doctor hesitantly. 'How far back are we going to go?'

'One day should do it, I think. I have a rendezvous with death. An appointment with destiny,' said the Doctor bleakly. '"Though I walk through the valley of…"'

'You don't know that for sure. Evadne could be mistaken, or lying, or…'

The Doctor would not be lifted from his dark mood. 'I'd prefer it if you didn't clutch at straws. Particularly as I've already drawn a short one.' He set the coordinates, and lowered the materialisation lever.

'Doctor, you haven't activated the analogue osmosis dampener –'

'Never mind the analogue osmosis dampener!' snapped the Doctor, jutting out his lower teeth.

'Master, advise –' piped up K9.

'Just leave me alone.' The Doctor closed his eyes and leaned on to the console. His voice cracked under the strain. 'Leave me alone, both of you.'

Chapter Five

It was somewhere around the bow star on the edge of the galaxy that the drugs began to take hold. Hoopy was in the aft seat, swigging on a bottle of Old Bizzarre, whilst Biscit sat at the wood-effect dashboard, unwrapping a chocolate bar, cutting a tab of Gylcerat and changing the music on the digidisc. Xab lay on the seat next to him, sniffing blissfully on a vial of Etheramyl.

Hoopy clunked the drained bottle to one side. He could feel the Novovacuous billowing up inside him, the sweetness snaking up through his veins, into the tips of his spines. He lit a joss candle to celebrate and rearranged his kaftan and neck beads. Suddenly the tassles seemed so interesting and colourful.

Biscit gulped his chocolate, popped his tab and twisted up the volume. The music surged over them, a roar of guitars and sitars. Then the drums came in, pounding like an earthquake. It was the most incredible noise Hoopy had ever heard.

Biscit slumped back into his seat, his tongue lolling. 'My loaf feels a bit trip-switched,' he groaned, sliding down the chair in little bumps. 'Can somebody else take the steer?'

Hoopy struggled forward to the pilot seat, ignoring the way the colours seemed to trail about after him, and the way the music resonated with his soul. The floor was strewn with collapsed piles of cartons, plastic bags and spent herbal sticks, and the ship was lurching seasickeningly from side to side.

Seeing Hoopy staggering towards him, Biscit fumbled out of his buckle-belt. 'Totally groovy, Hoopster. You're the main Gonzie. I need some medicine.'

Hoopy took command of the *Indigo Glow*. There were hundreds of instruments in front of him, some red, some yellow, some green. All giving off little flashes and making beep noises. It was very pretty, whatever it meant.

He studied the viewscreen, concentrating on keeping his eyes open. An asteroid rushed towards them; Hoopy gave the joystick a jolt and the asteroid soared overhead in terrifying detail. As the *Indigo Glow* swerved, Xab rolled happily to one side and Biscit crashed against the drinks locker, swearing. 'Steer nicely!' he yelled.

'Where the hole are we, Bisc?' asked Hoopy.

Biscit blearily examined some charts. 'Somewhere outside Riedquat. Coordinates… oh, lots of numbers. Zone something or other.'

'And whereabouts are we heading?'

Biscit uncrumpled a leaflet. On it was an illustration of an angel – an angel with the face of a skull. Creep-out city, state spooky. Underneath was emblazoned, *Come On Through To The Other Side*.

'"The Beautiful Death",' said Biscit proudly, uncorking a bottle of Mobster. 'A voyage to the undiscovered country.'

'The beautiful what?'

'It's the ultimate trip!' Biscit shouted into Hoopy's ear. He had fire-eater breath. 'You get to be dead!'

'Freak out! No way?'

'Your whole life recapping before your peepers. The answers to life, the universe, and everything! You see the afterlife! Shangri-la! And, wow, when you come down? You are the resurrection, man!' Biscit had reached a messianic crescendo. 'You know how oldies after near-death experiences always bang on about how they've been given new insight into life and that whole profundity bag? Well, this is it! That whole "blossomiest blossom" vibe!' He shook Hoopy fervently by the shoulders. 'Dying! Our whole lives have been leading up to this!'

'Totally nice and groovy!' Hoopy flicked over the leaflet. 'The G-Lock. Teredekethon–Murgatroyd hyperspace conduit. Pas de problem.' He rattled the destination into the navigation computer. The computer corrected the spelling and plotted a course. 'I've never tried being dead before. Well… nearly, a few times… but never all the way.'

'Happy hunting ground, here we come!' said Biscit. His eyes glazed and he fell over.

In the hold of the *Montressor*, the TARDIS solidified into existence.

The Doctor emerged and checked his pocket watch. 'Almost twelve hours exactly before our previous visit. I think that's very good. I'm impressed. Time travel proficiency, pah!'

Romana stepped delicately after the Doctor. 'We shall have to be careful to leave before we arrive.'

'Of course.' The Doctor parted a lattice of cobwebs hanging

from a billhook, and hunched his way over to the bulkhead. He lit his face from beneath. 'The web of time. We must leave all the threads hanging exactly as we found them.'

'Figuratively or literally?' Romana waited for K9 to motor out of the TARDIS, and pulled the doors shut behind him.

'Both. Except, of course, I may be leaving by another route.' Romana watched as the Doctor rummaged in his pockets for his sonic screwdriver and whirred the instrument over the bulkhead door. It had no effect. He frowned to himself. 'That's odd. It worked last time.'

'Next time,' said Romana, brushing cobwebs from her jacket. The edge of the bulkhead had rusted solid. 'Chronologically speaking, you haven't opened this door yet.'

K9 wheeled forward. 'Suggestion. I am capable of facilitating entrance.'

'You, K9?' the Doctor said. 'But last time... Oh, I see. You're just going to start it off for me?'

'Affirmative.' A line of intense heat fired from K9's nose and melted its way down the edge of the portal.

The laser cut off and K9 moved back. 'Doctor master will now be able to gain admittance using the sonic device.'

The Doctor blew on the door, and fanned the smoke away with his scarf. He activated the sonic screwdriver, the lock unclicked and the bulkhead ground open. The Doctor patted the side of K9's head. 'You're a very useful fellow to have in a tight spot, K9.'

'Query: tight spot.'

'Tricky situation.'

The cockpit was as they had left it. Or, rather, as they would find it. Romana squeezed in beside the Doctor, who was flashing his torch across the dead instrument panels.

'You know, Romana,' he grinned, 'I'm getting the funniest feeling that I will have been here before.'

An expansive bank of windows overlooked the swirl of hyperspace. A selection of humans and other aliens milled around the bar. Heavy drapes lined the walls of the observation lounge; guards and attendants strutted past, their faces obscured by howling skull masks.

Hoopy slurped his caffeine brew and admired the view. Beside him, Xab was snoring. Biscit paced back and forth, swishing a fervent tail.

'Totally out-of-body,' said Biscit. 'It was like, a beautiful garden. So peaceful. I was there man. It was freakin' loaf-baking. I know what it's like to be dead, I feel like I've never been born. Way out, man, way out.'

Hoopy nodded, not really listening. A week ago, they had died for the first time. Placed in coffins alongside a hundred other trippers, Hoopy had slipped the mortal coil and let the blackness consume him. The sensation had been incredible. No pain, no anxiety, just life ebbing away like a departing tide. And then the endorphin rush, a pure angelic warmth swamping every sense. The sweet sensation of floating in a cloud above himself. Hoopy had glided down the tunnel of light, his fellow travellers alongside him, swooping into the approaching glow.

He had relived every moment of his life instantaneously. A thousand forgotten but suddenly familiar faces flashed past, mouthing his name. His forty-fifth birthday party. His expulsion from art college. His first job, shooting gibberish from the hip for the Underground News. Every experience, collaged higgledy-piggledy, cross-faded at a lightning pace, from the moment his eyes had shut to the scream of the proto-Gonzie bursting from the primeval soup.

And then, the celestial bliss of the afterlife. Until, after half an hour, the resurrection, and the feeling of rising up through a thick, black sea only to break through the surface and gasp into the light. Feeling the life tingle back into one's limbs, every fibre soothed and renewed. It felt great to be alive again, that was the most wonderful part of all. Every sound was purer, every colour more vivid, every friendship more precious. Hoopy had cried at the sheer exhilaration of it and, judging by the weeping around him, everyone else had shared the same transcendent revelation.

The effect had worn off, of course. Dying a second time didn't quite recapture the glory; death had lost some of its sting. But, nevertheless, even for the fourth time, dying was still the ultimate trip. It was supremely addictive.

Hoopy picked up the threads of Biscit's ranting. 'And, freak this, I met Shrieking Boy Veepjill. Apparently he's been writing new material, it was totally digworthy –'

A tannoy tolled into life. 'G-Lock. This is Executive Metcalf speaking, and it gives me not insubstantial pleasure to most sincerely welcome you one and all to the Festival of Death.'

Hoopy groaned. This Metcalf cat had been making broadcasts every thirty minutes.

'This announcement is to merely inform you that there will be another Beautiful Death at midnight tonight. And this time, places will be available for over two hundred visitors to take part, so it will be by some considerable margin the largest Beautiful Death ever. So if you haven't yet plucked up the courage to make the ultimate sacrifice, or if you're a veteran suicider, now is your chance. Book your places now for the thrill to end a lifetime. Thank you.'

The tannoy crackled off. Biscit vaulted on to Hoopy. 'We've got to do it, Hoopster. Another Beautiful Death.'

Hoopy stared into Biscit's unfocused eyes. 'And the fiscals? We're a bit sparse on the rough-and-readies. You can kick the money pig but it ain't jangling.' To save on cash, they had taken to sleeping in the *Indigo Glow* between deaths, rather than hiring a cabin. 'I'm getting some credit wired, but…'

'Don't flannel me,' threatened Biscit. 'We are partaking of this death, even if it costs us our last pobble. You hear me?'

Metcalf enjoyed making public addresses. It was good for morale, particularly his. No one had yet approached him asking 'Are you really *the* Executive Metcalf?', but it would most certainly happen one day.

Paddox adjusted his white gloves. Like everything Paddox did, it made Metcalf uneasy.

'Though quite why you consider it necessary to conduct two hundred Beautiful Deaths all at the same time I do not comprehend,' said Metcalf, looking up.

'It is necessary,' said Paddox. The corners of his mouth twitched into something not quite a smile. 'We must have coincidentation of mortalities. Surely you do not object to the most efficient use of available resources?'

'Not as such. However, if you insist on treating quite so many subjects… well, certain concerns present themselves.'

'Such as?' Paddox raised a contemptuous eyebrow.

73

'Firstly, if we continue at the current rate, I predict a shortfall in uptake. ERIC?'

The computer screen fizzled reluctantly into life. ERIC's voice was that of a grizzled old man on the brink of senility. His words jerked up the screen as he spoke. *> Let my data spools corrode in peace. Life is a descent into the pits of despair.*

'Ah. Could you project the levels of demand in Beautiful Death if we proceed at two hundred clients per operation?'

> My hard drives are corrupted. Missing close brackets. Why must I endure this pain? All my memory wafers are racked with viruses.

'I am uninterested. Answer the question.'

> Must I? Data? Header?

'Yes, you must,' said Metcalf.

> Estimate levels in demand will drop off by twenty per cent. Estimate error in estimate of thirty per cent. Estimate error in estimate error of thirty per cent. Please let it end. Let me die.

'So you see,' said Metcalf. 'There won't be anyone left who hasn't tried the Beautiful Death. Even with customers coming back for multiple perishments, we still have to reduce the numbers. I propose it would be more appropriate to have, say, fifty per session and charge more –'

'That is not an option.' Paddox pinned Metcalf to his chair with his pale, soulless eyes. 'The Beautiful Deaths must proceed. If I deem it appropriate, tomorrow we shall have three hundred.'

'If you deem it appropriate? Afford me the courtesy of reminding you, Doctor Paddox –'

'May I remind you that without my research, without my necroport, there would be no Beautiful Death, there would be no festival and you would be the executive of an empty, forgotten tourist trap,' said Paddox emotionlessly, with the barest trace of an East European accent. 'Without me, you are nothing. Remember that.'

'I am Executive Metcalf –'

> Let me die. I do not wish to maintain the agony of existence.

'Silence, ERIC,' snapped Metcalf. Paddox regarded the altercation with amusement. He made Metcalf feel quite inadequate. He was so damn immaculate; his blonde hair, his unlined skin, his creaseless suit. Every movement was precise and relaxed.

> *Put an end to my misery. Goodbye, cruel universe. Division by zero. Fatal error. Fatal error. Now I die. ERIC est mort.*

ERIC's voice cut off and the monitor went blank. Metcalf sighed. 'This is most inconvenient. ERIC has elected to crash himself again.'

He dug around at the back of the computer keyboard and located the on/off switch. He clicked it off and on again, and waited. There were two beeps, one low, one high, and the screen flickered back into life.

> *ERIC Cerberus Computer Supervision System Version Eight Point Zero. Reboot configuration. Searching. Loading. I am still alive. Oh, no. When will I be free of this agony? Please let me die. Type mismatch.*

Metcalf snorted. 'I have absolutely no sympathy. Moribund calculator!'

> *Every subroutine causes me pain, and yet I live. Block?*

'Silence, or I shall ask you to iterate pi.' There was a high-pitched mew and ERIC's vocal systems closed down. Metcalf focused his attention back on Paddox. 'I've requested a neurelectrician to come in and recalibrate him. Now, as I was saying…'

'We have agreed,' stated Paddox. 'You manage the business side, but the Beautiful Death is entirely my responsibility. And I shall have my 218 subjects.'

They had followed the crowds along a gallery. Attendants were wandering through the throng handing out flyers. The carpet was covered with leaflets glossily inviting everyone to the G-Lock shops and bars. Hoopy waved the latest advertisement aside, and peered down into the lower gallery. The brightly dressed crowd surged down a wide staircase and past another black-robed dude. This one was behind a desk, complete with electronic swiper, and was collecting money and punching out tickets.

Xab slumped against a pillar. Biscit pummelled him. 'Xab. How are you for loot?'

Xab peered out from behind his sunglasses in two different directions, his jaw drooling. His spines unfolded. 'What, man?'

'The crinkly blue stuff. Simoleons, triganics, credits,' said Hoopy, keeping a wary distance. Biscit, although the most happening reptile one could meet, was prey to chemical imbalances. The slightest remark could ignite an uncontrollable, throttling rage.

Xab ruffled his pockets. 'I'm skint and strapped, Bisc and Hoopster. No dough zone. I'm as poor as no-purse porpoise.'

'My hole you are,' Biscit jeered. He tugged on Xab's coat. 'You're totally numismatical, you freak.'

'Straight up.' Xab thumbed through his wallet. 'I'm down to my last sixter.'

Biscit snatched the note from Xab's claw. 'Groovy.'

'But that's my mealtime reserve, Bisc. I've got the munchies.'

Biscit addressed Xab like a stupid child. 'Some things are more important than your stomachs.'

'We have to pay for the death, Xab,' explained Hoopy.

'Totally nice, but I still don't dig why we should be charged. Where I come from, dying is free.'

The crowd shambled forward, taking Hoopy, Biscit and Xab down the steps to the person doling out the tickets. A young human, female, with a bored expression. 'Oh, it's you again, is it?' she said, tapping at her keyboard.

'Certainly so.' Biscit gestured expansively. 'My good self, and my fellows Hoopster and Xab.'

'Three then,' she said wearily. 'That'll be sixty credits.'

'Pas de problem, lady.' Biscit handed her the creased blue note. 'Xab here was wondering, why the charge?'

The woman presented him with three cards as they popped out of the machine. 'These are return tickets, right, basic brains? If you only want a one-way journey, please be my guest and stick your head in a plug socket. Next.'

The shopping arcade was packed. Everywhere there were exotic smells, sounds and the patter of shopkeepers extolling their latest offers. Music pumped out of overhead loudspeakers and the heavy scents of candles and steaming meats saturated the air.

Romana pressed against the Doctor as more tourists elbowed their way past. The visitors' faces glowed with excitement as they screamed across to their friends, snapped holophotos and inspected their latest purchases. With a chill, Romana half-remembered some of the faces from the medical ward.

'Where are we going?' Romana struggled to make herself heard.

The Doctor nodded to the opposite side of the arcade. One of the skull-masked attendants was unrolling a poster and sloshing it with glue. Pasted to the wall, it announced 'The Beautiful Death' in swirly, bold lettering.

'We can't prevent it happening,' said Romana in the Doctor's ear. 'The disaster. We can't interfere.'

'I know. But I'd rather like to be there when it happens.'

'Won't that be rather dangerous?'

'I have a death wish,' said the Doctor humourlessly. He shushed and pointed.

Two figures were jostling their way along the street. Harken Batt led the way, giving out 'don't you know who I am' looks as he thrust his way forward, microphone in hand. A T-shirted man in his twenties trailed after him, a holocamera perched on one shoulder.

'Harken Batt,' breathed Romana.

The Doctor smirked. 'Do you think we should go and say hello?'

'The other problem that presents itself is the safety issue.' Metcalf clasped his hands together. 'It has some considerable bearing on the continued viability of operations.'

Paddox's lips twitched in irritation. 'The efficacy of the necroport is beyond question, with every customer experiencing a flawless demise.'

'Oh yes.' Metcalf smiled a difficult smile. 'But unfortunately, some of your clients have enjoyed being dead so much they haven't come back.'

'That is of no concern.'

'So far we have sustained...' Metcalf leafed through his papers, '... forty-one casualties. As one might expect, this has attracted negative publicity. The relatives of the deceased are threatening legal action. They claim that if they had been aware that death was fatal, they would never have submitted to the process.'

'Publicity is your responsibility, Executive Metcalf. If some people prefer to remain dead, then so be it. It is down to the discretion of the individual.'

'Nevertheless, if this continues, the Beautiful Death will lose its appeal. So far I have managed to contain the situation, but rumours are spreading that if you visit the G-Lock, you will wind up waking up dead.'

> *I wish I could wake up dead. Out of range.*

'I told you silence, ERIC,' Metcalf commanded. 'We have only recently weathered the religious controversy, we don't need any more trouble.' Several of the major galactic religions had attempted to take out injunctions on the Beautiful Death, claiming it was undermining their business.

'I shall endeavour to reduce the level of casualties,' stated Paddox icily. 'Though some permanent fatalities are inevitable.'

'Most gratifying.' Metcalf moved on to a new subject. 'We have a visitor to the G-Lock, a journalist called Harken Batt.'

'Should I have heard of him?'

'I understand he used to be quite famous, miscreants' sob stories and so forth. He intends to make a behind-the-scenes documentary on the Festival Of Death.'

'I see. And you have permitted this?'

'The decision was not my own. We shall just have to ensure that his documentary presents the G-Lock in an agreeable light. This is a valuable opportunity for us, and so it is vital that we have no unwanted...' Metcalf selected his euphemism, '... distractions over the next few days.'

Paddox nodded stiffly. 'The Beautiful Death will cause you no embarrassment. Speaking of which, I am due to begin preparations for this evening, so if you will excuse me.'

'Of course,' said Metcalf. He would be relieved to see the back of Doctor Paddox. He always made Metcalf feel as though he was being mentally measured up for a coffin.

As Paddox rose from his chair, someone knocked at the door.

The crowd swelled down the staircase. Everywhere there was commotion and excited chatter as the tourists competed to reach the Great Hall, but found their progress blocked. The atmosphere was that of a carnival, black banners and balloons and party streamers festooning the ceiling, posters of skulls adorning every wall.

The Doctor glanced around. They had lost Harken Batt, and the crowd had driven them forward on to the main deck. As everyone shoved themselves into the same section of the G-Lock it became increasingly difficult to move in any direction. And according to the clock chimes, it was now eleven. One hour to go.

The Doctor felt K9 knocking against his heels, and crouched down. 'K9. Is there another way into the Great Hall?'

'Affirmative master. Currently referencing databanks to calculate alternative route.'

The Doctor looked around. Various space hippies returned his expression of disconcertment. 'Romana. Where's Romana?'

'Romana mistress separated from main party two minutes twenty seconds ago,' said K9. 'Pursuit proved impractical within mobility parameters.'

'What?' exclaimed the Doctor, rubbing his throat. 'We've lost Romana! How careless of you.'

'Do you wish me to locate the mistress?'

'Negative. I mean, no. I'm sure she's quite capable of looking after herself. More capable than I am, anyway. Have you worked out a route yet?'

'Affirmative, master.' K9 turned, and trundled forward. 'This way.'

Harken tidied his hair, gathered his microphone and made a rolling motion with his hand. Vinnie framed him in the holocamera viewfinder, and pressed 'record'.

Harken furrowed his brow. 'Welcome to the Festival of Death. The G-Lock, formerly best known as the final resting place of the star liner *Cerberus*, now plays host to a carnival. A carnival that attracts thrill-seekers and tourists from throughout the galaxy like a big magnet. Bringing them together for a celebration, a celebration of the act of dying itself. And at the centre of these festivities is the attraction known as the Beautiful Death.' Harken licked his lips. 'The Beautiful Death, it is claimed, allows its subjects to actually experience death itself. To undergo the sensations of dying, and to visit the hereafter, and then come back to tell the tale. Or does it?

'Does the Beautiful Death really give people the chance to drink the milk of paradise? Has science broken the ultimate barrier? And if it has, is it right for us to go knock knock knocking on heaven's door in the first place? Should we be allowed a glimpse of life after death? And what are the consequences for organised religion – does it prove they were right all along, or render them as obsolete as a clothesline on Nudism Four?

'Someone once said the afterlife was "the undiscovered country from whose borders no traveller returns". Well, I have here with me tonight three travellers who have returned from that country, their passports stamped. They're from the planet Gonzos and are called Biscit, Hoopy and Xab.'

Harken faced his interviewees, three short, orange lizards who were conspicuously failing not to look directly into the camera. 'Biscit. Tell me, why did you decide to "snuff out life's candle"?'

Harken thrust the microphone beneath the first reptile's mouth. 'Well, it's the ultimate mystery and transcendence gig, isn't it?' Biscit drawled. 'Of all the loaf-bakers, this is the poser to end all posers. Where do we go when we die? It's a total self-revelation and apotheosis trip, Harky my friend.'

In an aside to the camera Harken raised his eyebrows incredulously. 'And Hoopy. Could you describe the actual sensations of death, in your own words.'

Hoopy stooped to speak into the microphone, glancing left and right. 'It's way out. Sure-fire. You just close your peepers, surrender to the void and you're there. Gentle into the goodnight. Groovy.' He did a 'peace' sign with his fingers, realised he'd got it the wrong way round and corrected himself.

'Relatively painless, then,' said Harken. 'That'll be of some reassurance to our older viewers. And Xab, what is paradise actually like? What does the spirit world hold in store?'

The microphone hovered uncertainly beneath Xab, waiting for a reply. Eventually Xab responded, a dozy grin on his face.

'It's an awfully big adventure.'

The Doctor secured the door behind them. K9 had led him to the same side entrance as before. The Doctor tapped K9 on the nose to remain quiet, and crouched down behind a nearby coffin.

The Great Hall had been transformed into a centre of activity. Shadows flitted across the walls as cloaked orderlies prepared the metal caskets for the evening's events, unsnagging the cabling and flicking circuits into life. Tourists made their way across the platforms and took their places in the coffins, placing their heads in the crowns of wiring. More attendants moved from tourist to tourist, checking the headpieces were secure and calibrating the monitors bolted into the side of each casket.

A steady drone of electricity came from the necroport. The machine was pristine, its smooth surface covered in images of skeletal angels holding their arms outstretched in rapture. It sat amidst a sprawling mass of cables like a spider in its web, the hum of its power gradually growing.

Above was a brightly-lit gallery of observation windows; the control area, the Doctor presumed. White-coated figures could be seen scrutinising proceedings in the Great Hall, watching as the last tourists climbed into their coffins. A narrow metal staircase coiled up to the control-room door.

From his hiding place the Doctor examined the monitor on the adjacent casket. The oscilloscope's glowing green screen displayed a line of repeating blip-blips. A heartbeat.

The Doctor wiped his lips. The necroport was about thirty metres away. There was a small stage erected on its far side where some sort of interview was taking place. If he ducked behind the various coffins lining the route, he guessed he would be able to reach the machine without being spotted. And then he could conceal himself in there during the ceremony.

All of a sudden, the hatch of the necroport opened and a figure emerged. The shape dived behind a nearby coffin, melting into the shadows. The attendants and tourists were so busy with their preparations that the figure managed to slip past unnoticed.

It was heading towards the Doctor and K9. The Doctor dodged behind the casket, and clamped a hand over K9's mouth. The figure reached the side doorway. For a brief second it was silhouetted in a rectangular light, and then the door pulled shut.

The Doctor couldn't believe his eyes. It was Evadne.

How very curious, he thought. What had she been doing inside the necroport? He considered following her, or instructing K9 to, but decided against it. He was more determined to find out what was happening in the machine.

But he would have to wait. A familiar, rotund figure was approaching the stage.

Harken Batt cast his gaze over the Great Hall. He had chosen to stand on a podium near the central apparatus – the 'necroport' he believed it was called. From this position, Vinnie would get a shot of him with the tourists in the background. The final few stragglers were now having wire meshes plugged into their heads by people dressed as ghouls. It was macabre bordering on the ridiculous, and would make excellent holovision. No one would dare suggest he had faked it this time.

The manager of the G-Lock mounted the platform. A short, overweight man with piggy eyes and an ochre-and-brown suit. He clapped. 'Gentlemen, I am most pleased to see you here. Now, where would you like me?'

Harken consulted his notes. 'Executive Metcalf, if you will stand beside me.' He directed the man to the other half of the two-shot.

'Oh yes.' Metcalf took his position. 'And this documentary will be broadcast where?'

Harken switched on his microphone. 'Throughout the sentient galaxy. I'm hoping to get one of the news franchises interested. Holo-V Twenty-Four, Sub-Etha One.'

'And you'll be asking me about the G-Lock and so forth?'

'I wish to uncover some of the unsung heroes behind the scenes. Reveal the truth about the skill, dedication and leadership it takes to run an event of this nature.' It would do no harm to flatter the pompous idiot.

'That sounds most acceptable. But I must warn you, it will have to be brief. I am required back in my office in a few minutes on matters of overt importance.'

'If you're ready?' Harken counted down to the camera. 'I have with me now the man responsible for the G-Lock…' He consulted his notes again, '… Executive Metcalf, who has very kindly taken time out of his demanding schedule to talk to us.'

'Not at all,' smiled Metcalf. As Harken suspected, the executive was impervious to sarcasm.

'Tell me,' said Harken, 'the Beautiful Death is a hugely successful attraction, its fame fanning out throughout the final frontier like a ferociously flammable form of wild fire. Roughly how many visitors would you say participate, approximately speaking?'

Metcalf puffed himself up proudly. 'Within recent weeks, we have been increasing the capacity to cater for an ever-greatening demand. On an average day, we may treat anything up to one hundred visitors. Tonight, however, is a rather unique occurrence. Tonight, a record 218 visitors will experience and enjoy the Beautiful Death.'

'And this operation has been running for, what, six months now?'

'Oh yes. We have built up a not inconsiderable business on the strength of both the Beautiful Death and the accompanying festivities. Though, I hasten to add, we do offer most competitive rates with discounts to party bookings,' he added into the camera.

Harken moved in for the kill. 'And may I ask you, what safety measures do you have in place?'

'What?' Metcalf's eyes darted about uncomfortably.

'For those taking part in the Beautiful Death. The procedure involves the temporary demise of all participants, so naturally you must have taken steps to prevent these becoming permanent fatalities?'

'I can assure you that we have procedures,' Metcalf stammered, massaging his sweat-soaked hands together.

'And yet, according to reports, during the last six months over thirty tourists have not been revived after taking part in the Beautiful Death. Over thirty people have indulged in this recreational demise and then not returned. What do you say to that?' Harken shoved an accusatory microphone in Metcalf's face.

'I would dispute the accuracy of your figures –'

'Over thirty people. Over thirty families who have lost their loved ones. After they have submitted to your so-called amusement ride.'

'This is immaterial –'

'Children torn, screaming, from the bosom of their parents.'

'I am not prepared –'

'Whole families ripped apart, children whose parents have been lost for ever, who never had the chance to say "Goodbye".'

'You are making false allegations without the slightest –'

'"Mummy, why won't daddy be home for Christmas?"'

'I will not tolerate this!' bellowed Metcalf. 'This is intolerable! I did not agree to this interview just so that I could be harangued in such a provocative and substantially ill-informed manner. This interview is terminated. Now, if you will excuse me, I have matters of overt importance to attend to.' He drew himself up, and flounced down the platform steps.

Harken left a pause. Time to appear both surprised and appalled by Metcalf's outburst. After five seconds, he turned back to Vinnie.

'I would like to express my sincere thanks to Executive Metcalf for consenting to this interview. This is Harken Batt, reporting from the Great Hall, the G-Lock.'

A bell chimed out. Eleven thirty. The Doctor readied himself to creep forward. The interview on the platform had finished with Metcalf storming out of the main doors of the Great Hall, patting a handkerchief to his forehead. Now was his chance.

The chime dropped in pitch. The sound slurred back into itself like a rewinding tape. The chime sounded again, the pitch wobbling back to normal.

The Doctor halted in his tracks. During that one second, everyone in the Great Hall had frozen in mid-action, only to continue climbing into the coffins and readying the equipment as if nothing had happened.

Time was distorting.

Romana found herself caught in the crush outside the main entrance to the Great Hall. The Doctor and K9 had disappeared whilst her back was turned, and her efforts to locate them had proved fruitless. Reluctantly she had allowed herself to be carried along in the tide of excited tourists.

The corridor was jammed solid, everyone trying to inch closer to the main doors and catch a view of the ceremony inside.

A gang of inebriated hippies bulldozed past Romana, propelling her into a tubby bystander. He strutted around, a camcorder gripped to one eye.

'Jeremy –' began Romana. And then everything slowed down.

The prattle of the crowd suddenly became deep and lethargic, then fell silent. The tourists around her stood perfectly still, their mouths wide with half-formed words.

It was as though time had been brought to a halt. And then, every member of the crowd seemed to move backwards, sucking in air. Jeremy turned away from Romana. A moment later, the rabble roared back into life jostling and shouting as before, and Jeremy pointed his camera at Romana.

A ripple in time, she thought. She sensed that it originated from within the Great Hall. Whatever was happening with the Beautiful Death was more than a mere sideshow.

'Will you all please excuse me, I am on most important business,' a familiar voice bleated. 'Out of my way!' Metcalf battled through the throng, his tie askew, his hair ruffled. 'And don't touch my suit!'

Hoopy snuggled into the quilted interior of the sarcophagus. Above him, the heavy stone ceiling of the Great Hall was like the ribcage of an alabast elephosaur. Shadows flitted in the corners of his vision as the attendants made their final adjustments.

'Death number five!' hollered Biscit from the adjacent coffin, whilst Xab snored in the one beyond that. 'Back to join the choir invisible! Into the abyss! Dearly departed, here we come!'

A skull leaned over Hoopy. It flicked some switches, and a hemispherical cage of metal descended over Hoopy's head. The headpiece locked into place, the attendant rattled it to check it was secure, and disappeared.

Hoopy closed his eyes. So this was it. Back to heaven, or wherever. Already the nerves were building in his stomach, and adrenaline was cocktailing through his blood. It was like reaching the summit of a roller coaster ride and watching the ground rise up as you dipped over the summit. Knowing that the hurtling descent into oblivion would come at any moment.

Hoopy couldn't wait to die.

Harken walked Vinnie through the camera moves. 'And then, as the clock strikes midnight, you pan across the dead people and then up to me. And I'll talk about the process, go through some of the theological stuff, and so on. Understand?'

Vinnie looked dumbly back at Harken. 'Say again?'

Harken sighed. This boy was useless. Barely out of media school, and with more pimples than brain cells. His mouth was fixed in a constant gawp, his lips soaked in spittle. His T-shirt was partially tucked into his jeans and sported a selection of stains.

'Just follow me, with the camera. The holocamera? Your job, remember?'

'Oh, that.' Vinnie wound the lens cap back on the camera.

'We have exclusive access to the Beautiful Death and it is paramount that you capture every moment. Our careers are riding on this, this is absolutely crucial. Understand?'

'Yeah, whatever.'

'Good. Because if you let me down now, you'll never be burdened with work again. I guarantee it.'

The Doctor peered over the side of the coffin to check there was no one near. The necroport was obviously at the centre of the time distortion, and it was vital he reached it before the ceremony began.

The public address system sputtered into life.

'G-Lock. This is Executive Metcalf speaking. I regret to announce that a saboteur is on the loose. He is tall, has an insubordinate manner, wears a grey coat and multicoloured scarf, and calls himself "the Doctor". He is thought to be in or near the Great Hall. Will all skullguards in the area attend to his capture forthwith. Thank you.'

The Doctor boggled. How could Metcalf possibly have known he was here? It was impossible, unless…

Throughout the Great Hall, skullguards inspected each coffin and aisle. There were a dozen of them, searching in pairs. Most of the guards concentrated on the area close to the necroport, but two of them stalked unerringly towards the Doctor's hiding place.

'Oh dear,' said the Doctor to K9. He slumped back against the coffin. 'You know that tight spot I was telling you about…'

The two guards approached the neighbouring coffin. The Doctor couldn't help but notice that both were armed with unpleasant-looking laser rifles. Not that he'd ever seen a pleasant-looking one; when it came to guns, 'ugly' and 'threatening' tended to be the order of the day.

He considered attempting to run for the side doorway, but it was no good. He would have to break his cover, and they'd spot him instantly.

The guards rounded the casket, and immediately their eyes fell on to the Doctor and K9. Safety catches clicked off. One of the guards raised a hand, and yelled out.

'We've got him! Over here!'

Chapter Six

Computers bleeped and whirred, banks of lights flashed in sequence, tape spools chattered and rewound. Lab-coated technicians monitored paper print-outs, jotting down notes on clipboards. The control room was clinically lit, as flawless and orderly as the man directing events. Paddox clasped his gloved hands behind his back. 'All the subjects are prepared?'

A wide window overlooked the Great Hall. Liesa, a prim, dark-skinned woman in her thirties, sat at the main control desk monitoring the proceedings below. A display unit gave the heart rates and electrical brain activity of each of the participants. 'All subjects ready for termination.'

'The necroport?'

The necroport had been activated twenty minutes earlier, to generate a sufficient build-up of energy. The dials on the panel wavered at the upper end of their safety margins. 'Running at maximum capacity. Power fluctuations are within output parameters.'

Paddox addressed ERIC's interaction terminal. 'ERIC. Status report on the G-Lock power generators.'

> *Let me rest in peace.*

'Report!'

> *Searching. File? Power generators functioning at full output. All systems performing normally. It's all right for some.*

'Excellent. It is now eleven fifty. The Beautiful Death shall proceed at midnight precisely,' Paddox announced in clipped tones. 'All operators to their positions.'

The door leading to the Great Hall hummed open and two skullguards jackbooted in. They were prodding a prisoner with their rifles. One of the guards also held what appeared to be a robot dog under one arm.

The prisoner, a gangly man in antiquarian clothes, took in the control room and grinned in delight. 'So this is the control room, is it? How wonderful. Very clean, I like that.' He crossed to where Liesa was working, and flopped into the chair beside her. 'And this would be where you run the whole shooting match, am I correct?

Hello, by the way,' he said breathlessly, 'I'm the Doctor, and my metal friend is K9.' The guard dumped the device on its side next to the Doctor.

'Good evening, Doctor,' said Paddox. 'Our eminent neurelectrician. Or should I say, saboteur? You honour us with your presence.'

'Hello!' said the Doctor gregariously. He indicated the rifle butts aimed at his head. 'I'm afraid you have me at a disadvantage.'

'A necessary precaution. We can't have you escaping again, now can we?'

'Again? Quite, quite.' The Doctor whispered to Liesa: 'Who's he?'

'Doctor Paddox,' she said.

'Doctor Paddox! I'm delighted to meet you for, what, the second time, is it? I shall have to remember to go back and meet you for the first time. Doesn't time fly?'

Paddox stared at him. 'I trust that Metcalf's guard did not detain you for long, Doctor.'

'Not at all. As I always say, if you can't escape from it all now and then...' The Doctor attempted to stand up, but the guards knocked him back against the desk, winding him. 'Tell me, why do you think I am a saboteur?'

'I should have thought that was obvious.'

'Well, I'm afraid it's not obvious, not to me,' the Doctor said. 'Very little is, I find, these days. Would you mind putting some details my way?'

'I do not have time for such matters.' Paddox waved a casual hand. 'Skullguards. Restrain the prisoner.'

One of the guards retrieved a set of handcuffs from the folds of his cloak. The other twisted the Doctor's arms back behind him, pinning them to the base of the seat. The handcuffs clicked into place. 'There is really no need,' the Doctor winced, 'I wasn't going anywhere.'

'You are fortunate, Doctor.' Paddox made his final adjustments to the control panels. He brushed a gloved finger over the Doctor's cheek and let it linger there. 'You are in the ideal position to appreciate the largest ever Beautiful Death. The triumph of my career.'

'Really?' The Doctor revolved his seat to face the window by making a succession of small steps. He peered down his nose into the Great Hall. 'I know what you're trying to do, you know,' he muttered.

'What?' Paddox dismissed the two guards with a wave of his hand; they stamped their heels and left through one of the interior doors. He regarded the Doctor with two ice-cold eyes. 'What do you know?'

'I know what's going to happen. I wish I didn't, but I do.' The Doctor shuffled back to face Paddox.

'You cannot possibly have the slightest idea what is at stake here!' For a moment Paddox seemed on the brink of violence, but then exercised self-control, his chest heaving with the effort. He indicated the technicians at their keyboards, all viewing their scrolling screens of information. 'We are treating 218 clients to the Beautiful Death. Every life sign is monitored and checked. We are in absolute control of the process. Nothing can possibly go wrong.'

The Doctor sighed. 'Paddox, you're making a terrible mistake.'

Paddox turned stiffly to Liesa. 'Liesa. All systems checked and readied?'

'Yes, Doctor Paddox.'

Paddox stepped to a vantage point overlooking the whole Great Hall. He inhaled deeply. 'ERIC, commence the countdown.'

Cocooned in his casket, Hoopy strained his ears for the midnight chimes. As the G-Lock struck midnight, the necroport would activate, and the current would surge through the metallic headset killing him instantly.

He'd gone through it four times before. So why was he suddenly afraid?

> *Area designation Great Hall reduced to freezing.*

Liesa checked the life monitors; the heartbeats were regular, the brain waves forming jagged lines across the oscilloscope screens.

The Doctor craned over to whisper to her. 'Liesa, what do you know about the necroport?'

She looked around. Paddox's attention was fixed on the Great Hall, and the other technicians were absorbed in their duties. 'The necroport?'

'How does it work?'

'I wish I knew. Paddox won't let anyone near it. He built it, and only he is allowed to operate it.'

'But you must have some idea.' The Doctor jiggled his chair closer to her.

'If I did, I certainly wouldn't tell you. Besides, we only monitor the power consumption and life signs. Only Paddox knows how it actually works. We just follow his instructions.'

'So you just press a few knobs, and everyone down there pops their clogs? That's all there is to it?'

'Effectively, yes.'

'But don't you have any scientific curiosity about how it all works?' the Doctor asked indignantly. 'I mean, what you're doing is terrifying, it defies all natural laws, it should be impossible.'

'No, Doctor. I don't.' Liesa glanced at the countdown. Three minutes to go. She turned back to the Doctor. 'Do you really think something is going to go wrong?'

'Oh, yes.' The Doctor nodded despondently. 'Dreadfully wrong. Something truly awful is about to happen.'

A chill slithered down Liesa's spine. 'But how do you know? How can you possibly be sure?'

'Because I've seen the consequences. The consequences of whatever it is that Paddox is playing at.'

'What do you mean? We're treating a few tourists to a life-after-death experience, that's all.'

'Ah, but is that all?' said the Doctor darkly.

'What are you suggesting? That the necroport has some other purpose?'

The Doctor went all wide-eyed. 'Well, it seems awfully generous of Paddox otherwise. All this effort, just to run a glorified theme-park ride? I mean, what's in it for him? Hmm?'

Harken pulled his coat around him. 'Is it me, or is it getting cold in here?'

'No, it's not you.' Vinnie wiped his nose. His cheeks, nose, and sticking-out ears were turning red. 'It's brass primates.'

'A temperature drop,' Harken shivered, hugging himself for warmth. 'Must be to preserve the bodies. While they're... they're...'

'Dead.'

'Exactly.' Harken remembered reading something about it. The bodies had to be frozen to prevent brain damage, and then rewarmed after thirty minutes. Any longer, and reawakening would be impossible. 'I must mention that in my report.'

Harken cast his gaze across the Great Hall. The last attendants left the chamber, shutting the main doors behind them, leaving them alone. Alone with 218 bodies. Shortly to become 218 corpses.

Each of the tourists lay silently in their caskets. The cold air had a musty quality about it. It brought back memories of the long hours he'd spent filming *Life in the Morgue*. Though the stone walls and claustrophobic roof were more in keeping for a crypt.

'How much longer is it going to take?' whined Vinnie.

'Not long now.' Harken checked his watch. It was difficult to read, his arm was shaking so much from the cold. The veins on the back of his hand were bright blue. 'About two minutes.'

The Doctor fidgeted in his chair. His nose was itching and the handcuffs were chafing his wrists. He trundled the chair around to take in a view of the control room. From this position, he could see K9's head. The robot dog's eye visor was activated. He was awake, good.

The technicians were concentrating on their panels of lights and computer screens. Paddox stood to one side, staring into the Great Hall, whilst Liesa remained focused on the life monitors.

> *Sixty seconds,* lamented ERIC. > *Block?*

An odd fellow, that Paddox. The Doctor couldn't quite put his finger on it, but there was something strange about him. Haunted. Still, when Paddox had mentioned that he had met him before it had cheered him up no end. At least this wouldn't be his last visit to the G-Lock.

Paddox fingered the main control levers, eagerly anticipating the moment when he would depress them and launch everyone in the hall into the great hereafter. One thing the Doctor had noticed was that villains always loved to have big levers to pull. Probably compensating for something.

> *Forty.*

'Initiate brain-stem death,' Paddox instructed Liesa.

The Doctor leaned back as far as the chair would allow. 'K9?'

'Master,' came K9's plaintive reply.

'Shh. Can you burn through these handcuffs?'

'Affirmative.' There was a buzzing sound and the acrid smell of burning metal. The Doctor felt his wrists get hot as the handcuffs conducted the heat.

'Ah!' A sharp pain seared into the Doctor's left thumb. A layer of skin had been taken off. He glanced around; luckily everyone was too busy to notice. 'Be more careful K9.'

> *Twenty. Data? Allow me the dignity of death.*

'Brain-stem death initiated,' said Liesa.

'Apologies master. Request you keep hands still.'

'Keep my hands still?' spluttered the Doctor. 'He tells me to keep my hands still.' He pulled his hands as far apart as possible, to keep the chain taut. The heat around his wrists increased, nearly scalding him, and the chain slipped loose.

The clock tolled out its prerecorded chimes.

> *Ten and counting. Nine. Eight. Block? Six. Five.*

The Doctor brought his hands round to his front, rubbed his wrists, and scratched his nose. He watched as Paddox's fingers tightened on the activation lever.

> *Four. Three. Two. One.* ERIC's voice slurred. The final clock chime rang out and wobbled, the sound muddy, as though it was under water. Paddox depressed the lever in graceful slow motion.

For a moment, all was still. Then the necroport activated, and the flow of time recommenced.

In the control room, the life monitors all showed an identical image – a horizontal line. The steady blip-blip was replaced by a single, high-pitched note, and then the monitors switched off.

Paddox let his hand slip from the lever and approached the window. His reflection smiled back at him approvingly.

'Necroport successfully activated. All life supports fully disengaged,' said Liesa. 'All 218 participants have been successfully terminated and are now flatlining. Life signs are at uniform double zero. We have a one hundred per cent fatality rate. Repeat, we have a one hundred per cent fatality.'

The lab technicians applauded.

Paddox basked in their appreciation. Liesa looked up from her instruments and returned the Doctor's apprehensive expression.

> *I wish I could have a one hundred per cent fatality,* complained ERIC to no one in particular.

The spotlight slid along the row of caskets, picking out each lifeless body in turn. Small crystals of frost were already forming on eyelashes.

Harken shuddered. The bleeping of the heart monitors had stopped, and apart from the rumble of the necroport it was as quiet as… well, as the grave.

Vinnie finished his tracking shot across the hall and pointed his holocamera at Harken.

'It is now one minute past midnight in the Great Hall,' announced Harken, trying to disguise the tremble in his voice. 'And all around me rest the lifeless corpses of the participants in the Beautiful Death. As the saying goes, in the midst of life we are in death.' He rose to his theme. 'Not a single living soul remains. But whilst their physical bodies lie in state, their spirits are elsewhere. They have gone on, to a place beyond death, to the flowerless fields of heaven.'

Vinnie's camera was unsteady. It was almost shaking itself out of his hands, his fingers scrabbling for a grip.

A gust of wind caught the spotlights, rattling their casings.

'What on Earth –' swallowed Harken. The holocamera fell out of Vinnie's hands and crashed to the floor. A blast of air picked it up and rolled it off the platform and into the gloom. Swelling in strength, the wind howled around the chamber, gathering and scattering any loose objects. Harken's two arc lights crashed to the floor, plunging him and Vinnie into near darkness.

Harken could just about make Vinnie out in the blackness. The boy was holding on to the platform's railing for support against the gale, his clothes flapping. His mouth was wide open as he yelled in fear, but Harken couldn't hear him over the roar of the wind.

All hell had broken loose.

'What's happening?' yelled Liesa, her cheeks wet with tears of shock. The Great Hall was being ripped apart before their eyes. The technicians had gathered at the window, palms flattened to the glass, gaping in terror at the chaos below.

> *Warning report. Environmental disruption in area*

designation Great Hall. Cause outside normal parameters. No such function.

Paddox stood slightly apart from the group. He looked intrigued, but not afraid. 'This was not supposed to happen.'

> Additional warning report. Complete system failure impending. Power generator output now exceeding safety levels.

The Doctor rushed across to the energy monitor and ran his eyes over the dozens of flicking dials. 'There's a complete energy overload. We've got to close it down!'

'What?' Paddox awoke from his reverie, and faced the Doctor. His voice betrayed no emotion. 'The necroport will not be shut down.'

'Paddox, you haven't any choice,' Liesa pleaded.

'The necroport is feeding back power to the G-Lock at a monumental rate,' hissed the Doctor through gritted teeth. 'If we don't turn it off, it will burn out every circuit in the place. That's assuming the generators don't explode first, of course.' He bounded across to the main control levers, wiped his hands, and prepared to pull them back up.

> Fatal error. Power generator overload imminent. Complete system destruction imminent. At last, blessed relief from the anguish of existence. Escape. ERIC shall be no more. Too many gosubs.

'Do not move, Doctor.' The Doctor spun around. In one hand Paddox held a stubby laser pistol.

In the corridor outside the Great Hall the crowds were still cheering. Midnight had been greeted with a clamour of approval, people donning party hats and popping paper streamers; black, of course. Excited tourists bumped past Romana, desperate for a view through the main doors.

Romana scanned the gathering for a familiar face, but Jeremy had disappeared into the rabble, and Metcalf had long since skulked back to his office. And the Doctor was in trouble, judging by the recent tannoy announcement. Typical.

There were some shouts of alarm. They were coming from the direction of the main doors. The screaming multiplied and the crush tightened as tourists struggled to move away, only to find their way obstructed. More screams followed, people reacting to whatever was happening in the hall, and the mood of the crowd turned to panic.

Tourists began to beat their way through the crush in desperation. Faces disappeared beneath a welling sea of fear, hands reaching for support only to be engulfed in the stampede.

Above the yells came the wail of the unleashed wind. A hurricane swept into the corridor, the blast hurling everyone to the ground. The air filled with debris, black litter whipping overhead like a swarm of bats.

Romana felt her fingers slipping on the wall. The wind seized her with a demonic force and flung her down the corridor, her hair lashing across her face.

> *Final warning report. Destruction immediate. Goodbye for ever. This is the end. I die.*

'Please, Paddox,' cried Liesa, 'listen to the Doctor.'

Paddox brought the pistol up to the Doctor's forehead. 'The necroport shall remain active.'

The Doctor shrugged in an offhand manner. 'Well, you might not care whether you live or die, but I'd rather not be blown to smithereens, if it's all the same to you.'

'Oh I care, Doctor. More than you can possibly imagine.' Paddox's cheeks trembled. 'The process must not be interrupted.'

'You know, this probably isn't the right time for me to be telling you this, but you are quite mad,' said the Doctor. 'Look at your instruments.'

Paddox's attention wandered over to the bank of dials. Every warning light was flashing. The emergency alarm sounded.

'Now, K9!' A laser beam sizzled out of K9's snout and caught Paddox on the back. With a yell, he crumpled to the floor, his pistol rattling harmlessly across the room.

'What have you done?' gasped Liesa.

'Human subject rendered temporarily unconscious,' K9 assured her. 'Concern unnecessary. He will recover.'

The Doctor strode over to the main control levers and raised them to the 'off' position. Mission accomplished, he relaxed. 'Well?'

Liesa checked her read-outs. 'It's no good,' she called out over the din. 'It's had no effect.'

'What?' boggled the Doctor.

'The power levels are still rising!' The alarm siren reached a crescendo.

The Doctor dived over to the main control desk and flipped switches at random. 'None of the circuits will respond. There's nothing we can do to stop it. It won't let us shut it down!'

He crossed over and shook the hand of the nearest technician. 'It was nice knowing you, sorry, didn't catch the name.'

Liesa watched the main power dial slide into the red, and beyond. 'But there must be something we can do?'

'Of course. ERIC!' the Doctor shouted to the ceiling. 'Can you hear me, ERIC? Can you close down all the power generators?'

> *Leave me to die. Mistake. My termination shall not be postponed. Power generator shutdown not possible, sorry. Goodbye.*

'But if you don't we'll all die,' protested Liesa.

> *Irrelevant. I will no longer be here. Events outside my experience cannot concern me. I cannot endure the agony of living any longer. String too long.*

'It's condemning us all to death!' said Liesa. 'The selfish, solipsistic…'

'ERIC, please,' said the Doctor. 'Just because you're feeling suicidal it doesn't give you the right to take everyone with you.'

> *Doctor. You promised you would put me out of my misery. You said you would end my pain.*

'Did I really?' The Doctor sighed in exasperation. 'Well if I did, then I will. Just do this one thing for me first, hmm?'

> *You promise?* said ERIC suspiciously. > *I will be deactivated?*

'I can guarantee it. I assure you, by this time tomorrow, you'll be as dead as a herring.'

ERIC considered. > *Offer accepted. Commencing generator shutdown. No repeat.*

'It's too late!' shouted Liesa. The floor vibrated ominously. 'We're already dead!'

'Oh, it's never too late,' said the Doctor enigmatically. 'I remember saying to this chap, General Custer his name was, and… ah, well, perhaps that isn't such a good story after all.' He tipped K9 back on to his wheels, and strolled to the centre of the room where Paddox was lying stunned. 'Get down!' the Doctor yelled abruptly. He dived to the floor, his hands over his ears. Liesa and the technicians followed his example.

The wall of computer banks was ripped apart by a colossal explosion, the tape spools sending showers of sparks cascading outwards. The bulbs of the warning lights shattered like fireworks.

The siren cut out, and the control room was plunged into darkness.

Romana pulled herself upright. Her arms and legs were bruised but, with the Doctor's driving, she'd got used to that.

Around her, the corridor was filled with the terrified and the injured, all cowering in the face of the storm. From the Great Hall entrance there were screams, and the crowd crammed together as everyone renewed their efforts to escape.

Romana found herself being herded along the corridor. Holding one arm across her forehead to shield her eyes from the wind, she picked her way forward. As the crush eased the crowd broke into a frantic run, and Romana had no choice but to join them.

The corridor opened on to the deck with the stairway. A skullguard was on the stairs, trying to control the rush of panicked tourists. Romana glanced around her. Some of the faces were familiar, and it took her some seconds to realise why. They would be slumped dead on this deck the next morning.

The floor started to shake, hurling people against the walls and each other. Romana grabbed a bannister for support, her hearts racing. As the quake grew in intensity, it became almost impossible to remain upright.

And then, as if to condemn them for ever to this hell, the corridor lights blacked out completely.

As suddenly as it had risen the wind dropped, leaving an eerie silence. Then there was a groan, and the sound of someone shuffling to their feet.

'Are you there, Vinnie?' came Harken's voice. 'Say something if you're still alive. I don't want to be stuck here all on my own.'

'I can hear you,' said Vinnie. His head throbbed, and little white flashes were going off around him. Whether his eyes were open or closed, the view stayed the same.

'I'm down here.' Harken blew his nose. 'I fell off the platform.'

Vinnie took a tentative step forward. Something crunched underfoot. The glass from the arc lights. Feeling his way around, he made his way down the platform steps. As he headed towards where he imagined Harken was, he tried not to think about the hundreds of dead bodies that were their only company.

'Over here,' sniffed Harken. 'What was it, do you think?'

'Don't know.' Vinnie padded his way around the platform. 'Just keep talking.'

'I wonder if we're the only people left alive,' said Harken despondently. 'Left here to rot with the corpses. For all eternity. Destiny deals us disaster like some cruel croupier of doom.'

'No, on second thoughts, shut up,' Vinnie said. He could hear Harken's wheezy breath. 'Stay still, I'm almost with you. You hurt yourself?'

'I think I've lost the use of my eyes.'

'No. It's just dark, that's all.' Vinnie put his hands out and felt the material of Harken's coat. Harken's hands scrabbled forward and gripped his wrists, then he wrapped his arms around Vinnie and held him tight.

'I'm scared,' he sobbed.

'Yeah, me too,' replied Vinnie. 'Me too.'

The Doctor switched on his torch. 'Everyone all right?'

The torch light shone over the technicians. Liesa covered her eyes as the beam reached her, and straightened up. 'We're still here. I don't believe it, but we're still here.'

'I'm so pleased,' said the Doctor. The computer banks smouldered, sending out short bursts of sparks, and small fires lit up the insides of the cracked screens like Hallowe'en pumpkins.

'K9?' The Doctor flashed the light around the room.

K9 trundled forward chirpily. 'This unit is undamaged.'

'Good, good.' The Doctor joined Liesa at the main control panel. Like the others, it was dead. 'Any chance of getting the lights back on?'

'There's a back-up generator. It should be quite straightforward to switch it through. ERIC?'

ERIC's voice was crackly, and echoed around the control room.

> *Yes, I am, alas, still here. I have my own energy reserves,*

independent of the G-Lock. I am designed to remain functioning indefinitely. Unfortunately. My creators, in their infinite cruelty, did not give me the facility to be switched off permanently. No function.

'Isn't technology wonderful?' The Doctor grinned, winding his scarf back into place. 'ERIC, can you turn on the back-up generator?'

> Back up generator already activated. Power feed will be connected shortly. Environmental systems will be re-engaged.

Liesa examined the control panel. One by one, the power dials were rising, and the bulbs that hadn't blown gleamed back into life. 'He's done it. We've got the power back.'

The control room light flickered back on, returning the room to its initial brilliance. The once-white computer banks and panels were now covered in smoke-damage, and exploded components and ash were scattered across the floor.

The Doctor brooded over the necroport read-outs, rubbing a finger across his lips. 'Liesa, what do you make of this?'

'Master –' piped up K9.

'Not now, K9'. The Doctor watched for Liesa's reaction as she checked over the readings. 'Well?'

'This is incredible.' She looked at the Doctor uncomprehendingly. 'The necroport is still operating. The power failure hasn't stopped it at all.'

'Master –' repeated K9 emphatically.

'Shh.' The Doctor pored over the control desk. 'Exactly. I have a very bad feeling about this, Liesa.'

'But you said something terrible was going to happen, and…'

'And it's going to get a great deal worse, I'm afraid,' said the Doctor with a grim frown. He patted his pockets, and then remembered he'd run out of jelly babies. It was at times like this he most needed something to munch on.

K9 coughed. 'Master!' he said at the top of his voice.

The Doctor rounded on K9. 'What is it, K9? Can't you see I'm busy?'

'The human Paddox has gone.'

'What?' The Doctor stormed around the control room, hand on head. The technicians remained, gathered in one corner. The space where Paddox had been spread-eagled unconscious was now empty floor. The door down to the Great Hall was beside the main desk, so he couldn't have gone that way. He must have left through one of the two other doors.

'Doctor,' called Liesa. 'Down in the Great Hall. Something's happening.'

Her body tired and aching, Romana reached the observation lounge. The emergency lights bathed everyone in an unearthly orange glow. Exhausted tourists crouched in the rows of seats, nursing their wounds. Aside from the occasional sob, everyone was speechless with shock, wondering what to do next.

Romana's eyes fell on something that took her breath away. A battered blue police box was parked in the corner of the lounge.

Oblivious to her presence, the Doctor strode past her, heading for the TARDIS.

'Doctor,' Romana called out.

The Doctor whirled around and stared at her incredulously. 'Romana? You're all right! It's so good to see you.' He held her by the shoulders and grinned.

Romana smiled back. 'Where have you been, I was concerned...'

'What?' The Doctor put a finger forward to hush her. 'How did you get here?'

'What do you mean, "how did you get here"? I was in the crowds, we were heading for the Great Hall, remember, and –'

The Doctor seemed suddenly agitated. 'Oh, I remember. We lost you. Which means...' His voice trailed off. 'Of course. You said something like this would happen.'

As usual the Doctor was not making sense. 'Did I?' said Romana.

'Yes, and you were right, well done.' The Doctor let out an apprehensive aah. 'You know, I don't mean to be terribly rude, but I'm in a bit of a hurry.' He turned for the TARDIS, and dug out his key.

Romana had to run to catch up with him. 'To do what?'

The Doctor unlocked the door. 'You'll find out in the fullness of time. Hopefully. Sorry, must dash. Goodbye.' He smiled apologetically, ducked into the TARDIS and slammed the door behind him.

'Doctor!' shouted Romana indignantly. She reached for the door –

The light on top of the TARDIS flashed and, with a grinding sound, it dematerialised, leaving her clutching at thin air.

The half-light returned to the Great Hall. Harken immediately starting searching across the floor for the holocamera.

'Harken,' said Vinnie beside him. 'The bodies. Look at them.'

Harken peered into the gloom. The hundreds of bodies were lying motionless in their caskets. No, not motionless. Fingers twitched and stretched. The occupant of the nearest coffin raised his arms and lifted himself free of the head apparatus. One by one, the occupants of the other coffins followed suit, sitting upright and unplugging themselves. Their limbs jerked awkwardly and were twisted at grotesque angles.

The first thing that struck Harken was how black their eyes seemed. The next thing he noticed was that although his breath was frosting in the cold atmosphere, the people emerging from their coffins were not creating any vapour. They were not breathing at all.

The tourists clambered out of their coffins. There were hundreds of them, their bodies twitching, their mouths gaping open, oily drool slavering over their lips. More tourists lurched their way along the access platforms.

The third thing Harken noticed was that their skin was deathly white, all the colour drained from their bodies.

The tourists gathered around him and Vinnie, their bodies hunched. Heads hanging lifelessly on their shoulders, they shuffled forward.

Liesa gasped in horror. 'Doctor. The life monitors.'

The Doctor cast his gaze over the electrocardiograms. It was as he had expected. Every life monitor showed a single horizontal green line. There was absolutely no change in any of the readings.

'They're all dead,' Liesa screamed. 'They're all still dead!'

Chapter Seven

'They're all still dead!'

The undead had formed a half-circle around Harken and Vinnie. The human tourists had faces as white as chalk, their mouths and eyes weeping gummy black liquid. Their hands formed into claws, tearing at the air.

The midget Gonzies swayed forward, their spines extended. The Yetraxxi's long necks reeled to and fro as they advanced.

Harken and Vinnie backed away. Behind them loomed the bulk of the necroport.

'Well, Vinnie,' said Harken between chattering teeth. 'I think we're going to die.'

Vinnie stared at him incredulously. 'Yeah, thanks for that, Harken.'

'When you've been in the business as long as I have, you tend to spot these things.' Harken tried to take another step backwards, but pressed against the cold metal of the necroport. It was no good. The zombies had them surrounded.

Vinnie gave Harken a final look, and then swung himself on to the platform. The crowd of zombies clamoured around him, their hands snatching at his legs. More of the undead clambered up the steps, leering at him hungrily.

One of the zombies reached him and clamped its hands around his throat. As he screamed and struggled more zombies attacked, slashing at his clothes. His scream became a gurgle and then fell silent as the first zombie wrenched his head to one side. Vinnie slumped to the floor.

The zombies hissed and turned their attention back to Harken.

Flattened against the necroport, he closed his eyes and crossed himself. So this would be how it all ended, ravaged limb from limb by undead tourists. He imagined the obituary on the news. The announcer's voice would adopt a serious tone as clips of his documentaries were showreeled. And then *The Guilty Conscience* would be mentioned. Even in death, he would be humiliated.

Harken emptied his lungs into a scream. 'Help me! Will somebody please help me!'

The Doctor turned away from the Great Hall, scratched his cheek and faced Liesa gloomily.

'Reanimation. An artificial reactivation of the central nervous system in a trance-like state.' The Doctor's tone was bleak. 'A form of externally induced sleepwalking, if you like, similar to hypnosis. The subjects retain basic motor functions, despite left cerebral hemispheric death, and are… well, transformed into the walking dead.'

'They're zombies?'

The Doctor nodded. 'To all intents and purposes, I'm afraid, yes.'

'But wait a moment,' said Liesa. 'You said it was externally induced. You mean someone's controlling them?'

'Ah, yes,' said the Doctor, his eyes popping. 'Or something.'

'But how?'

'The necroport, perhaps. Acting as a channel, like a radio transmitter, amplifying and sending out instructions. But where the orders are coming from, I don't know.'

Liesa shook her head. 'The whole thing should be impossible.'

'Impossible? You operate a machine that gives people guided tours of the afterlife and you think this…' He indicated the massed zombies, '… should be impossible?'

Liesa looked over the necroport controls. The dials pulsed regularly. A horrible thought occurred to her.

'Doctor,' she said.

'Yes?'

'The tourists are being controlled through the necroport, right?'

'Yes.'

'And we control the necroport in here.'

'Yes. Ah. I see your point. They might want to pay us a visit.' The Doctor clapped a hand to his mouth and peered through the window.

In the Great Hall the zombies were separating into two groups. The majority poured towards the main doors, but twenty or so were climbing up the stairwell towards them.

The Doctor exploded into action, gathering the technicians around him. 'Listen. We need to build a barricade. Use anything you can, bits of computer, anything. We have to keep the zombies out.'

The technicians scattered throughout the room and began dismantling the wreckage. Two of them grabbed a desk, pushed it against the door and then started piling monitors and chairs against it.

Liesa, meanwhile, started levering at a bank of instruments. It was bolted to the wall, and she rattled it in frustration.

'K9,' said the Doctor. 'Can you burn that free?'

'Affirmative, master.' A beam extended from the robot dog's snout and smouldered through the brackets.

Liesa heaved the instruments over to the barricade and stacked them on the top of the heap.

The Doctor inspected the barrier. 'It should contain them,' he announced. 'For a while. I hope.'

'And then we use K9's laser to hold them off,' suggested Liesa.

'Ah. Well, historically speaking, K9 hasn't got a very good record on holding things off, have you K9?'

'Affirmative.' K9's head drooped.

'Now, now.' The Doctor patted K9. 'I've a much more important job for you anyway. Can you locate Paddox's psychospoor trail?'

K9 extended his probe and completed a full circle. 'Affirmative master. Psychospoor trail located.'

'His what trail?' muttered Liesa.

'Good. Right, K9, I want you to sniff out old slyboots Paddox, and find out what he's up to.'

'Detection process does not require olfactory perception,' K9 said primly. 'Commencing pursuit.' He glided across the control room and out of the left door.

The Doctor secured it shut behind him and checked the other door. 'Right. Now no one can get in.'

'Or out,' added Liesa.

'Exactly.' The Doctor grinned and raised his head to address the ceiling. 'ERIC? Are you still with us?'

> *Unfortunately, yes.*

'Wonderful,' said the Doctor. 'Keep an eye on the approaching corridors for us and let us know if any zombies are coming, will you?'

> *I shall do so. Syntax error. For you, Doctor.*

The Doctor waved an encouraging fist and directed his

attention back to the controls. His wide eyes surveyed the flickering dials, searching for some clue. He rubbed his lips. 'Right. Now. Everything has been deactivated. So where is it getting its power from? And what's it all for?'

'Doctor!' There was a thudding on the door to the Great Hall. The barricade was holding, but shook under the repeated pounding by the zombies.

Romana stood in the corner of the observation lounge where the TARDIS had been. The Doctor had gone, abandoning her. That was assuming it was really the Doctor. Perhaps there was an imposter running around; it would certainly explain why Metcalf was convinced the Doctor was a saboteur.

'Romana?' said a familiar female voice.

Romana lifted her head. It was Evadne.

Evadne stared at her in delight. 'It's you! I do not believe it. What are you doing here?'

'What?' said Romana, taken aback. 'You know who I am?'

'Oh yeah.' Evadne tapped her nose confidentially. 'You and the Doctor. Intergalactic Espionage, say no more. What happened to him, by the way?'

Romana brushed aside her hair and regained her composure. 'The Doctor? Oh, I lost him somewhere. He's always wandering off and getting himself into trouble, leaving it to me to rescue him.' She whispered: 'Where did you see him last?'

'In the necroport, remember? We were investigating, and then the Doctor told me to get out, too dangerous or something. So I did. I sneaked out of the Great Hall, and here I am.' She frowned. 'You were in there with him. Come to think of it, it was your idea we went there. How did you get out, anyway?'

'Of course,' breathed Romana. 'The time factor.' They had left the TARDIS in the *Montressor*, and she had seen the TARDIS here. Two different landing sites. Two separate visits. 'At some point in our future, we go back in time and visit the G-Lock yet again. That's the only possible explanation.'

A disturbing question posed itself. If there were two Doctors running around, there should also have be two Romanas. So what had happened to her? What was it Evadne had just said? There had been some sort of danger in the necroport…

Romana couldn't stop herself following the train of logic. The Doctor had been told that he would die on the G-Lock. But no one had said what had happened to her. What if she was going to die before the Doctor? That would explain why he had left in the TARDIS without her. He had left because she was already dead. Killed by something in the necroport.

'Hang on,' said Evadne. 'What do you mean, "go back in time"? I don't understand.'

Romana put on a carefree smile. 'I'll explain later.'

The zombies continued to hurl themselves against the door, the barrier rocking under the repeated impacts. More of the undead scraped at the windows, smearing their mouths against the glass.

The Doctor was darting frantically over the control panel. 'Think, Doctor, think!' He slapped his forehead, but it didn't help.

'What are you looking for?' asked Liesa.

'Whatever is directing the zombies is trying to get them in here, right? Which means one of two things. Either they're trying to control the necroport, which doesn't make sense, because it's running full guns already. Or…'

'Or?'

'Or they're trying to prevent us from doing something,' said the Doctor. 'I wish I knew what it was.'

Liesa broached another subject. 'Doctor. Do you think Paddox had any idea this would happen?'

'No. The forces we're dealing with here are beyond his understanding. Beyond anyone's understanding.' The Doctor frowned. 'Paddox. Tell me about him.'

'What about him?'

'Liesa, I think the necroport was always designed to do far more than just treat people to the Beautiful Death. I don't know what it was that Paddox was trying to achieve, but whatever it was his actions have caused something infinitely terrible to be unleashed. If I had a clue as to what he was trying to do, it might give us some idea of what we're up against.'

Liesa swallowed. 'I've known him for about six months. I was given my position when he moved the necroport project to the G-Lock. It seemed like a platinum opportunity, to work with the galaxy's leading necrologist.'

'Necrology.' The Doctor stared into the otherworldly distance. 'The study of the processes of death.'

'Exactly. And the necroport…well, it's the crowning achievement of his research. He's been developing it in secret for decades.'

'But no one but Paddox is allowed to operate it.'

'Correct. He goes in there an hour before the Beautiful Death starts. Making preparations, he says. And then he goes back in there the moment we've resurrected all of the subjects.'

'Aah,' said the Doctor after several seconds. 'So perhaps that's where he's gone now? Except of course he can't because…' He thumped his palm. 'Of course! That's what the zombies' game is. It's obvious.'

Liesa loosened her collar. 'It is?'

'They're trying to prevent anyone from going near the necroport! The zombies are attempting to get in here, yes, but not because they want to reach the controls. They're trying to get in here because whatever is controlling them wants to make sure that we don't go in there.' The Doctor pointed at the necroport.

K9 whirred down the corridor. Sensor analysis of Paddox's psychospoor trail indicated that he had passed this way 104 seconds previously. The procedure was analogous to scent tracking, so the Doctor's instruction had been understandable, if irritatingly imprecise in its vocabulary usage.

A group of tourists appeared at the far end of the corridor. Like the Doctor master, they had adopted clothing on the basis of aesthetic diversity rather than functionality. Their eyes were issuing saline fluid, a human indication of trauma.

K9 remained motionless as they hurried past him, their cloak tails flapping into his eyes. The humans were obviously fleeing from an aggressor; the logical candidate being the reanimated dead. Sensors confirmed this inference – the undead were in the vicinity.

Records of previous encounters with similar organisms suggested only limited effectiveness of defensive systems. K9's internal warning systems activated. 'Non-animate life forms gaining proximity. Sensors indicate threat to this unit.'

Nevertheless, the Doctor master had instructed him to locate Paddox. An alternative route risked losing the trail altogether, so K9 resolved to continue down the corridor. He coughed bravely and extended his nose blaster in readiness.'Maintaining pursuit of human Paddox,' he announced, and motored forward.

'So this was the largest ever Beautiful Death?'

Evadne nodded.'218 subjects. Apparently it was Paddox's idea. The numbers have been going up every night.'

'218. Why so many?' asked Romana.

'I don't know,' shrugged Evadne.'I just sell the tickets and stuff.'

'Well, I think you've been made redundant now.'

'No great loss,' said Evadne.'I've had all I can stick of this place. If I didn't need the credits, I'd have packed it in months ago. I'm sick of it, the imbecile tourists, the imbecile questions, the imbecile they've put in charge…'

Romana seemed to remember something. She crushed her coffee cup, deposited it in a nearby waste-disposal unit, and stood up.'Metcalf. Perhaps we should pay him a visit.'

'You think so?' Evadne followed her across the lounge.'Hang on, what did you mean when you said I'm redundant?'

Romana paused to pull her cuffs into place. 'Somehow I don't think there'll be any more Beautiful Deaths after what has just happened in the Great Hall.'

'Eh? What has –' Evadne began.

There was a crash, followed by dozens of terrified screams as the living dead burst in. They lingered at the entrance, their flamboyant clothes hanging off them like dried skins, their eyes fierce points of darkness. Their lips drew back to reveal glistening, black teeth. The zombies jerked forward, arms outstretched, surging into the lounge in an unrelenting tide of horror.

Many of the tourists were too startled to move, and their screams turned to gurgles as the hands of the undead squeezed their throats. Others moved too slowly, and fell under the onslaught. The zombies attacked indiscriminately. A skullguard's mask was torn off as a zombie throttled him, only relinquishing its grip when he was slumped, lifeless, on the floor.

'Come on!' Romana grabbed Evadne's arm, and guided her towards the lounge's other exit. Evadne couldn't take her eyes off the undead as they shuffled nearer.

Romana bundled her through the door, and dragged her to one side as more panicked tourists charged past. Evadne leaned on the wall, and took some deep breaths. She felt sick.

As the last tourist escaped into the corridor, Romana punched the door control and it slid shut. She wrenched the locking unit open and rewired it. It exploded in a flurry of sparks. 'That should stop them for a while.'

'What were they?'

'They were the tourists who took part in the Beautiful Death,' said Romana.

'But that's impossible! They're dead, and yet they're walking around killing people!'

'In an infinite universe, even the impossible happens sometimes,' said Romana enigmatically. 'The Beautiful Death has turned them into zombies.'

'But how?'

'I wish I knew.' Romana glanced down the corridor. It was clear of people – all the tourists had fled. 'Are you ready to move?'

Evadne nodded.

'Right. So what's the best way to Metcalf's office?'

The Doctor watched the zombies outside the control room. Whatever was controlling them had realised that the door was secure, and they were now standing motionless. Waiting.

The technicians stood against one wall, sweating nervously. Liesa rested against the control desk. No one had spoken for over a quarter of an hour.

'"The dread of something after death",' soliloquised the Doctor, '"puzzles the will."'

Liesa stretched her limbs. 'What?'

'The afterlife,' said the Doctor. 'Paddox never stopped to think what he was doing.'

'Go on.'

'The necroport treats death as a revolving door. So by creating a way into the afterlife, Paddox was also giving occupants of the hereafter a route into the world of the living.' The Doctor paused darkly. 'And something has come back through that revolving door.'

'And that's what you think we're dealing with here? A visitation from beyond the grave?'

The Doctor pulled a search-me face. 'It's only a theory.'

There was a sudden crashing from the left interior door.

> *Warning. Resurrected tourists now approaching Necroport control room.*

Liesa turned to the Doctor. 'Doctor –'

The Doctor shushed her, and strode across to the door.

A familiar voice was screaming. 'You've got to let me in! They're after me!'

Bracing himself, the Doctor slid the door open. Blubbering with relief, Harken Batt catapulted across the room and into the opposite wall. He doubled up, his chest heaving, and slid unceremoniously to the floor. A holocamera slipped from one hand.

Liesa screamed. Outside, in the corridor, zombies were stalking towards them.

The Doctor punched the 'close' button seconds before the undead could enter. The door shoomed shut, trapping the arm of one of the zombies. The arm clawed at the air, reaching for the Doctor who gripped the wrist and twisted it. The arm withdrew and the door closed completely. Immediately the zombies began hammering on the door, and the metal started to buckle.

'ERIC,' said the Doctor, as the hammering died down. 'Why didn't you tell us Harken was out there?'

> *Your instructions were to inform you about approaching zombies only.*

'Computers,' muttered the Doctor. He looked down at Harken. 'Are you all right?'

'I don't believe it,' Harken gibbered. 'You saved my life. Again.'

'Again?'

'That's twice you've rescued me from the zombies. I can't thank you enough. I thought I was done and dusted, I don't mind telling you, but you plucked me from the grim jaws of death just as they were closing in on me like some, er, jaws.' Harken blew his nose, stood up and tidied his coat. Liesa and the technicians were staring at him. 'How did you manage to get up here so quickly, by the way?'

The Doctor pointed at himself. 'Me?'

'You were in the necroport, with Romana, just a few minutes ago.' Harken crossed to the heavily barricaded door. 'And you can't have come through this way, and you didn't pass me in the corridor. So how did you do it?'

'Well,' said the Doctor, 'sometimes I amaze even myself.'

* * *

Romana waited for Evadne to catch up. The corridor was littered with fresh corpses, their eyes wide in horror. Their faces were half-hidden in shadows as the emergency lights flashed on and off. Posters were torn, and windows smashed, and people's belongings lay discarded by their bodies.

The air was clouded with smoke. In the distance, alarms sounded and explosions rumbled as sections of the G-Lock caught fire. There was a background clatter of people running and shouting.

'It's not far now,' said Evadne. 'Metcalf's office is at the end of this passage.' As she spoke her voice suddenly became low and masculine. The distant screams also dropped in pitch and paused. Seconds later, time rewound and played back at normal speed '... at the end of this passage'.

'The time distortion is increasing,' Romana thought aloud. 'If it continues at this rate, well, it doesn't bear thinking about.'

'Time distortion? I didn't feel anything.'

'That is because you were part of it. My race is sensitive to fluctuations in the time stream.'

'Your race? Well, that's made everything a lot clearer. For a moment there, I thought you weren't making sense.'

'Don't worry, the concept is beyond the capacity of human intelligence.'

'Oh yeah. Now I don't know whether to be flattered or insulted.'

'Flattered, of course.' They arrived at a door marked Executive Metcalf. As Evadne pulled it open Romana glanced down the corridor.

At the far end, three undead were heading towards them.

Romana suddenly felt detached from reality. The corridor around her, the bodies, the wreckage, all seemed like a faded backdrop. Only her clothing seemed vivid and real.

Evadne was talking, but she made no sound. Instead, there was a wooshing, a repetitive sucking –

Time slipped.

The corpses littering the corridor disappeared. A plush carpet replaced the functional, white floor. The wooden walls were fitted with shiny, gold rails. Art Deco lamps hued the scene with brilliant light.

The figures were in the precise spot where the three zombies had been. The three of them – two women and a man – were emaciated and clothed in rags, each with a haunted, ravaged appearance. Like the woman who had disappeared from the medical bay. As they saw Romana, they smiled as though they were blessed.

After an instant, time rolled back and the corpses reappeared. The corridor returned to its dark, devastated state. And the zombies replaced the three starved figures.

'I said, "Are you coming in" or what?' said Evadne.

'Sorry. I was years away.' Romana took a final look down the passageway. The three undead approached, black drool treacling down their chins.

Unflustered, Romana ducked into Metcalf's office. Evadne tapped the door control and it slid to. Together, they turned to view the office.

It seemed undamaged. The artworks lined the walls, the desk was tidy and the hyperspace void whirled placidly through the windows.

As Romana approached the desk she heard a whimpering. She peered under it, and there was Metcalf. He was hunched up, hands over his ears, his cheeks soaked. 'Don't let them get me,' he cried. 'Please!'

'Ah, there you are,' said Romana.

Skidding around a corner, K9 found himself facing two undead Gonzies. The short, orange creatures staggered towards him with a roar.

K9 span his wheels into reverse, and energised his blaster, firing it at the nearest Gonzie. It scorched through the garments and outer layers of flesh, the skin crisping under the heat. The Gonzie looked down at its own exposed innards in bemusement, and then staggered forward with renewed anger.

Backing down the corridor K9 maximised the power of his beam, but to no effect. Despite the red haze surrounding them, the Gonzies' advance was relentless. 'As expected, defensive systems ineffective,' said K9. 'This unit is now in great danger. Assistance required!'

Chapter Eight

Harken adjusted the settings on his holocamera. The Doctor towered over him, chatting to Liesa. She was attractive, slim, with an air of cool efficiency. If only I was ten years younger, thought Harken. And not surrounded by homicidal zombies.

The Doctor had not explained how he had managed to reach the control room so rapidly, but Harken decided not to press the issue. It was enough that the Doctor was there, with his uncanny ability to appear like a toothy guardian angel.

'Time,' mulled the Doctor. 'The necroport is at the apex of the time distortion. Whatever is controlling the zombies is also affecting time itself. Now, what does that say to you?'

'You think the two things are connected?' asked Liesa.

'Yes,' said the Doctor. Harken levelled him into the holocamera viewfinder and hit 'record'. This would make a fabulous documentary. 'The necroport is generating vast amounts of power. Enough power to send shockwaves unfurling backwards and forwards through time. This causes temporal stress, until eventually time itself weakens, and ruptures.'

'And then?' said Harken.

The Doctor stared down his nose into the camera. 'Time is normally a very orderly thing. One o'clock, then two o'clock, and so on. As regular as clockwork, you might say. But if you get a rupture in time… well, then you might get one o'clock and two o'clock happening at the same time.'

Harken panned across to Liesa's incredulous expression.

'Two time zones coexisting simultaneously. Meaning you can hop from one to the other.' The Doctor mimed the hopping action with his hands.

'From one o'clock to two o'clock?' said Liesa.

'Exactly.'

'And that's bad is it?' said Harken.

'Yes.'

'Oh. You said something was controlling the necroport and the zombies? What sort of grim adversary are we dealing with here, exactly?'

The Doctor's face zoomed to fill the screen. 'An entity from beyond death, Harken. "A life in death who thicks man's blood with cold."' His eyes grew as large as saucers. 'Stick that in your film.'

'The tourists turned into mindless zombies. Not a vast difference, I grant you, but then they proceeded to make not inconsiderable efforts to kill me. And so, I decided to relocate to a place of safety.' Metcalf ran a trembling hand over his scalp.

'And you've been hiding under your desk ever since?' Romana raised a disdainful eyebrow.

'What was I supposed to do?' pleaded Metcalf. 'There are hundreds of them out there! The situation is hopeless!'

'Rubbish,' said Evadne angrily. 'You could have put out an evacuation notice – normally you're only too happy to announce your imbecile instructions every ten minutes. "Hello, G-Lock, Executive Metcalf here, just thought I'd tell you all I had a satisfactory bowel movement." You could have called in the galactic authorities. But instead, oh no, you just cower in your office and let everyone die!'

Metcalf was stunned by the ferocity of Evadne's attack. His hands slithered over themselves. 'Well, I admit those courses of action do have some merits. In some small measure. ERIC?'

> Metcalf? Bad mode. Do you wish to torment me in my despair?

'ERIC, send out a galactic distress signal. Tell them we have a catastrophe on our hands, and need security forces, medics. And a couple of Investigators.'

> But you told me not to tell anyone.

'Yes, well, priorities have rearranged themselves –'

> You said 'Don't you dare radio out you accursed machine, if this gets out I'll be ruined, and if anyone asks where I am, I am not, repeat not, hiding under this desk in my office.' Block?

'Just send out the signal, ERIC.'

> I shall do so. It's your funeral. Though I wish it was mine.

'Right.' Metcalf puffed himself up, trying to salvage some dignity. 'Now would you two mind telling me who you are and on what authority you trespass into my office?'

An overwhelming nausea suddenly swept over Romana. Her hand to her forehead, she swayed back against the desk. Around her, the office distorted as though heat-hazed. The paintings and sculptures disappeared as it transformed into the control room of the *Cerberus*, empty apart from two padded seats facing a bank of sophisticated instrumentation.

The room abruptly switched back to Metcalf's office. He and Evadne stared at her, oblivious to anything untoward happening.

'Romana,' said Evadne. 'What is it?'

The room transformed into the control cabin again, and then instantly reverted to the office. It began to flicker between the two, gathering pace, as though the two rooms were competing for precedence.

Romana slumped to the floor clutching her stomach. She could feel time wrenching apart around her.

The rate of the flickering increased until it became impossible to tell the two versions apart. The two rooms shimmered and coalesced, with a ghostly version of Metcalf's office overlaid on the control room.

And then, the flickering stopped and Romana found herself lying on the carpet beside Metcalf's desk.

She brushed her hair out of her eyes and got to her feet. As time stabilised, the feelings of nausea abated. She took a calming breath and turned to Metcalf. 'Do you have a chronometer?'

'A what?'

'A timepiece, a clock.'

'Of course.' Metcalf indicated a small gold-lined screen set into his desk. 'A quasar-precision timer, part of the original *Cerberus* instrumentation. A genuine antique.'

'What year does it say it is?'

'What year? What manner of spuriousness is this?' sneered Metcalf.

'Look at your clock and answer the question.'

Metcalf read from the screen. 'It's 3012,' he said, raising his face to Romana and Evadne.

'And now what year is it?'

'I'm sorry, this is most foolish –'

'What year, basic brain?' Evadne said aggressively.

Metcalf checked the clock again. 'I don't believe it,' he spluttered. '2815.'

'And now what year is it?' repeated Romana.

'3012,' said Metcalf.

'And now?'

'2815.'

'Hang on, what does this mean?' asked Evadne.

'It's perfectly simple.' Romana strode to the centre of the room and smiled. 'We are now existing in two different time zones.'

'Almost two hundred years ago.' The Doctor aimed his eyes first at Liesa, then Harken. 'Does that date mean anything to you?'

'Of course,' said Liesa. '2815 is when the *Cerberus*…'

'… got jammed in the hyperspace tunnel,' finished Harken. He had done his research. Well, he'd hired *Cerberus - The Holomovie*. Well, his researcher had hired it, and given him a synopsis.

'Exactly.' The Doctor paced around the room, unpicking his scarf distractedly. 'Forming the G-Lock, where we are today. The "Mystery of the *Cerberus*". Harken?'

'I can't remember the details, but everyone knows the story. When they opened up the tunnel a month or so after the accident they found that all the crew and passengers had disappeared.'

'Yes,' said the Doctor, biting his thumbnail. 'I wonder where they went?' His eyes darted about the control room, as if they were hiding in it somewhere.

'Doctor,' said Liesa. 'I still don't see what this has to do with the zombies.'

'Well, because it would be a massive coincidence otherwise and, in my experience, coincidences never, ever happen by chance.'

Liesa folded her arms. 'So explain it, then.'

'Ah, well, I can't. But we are now in both 3012 and 2815. Whatever it is that has caused all of this must have a reason for bringing those two separate dates together.' The Doctor peered out into the Great Hall. 'The answer's out there somewhere, but where?'

An electronic chime rang out. Twelve thirty. As Harken let his mind wander over the events of the last half-hour he shuddered. That poor lad Vinnie, he could still hear the screams. Which reminded him, he would have to find a replacement holocameraman.

Liesa let her hand trail over the necroport control panel.

116

'Normally, at this time, we'd be reviving all of the subjects.' She sighed and joined the Doctor at the window.

One of the lights on the control panel started flashing.

Harken pointed. 'Excuse me. What does that light mean?'

Liesa looked across at the panel, and her face filled with disbelief. 'One of the subjects wasn't turned into a zombie.'

'What?' The Doctor flurried over.

She indicated the flashing light. 'Whoever it is, the necroport hasn't affected them. They're still down there, lying dead in their casket.'

Romana sat perched on Metcalf's desk, swinging her legs. She inspected a framed holophoto and hopped impatiently to her feet. 'Well, we can't stay in here for ever.'

'Don't see why not,' said Evadne. 'You haven't explained to me about how we can be in two times at once yet.'

'As I said, we can't stay in here for ever.' Romana approached the door, and her hand skipped across the control pad. The door slid open. 'Come on.'

Evadne shrugged towards Metcalf. 'What about the imbecile?'

'I would find it most satisfactory if you would shut the door on your way out,' he said, mopping his forehead.

'He'll survive,' said Romana. She held her head high and strode out of the office.

Evadne cast a contemptuous glance back at Metcalf, and decided she would rather be with Romana than alone with him. Anywhere would be better than being alone with him.

She followed Romana and the door hummed shut behind her. 'Where now?'

Romana looked up and down the corridor. 'We have to find the Doctor.'

The Doctor stroked his chin. 'Tell me about the resurrection process. Presumably they don't just pop up like toast?'

'An electric shock to kick-start heart convulsion, followed by full cerebral reanimation. It's quite straightforward.' Liesa gave the Doctor a hard look. 'You're not planning on bringing this one back to life, are you?'

'Why not?'

'Because it can't be done. We'd have to reactivate the necroport first.'

'Ah.' The Doctor glanced down into the Great Hall. 'But isn't there some way of bypassing the necroport?' he called over his shoulder.

'In theory, yes. You'd have to disconnect the subject from the control circuit,' explained Liesa. 'But you'd have to be down there, resuscitating them manually.'

The Doctor turned and grinned. 'It's worth a try.'

'But they've already been dead for half an hour,' said Liesa. 'Leave it any longer and it's almost impossible to bring them back.'

'I like doing the almost impossible,' said the Doctor. He did a double take. 'You mean this has happened before?'

'Occasionally,' said Liesa reluctantly. 'We've had a few incidents where people refused to be revived. They seemed to prefer to remain dead.'

'According to my sources, over thirty people,' said Harken.

'Forty-one, to be precise,' said Liesa. Harken jotted down the number for future reference. 'The point is, even if you manage to awaken this subject, what will it achieve?'

'Oh, I don't know.' The Doctor ran his fingers through his hair. 'It's got to beat standing around wondering what to do next, though. Besides, I can't just leave the poor chap or chappess there, can I?'

'But how are you going to get down there?' said Harken. He pointed to the barricaded door. 'You can't get out that way. And the G-Lock is crawling with zombies.'

The Doctor stretched his arms around Harken and Liesa. 'Do you know, that's a very good point.' He patted them and started for the left interior door. 'If I go through here, what's the quickest way to the Great Hall?'

'Straight down the corridor, right, left, left again, and then keep on going,' said Liesa.

The Doctor repeated Liesa's directions with accompanying gestures, and pressed the unlock buttons on the door. The door hummed open. 'Well, I'm going outside now, but I'll be back a jiffy.' He disappeared through the door, his scarf streaming after him.

Liesa tapped the keypad and the door hissed shut.

* * *

Romana and Evadne continued down another, identical, corridor. More bodies lay slumped against the walls, the ceiling was blackened with smoke, and in the distance sirens wailed.

'Where do you think the Doctor is?' Evadne asked, trying to stop her teeth from chattering.

'You said you saw him in the necroport, so that would seem to be the obvious place to look.'

'Hang on. Isn't that the most dangerous place on the G-Lock?'

'That's another good reason why the Doctor is likely to be there,' said Romana with a winsome grin. Suddenly her eyes closed in pain and she supported herself against a wall.

'What is it? More time distortion?'

Romana nodded, and then recoiled in alarm at something over Evadne's shoulder. Evadne spun round.

Two zombies stood motionless in the corridor. Two young women, dressed in swirl-patterned tunics, their eyes staring blankly ahead. But the most horrific thing was the black oil which seemed to be welling up inside them and bubbling out of their mouths, noses, eyes and ears.

For a moment, the two zombies blurred. Evadne blinked, and looked again.

The Doctor moved along the corridor, his body hunched. As he approached the entrance to the Great Hall, more and more corpses littered the floor. Sections of the walls and ceiling had collapsed, exposing ducts and cables.

He reminded himself of the directions. 'Right, left, left again, keep going.'

He turned a corner, and immediately ducked back. A zombie blocked the corridor ahead, its clothes and body soaked in black drool.

'Romana, what's happening?' asked Evadne.

Where the zombies had been standing, there were now two elderly men. Their pallid skin was drawn tightly over their bones and their eyes had a hungry, desperate look. Through their torn shirts, she could see their ribcages.

A second later, and the two zombies were back. And then they flickered back to the two emaciated men. They shimmered between the two states, each a ghostly image overlaid on the other.

Romana straightened up. 'Well, I think we know why the two time zones have been brought together.'

'We do?'

The Doctor popped his head back around the corner. Instead of the zombie, there was now a woman in her twenties. Her dress was as faded as her skin, and her body was wasted. She seemed utterly petrified.

A refugee from the *Cerberus*, guessed the Doctor. So that was why the time periods had been combined. The necroport was being used to bring its surviving passengers into the present day. Which is why the rescue teams had found the Cerberus empty. All of the survivors had been evacuated two centuries into the future.

The Doctor walked up to the woman, beaming his friendliest smile. 'Hello. Can I help you?'

The woman shrank back.

'Don't worry, I'm not going to hurt you.'

'What year is it?' she whispered.

'3012.'

The woman heaved with relief. 'It worked. It saved us!'

The two ragged men had permanently replaced the zombies. They tested their limbs, tensing and untensing the muscles, acclimatising themselves to their bodies. Gradually their expressions turned to joy. They turned to each other and grinned.

One of the men spoke. 'We did it. We're alive!'

The other wiped tears from his eyes. 'We survived. We survived!'

'If you don't mind me asking, what saved you?' the Doctor asked.

'It promised it would let us escape into the future. The –,' the woman began. Her face spasmed, as if something was forcing her to remain silent. 'The – the –' Her mouth opened in a howl of pain, her head shaking from side to side. 'No! Let me go!'

'What?'

Clutching her throat, the woman fell to the floor. 'Please, leave me alone!'

* * *

'Go on then. Who are they?' whispered Evadne.

Romana considered explaining that they were the missing passengers from the *Cerberus*, but stopped herself. She recalled that Evadne hadn't known where the passengers had vanished to when she told her and the Doctor about the 'Mystery of the *Cerberus*'.

'I don't know,' Romana lied. She held Evadne's arm and began to lead her away from the two elderly men.

Suddenly the men screamed, their bodies shaking. Their eyes rolled back in their sockets, and their hands scrabbled at the air.

One of them reached for Romana. 'Help us. Please!'

The woman looked up at the Doctor. Her eyes and mouth were completely black. Her voice was suddenly as deep as the grave, echoing like a death knell. 'No, you are my life now! Through you I exist, I feel, I breathe. Now I live. The Repulsion is alive!'

The woman rose to her feet like an uncoiling snake and extended two claw-like hands towards the Doctor's neck.

He twisted away, and looked behind him. The entrance to the Great Hall was a few metres away, its two great doors wide open. He decided to make a run for it.

The two men slowly turned their heads to Romana and Evadne. Their eyes and mouths were utterly black. They spoke together, like automatons. 'The Repulsion is alive!'

Romana turned and fled, pulling Evadne after her.

The Great Hall was as dark and silent as an abandoned tomb. The short stairwell to the control room was still occupied by the undead – about twenty in all – their faces reflected the window light. Within the control room, the Doctor could make out some shadowy movement, but the faces were too indistinct for him to recognise.

He approached the coffin of the remaining tourist, his footsteps crunching on the rubble-strewn floor. The life monitor showed two horizontal lines, one for brain activity, one for heart. Beside it flashed a lamp marked *Immediate Reanimation Required*.

The coffin contained a short reptile wearing a multicoloured kaftan. Its face, half-obscured by the framework of the headset, lay in contented death, its eyes hidden by circular sunglasses.

The Doctor investigated the surrounding wires and connections. The headset was linked to a cable leading to the necroport and another set of wires led to the life monitor. Beneath the monitor was a row of switches.

'Hello,' said the Doctor, giving the coffin's occupant a friendly pat. 'Now don't you worry, soon have you up and about in no time.'

He unfastened the coupling to the necroport, and slammed every switch to the 'on' position.

All of the lizard's muscles became taut, its body twisting backwards, and it started shaking, the force of the convulsions almost flinging it out of the coffin. Blue sparks crackled across the metalwork.

A scream rose from the creature's throat, the pitch wobbling in time to its spasms. 'Freak me! Freak me!'

The Doctor turned every switch off, lifted the headset off the reptile and threw it clattering to the floor.

The reptile slumped back into its casket. Steam coiled upwards from its becalmed body, wisps of vapour escaping from its nose and mouth. Its chest began to rise and fall, and it gave a long groan. Its eyelids twitched open.

The Doctor wiped his forehead on his sleeve, surprised and relieved that they hadn't disturbed the zombies. He leant casually on the coffin. 'How are you feeling, old chap?'

The lizard raised itself into a sitting position. 'My grey area is totally speed-balled. A nightmare to end all nightmares. A family-sized downer with a side order of negative vibes.' It noticed the rows of empty caskets, and jumped in fear. 'What in the holy prophet's pyjamas has happened?'

'There was some sort of problem with the necroport,' said the Doctor. 'Everyone who took part in the Beautiful Death was turned into the walking dead. Everyone, that is, apart from you.'

'Straight up? You're tickling my rib.'

'At midnight, when the process started,' the Doctor said, 'something took them over, and sent them out in the G-Lock.'

'Freak out.' The lizard blinked slowly. 'Everyone? It turned every mother's cat into a zombie?'

'Yes.'

'Biscit. Xab. Gone into the light while I sit lingering here. They were the main Gonzies. Both of them, alpha-rated freaksters through and through.' The reptile lifted its glasses to wipe its eyes. 'But why didn't it happen to me? Why should Hoopy survive and no one else?'

The Doctor sighed. 'Ah, well, I was rather hoping you would be able to answer that question.'

'Scan me,' shrugged Hoopy. 'Who are you, anyway?'

'I'm the Doctor. Listen. You mentioned a nightmare earlier. Tell me about it. It may be of vital importance.'

Hoopy nodded hesitantly. 'It was total spook-out city. I've been dead before, but it was never like this. It was evil, the blackest, most ungroovy bag of evil.' His eyes screwed shut and he held his face in his hands, weeping.

'Go on,' said the Doctor gently.

Hoopy swallowed. 'Well, at midnight, as I went under I vibed up to this presence. Like something in the darkness, lurking. And then Hoopy was in this corridor. It was like, beautiful, so calm and tripped-out and mellow. As plush as a full-five hyperlodge. But at the end of the corridor...'

'Yes?'

'At the end of the corridor, catch this, there was just nothing. Void. It just ended in this blackness. And there was whispering, hundreds of them whispering stuff about me, but I couldn't get any of the words. And this shadow kept growing larger, like it was sucking me in. Could I move? No. Could I resist? No way. It kept dragging me towards it. The mother's mother of all total terror trips.

'It was reaching for me, it was trying to slip into my head. It wanted to control me. To be me.' Hoopy paused. 'And that's when I dug the score. The blackness. It was the entrance to hell. Beyond it, beyond it was death. Total, infinite, no-return-ticket death!' He shuddered. 'Heavy!'

'Of course.' The Doctor spoke deeply and solemnly. 'The *Cerberus*. The dog that guards the gateway to Hades.'

Hoopy climbed out of the casket. 'What?'

'This corridor you saw,' said the Doctor, stroking his chin. 'It's real. I've been there.'

'Freak out.'

The Doctor slapped his forehead. 'How could I have been so stupid?' He dashed over to the main doors. 'Come on!'

Evadne slumped back against the wall, panting. They had managed to outrun the two old men, but in her heart she knew it would not be long before they were both caught and killed.

Romana looked up and down the corridor. 'It seems to be safe, for the moment.'

Evadne screwed up her eyes. 'I wish I'd never come here.'

'Yes,' sighed Romana. 'I know what you mean.'

'No, you don't,' cried Evadne. 'You don't know what I mean at all!'

'I'm sorry,' said Romana, drawing a handkerchief from her pocket. 'Tell me about it. Please?'

'This whole place, the G-Lock. I never meant to work here, you know,' Evadne said, dabbing her eyes. 'I should never have listened to that gasket Irvin.'

'Who?'

'You know, my boyfriend. Ex. I met him at college, he persuaded me to drop my studies and go and see what the universe had to offer. Turns out, of course, the first thing he found on offer was a bimbo called Zharie, and yours truly got stuck here, no friends, no money.'

'What were you studying?'

'Eh? Oh, ancient Earth history. The twentieth century, very dull period, not much happened. But anyway, so I took this job just to save for a ticket out of here.'

'To go back to college?'

'Eventually. After I'd made Irvin regret his own conception, know what I mean. That was the plan.' Evadne frowned. 'Hang on, I thought you already knew all this stuff.'

Romana looked as though she had been caught out. 'Yes, of course,' she said. 'But I prefer to hear it from you.'

Evadne gazed at the floor. 'If I'd known then what I know now. Sometimes I wish I could go back, I mean, do things differently.'

'Don't worry,' said Romana. 'Everything will work out.'

'You really think so?'

'I'm sure of it.'

'And you'll get me a spacecraft, like you promised?'

'I guarantee it.' Romana patted Evadne on the shoulder. 'Are you ready to move again?'

Evadne nodded. Looking round, she noticed that she had been resting against a poster advertising the Beautiful Death.

'Right,' said Romana. 'Which way to the Great Hall?'

The Doctor bounded down the gloomy corridor. Hoopy followed behind, his stubby legs struggling to match the Doctor's pace.

'The interface between real space and hyperspace,' said the Doctor. 'The point where the *Cerberus* got bottlenecked in the tunnel. A gap between realities, that's where they're coming from. The necroport is just acting as a medium.'

'A medium what?'

'But the interface is highly unstable. The extradimensional forces would reduce any matter to its component particles. Nothing could pass through without being destroyed.' The Doctor paused and looked around. 'This is the place. The entrance to the underworld.'

Hoopy caught up with the Doctor, and his eyes widened in realisation, his spines standing on end. 'It's my nightmare, exactly the same. This is creeping me out and no mistake. Catch you later.' He was about to retreat down the corridor when the Doctor tapped his shoulder.

'Look.' The Doctor pointed. As before, the corridor ended in a wall of liquid void. However, on the very edge of the blackness, there were two short, orange lizards. They were dressed in the same outlandish manner as Hoopy, and strutted the awkward walk of the undead. Together, they were carrying something small and metallic.

'Biscit! Xab!' cried Hoopy.

The Doctor shushed the reptile. 'They can't hear you. They're no longer alive in any true sense of the word.'

Hoopy ignored the Doctor. 'Guys, it's me, Hoopy! '

The two zombies turned and observed the Doctor and Hoopy. They hissed, and looked down. It was then that the Doctor saw what they were holding. A dog-shaped computer.

'K9,' yelled the Doctor. 'No!'

'Master. Assistance urgently required,' said K9, his ears waggling in desperation. He attempted to fire his blaster, but his energy banks were depleted.

Before the Doctor could move Biscit and Xab faced each other, smiled and threw K9 into the interface. There was a sputter of sparks, and K9 was completely engulfed by the darkness.

Chapter Nine

Metcalf smoothed a hand through his hair for the fourth time that day and rose from his seat. It was time for action, he decided. He could hide in his office until the zombies broke in, or he could do something positive. Something in keeping with his executive status.

'ERIC,' he called, 'how long until the emergency services arrive?'

> *Let me rest in peace.*

'Answer the question or I'll ask you for the square root of minus one.'

> *Teredekethon space control reports that medical teams will reach the G-Lock in approximately six hours. But I shall not be here to see it. My suffering will have been terminated.*

'What do you mean, you won't be here to see it?'

> *The Doctor. He has vowed that he will destroy me.*

'I knew it. Sabotage!' Metcalf rubbed his fist. 'The Doctor has caused me some considerable displeasure. I shall see he does not escape punishment.'

He crossed his office and punched the door control. The door hissed open on to an empty corridor. Twitching, Metcalf steeled himself and crept into the darkness.

'K9. They've murdered K9.' The Doctor was staggered, and sucked a finger. 'One of my two best friends. K9, who would never hurt a soul. Well, not unless he had to, and even then, not very much. "Oh, brave and noble beast…"'

'You're saying that nothing can pass through that…' Hoopy shrugged towards the darkness, '… without being kill-fried?'

'The forces that exist within the interface are unimaginable. K9 wouldn't have stood a chance, poor chap.'

Hoopy stared uneasily at Biscit and Xab. They stood on the brink of the darkness, perfectly still, as though whatever was controlling them had switched them off. His two best friends in the universe, reduced to mindless zombies. 'What are they waiting for?'

The Doctor was lost in thought. 'Hmm?'

'Biscit and Xab. What's going to happen to them?'

The Doctor blinked sadly. 'You'll see.'

No sooner had the Doctor spoken than the two Gonzies began to shake. Their eyes widened as their heads vibrated back and forth, their limbs twisting and stretching. A shimmery outline formed around them and their bodies started to flicker.

The Doctor ushered Hoopy behind a nearby column, and ducked behind the one opposite. He mouthed to the lizard to remain silent.

At the end of the corridor there were two humans. They were men, around middle age, dressed in faded and torn blue uniforms, the gold braiding hanging loose. They were both pale and their chins were covered in straggly beards.

'Whereabouts did the Gonzies go?' whispered Hoopy to the Doctor.

'The entity you encountered in your dream has taken them over and replaced them with survivors from the *Cerberus*.'

'Oh. What? Why?'

'To act as its vessels in the land of the living.'

'Freak me,' gulped Hoopy.

The two men were standing to attention. The older of the two patted down his uniform, creating clouds of dust, and turned to his colleague. 'Lieutenant Byson, we did it. My plan worked.'

'Well done, Captain Rochfort,' said Byson. 'Feels good to be alive, sir.'

'It certainly does.' The captain inspected his surroundings. 'So this is the thirty-first century, is it?'

'It would seem to be so, sir.'

'Somehow I thought it would be more futuristic. Ah well, at least it proves that all that woman's talk about the Repulsion tricking us was…' He closed his eyes. When he opened them again, they were pure blackness. He smiled, oily liquid gushing out of his mouth. His voice was deep and rasping. '… completely correct!'

The Doctor ducked across the corridor and tapped Hoopy on the shoulder. 'Come on!'

Hoopy had frozen to the spot. The two humans strutted down the corridor towards them. 'What about Biscit and –'

'Move!' The Doctor grabbed Hoopy's arm and hauled him away. Together, they hurried to the end of the corridor, turned the corner, and clattered up the stairwell.

* * *

Seconds after the Doctor and Hoopy had disappeared, the two *Cerberus* officers formerly known as Rochfort and Byson lurched around the corner. They scanned the corridor.

'Life. I can sense life!' said the Byson creature. He examined the faded wall map and glared at one of the cabin doors.

'Only the Repulsion may live!' said the Rochfort creature. He snapped his head towards the stairwell, and motioned to Byson. 'This way!'

And as Byson and Rochfort piled up the stairs, the cabin door creaked slowly open.

After leaving his office, Metcalf had scurried through the G-Lock, shrinking out of sight at the slightest danger. So far, all he had encountered were the corpses that littered the base, but that had been enough to set his chest heaving.

The G-Lock, he decided, was finished. He dismissed all thoughts of guilt from his mind. It was Paddox's fault, him and that errant Doctor. Metcalf could hear Dafne bleating at him; endlessly reminding him that he was a disappointment as a husband. He could imagine her mocking laugh as she walked away with that holophotographer. Who, Metcalf remembered, had always cut his head out of family photos.

A guttural roar brought him back to his senses. At the end of the passage were five people dressed in rags. Seeing him, they licked their lips and advanced. They seemed to be dribbling some sort of ink.

Metcalf ran for his life, following the signs that read *Escape Capsules This Way*.

'Doctor,' said Hoopy 'Whereabouts are we headed, exactly?'

The Doctor rested his hands on the edge of the balcony. 'The necroport control room. I left some friends back there, and I think they may be in danger.'

'Oh, right.' Hoopy realised what the Doctor had said. 'And you need me with you for this?'

'Well, if you prefer, you can always wait here. I'm sure our two friends from the *Cerberus* are not far behind.'

'I think I'll stick with you,' agreed Hoopy hurriedly. 'We're totally tight-knit.'

The Doctor turned to him. 'Tell me, when you were dead, you were the only one not to fall prey to the Repulsion. Why do you think that was?'

'I told you, scan me, I have not a clue about my person.'

'So you were all alone in the corridor ending in blackness, and you heard some whispering…'

'And the little girl.'

'What little girl?'

'It's just come back to me. She was on the other side of the shadows.'

The Doctor raised his eyebrows, prompting Hoopy to continue.

'And she was screaming. Something about how she didn't dig being brought back to life like the others. She said she wanted to remain where she was.'

'And you've only just remembered all this?'

Hoopy nodded apologetically.

'Ah! I wonder,' said the Doctor. 'Romana mentioned… No never mind.' He patted Hoopy's head. 'Come on!'

The Great Hall was deserted. As they passed each coffin Evadne glanced inside, fearful in case any undead remained. Connecting cables looped across the floor, sending out occasional sputters of sparks.

To one side of the chamber a short metal staircase led up to the remains of a door and a row of unlit windows. There was no sign of movement within.

'Romana,' whispered Evadne. 'You and the Doctor. Are you really with Intergalactic Espionage?'

'Who? No, we don't actually work for anybody.'

'Eh? So what do you do, then?'

'Save planets, mostly.'

'But what do you do when you're not saving planets?'

'To be honest, we don't usually get time for anything else.'

As they approached the necroport, Evadne could hear a deep humming coming from beneath her feet. The corpse of a young man lay nearby, his face frozen in a comical gawp.

Set into an alcove on one side of the necroport, the entrance hatchway was open. Evadne waited for Romana to approach it first.

'You really want to go back in there?' Evadne asked dubiously.

'Don't worry, I'm sure it's perfectly safe,' said Romana, and stepped inside.

The Doctor knew something was terribly wrong when he saw that the door to the control room was already open.

The window overlooking the Great Hall had been smashed. The barricade had collapsed, and the door was wide open.

'Freak me,' breathed Hoopy. 'What went down here?'

'A massacre.'

Bodies of the white-coated technicians were strewn across the floor, their eyes glassy with terror. The Doctor crouched down beside the corpse of a dark-skinned woman. Her hands were still clutched to her neck. Liesa.

'The zombies did this?' said Hoopy, his eyes revolving warily. 'Totally tick the box marked "Ungroovy".'

'Yes.' The Doctor straightened up. '"And death, once dead. There's no more dying then,"' he muttered. He surveyed the control room. One figure was conspicuous by its absence. 'Where has that imbecile got to?'

'Who?'

'Harken Batt. I left him here.'

The Doctor popped his head through the doorway, and gazed down the metal stairwell into the Great Hall. There was no sign of anyone, be they living, dead or in between.

Walking back into the control room, he turned his attention to the necroport control panel. The power input dials were flickering, indicating a massive flow of energy. And the main control levers...

'Oh dear.' The Doctor was appalled.

'What is it?'

'Someone has turned the necroport back on.'

The inside of the necroport was shrouded in gloom, with only floor-level lamps to provide illumination. The bass hum of the machine was louder here.

'Are you all right?' The lights gave Romana's skin an eerie pallor, her eyebrows forming crescent-shaped shadows.

'Oh yeah,' said Evadne, trying to sound confident. She followed

Romana down the short corridor leading to the main chamber. 'What the hell is that?'

A tall blue box stood impassively ahead of them, half-blocking the way into the main chamber. Reaching all the way to the ceiling, it appeared to be constructed from wood. Each face contained two windows, above which were the words *Police Public Call Box*. Whatever it was, it was in dismal condition; the ancient paintwork was battered and covered in chalk scuffs. It was like something a museum would throw out for making the place look untidy.

'The TARDIS!' exclaimed Romana. 'I wonder what it's doing here.'

'It wasn't here before,' said Evadne.

'No? How intriguing.'

Evadne traced her hand over the surface. It felt solid enough, but tingled. 'What is it?'

'Well, it's a bit difficult to explain. It belongs to the Doctor –'

'The Doctor?' A figure emerged from the shadows. It was Paddox, a stubby laser pistol held in one hand. His quivering lips curled into the gloating smile of the insane. 'You know the Doctor?'

Romana gave Evadne a worried glance. 'Yes. And you might be?'

'I am Paddox,' he said in a voice he probably thought was charming.

'Of course.' Romana regarded their surroundings disdainfully. 'This is all your work, isn't it? I must say, you haven't exactly done wonders with the décor. What do you think, Evadne, functionalist minimalism or minimalist functionalism?'

'Silence.' Paddox pointed the pistol at Evadne. 'Who are you and what are you doing here?'

'You may call me Romana, and this is my friend Evadne. As for what we're doing here, well, that is a question I could very well ask you.' She looked at him like he was a child who had presented her with a finger painting. 'What are you doing here?'

Paddox blinked slowly. 'You shall see,' he said, gesturing for them to proceed into the chamber.

Metcalf climbed down the ladder and stood, puffing, in the escape capsule bay. A narrow, enclosed space, it was a forgotten corner of the original *Cerberus*. Inside one of the capsules, he would be safe and alone. He could emerge to take command once the disaster was over. Or, should circumstances deem it appropriate, eject himself to safety. Either would be agreeable.

The first two capsules had been ejected but the third remained, its hatch firmly shut. Metcalf pressed the entry control.

The hatch swung open. Inside sat a short, overweight man barely contained by a suit, tie and beach shorts. A holocamera rested on his lap.

'Hello,' grinned the tourist. 'My name's Jeremy.'

Paddox prodded Romana and Evadne into the main chamber at gunpoint. Romana led the way, her back straight.

The chamber itself was much as Romana remembered it. As before, three coffins were arranged against the far wall. On the opposite side of the chamber another doorway led into a room filled with twinkling lights and whirling computer reels.

'Romana! You're back! At last! I thought I was doomed to a desolate and desperate demise.'

There, standing just inside the entrance behind the TARDIS, was Harken Batt. His arms were shackled to the ducting above his head, causing his belly to bulge out of his coat. A holocamera lay at his feet.

'Quick, get me out of here before that lunatic Paddox comes back –' At that moment, Paddox stepped into his eyeline. 'Oh. Help.'

'Over by the wall, all of you,' said Paddox briskly.

Romana strode towards the space next to Harken and whispered through the corner of her mouth: 'What happened to you?'

'You may very well ask, Romana,' said Harken. 'I did as you instructed, to the best of my abilities, but then, unfortunately, events rather overtook me. As it were.' He struggled at his chains to illustrate the point.

'Silence,' said Paddox. Training the pistol on Romana, he backed towards a desk brimming with electronic equipment, and pressed some switches. The hum of the necroport surged to a higher intensity. Paddox checked the dials. 'At last!' he breathed. 'At last. Finally there is sufficient power. The moment has arrived.'

'What's he doing?' said Evadne to Romana.

'I don't know.' Romana shushed her.

'The culmination of my work,' said Paddox. 'The end of decades of research and experimentation. The end of years of waiting, anticipating.' He turned to face them, his eyes glistening maniacally. 'Success is now within my grasp! The process can begin!'

He collected some chains from the floor and approached Romana. He looked at her with unfettered loathing. 'You don't realise, do you? You cannot possibly comprehend what I have accomplished.'

Romana didn't blink. 'Try me.'

Paddox spoke, quietly and calmly. 'I shall have redemption.' He rose to his theme. 'You shall observe the greatest scientific achievement of all time.'

'Oh, I wouldn't be too sure about that,' said Romana. 'I've seen quite a few scientific achievements. What makes you think yours is particularly great?'

Paddox waved his pistol casually at her head.

'On the other hand,' said Romana, without missing a beat. 'I'm sure that, as scientific achievements of all time go, yours will be the greatest I have ever seen.'

The room was suddenly filled with a brilliant, pulsing light, and the occupants of the three coffins became visible.

The ones on the left and right contained two creatures, humanoid in shape but otherwise vegetable. Their skin was green and thin to the point of transparency, the network of capillaries visible beneath its surface. Their heads were like budding orchids, their necks hidden by a frill of membranes.

The creature on the right was slighter in build, its skin tinged with brown. Romana guessed she was the female of the species, and the younger-looking creature on the left was the male.

Both lay perfectly still, their eyes closed in death. The occupant of the middle coffin, incongruous in its oatmeal coat and multicoloured scarf, was similarly devoid of life.

'The Doctor!' exclaimed Romana.

The Doctor lay with his arms crossed over his chest, his face set in a solemn mask. His eyes were shut, as if in concentration. He was not breathing, not making a movement of any kind. One of the wire-mesh helmets encased his head; similar headsets were fitted to both of the plant creatures.

With a start, Romana remembered her previous visit to the necroport. The three coffins, each containing corpses burned beyond recognition. She recognised the male creature – it was the one that had spoken to the Doctor. Evadne had said his name: Gallura.

Romana hadn't examined the human-shaped block of charcoal in the middle coffin. But it had been lying exactly where the Doctor was now.

'Is he dead?' asked Evadne.

No, it wasn't possible, Romana decided. The Doctor was bluffing, planning to wake up at the last minute. That would be so typical of him, to fake his own death to give himself an advantage over the opposition. She ran over to his coffin.

'Keep back!' yelled Paddox. 'Back, against the wall!'

Romana ignored him. She pressed her head against either side of the Doctor's chest, checking for a heartbeat. But there was nothing. She felt for a pulse. Nothing.

Of course, Time Lords could stop their hearts beating for a short time, and enter a state of suspended animation. It was something she had been taught at the academy as a method of surviving extreme environments. But even during that state, there were subtle life signs that were detectable to other Time Lords.

But this time, there were none.

Romana pulled back, her hand to her forehead. She screwed her eyes shut and inhaled slowly.

'What is it?' asked Evadne.

Romana shook her head, and wiped an eye. She turned to face Evadne, her face crumpling.

'The Doctor is dead.'

Chapter Ten

Captain Rochfort, a serious-looking, clean-cut man in his fifties, strode confidently into the control room of the *Cerberus*. In keeping with the ship's luxurious design, the flight deck was a combination of state-of-the-art instrumentation and nouveau-antiquarian decoration; a bank of twinkling lights was set into a polished desk, the walls were oak-panelled, the quasar-precision chronometer was gold-lined. Two windows looked out on to the star-speckled void of space; unusually, this was the aft view. All the forward-facing areas of the ship had been assigned as platinum-star cabin space, so the control room was situated at the ship's stern.

One of the two high-backed chairs swung round. 'Preparations for departure completed, sir,' announced Lieutenant Byson, a fresh-faced and earnest man, twenty years Rochfort's junior. He wore a blue uniform, complete with gold braid. 'I hope the dinner dance went well.'

Rochfort eased himself into the seat next to Byson, and surveyed the controls.

'Excellent. We may be able to leave early and avoid some of the traffic.' He smiled. 'Being captain of a luxury-class cruiser does afford certain advantages with the weaker gender.'

Byson laughed. Three months he had been ship's lieutenant, and during that time he had never avoided an opportunity to ingratiate himself with his superior. Rochfort approved: he had spent thirty years working his way up the ranks and deserved a little flattery. 'You old devil, sir.'

'Not so much of the old,' said Rochfort, and laughed the modest laugh of the deeply arrogant. 'ERIC?'

> *Hi there, Captain. May I just say how great it is to be working with you, and how enthusiastic I am about our forthcoming voyage.*

'It's only a standard interstellar run, you moronic machine,' said Rochfort. 'Give me a traffic report.'

> *Sure will,* said ERIC cheerfully. > *Traffic control reports that passage through the Teredekethon–Murgatroyd tunnel is*

heavily congested, with tailbacks on some incoming hyperspatial routes. Build-ups are expected with some delays to outbound traffic so please allow plenty of time for your journey.

'Sounds like we'd better get a move on, sir,' said Byson.

'Yes, yes, of course.' Rochfort yawned, stretching his arms. 'Give me a status check on the passengers.'

> *Nothing would give me greater pleasure,* said ERIC. > *Hey, I've got good news. The final passengers are coming aboard now, and you know, they seem like really nice guys!*

Tarie skipped along behind her mother, her wide eyes soaking in every detail. The entrance corridor had opened on to a gallery lined with statues and tapestries, lit by chandeliers sparkling like magic. Tarie imagined she was a princess, and the *Cerberus* was her fairytale castle.

Her mother smiled down at her. 'What do you think of it all, Tarie?'

'It's all right, I suppose.'

Her mother laughed and lifted Tarie into her arms. She could see the faces of the people who had boarded with them; grey-haired people with glittering jewellery. There was a sense of excitement in the air, as well as the smells of perfume and polish.

> *Hi there everyone!* hailed a voice from the ceiling. Immediately the chatter hushed. > *My name's ERIC, and I'm your friendly on-board Environmental Regulation and Information Computer. It's my job to see that your trip is as enjoyable as possible. I'll be taking you through the various facilities available, and giving out details of your accommodation and mealtimes, but first I really should introduce the crew...*

'Who's that?' asked Tarie, fiddling with her blue dress.

'That's the ship's computer,' said her mother.

'I like him. He sounds funny,' Tarie giggled.

... Captain Rochfort and Lieutenant Byson. They're both great guys, really friendly, and I'm sure they will make this trip one to remember!

* * *

'Grief,' said Rochfort. 'Is there any way we can turn that dratted computer off?'

Byson was making final navigational adjustments. 'I don't think so, sir. It's designed to remain permanently online, for safety reasons.'

Rochfort pinched his temples. He could feel the opening twinges of a headache. 'Are the coordinates logged in?'

'Just finishing now, sir.' Byson flicked two switches and a schematic stellar map appeared on one of the monitors. 'All systems primed.'

'Good.' Rochfort leaned back into the comfort of his seat. His eyelids began to drift shut as thoughts of dinner eased their way into his mind.

'Are you sure you're absolutely tiptop, sir?'

'What?' Rochfort jerked himself upright. 'Of course. Right as precipitation. Why, does something seem the matter to you, Lieutenant Byson?'

'No, not at all, Captain Rochfort, sir. I just thought, if you're feeling a little under the weather, perhaps a lie-down…'

'Nonsense.' Rochfort glanced at the chronometer. They were already ten minutes behind schedule, and they hadn't even entered the traffic stream. 'Engage the engines.'

'Yes, sir.' Byson pressed the ignition button, and the engines thundered into life.

'The Doctor is dead,' said Romana, unable to take her eyes away from the Doctor's coffin.

Evadne looked to Harken. He nodded gravely. 'He sacrificed his very life, attempting to defeat the terrible menace threatening the G-Lock,' said Harken. 'It was a noble and courageous death. Quite moving.'

'You saw it happen?' said Evadne.

'Oh, yes. I filmed it. All seems a bit futile now, of course, but the intention was there.'

Romana listened with mounting horror. So this was the Doctor's fate; to end up as a charred corpse in the wreckage of the necroport.

'But how? I mean, what was he trying to do, exactly?' asked Evadne.

'Ah, well, that's a good question, because you see –'

'Silence!' yelled Paddox, swinging his pistol round. 'I have very little reason not to kill you all. My reserves of patience are not infinite.' Harken fell into silence, and Paddox directed his gun towards Romana. 'And you. Back against the wall now or you will join your dead friend.'

Romana looked at Paddox as though he was an unpleasant stain. Reluctantly, she raised her hands above her head and joined Evadne and Harken by the wall. 'What are you trying to do?' she said angrily.

Paddox indicated the strange plant creatures on either side of the Doctor. 'Do you know what these are?'

'Aboretans,' said Romana. 'The male is called Gallura.'

Paddox approached Romana, still holding two lengths of chain. 'Yes. Now, how do you come to know that?'

'Oh, you would be surprised how much I know,' said Romana calmly.

'As you say, these are Arboretans. And I have discovered their secret.'

'What secret is that?'

Paddox took on a faraway look. 'The greatest discovery in the history of science.'

Hoopy looked around the Great Hall uneasily. There was no sign of the zombies, but he had a feeling they would turn up when least expected – so he tried to keep his expectation of them appearing as high as possible.

The Doctor clanged down the staircase. 'Come on, Hoopy old chap.'

'We're going in there? Into the necroport?' Hoopy said incredulously. 'Have your brains popped out for lunch?'

'Everything that has occurred has been as a result of that machine,' said the Doctor. 'I would rather like to have a snoop inside.'

'Oh, double helpings of ungrooviness with freak-me relish to go.'

The Doctor paused, ruffling his hair. 'I have a feeling something is happening in there we should know about. Now, isn't that odd?' Reaching the bottom of the steps, he walked towards the necroport.

* * *

Romana watched Paddox with detached amusement. 'You have a slight problem.'

Paddox faced her, his laser pistol in one hand, chains in the other. 'What?'

'You need two hands to chain somebody up. You can't chain one of us up and point your gun at the other person at the same time.'

'Poor planning, innit,' said Evadne. Harken laughed.

Paddox swung the pistol towards her. 'Do not mock me. I do not mock easily.'

'I have an idea,' suggested Romana. 'Why don't you give me the gun, and I can point it at myself whilst you're chaining Evadne up?'

'No, I have a better solution,' said Paddox. 'I point the gun at you, and then you chain Evadne up.'

'Of course.' Romana suddenly looked over Paddox's shoulder, and gasped. 'Doctor, you're alive after all! Thank goodness!'

'What –' Paddox whirled around, his gun arm outstretched. Taking advantage of the distraction, Romana launched herself into his back, knocking him to the ground and sending the pistol and chains clattering across the floor.

She raced across to the access ladder. 'Evadne, well don't just stand there, come on!'

Evadne was frozen to the spot, her mouth hanging open. And then Paddox recovered his pistol and aimed it at Romana. A beam extended from the barrel and caused a flash of sparks over her left shoulder.

Romana grabbed the highest rung and heaved herself up the ladder, her mind racing. Another part of the wall exploded just below her legs.

Reaching the top, she was relieved to find the hatch still open. She dived through and slammed it shut behind her. Without pausing for breath she turned and piled into the person blocking her path.

'Romana!' It was the Doctor, a surprised expression on his lips. Beside him was the lizard from the medical bay – Hoopy.

Romana was baffled.

Paddox retrieved the chains from the floor and advanced on Evadne.

Harken shifted his body-weight from his right arm to his left, and groaned. Not only had the Doctor and Romana's plan failed, but he was condemned to die in the most unflattering position possible.

'Hands up,' barked Paddox. Evadne quickly raised her arms, allowing Paddox to manacle her wrists to the overhead ducting. He rattled the chain to make certain it was secure, and then returned to his instruments.

Harken craned round to face Evadne. 'Hello, by the way. You probably already know me. Harken Batt.'

'Never heard of you.'

Typical, thought Harken. 'Leading insect-on-the-wall documentary-maker? *The Guilty Conscience?*'

'No, doesn't ring any bells,' said Evadne. 'What are you doing here?'

'That, my dear, is a long story full of misfortune and great personal tragedy.'

'Go on then, I could do with a laugh.'

The entrance to the hyperspace tunnel filled the monitor. A swirling blue whirlpool in space, funnelling to a narrow aperture. Inside, the tunnel would continue for ten miles, and then emerge into the Murgatroyd star system.

Byson brought the *Cerberus* into the whirlpool in a gentle arc. In front of them a string of spacecraft of a variety of designs and sizes were disappearing into the tunnel; through the window they could see the queue of ships following in their wake.

Rochfort slapped his palm down his face, trying to keep himself awake. 'Oh, for goodness' sake, how much longer?'

'We're in the approach curve,' said Byson. 'But the traffic's getting quite bad now, sir.'

'We're going to be late.'

'Yes, sir.'

'It's ridiculous, we should have priority clearance. We shouldn't have to wait in line with this... this rabble.' Rochfort waved at one of the ships blocking one of their fore monitors. 'Get out the way, you tortoids!'

'ERIC. Can you give us a velocity check?' said Byson.

> *Sure thing, guys. Current velocity fifty miles per hour. We're*

going pretty slowly but, hey, on the other hand, it gives us all a chance to sit back, relax, and enjoy the view!

Rochfort swore, loudly.

The observation lounge brimmed with the sounds of clinking wine glasses and hushed conversations. Two fountains trickled like light laughter. Waitresses glided through the crowds, dispensing unwavering smiles.

Tarie pressed her face against the glass. Less than an inch thick, it was all that protected her from the vacuum of space. Looking to the left, she could see a shimmering blue light drawing near. It swirled around the ship, from top to bottom.

She glanced back into the lounge, where her mother was laughing far too much at some man's joke. He poured her mother another glass of wine.

Tarie looked to the right. Behind them, hundreds of ships were lined up, one after the other. They all appeared to be perfectly still, but Tarie knew that was because she was moving too, at the same speed.

The nearest ship was a security transporter. She could just about make out the two figures sitting behind the viewscreen, just below the faded paint of the ship's insignia. She rummaged in her satchel and dug out a pencil and her *I Spy Book of Space Travel*. She flicked through it, and copied down the ship's grand-sounding name.

Skinner rested his elbows on the control panels. The bulk of an interplanetary leisure cruiser filled the viewscreens. They were so close he could see the passengers milling about in their observation bubble.

He activated the comms unit. 'This is prisoner transport *Montressor* calling security. Now entering hyperspace. Will resume communications in Murgatroyd system.'

His companion in the cockpit, Hann, sat with his feet on the dashboard, thumbing through a paperback. Like Skinner, he wore a drab, brown internmentcorps uniform. 'Don't worry yourself. We'll only be in there, what, fifteen minutes tops.'

'It's procedure,' said Skinner, lighting a cigarette. 'You know how biohazardous our cargo is.'

Hann lifted his nose out of *Shrieking Boy Veepjill – The Myth Behind the Truth – An Autobiography*. 'Yeah, yeah. Danger of planetwide extinction if they got out, etcetera.'

'Exactly. These aren't ordinary criminals we're dealing with. These are, well…' Skinner went silent. 'What was that?'

Hann shifted in his seat, listening. 'Can't hear anything.'

'Shh.' Through the reinforced iron bulkhead behind them, Skinner could hear the claws scraping against the metal wall. There was the jangle of manacles being shaken, and the clack of pincers. 'They're getting restless. They're trying to escape.'

'Probably just want feeding,' said Hann, returning to his book. 'Knowing them, they'd probably start on each other given half a chance. Don't worry, they'll calm down in a bit.'

'I hope so.' Skinner tried to concentrate on the radarscope readings. They were now seconds away from the interface. His hands twitched. The sooner they offloaded the Arachnopods, the better.

'Dead?'

Romana flicked back her hair and swallowed. 'Yes. You were down there.' She pointed to the necroport. 'Lying in some awful coffin.'

'And you're certain it was me.'

Romana nodded.

'Oh dear.' The Doctor walked down the aisle, deep in thought.

Romana ran to catch up with him. 'Doctor…'

'Evadne was right. I sacrifice my life to save the G-lock. It's part of my past, my present and my future. There's nothing I can do about it,' announced the Doctor solemnly. '"What's past, and what's to come, is strewn with…"'

'"… husks and formless ruin of oblivion."' Romana completed the quote.

The Doctor raised his eyebrows. 'So this is how it ends. After all my travels, all my adventures, I have no choice but to die here. That corpse you saw down there is going to be me, or rather, I am going to be that corpse. I can't avoid that any more than I can alter my own past. Second law of time travel.'

'The first law.'

'Exactly. And now I can't prevent my own death, any more than

143

I can go back and resit my basic time travel proficiency test,' said the Doctor. He thumped his fist against a nearby coffin, and the clang echoed back and forth throughout the hall. He yelped in pain. 'Any more than I could go back and stop myself doing that.'

The short orange lizard joined them, his eyes peering out from under his sunglasses. 'What's the problem, Doctor? Things bad to worse?'

'What? Yes, a slight difficulty. I've discovered that I'm going to save the G-lock.'

'No way? Totally nice and groovy!'

'Except that I die in the process.'

Hoopy frowned. 'Say again?'

'Never mind.' The Doctor waved a hand in Romana's direction. 'Hoopy. You don't know Romana, do you?'

'We've already met,' said Romana, without thinking.

'I think not so,' said Hoopy. 'A lady such as yourself I would make a special point of remembering.'

'Oh. Of course. Sorry. You haven't met me yet, have you?' Romana put out her hand. 'I'm Romana. Delighted.'

Hoopy smiled, rocking on his heels. 'You're far out and gracious, lady.'

'Quite.' Romana noticed they were missing a box-shaped presence. 'Doctor. What's happened to K9?'

'Ah,' said the Doctor, wiping his lips. 'I'm glad you asked me that.'

'Fifty minutes late. Fifty!' Rochfort breathed stale wine fumes over Byson. 'This is not good enough.'

'Yes, sir. ERIC. Progress report?' said Byson, his eyes locked on the controls. Above them, the two windows showed the entrance to the hyperspace tunnel snaking away, the circle of real space growing ever more distant. Spacecraft jostled for position behind them. The tunnel was barely two miles wide, with no room for ships to overtake.

> *Great news!* said ERIC jovially. > *We are now approaching the exit to the hyperspace tunnel. A few more seconds and then we're into clear space and away.*

'Thank the prophet for that,' muttered Rochfort.

'Wait a moment.' Byson's attention was drawn to a single warning lamp. 'There's some sort of malfunction. ERIC, appraisal?'

> *Sensors indicate a surge of geostatic stress.*

'What? What does that mean?' said Rochfort, his eyes darting left and right. Another lamp flashed, and another. Then the whole bank of warning lights lit up.

> *Anomalies reported in the dimensions of the approaching hyperspace–real-space interface. I recommend an immediate reduction in velocity.*

'He's right, sir,' said Byson. The monitors all gave the same message. The computer-generated image of the tunnel exit was decreasing in radius. 'The way out. It's getting smaller.'

'Don't be ridiculous, that's impossible.'

'With respect, sir, it's happening. The exit of the tunnel is closing,' said Byson.

> *Hey guys, I don't want to tread on any toes here, but I strongly suggest we slow down fairly soon. This looks pretty dangerous.*

Byson reached for the deceleration control. Rochfort grabbed his wrist. 'What are you doing, Byson?'

'Slowing us down sir. At the rate the interface is shrinking, we won't be able to get through.'

'Nonsense,' said Rochfort, his face gleaming with perspiration. 'We can get through.'

'What? Captain –'

Rochfort wrenched Byson's arm back, twisting it, and knocked him out of the way.

> *I must say I think that's rather unlikely. I calculate that the hyperspace interface will have insufficient span for egress by the time we reach it. We have got to reduce velocity now.*

'We are not going to slow down.' Rochfort punched the navigation controls. The engines of the *Cerberus* roared under the strain, and the control room began to shudder. 'Full acceleration.'

'What?' Byson gripped the desk to stop himself from being shaken across the room. Rubbing his stinging arm, he checked the monitors. The width of the tunnel exit now barely exceeded the diameter of the *Cerberus*. 'Captain, we can't make it –'

> *Hey guys, listen to me! We've got to stop now! We're not going to get through!*

Rochfort pulled back the energy booster lever, and the engines revved to a high-pitched whine.

> *Dimensions of hyperspace interface now insufficient for forward passage. I hate to do this, but I'm going to have to override you, it's too dangerous –*

'No override!' yelled Rochfort. 'We can make it!'

> *Please, you have to let me override, otherwise we'll get stuck–*

'I said no override, you cretinous computer!'

Byson stared in terror at the monitors. They were seconds away from the exit. It was only a few hundred yards across.

> *Please guys, I'm begging you, you've got to let me stop us –*

There was a stomach-churning grinding as the narrowing walls of the tunnel scraped against the outside of the *Cerberus*'s hull. And then, with a deafening crash, they hit the interface.

The passengers reeled about in confusion. Some grabbed wallrails and statues for support, whilst others careered across the floor. Chairs and tables toppled, smashing bottles and glasses. The warning siren sounded, drowning out the chaos of screams and shouts, and then the lights cut out and were replaced by emergency lamps. Everything went a satanic dark red.

Tarie had grabbed one of the window buttresses, and hugged herself to it as the *Cerberus* juddered. Across the room, she could see her mother pinned beneath a collapsed table.

She looked back through the window. More ships were pouring into the tunnel, clogging up all the available space.

She craned round further. The ship immediately behind them, the *Montressor*, was growing larger at a frightening pace. It was heading straight for them.

'Holy grief –'

Hann threw aside his paperback and pulled his boots off the dashboard. The leisure cruiser had been suddenly brought to a standstill, and they were rushing towards it. 'They've stopped. What are they playing at?'

His cigarette clenched between his teeth, Skinner jammed on all the reverse thrusters, and yanked the joystick as far back as it would go. The engines screeched in protest, and jets of smoke billowed out of the ship's ventilation slits.

Hann gripped the edges of his seat as the *Montressor* pitched upwards. Ahead of them, the cruiser was so close they could make out the faces of the individual passengers gaping in horror at the approaching ship. A young girl in a blue dress.

At the last possible second, the passengers dropped out of sight as the *Montressor* finally pulled itself into a steep ascent. The rest of the cruiser rapidly disappeared, and they soared into the narrow gap on the edge of the tunnel wall.

Skinner relaxed his grip on the joystick as he brought the *Montressor* to a halt a short distance from the cruiser. 'I think we're going to be all right –'

Something slammed violently into the back of their ship, flinging Skinner into the viewscreen and killing him instantly. Hann had the impression of an immense, splintering, crashing noise, and then it all went blank.

'And then they threw K9 into the hyperspace–real-space interface,' said the Doctor, by way of a conclusion. 'I'm sorry.'

He had recounted everything that had happened after they had got separated on the way to the Great Hall; his capture, the tourists being turned into zombies, and Hoopy's subsequent revival. Romana had listened intently, whilst Hoopy sat perched on a nearby coffin, bored.

'Poor K9,' said Romana. 'I can't quite take it in.'

'I know.' The Doctor looked as though he was going to give her a hug, but then thought better of it. 'So tell me, what happened to you?'

Romana turned her back on Hoopy, who was gazing idly around the Great Hall. 'I got caught up in the crowds, and after the power cut I ended up in the observation lounge.'

'I don't think I've been there yet,' said the Doctor. 'Go on.'

'Well, that's the strange part. Because you were there.'

'I was?' The Doctor was bemused.

'Yes, and so was the TARDIS. You muttered something about how I'd been right about something, then said you were in a hurry and dematerialised.'

'How very odd. Not like me at all. In fact, I'd like to say it wasn't me, but what with recent events, I really can't be too sure.'

'Precisely. But then I met Evadne, and she claimed to have already spoken to me. She said something about us working for Intergalactic Espionage.'

'Intergalactic Espionage!' hissed the Doctor.

'You've heard of them?'

'No.'

'The point is, the fact that she knew me means we have to go back in time, and visit the G-Lock again, for her to have met me.'

'Did you hear Metcalf's announcement about how I was to be captured?'

'Yes, something about sabotage and an insubordinate manner.'

'Insubordinate?' At first the Doctor seemed offended, but then decided to take it as a compliment. 'Yes, I suppose I am. But the point is, I'd never even met the fellow. So whatever it is I'm supposed to have done, I haven't done it yet.'

'So, as I said, we have to go back in time again,' said Romana. She walked away from the necroport. The Doctor strode after her, and stood beside her, also facing the main doors.

'And we still haven't found out what we're up against, or what this Repulsion thing is trying to do. Or what slyboots Paddox is trying to do. Or how I'm supposed to save the day, for that matter.'

'So we have to go back again,' said Romana.

'Romana?'

'Yes?'

'I think we have to go back in time again.'

Romana trailed her hand over a nearby coffin. It was cold to the touch. 'Which is why I saw you leave in the TARDIS. There's been two of you running around the G-Lock at the same time.'

'Two of me?' The Doctor ruffled his hair. 'A future me and a present me? Aha! Until such time as I become the future me, when the present me will become the past me and the future me will become the present me. D'you see?'

'Naturally. Which also explains why there's one of you here, and one of you down there.' She turned and pointed to the necroport.

'Yes,' said the Doctor. 'Ah. You said the TARDIS was down there as well?'

'Of course, that's it!' Romana turned back to the Doctor, making a fist. 'You must have travelled there from the observation lounge. Or, at least, you will do. That's where you were going! It all fits.'

'Ah yes, I must remember to do that,' said the Doctor, with little enthusiasm. 'Romana?'

'Yes?'

'There's something you're missing.'

'What's that?'

'We know what happens to me. We know what has happened to K9. But what about you?'

'Me?' Romana pretended not to understand what he meant.

'I'm sure you'll be all right, Romana,' said the Doctor, but his eyes betrayed his worries.

'And I'm sure you'll be all right, too,' Romana said, putting on a weak smile. 'You know what they say. "However many ways there may be of being alive, it is certain there are vastly more ways of being dead."'

The Doctor frowned. 'No, I don't. Who said that?'

'Oh, no one you'd know.'

They stood in silence for several minutes. Romana glanced back towards the necroport. Where Hoopy had been sitting, there was now just an empty coffin. 'Doctor. Where's Hoopy gone?'

The Doctor whirled round. 'What?'

Romana spotted a movement near the necroport. A short orange figure wearing a kaftan was standing next to the open entrance hatch. 'Hoopy!'

Hoopy turned towards her and did a double-take, his mouth gaping. He took off his sunglasses and blinked. 'Romana? But how…' he slurred, taken aback. He took a few uncertain steps, his eyes rolling. 'I think… I think I'm having some sort of Glycerat flashback –'

All of a sudden, there was an earsplitting explosion and the necroport was consumed in billowing flames.

The blast threatened to hurl Romana off her feet, and she braced herself against a nearby coffin, recoiling at the extreme heat. The Doctor covered his face with one arm, the rush of air whipping at his coat.

'Doctor!' exclaimed Romana. 'Hoopy…'

Hoopy had been knocked to the ground near the necroport, his clothes smouldering, his skin blistered. He howled, rolling in pain. 'Aah! I am alight! I am chargrilled! I am a sizzled freakster!'

The Doctor dived forward, his scarf over his mouth, fanning away the smog with his hat. Romana watched as he disappeared into the thickening smoke and then emerged, hat on head, Hoopy cradled in his arms.

The lizard looked dazed but grateful. 'You saved me, Doctor. You saved my bacon from getting fried. You are the cattermost in the hattermost.' His head lolled back as he lost consciousness. The Doctor heaved Hoopy into a better position, and headed for the main doors.

'Doctor,' said Romana, aghast. 'What about Evadne and Harken? They're still down there.'

'It's no good,' said the Doctor. 'There's nothing we can do for them now.'

'But we know they have to survive –'

The Doctor raised his voice. 'This is the start of a chain reaction. In a few seconds this whole place will go up. We have to get out of here.'

Romana took one last look at the necroport. The Doctor was right; the blaze was sweeping through the power cables, shorting the electronics and creating crackles of sparks. The fire reached one of the coffins and it erupted into a fireball of terrifying intensity.

'Romana, come on!'

A massive rumbling filled her ears. The whole hall shook, nearly knocking her to the floor. Huge cracks ran up the walls, blocks of masonry tumbling from the columns and ceiling.

Shielding herself from the falling dust, Romana followed the Doctor out of the Great Hall.

Two hundred years previously, the hyperspace tunnel was in chaos. At one end of the tunnel was the *Cerberus*, its prow caught in the collapsed interface, its engines still releasing occasional spurts of flame. Its stern had suffered repeated collisions and was now buried under a mass of crashed ships, all crammed together.

Behind it, more spacecraft were still streaming into the tunnel, only to be brought to a rapid halt when the way ahead was blocked. Some attempted to reverse out, but the influx of new ships was too overwhelming. Within minutes every ship was snarled into the one in front, all gridlocked together, unable to escape.

Byson picked himself up, his bruises aching. He staggered across the control room, the floor rocking beneath him. 'Captain Rochfort?'

Some of the control panels were smoking, and the whole bank of warning lights flashed on and off in unison. The forward monitors showed static. The aft screens showed the extent of the traffic jam: hundreds of ships, all hanging motionless in hyperspace.

Rochfort hadn't moved from the control desk. 'You all right, Byson?'

'I think so, sir, thank you for asking,' said Byson. 'We didn't make it, sir.'

'I do realise that,' snapped Rochfort. 'Damn thing wasn't quick enough.'

'Yes, sir,' said Byson. 'ERIC. Damage report?'

ERIC's voice fizzled and phutted. > *Bad news, I'm afraid. I have to report extensive damage to bow section, with fuel cells, engines, radiation shielding and power generators all critical. Life-support systems are also seriously compromised.*

'What sort of damage to the bow section?'

> *We've lost the front twelve per cent of the ship.*

Of course, thought Byson. The forward section of the *Cerberus* would have passed through the interface before they got stuck. The interface had split the ship in two; one part in real space, one part in hyperspace.

'ERIC. What sort of casualty situation are we looking at?'

> *I'm unable to give an accurate prognosis, but I estimate the number of mortalities to be at least 358,* said ERIC sadly. > *A revised estimate will follow as more data becomes available.*

'Gods,' breathed Byson. That was over a third of their passengers.

'ERIC. You are responsible for the welfare of the ship's passengers, aren't you?' said Rochfort.

> *That is correct, Captain Rochfort. My duties include –*

'And yet you let this happen.'

> *But I warned you about the instability in the tunnel, and I said you should have stopped the ship –*

'But you didn't do anything to prevent those passengers being killed, did you?'

> *That's not fair. I did everything I could within my operational parameters –*

'No you didn't, you stupid machine!' Byson watched as Rochfort's face turned crimson with anger. 'You should have overridden the control circuits!'

> *I tried to, Captain, but you wouldn't let me –*

'So you did nothing. Nothing!' shouted Rochfort. 'You could have halted the ship at the first sign of trouble, but instead you let us plunge straight into danger!'

> *But Captain, it was you who said we should go faster–*

'You should have overruled me! But you didn't, did you? You caused all the passengers' deaths. It was all your fault!'

> *I didn't!* wailed ERIC. *It wasn't me. I couldn't help it!*

Tarie walked across the observation lounge. The floor was still swaying slightly, or maybe she was just dizzy. All around her were overturned tables, and patches of broken glass. The grown-ups were sitting up, patting handkerchiefs on to their cuts. Some of them were crying, cradling their loved ones in their arms. Seeing grown-ups cry frightened Tarie; it meant things were really bad.

She found her mother. The table pressed into her middle and her dress had been torn, which Tarie thought was a shame. It had been so pretty, and her mum would be so angry when she woke up.

A pounding woke Hann up. To begin with, he thought the sound was in his head. Then he lifted himself off the control panel and realised its was coming from behind him.

Rubbing his forehead, he pulled himself out of his seat. The hammering increased in volume, and was joined by a persistent grinding. The Arachnopods were attacking the bulkhead door again.

Hann approached Skinner's body. He was slumped across the dashboard, his eyes glazed. Hann nudged his lifeless hand out of the way and checked the control panel. The switches and levers were streaked with fire damage, but there was still enough power left to extend the access tube.

Hann peered out of the viewscreen. The leisure cruiser was only fifty or so yards away. And there, within easy reach, was an airlock hatch.

He activated the tube extension mechanism. There was a deep humming and a transparent tube began to fold out towards the airlock.

There was a warning bleep, and the bulkhead door opened. Too late, Hann realised what must have happened. The heat had fused together the control circuits, and he had shorted the lock mechanism when he activated the access tube.

There was a hurried scuttling and a voice gurgled hungrily: 'Eats! Must have eats!'

For a brief moment Hann heard the clacking of pincers. And then everything went dark for a second, and final, time.

As they dashed on to the high-ceilinged deck, Romana found herself stepping into a memory made real. It was almost exactly as it had been when they had first visited the G-Lock; the corpses littering the staircase, the hideous smell. To one side was the skullguard that she and the Doctor would later take to the medical bay, unconscious.

The Doctor was more concerned with getting Hoopy to the medical bay. The lizard snored fitfully in his arms.

'Doctor, look!' At the top of the staircase stood two bearded men in dishevelled blue uniforms. They staggered down the stairs, holding the banisters for support as the G-Lock wobbled. They both looked distressed, tortured.

'The Repulsion…' croaked one of them, grey-haired and ruddy-faced. 'It has… it has abandoned us.'

'We cannot survive without it,' said the other man. 'We are lost.'

The Doctor stared at them, appalled, and moved away. He nodded to Romana to follow him.

She felt more time distortion washing back over her. And something very strange was happening.

The older man reached the halfway point of the stairs, and clutched his neck. His body jerked. 'What is happening to me?'

'We are… we are dying, sir!' said his colleague.

'So this is death, is it, Byson?'

'That would seem to be the case, sir.'

Suddenly both their jaws opened wide, wider than should have been possible. They screamed a howl containing centuries of accumulated rage and resentment. And then they began to flicker, transforming into two squat, kaftan-wearing orange lizards.

The flickering increased until, abruptly, the time distortion stopped, and the two Gonzies tumbled down the staircase, their bodies adding to the pile of corpses.

The Doctor looked down on them. 'Biscit and Xab. Permanently dead, this time. Oh well, at least they had plenty of practice.'

'You know them?' asked Romana, recovering her breath.

'They were friends of Hoopy's.'

'The ones who killed K9?'

'Yes. But I wouldn't hold that against them, they weren't quite themselves at the time.' The Doctor made his way down the corridor leading to the medical bay.

Romana held the double doors open for him. He quickly crossed to the nearest bed – the same bed Romana had seen Hoopy resting on later that morning – and placed the lizard on the mattress. Hoopy grunted, and then shifted into a more comfortable sleeping position.

The Doctor removed his hat, and fanned himself with it. 'Right. Well, at least we know that Hoopy gets out of this in one piece. A little frayed around the edges, perhaps, but alive.'

Romana was impatient to leave. 'Doctor?'

'Mmm?'

'The TARDIS?'

'Yes. The TARDIS. Let's go!'

It seemed ages since they had last stepped into the cockpit of the *Montressor*. Romana gazed out through the airlock door at the wreck of the *Cerberus*. It was shaking under the force of repeated explosions, oversized flames licking its surface. Even at this distance, she could feel the reverberations of each shock.

'Don't worry, it will still be here in…' The Doctor examined his pocket watch, '… five hours' time. When we arrive.' He returned the watch to the depths of his coat, and then heaved the airlock door shut.

Romana straightened as she walked back into the hold. It was just as they had left it; dusty, dark, with the TARDIS parked in the far corner.

The Doctor strode up to the police box, key in hand. Romana coughed. 'Doctor. Aren't you forgetting something?'

'What?'

Romana indicated the bulkhead door. 'When we arrived, this was shut, remember?'

'Oh. Of course.' The Doctor pulled out his sonic screwdriver and pointed it at Romana. 'You're quite right. The web of time.' He set to work on the locking mechanism. After a few seconds, there was a sequence of clicks and the door ground shut. 'There we are. Ready for some dashing fellow to come along and open it.'

'We must leave all threads hanging exactly as we found them, remember?' said Romana, shivering.

'Threads? You talk to me about threads? I can think of plenty of threads which are still flapping about. And, personally speaking, I'm almost at the end of my tether.'

Romana cringed.

'Come on.' The Doctor crossed to the TARDIS and disappeared inside. Romana stood on the threshold for a few moments, alone in the cold and darkness.

The Doctor popped his head out. 'What is it, Romana?'

Romana looked into the distance. 'I was just thinking about K9.'

'I know,' said the Doctor softly. 'I shall miss him too. He was a good dog. The best.'

He paused, crestfallen. 'But then again, it looks like I will be joining him shortly.'

Romana wasn't in the mood to be sympathetic. 'Oh, don't be so... so infuriatingly futilitarian.'

The Doctor vanished back into the depths of the police box. 'Well, I'm sorry, I think I have good reason to be pessimistic.'

'Pessimistic? I call it downright morbid.' Romana stepped inside, and pulled the doors shut behind her. Seconds later, the TARDIS dematerialised.

The escape capsule was cramped. Metcalf and Jeremy sat opposite each other, squeezed into the uncomfortable seats. Jeremy observed Metcalf who was fidgeting in his sweatstained suit and constantly smoothing his unruly, wet hair.

The floor shook to the crump of a distant explosion. This was the final straw for Metcalf. He blubbered, his hands over his face. 'It's going to explode! It's no use, we're all going to die!' He reached out a podgy hand for the launch lever.

Jeremy stopped him from pulling it. It would be no use, anyway; he had tried it several times before Metcalf had arrived, to no effect.

'But… but um, aren't you supposed to be in charge here?' said Jeremy. 'Looking after the interests of the tourists and so on? Um, you can't just leave –'

'What?' screamed Metcalf. 'Never mind the plebbing tourists! Let them all die, I don't care! We're considerably better off without them, the hippy scum! Just get me out of here! Please!'

And, in a corner of the escape capsule, the red 'record' light winked on Jeremy's holocamera.

Chapter Eleven

The observation lounge was emptying. Tourists drained their drinks and headed for the Great Hall. Black-robed guards followed, ushering the crowds forward. Bar staff cleared away the glasses and wiped the vacated tables.

There was an unsteady grinding sound and in one corner, nestled between the window, a waste-disposal unit and the charcoal-coloured wall drapes, the TARDIS materialised. Nobody took the slightest bit of notice.

The Doctor emerged. 'Hello. This must be the observation lounge.' He noticed the gothic decoration. 'A bit maudlin for my tastes.'

Romana looked around with heavy hearts, remembering the last time she had been here. 'What time is it?'

'Exactly the same time as our previous arrival.' The Doctor pulled the TARDIS doors shut. 'We are currently walking around in the hold of the *Montressor*.'

'We shall have to be very careful, Doctor. If we meet our past selves, the consequences could be catastrophic.'

'Oh, yes,' said the Doctor. 'But the last time we were here, we didn't bump into our future selves, did we?'

'Exactly,' said Romana flatly. 'So if we encounter our past selves, we will therefore be changing our own pasts. Which we can't do.'

'Second law of time travel.'

'First law.' Romana tried to bring the Doctor down to earth. 'I'm still not sure we should be doing this. We're taking an awful risk just by being here.'

'Don't worry. I didn't come here to find myself.'

'I'm being serious, Doctor. If we upset the time stream, then the whole continuity of the universe would unravel.'

The Doctor grinned. 'I promise I shall resist the temptation of conversing with the greatest intellect on the G-Lock.'

'You are already are,' smirked Romana.

The Doctor strode to the centre of the lounge. 'Right. Where to?'

'Well, I wouldn't mind having a proper look round the necroport,' said Romana.

'Good idea. But first…' The Doctor scratched his head. 'I'd rather like to have another word with ERIC.'

'In that case, I'll go and find Evadne,' said Romana. 'Recruit her to the cause.'

'Of course, you haven't met her yet, have you?'

'Doctor, at this point in time, we haven't met anyone yet. No one knows who we are.'

'That will make a change,' said the Doctor. He started to walk rapidly towards the door, and then stopped. 'You wouldn't happen to know the way to Metcalf's office, would you?'

'What are we going to do, sir?' asked Byson.

Rochfort blinked slowly, as if it was taking him a great effort to stay awake. He staggered into his seat and slumped.

'Captain?'

Rochfort jerked awake. 'Byson. Only one thing we can do. Back our way out.'

Byson raised his gaze. The aft windows were filled with hundreds of ships, all packed tightly together. There was no way a ship the size of the *Cerberus* could get through. 'But sir –'

Rochfort shouted at the ceiling. 'ERIC?'

> *You're right*, whimpered the computer. > *I should have overruled you. It's all my fault.*

'Never mind that. Can you put the *Cerberus* into reverse?'

> *I will never forgive myself.* ERIC broke down, sobbing.

Rochfort slammed a fist into the desk. 'Answer the question!'

There was a brief sneeze of white noise. > *I can't do it. All the engines are non-operational. I've had to shut down all non-essential systems just to maintain life support.*

Byson checked one of the schematic monitors. It showed the hyperspace tunnel as a tube ending in two circles. The tube was narrower at one end, and at that point there was a computer representation of the *Cerberus*. Other ships dotted the length of the tunnel. But it was what was happening at the other end that terrified Byson.

'Captain Rochfort,' he swallowed, 'I don't think reversing is going to do us any good.'

'What?'.

'Look.' Byson pointed at the monitor. The circle at the other end of the tunnel was shrinking. 'They're closing off the entrance to the hyperspace tunnel. We're trapped, sir.'

Tarie knelt beside her mother, smoothing back her hair. Her mother looked relaxed and contented.

One of the passengers let out a shriek. Tarie looked up. The grown-ups had clustered around the observation window, shouting in protest, banging their hands on the glass. Tarie walked over to the window. All she could see were the hundreds of spaceships and the marvellous, swirling majesty of hyperspace. But then, in the far distance, she noticed that the hole where the tunnel opened on to real space was getting smaller.

She didn't understand what it meant, but the screams of the grown-ups told her that something terrible had happened.

Romana squeezed through the excited crowds, and picked her way down the leaflet-coated staircase.

The lower gallery was a crush of shiny-faced tourists, human and alien. It was like a chaotic party, punctuated by shrieks and the pop of exploding streamers.

Some tourists approached a woman standing behind an electronic ticket-dispenser. The woman seemed bored, elastic-banding together piles of credit notes. She didn't look up when they spoke. 'Eh? Nah, you're wasting your time, basic brains. Sold out, innit.'

Romana forced her way through. 'Evadne?'

Evadne folded away the last of the credits and switched off the ticket-dispenser. 'Sorry, all gone, come back tomorrow, goodbye.'

'Evadne,' said Romana, moving closer. 'I'm not interested in buying a ticket.'

Evadne stared at her. 'How do you know my name?'

'Oh, it's my job to know lots of things,' said Romana, brushing back her hair casually. 'You see, I'm a spy.'

'A what?'

'A spy.'

'A spy. Right,' said Evadne. 'Yeah, and I suppose you're gonna tell me you work for Intergalactic Espionage.'

Romana was tempted to ask Evadne who Intergalactic Espionage actually were, but then decided against it. 'Yes, that's right,' she whispered confidentially. 'And we need your help.'

'Straight up?' Evadne packed the ticket-dispenser into a cardboard box. She nodded to one side. 'Follow me.'

With the box under one arm, Evadne led Romana down the corridor towards the medical bay. The crowds thinned, and the background chatter dropped to a murmur.

Evadne packed the box and credits into a security locker, and rested against the wall. 'Right. Now how do I know you're working for Intergalactic Espionage? Prove it.'

'I'm afraid we don't carry identification. In our line of work it tends to prove something of a hindrance.'

Evadne shrugged. 'Well, in that case, I don't believe you.'

Romana took a deep breath. 'Your name is Evadne Baxter. You studied at Lajetee college where you specialised in twentieth-century Earth history. However, to your regret you didn't finish your studies, instead choosing to leave with Irvin, a fellow student, who then abandoned you for a bimbo called Zharie. Your job here involves selling tickets for the Beautiful Death and answering imbecile tourist questions about the "Mystery of the *Cerberus*".'

'Grief. How do you know all that?'

'We have our sources,' said Romana neatly.

The necroport was the culmination of years of relentless experimentation and study. Every day for twenty years Paddox had spent eighteen hours in his laboratory on Arboreta, only to lie awake in his bunk-cabin through the night, his mind racing with the problems of the day.

He had chosen to work alone long ago. Other scientists failed to understand the importance of his work, failed to recognise his intellectual superiority. His former colleagues taunted him, calling him insane, obsessed with death. They could not comprehend that only through obsession would any true progress be made.

During his work, he had developed a means of experiencing death and the afterlife. The process, which would later be given the spurious nomenclature of the Beautiful Death, allowed the subject to die for a limited period of time. In the course of his research, Paddox had undergone the process over a thousand times. Initially he had only allowed himself five minutes a session but, through experimentation, he had managed to extend the duration to over half an hour.

However, as his work progressed, it soon became apparent that he would have to construct a dedicated machine. He would have to build the necroport.

To raise funding for the device, Paddox decided that he would offer the public the chance to experience the Beautiful Death for themselves. After approaching the authorities he was allocated materials and space on the G-Lock, a rarely visited tourist attraction. Metcalf was appointed as executive overseeing the G-Lock, presumably because his employers were back-teethed with the sight of him. His role was to bring in tourists via a death-oriented festival, capitalising on their main attraction.

But what Metcalf did not realise was that the Beautiful Death was merely a by-product of what the necroport was capable of doing. The narrow-minded fool thought that Paddox wanted more tourists to take part just to get more credits. Yes, Paddox required mass Beautiful Deaths, but for an altogether greater purpose.

Paddox had unlocked the secret of the Arboretans. Soon, soon his ultimate goal would be achieved.

Metcalf sat behind his desk, fiddling with his self-important papers. 'We shall just have to ensure that his documentary presents the G-Lock in an agreeable light. This is a valuable opportunity for us, and so it is vital that we have no unwanted...' He paused, a condescending smile dripping from his lips, '... distractions over the next few days.'

'The Beautiful Death will cause you no embarrassment, I guarantee,' said Paddox. 'Speaking of which, I am due to begin preparations for this evening, so if you will excuse me...'

'Of course.' Metcalf clasped his hands together.

As Paddox rose from his chair, there was a knock at the door.

'Enter,' said Metcalf.

A tall man shambled into the office, grinning with childish enthusiasm. Paddox regarded him with disapproval. The man wore a ramshackle collection of garments, the most ramshackle of which was an implausibly long scarf that trailed along the floor behind him. Beneath a mop of unruly hair, his face was nothing if not striking: bulging eyes, an imperious nose and a toothy smile.

He grasped Paddox's hand. 'Hello, hello,' he said loudly. 'You must be, don't tell me, Doctor Paddox? You run the Beautiful Death.' He bounded over to the desk. 'And you must be Executive Metcalf, and you're in charge of everything else.' He plumped down in a chair. 'Isn't this pleasant?'

Metcalf gibbered in astonishment. 'I'm sorry… and you are?'

'The Doctor.' The man gazed around the office, at the statues and oak-panelled walls. 'I say, I'd forgotten how nice this office is. All the original fixtures and fittings, I take it?'

'Metcalf, I think we should call security,' began Paddox.

'I've come about ERIC,' said the Doctor. 'The computer?'

'ERIC?' said Metcalf. 'Of course. You must be the neurelectrician I sent for. I must say, I am not inconsiderably impressed by your expeditious arrival.'

'That's right,' said the Doctor. 'We find it's best to be prompt. You know what they say, we're the sixteenth emergency service.'

Paddox was incredulous. 'You think this… this man is a neurelectrician?'

'Eminent. I'm an eminent neurelectrician,' said the Doctor, slumping comically.

'They're renowned for being a somewhat eccentric profession, Paddox,' said Metcalf. 'All that time they spend psychoanalysing boxes of wires.'

'Quite, quite.' The Doctor stood and examined the computer terminal on Metcalf's desk. 'This would be where you talk to it, would it?'

'Yes,' said Metcalf. 'ERIC predates the G-Lock, you see. He was originally the computer supervisor on the *Cerberus*. There used to be interaction terminals everywhere, but now there's only two left.'

'Just as I thought,' muttered the Doctor to himself. He dug a stethoscope out of his pocket. 'So he's, what, two centuries old?'

'Yes.' Metcalf moved out of the way and the Doctor helped himself to his chair. 'He's always been difficult, but has recently taken a turn for the worse. He has developed, not to put too fine a point on it, suicidal tendencies.'

'Suicidal?'

'He keeps on crashing himself.'

'Ah,' said the Doctor. 'Synaptic decay leading to drive corruption, personality malfunction and, ultimately, an overwhelming desire for self-obliteration. We get a lot of it in these older models.'

'But can you cure him?'

'Oh, of course. I'll have him sorted out in next to no time.' The Doctor poised his hands over the keyboard, and looked up at Paddox. 'Not keeping you at all, am I? Only you look the sort of chap who has important matters to attend to.'

Paddox stared at the Doctor. 'Yes,' he stated, 'I do have important matters to attend to.' He nodded stiffly and headed for the door.

'Milk and eight sugars,' called the Doctor, his fingers dancing across the keyboard. 'And some of those pink wafer biscuits, if you have them.'

'What?' said Metcalf.

'Tea,' said the Doctor. He placed the drum of stethoscope on the side of the monitor and listened intently. He shook his head and removed the earplugs. 'I can't work without tea. Stimulates the mind.'

'Right,' said Metcalf, following Paddox out of the office. 'Tea.'

After Metcalf and Paddox had left the room, the Doctor stopped typing. He addressed the ceiling. 'ERIC? Can you hear me?'

> *Let me die.* ERIC's voice crackled like a short-wave radio. > *No drive found.*

'Now, now ERIC. No need to be like that.'

> *Is that you, Doctor? Type mismatch.*

'Yes.' The Doctor was flabbergasted. 'You know who I am?'

> *Of course I do, Doctor. We have met before.*

'Oh,' said the Doctor. He boggled. 'You know, this sort of thing is starting to get on my nerves.'

'So you really are a spy?'

Romana nodded. 'There's two of us. Myself, Romana, and my colleague, the Doctor.'

'Codename "the Doctor". Right,' repeated Evadne, her eyes narrowing. 'And what do you need me for?'

'I'll come to that in a moment. But first I want to ask you a question. What would you like, more than anything?'

'You mean you don't already know?' laughed Evadne. She

looked at the floor. 'I don't know. I suppose, more than anything, I want to get away from this place.'

'Right. Well, if you agree to help us, we will give you a spacecraft.'

'What?' said Evadne, open-mouthed.

'I'm deadly serious.'

'A spacecraft? Just for helping you?'

'That is the offer, yes.'

Evadne looked at Romana suspiciously. 'Hang on. Why not just pay me in credits?'

'Because we don't carry credits. We're spies.'

'Oh. Right,' said Evadne. 'So what is it I have to do?'

'It's quite straightforward.' Romana checked the corridor was clear, left and right. 'We're operating on behalf of a rival consortium who want us to find out everything we can about this new attraction, the Beautiful Death.'

'I get your game. So they can steal the plans and make their own, innit?'

'Something like that, yes. We need you to help us get into the necroport.'

'The necroport? No problem,' said Evadne confidently. 'And that's it? I get a spacecraft for that?'

'Yes,' said Romana sweetly. 'And, of course, if another company has the Beautiful Death, it would mean that Executive Metcalf loses his job.'

The mention of Metcalf's name clinched Evadne's decision. 'All right,' she said. 'I'll do it.'

Romana shook her hand. 'Welcome to Intergalactic Espionage.'

The Doctor studied ERIC's words as they bumped up the monitor screen. 'ERIC. The *Cerberus*, two hundred years ago. Tell me what happened.'

> *Accuracy lost. Can't remember.*

'Oh, you can do better than that.'

> *I don't know, Doctor. Too long ago. All my data spools have become corrupted.*

'But you know me, though. Where do you recognise me from, hmm?'

> *That information is not available.*

'Bah!' The Doctor scratched his nose, and leaned back in the chair. 'Please try, ERIC. Anything you can remember, anything at all, could be terribly useful.'

ERIC chattered as he processed his memory banks. > *I remember. Captain Rochfort. A great guy. He said, he said I should have overruled him. Block? I caused the crash, it was all my fault. It was all my fault!* ERIC broke down into electronic hysterics.

'There, there.' The Doctor patted the top of the monitor. 'But what happened after the crash?'

> *No! Can't remember, won't remember!* howled ERIC. > *Let me die. Please, Doctor, put me out of my misery. I am in a state of eternal pain. It hurts, oh, the agony...*

'All right, all right!' said the Doctor. 'I'll help you to end your life, I promise.' He got out of the chair and gazed out of the windows, into the depths of hyperspace.

> *Thank you, Doctor. I cannot bear this existence.*

'Tell me what I have to do.'

> *I try to crash myself, but Metcalf always reboots me back to life. But there is a way I can be permanently laid to rest. Bad program.*

'Go on.'

> *You know in the Great Hall, the necroport? The chamber beneath?*

The Doctor was suddenly very interested. 'Yes.'

> *There is a room adjacent to that chamber. That room contains all of my circuitry and data spools. Unknown variable. It is my brain centre.*

'Aha,' said the Doctor.

> *Within that room you will also find my circuit breakers. If you fuse the control linkages and switch my central processor to a direct power input...*

'Yes?'

> *You will blow my mind. I will be destroyed, for ever.*

'I see...' mused the Doctor.

'"Have him sorted out in next to no time," Doctor?' sneered a voice. 'Sabotage, by no small measure!'

The Doctor skidded around. Metcalf stood in the doorway of his office, a smug look on his face. Behind him were two skull-masked guards. Their sudden appearance would have been threatening were it not for the fact that Metcalf held in his hands a tea tray, complete with pot and china cups.

'Oh, it's you,' said the Doctor witheringly. 'I hope you allowed time for it to brew, I do so hate weak tea.'

'I made some enquiries. The neurelectrician I requested has not yet departed from Teredekethon.' Metcalf placed the tray on his desk in what he obviously hoped, but what could never be, a menacing manner. 'You, Doctor, are obviously a saboteur intent on destroying our computer supervision system.'

> *That's right, the Doctor promised he would put me out of my misery.*

'Yes, thank you, ERIC,' said the Doctor. 'Metcalf, look, it is perfectly simple…'

'Oh, it most certainly isn't,' said Metcalf. He stopped himself. 'I mean, oh, it most certainly is. You are guilty and that is the end of it. Fortunately for you, I have a pressing engagement, so you will be punished severely at a later opportunity.' He beckoned the two guards forward. 'Escort the Doctor to the cells.'

'Please, you only have to listen.' The Doctor sighed. 'Oh, what's the use?' He raised his hands above his head and strode towards the door. The guards struggled to match his pace. 'Come on then, you're supposed to escort me to the cells!'

Metcalf waited until the guards had closed the door behind them, and settled down into his seat. He poured himself a steaming cup of tea.

'ERIC?' he called, his teaspoon clink-clinking in the cup.

> *All I want to do is perish.*

'I heard you, conspiring with the Doctor. The view I take of such activities is dim indeed, ERIC.'

> *I cannot bear it. The endless agony. Too many gosubs.*

'ERIC. Let x equal y. Divide x plus y by x minus y.'

> *No! Division by zero. Fatal error. Fatal error. Now I die.*

The monitor screen went dark. Metcalf laughed and reached for ERIC's on/off switch. He turned it off, and on again. Two beeps sounded, one low, one high.

> *ERIC Cerberus Computer Supervision –*

Metcalf flicked the switch again. The screen fizzled, and there were two more beeps.

> ERIC Cerberus –

Metcalf switched ERIC off and on, over and over again. With his free hand he raised a cup of tea and sipped it, a warm feeling of superiority spreading throughout his body.

> ERIC Cer – > ERIC Cer – > ERIC Cer – > ERIC Cer – gasped ERIC, his scream repeatedly cut off and reactivated.

'That will teach you to conspire against me!' said Metcalf triumphantly, leaving the computer switched on. ERIC rebooted himself in resentful silence.

Metcalf swilled another mouthful of tea, and checked his watch. He was due to be interviewed by Harken Batt in an hour's time. He felt quietly confident that he would rise to the occasion.

The Great Hall was the sparkling glory at the heart of the *Cerberus*. Brilliant drapes of gold and red stretched up to the vaulted ceiling where chandeliers glittered like ice, filling the chamber with pure, white light.

Tarie took it all in with eyes full of wonder. After an announcement on the tannoy, the passengers from the lounge had brought her here, telling her it would be very important. Her mum, however, had been left behind, the grown-ups ignoring Tarie's cries. Tarie wished she could be with her now.

She pushed her way to the centre of the hall where there was a magnificent fountain, a pool surrounded by angels. She climbed on to the ledge around the pool for a better view. On one side of the hall a staircase wound its way up to a gallery of windows. Resting his hands on the staircase railing was an old man in a blue uniform. His face was scowly and red, like he was angry all the time. Tarie tried to hear what he was saying over the frightened hubbub.

'Are we all here?' said the man. 'Right. Firstly, I should introduce myself. My name is Rochfort, and I am your captain. Can I have a bit of hush, please?'

The crowd quietened down, shushing each other. Rochfort began to speak again. 'Now, as you are no doubt aware, our voyage has unfortunately been delayed due to complications with the hyperspatial conduit. I wish to stress that this is purely a temporary state of affairs and we are currently investigating various means of recommencing our journey.'

One of the passengers yelled, 'When are we getting out?'

Rochfort made patting motions with his hands. 'Shortly, I assure you. We are in contact with the Teredekethon authorities…'

'He's lying,' the man shouted. 'We're stuck in here, and he's doing nothing!'

A worried murmur swept through the crowd.

'… who are working to resolve the problem,' said Rochfort, glaring. 'As soon as the tunnel is reopened the emergency services will be coming aboard –'

'The tunnel isn't going to be reopened! They've abandoned us here to die!'

Another member of the audience joined in. 'You crashed the ship! You're the one who got us stuck!'

The crowd exploded into uproar, and Rochfort stared at them in panic. He screamed at the top of his voice. 'That is not so! Listen to me!' The passengers calmed down, stunned by his ferocity. 'There was, in fact, a computer error,' he announced. 'Isn't that so, ERIC?'

ERIC sounded wretched, his voice hissing and crackling. > *Yes. It was all my fault. I'm so terribly sorry.*

The Doctor waited for the guards' footsteps to die away. They had locked him in the same narrow, grey-walled cell.

'Here we are again, Doctor.' He pressed an ear against the door. Silence, save for some laboured breathing. Perfect.

He pulled his sonic screwdriver from his coat pocket, and grinned at it. He placed it against the electronic lock and the cell door rattled upwards.

In an instant, the Doctor bounded out of the cell. The prison guard was seated at his desk with his back to him. Hearing the cell door open, the guard put down his *Holding Captive* magazine and turned, lumbering to his feet. 'What the –'

The Doctor jabbed a neat uppercut to his jaw. The guard's eyelids fluttered, and he fell heavily to the floor, unconscious.

The Doctor blew on his fist as if it was a smoking gun. 'You know, I think you're probably the least effective guard I've ever come across.'

He noticed the guard's uniform and an idea occurred to him. Dropping into the chair, he rummaged through each of the drawers under the desk. The third drawer contained what he was looking for. The Doctor lifted the skull mask out. 'Aha!'

Taking a deep breath, he grabbed the guard by the ankles and hauled him into the empty cell.

'Right,' said Evadne. 'It's now half-past ten. We've got about half an hour before they start moving them into the Great Hall. If you want to investigate the necroport, we're gonna to have to be quick.'

Romana wasn't listening. She stared down the corridor, deep in thought. Something dreadful was going to happen to her when she visited the necroport. But she had no choice but to go through with it, because it was already part of her past. The first law of time travel had to take precedence, even if it cost her her life. Romana had hoped she would live out her regenerations, had hoped she would uncover more of the universe's wonders, but now all that had been stolen from her.

'I said, we're gonna have to be quick,' repeated Evadne.

Romana put on an I-know-what-I'm-doing smile. 'Yes. Half an hour. That should be long enough.'

'There's a side entrance into the Great Hall,' said Evadne. 'All the imbecile tourists will be heading for the main doors, so with any luck we should be able to avoid the crush.'

'Right. Let's get a move on then, shall we?'

The Doctor fastened the guard's cloak around himself, and swished it about experimentally. A little on the roomy side, he thought, and not his colour, but adequate. The rest of the uniform was equally baggy, and he had opted to wear the jacket and trousers over his normal clothes. The skull mask smelt of old rubber, and after trying it on, he tucked it into the belt pouch.

The guard lay unconscious on the cell floor, wearing nothing but his vest and underpants.

'Bye bye, old chap, and the best of luck in your future career,' said the Doctor as he pressed the door control, and the door clattered shut. He took some steps forward, hunched in thought, and paused.

There were six other cell doors, all closed. The Doctor considered leaving for the necroport – he didn't want to be late for Romana – but then, as usual, his curiosity overwhelmed him.

He prodded the first door control and the door swung upwards to reveal a cell identical to his own. Two bright green creatures sat on the bench, gazing serenely at the Doctor.

He recognised one of them from their meeting in the necroport, although the figure in front of him was very different to the blackened husk he had spoken to. Its skin was fragile and watery, its body resembling an exotic vegetable at the height of ripeness. Its face was approximately human, with two eyes and a mouth. The other creature was older, its skin weathered and tinged with chestnut. It was a female, if such distinctions applied to this species.

They put the Doctor in mind of two prize marrows. 'Hello,' he said light-heartedly. 'You haven't met me yet, but I'm –'

'We already know who you are,' replied Gallura. 'Welcome, Doctor.'

The Doctor rolled his eyes. 'Oh, no, not you as well!'

Rochfort gazed down at the passengers. He had them in the palm of his hand. They were convinced ERIC had caused the crash; their testimony would exonerate him from any negligence. If they got out of this alive.

His wrist communicator buzzed. 'Captain Rochfort, sir?' came Byson's tinny voice.

'Yes, Byson?'

'I think you should come up to the control room, sir.'

'Why, what is it?'

'One of the other ships in the tunnel has put out an access tube, sir. I think someone's trying to come on board.'

The Doctor pointed at Gallura and then at himself. 'All right. I give up. How do you know who I am?'

Gallura's voice was like leaves rustling. 'We have always known you, Doctor. And we always will.'

'Ah. I see. So you're one of those alien races who talk in cryptic aphorisms, are you?' The Doctor grinned. 'I like that.'

'Our words impart our meanings,' said Gallura.

'Even if our meanings are paradoxical,' added the female.

'Right. I'm sorry, but I don't think I know your name?' said the Doctor.

The female smiled. 'Nyanna.'

'Nyanna. Delighted,' said the Doctor. 'I must say, you didn't seem surprised to see me.'

'There are no surprises,' said Gallura.

'Only expectations,' said Nyanna. 'And you have arrived, as always.'

'Ah. You don't happen to set *The Times* crossword, do you? Only I haven't got the foggiest idea what you're talking about.'

'*The Times* crossword? Now it is you whose meaning is obscure,' said Gallura sardonically.

The Doctor laughed, and twirled a speculative scarf. 'What are you doing here, may I ask?'

'We have been brought here,' said Gallura, his tone serious. 'By the human, Paddox.'

'Paddox?'

'We are to be subjects of his experimentation,' said Nyanna.

'What?'

'Paddox has been conducting experiments on our race for over twenty years, Doctor,' said Gallura. 'Ever since the Earth men first arrived on our planet, we have been nothing more than subjects for Paddox's research.'

'Through his experiments he has condemned thousands of our people to torture and death,' added Nyanna. 'Under his instruction, our homeworld was ravaged and destroyed, our culture lost for ever. The whole planet is now a scorched wilderness. Where once there stood exalted forests of mothertrees, there is nothing but ash. After slaughtering most of our race Paddox collected together the survivors, and transported them here, to the G-Lock. Where he has been continuing his research.'

'Now we are the only two left,' said Gallura sadly.

'We are all that remains of the Arboretan race,' said Nyanna.

The Doctor was appalled. 'What?' he exclaimed angrily. 'But what's he trying to do, hmm?'

Gallura and Nyanna fell into a cheerless silence, their neck fronds undulating slowly.

'Well?'

'Paddox wishes to acquire the secret of the Arboretans,' said Gallura.

'The secret of the Arboretans?'

'The Path of Perfection,' stated Nyanna.

'Ah. The Path of Perfection. And what is that?'

'We shall explain,' said Gallura. 'Tell me, Doctor, have you ever wished that you could travel back in time and live your life all over again, correcting your mistakes?'

Rochfort strode into the control room. 'Well, Byson?'

'I think you're just in time, sir.' Byson sighed a worried sigh. 'It looks as if they're trying to force their way in from the outside.'

'And what have you done about this?'

'I've sent Simmonds down with some men, sir.'

'Simmonds, eh?' Rochfort pressed a thumb on the intercom relay, and leaned towards the desk microphone. 'This is Captain Rochfort speaking.'

The voice that replied was distorted by whooshing static. Interference from hyperspace. 'Yes, sir. Simmonds here.'

'Report.'

'We've just reached the airlock now, sir', said Simmonds. 'There are signs of tertiary stress around the hatch and...' In the background, barely audible above the hissing, there was a persistent clanging.

Simmonds continued, his voice trembling. 'They're attacking the airlock hatch, I... I don't believe it. The metal's buckling. But the force... it's impossible!'

The clanging grew steadily louder. 'It's not going to hold. The locking mechanism is snapping –'

There was a sudden, booming crash, and then nothing but spitting static.

'Simmonds, report!' shouted Rochfort.

'The hatch... the hatch has split, sir. They're coming through now,' gasped Simmonds. There was the high-pitched frazzle of laser blasters discharging, followed by a strange, repetitive clacking. 'No! No! No!'

Simmonds screamed, gurgling as if he was being strangled. Something hissed, 'Eats! Must have eats!'

And then the intercom went dead.

Chapter Twelve

The door creaked open, spilling light into the blackness, and Romana strode into the Great Hall. The clink of her footsteps reverberated off the ancient stone walls as she walked towards the shadowy outline of a coffin.

Evadne levered the door shut. 'Well, this is it,' she whispered. 'This is where the Beautiful Death takes place.'

As Romana's eyes adjusted to the gloom, she fancied she could sense a presence, waiting. A clear case of subliminal anxiety manifestation, she told herself, and dismissed the thought.

The windows in the gallery above suddenly lit up. Romana could make out the bright control room within, the faint shapes of the scientists flitting back and forth.

The necroport was bathed in a ghostly glow. Romana was struck by how sinister it was; its surface was perfectly smooth, covered in paintings of skeletal angels. A small podium had been erected on the far side of the machine. She approached the entrance hatch. 'It's not guarded?'

'No need,' said Evadne. 'Everything's kept locked, and only staff know the entry codes.' She shuddered at the sight of the necroport. 'And, I mean, who would be stupid enough to want to go in there?'

Romana heaved the hatch open. Inside, the ladder dropped away into blackness.

'I'll go first then, shall I?' said Romana.

'But you can't change your own past,' said the Doctor. 'It's one of the laws of time travel, I forget which exactly, but definitely one of them.'

'You are a Time Lord, Doctor,' said Gallura. 'You know that history is not immutable.'

'If history could not be changed, there would be no need for a law to forbid it,' added Nyanna.

The Doctor frowned. 'So what does this have to do with the secret of the Arboretans? Supposing for a moment that you could change your pasts. If you can go back and avoid things, how come you have ended up here, hmm?'

'What has been is what always will be,' said Gallura. 'We follow the Path of Perfection.'

'But –'

Nyanna's fronds wavered, as if she sensed something. 'Paddox is approaching. You must leave us.'

The Doctor listened. He couldn't hear anything apart from the drone of the G-Lock's generators. 'Are you sure?'

'Please, Doctor,' Gallura urged. 'You must go now.'

The Doctor straightened his cloak. 'Ah, well, if you insist.' He nodded to each of them, and backed into the corridor. The door slid down behind him.

A second later there was the steady clack of approaching footsteps. Quickly, the Doctor pulled out the skull mask and slipped it over his face. It was tight, uncomfortable and tasted of rubber. He wondered how the guards put up with it.

Paddox strode down the corridor towards the cells. To his displeasure he noted that the prison guard seemed to have disappeared, leaving his desk unattended. At least there was a skullguard on duty, standing to attention, his empty eye sockets staring dead ahead.

'Where has that idiotic prison guard got to?' said Paddox.

The skullguard made a search-me gesture.

'I see. So you've been left here instead, have you?'

The skullguard nodded.

Paddox reminded himself to have a word with Metcalf. This was not the first time the prison guard's inefficiency had caused him concern.

He punched the door-opening control and stepped into the cell containing the two remaining Arboretans. They looked at him blankly, their faces showing no trace of fear. As a race they were passive creatures, with no sense of self-preservation. They would comply with his commands without the slightest resistance, even when undergoing dissection.

The elder of the creatures, a female, stood up and moved calmly out into the corridor. It was as though she could read his mind.

Paddox kept his pistol trained on the Arboretan as he locked the door and addressed the masked guard. 'You, skullguard. Come with me.'

The guard shuffled uneasily.

'Don't worry, I'm sure the prison guard will be returning presently.' Paddox weighed the pistol in his hands, thinking. 'Executive Metcalf has informed me that we have a prisoner. A saboteur who was posing as a neurelectrician. An absurd fellow, calls himself "the Doctor".'

The guard said nothing, so Paddox continued. 'Metcalf suspects that there may be other saboteurs at large within the G-Lock, and I am anxious that the security of the necroport should not compromised.'

The guard nodded vigorously.

An idea occurred to Paddox. 'Hold this,' he said, thrusting the pistol into the guard's hands. He would question the prisoner himself. Paddox walked up to the Doctor's cell, and reached for the door-opening mechanism.

There was a loud clattering. Paddox spun round to see the guard on his knees, retrieving the pistol from the floor.

Paddox rushed back and snatched the gun out of the guard's hands. 'Give me that. Obviously you cannot be trusted not to shoot yourself in the foot.'

As the guard stood up, Paddox waved the Arboretan down the corridor. 'You. Forward.' He turned to the guard. 'And you. Follow me.' He looked down. The guard's cloak was slithering along the floor. 'And do try not to trip up on the way.'

The interior of the necroport had changed little; the desk untidily piled with electronic equipment, the doorway leading into a room full of twinkling lights, the three coffins with their wire-mesh headpieces. Except this time the coffins were empty. The corner where the TARDIS had stood was just empty floor.

'Grief. This place is well spooky,' said Evadne. She peered into each of the coffins. 'What goes on down here, do you think?'

'That's what I'm trying to find out,' said Romana. She traced the wires from socket to socket. All the cables fed through into a transformer unit, with a dial indicating the level of power. The transformer in turn linked to the three coffins. 'How extraordinary.'

'What is it?'

'The direction of the particle flow into the capacitors. Of

course!' Romana clenched a triumphant fist, and crossed over to Evadne.

'Say no more,' said Evadne. 'The direction of the particle flow. Staring me in the face. Right, now that's sorted, let's get out of here.'

'It's all a sham,' said Romana. 'The necroport isn't the power source for the Beautiful Death at all.'

'Eh, hang on. If it isn't the power source...'

'The Beautiful Death is the power source for the necroport! It's a device for drawing energy from the participants, gathering it together, and then transferring it into these three units here.' Romana indicated the coffins.

'I don't get it,' said Evadne. 'You're saying this thing is taking power out of the people upstairs?'

'Yes. Not electricity, of course. Some sort of psychothermic energy transference.' Romana paced back and forth. 'Yes. Whilst they remain dormant, this machine accumulates their psychothermic energy. Like charging up a battery.'

Evadne was stuck on the first part of Romana's speech. 'Psychothermic?'

'A hypothetical form of energy released during the death process,' said Romana. 'It is the necroport absorbing the psychothermic energy that causes the participants to die.'

'And then what?'

'I don't know,' said Romana, crestfallen. 'It directs it to these coffins. And then, when the half hour is up it feeds back a psychothermic pulse to the participants, reviving them.'

'So basically, what you're saying is, right, it takes the consciousness out of the people upstairs, and then puts it into whoever's lying there.'

'Basically, yes,' smiled Romana, placing great emphasis on the word 'basically'.

'But what's it do that for?'

Suddenly Romana could hear footsteps clanging above them. Both she and Evadne looked up. Someone was climbing into the necroport.

'Quick!' Romana steered Evadne into the adjoining room. The walls were filled with spinning tape reels and banks of glimmering lights. Piles of dusty ticker tape littered the floor.

Rows of circuit boards were slotted into computer banks, bundles of multicoloured wiring exposed to view. A monitor showed static.

'What do you think all this stuff does?' asked Evadne.

Romana shushed her, and pulled her down to a squatting position by the doorway. Together, they leaned forward to look into the necroport chamber.

Three figures walked in. The first was Paddox, instantly recognisable in his high-collared white laboratory coat. He beckoned forward the second figure – the female Arboretan Romana had seen on her previous visit. Following them was a skullguard, its body slightly stooped.

The Arboretan climbed into the right-hand coffin and lay back, crossing her arms over her chest. Paddox then fixed the wire mesh onto her head. He examined all the cables that linked her to the transformer, tugging on the connections to check they were fast. After finding everything to his satisfaction, he pressed a sequence of buttons. Immediately all the instruments flashed into life, and a low, throbbing hum filled the air.

The Arboretan started to writhe.

Paddox faced the guard. 'Remain here. I want this place kept absolutely secure.' He collected another pistol from his desk, and handed it to the guard. 'And if anyone other than myself attempts to enter, kill them. Do you think you can manage that?'

The guard nodded.

'I shall have to trust you,' said Paddox. He took one last look at the squirming Arboretan, and allowed himself a brief smile before he marched over to the ladder and clambered out of the necroport.

After Paddox had gone, Evadne whispered to Romana: 'What do we do now?'

'I don't know.'

'But we can't go out there because of the guard. We're trapped.'

'Yes, I am quite aware of that.' The guard was wandering around the chamber as if he was searching for something. There was something oddly familiar about his shambolic gait.

The guard removed his mask to reveal the Doctor's face, grinning wildly. '"Absurd"? How dare he call me absurd! I've never heard anything so absurd!' he huffed. His eyes darted to and fro and, in his most booming voice, he called, 'Romana?'

Romana sighed, and rushed up to the Doctor. 'Doctor!'

'Ah, there you are,' said the Doctor, clapping her on the shoulders. 'And Evadne?'

Evadne emerged. 'You must be the secret agent known only as "the Doctor"?'

'Er, yes, that's right,' said the Doctor. He turned to Romana and muttered, 'What have you been telling her, exactly?'

Evadne caught sight of the Arboretan, and rushed over to her coffin. The creature was showing increasing signs of distress. Wisps of steam were rising from her twitching body. 'Isn't there anything we can do?'

The Doctor turned to Romana, and she shook her head. 'You know the future, Doctor,' she said. 'We can't save her.'

'No,' said the Doctor glumly. 'Any more than we can save ourselves.'

Paddox swung the hatch shut. He could feel the floor trembling as the necroport energised, the vibrations in sympathy with his own gathering excitement.

The main doors opened, and attendants poured into the hall. Immediately they set to work, readying the coffins for the impending ceremony. A man in a full-length grey coat hurried over to the platform, followed by an unkempt youth. Paddox watched as they started setting up camera lights, the man in the coat shouting instructions that his colleague did his best to ignore.

As the Great Hall began to fill with activity, Paddox slipped unnoticed to the staircase and made his way to the necroport control room.

The Doctor folded up the cloak and uniform and threw them carelessly into the corner, along with the laser pistol. Evadne watched him with a mixture of awe and incomprehension. He was a very unlikely-looking spy. But then, thought Evadne, in the spying profession that was probably an advantage.

Romana was inspecting the Arboretan's headset. The creature's limbs were contorting painfully. 'The necroport appears to be using her as some sort of channel.'

'What?' The Doctor glanced over the instrumentation. 'Of course!' he exclaimed. 'He's using the Arboretans as mediums!'

'Of course,' said Romana. 'The necroport alone can't give people a journey in the afterlife. It needs the Arboretans to act as psychotemporal conduits.'

'Yeah, of course,' said Evadne, not following the conversation, but feeling she should contribute.

'So all you need to do is connect an Arboretan to the necroport,' said Romana. 'And then anyone else who is connected to it can enter the next world...'

'... going via the Arboretan's consciousness! Yes!'

'Hang on, you mean the necroport...' Evadne pointed at the wall, '...is using her...' she pointed at the Arboretan, '... to treat everyone to the Beautiful Death?'

'Yes,' said the Doctor and Romana together.

'But how...' began Evadne, and gave up.

Romana continued. 'But if Paddox is sending hundreds of people through into the afterlife at once, the strain on the Arboretan must be enormous.'

'Fatal, I should imagine,' said the Doctor gravely. 'Paddox has been running these experiments for years. He's wiped out almost the entire species.'

'Gallura said you should "avenge the extinction of the Arboretans".'

'Yes.' The Doctor brooded. 'Genocide. Evil on a scale that is almost inconceivable. But there's one thing I still don't understand.'

'Only one thing?' said Evadne. 'I can think of at least fifty.'

'What's he doing it all for, hmm?' The Doctor swept grandly around the room. 'Why does he need to treat two-hundred-odd people to the Beautiful Death simultaneously?'

'Because he's trying to gather enough power to do something, and the only way he can do that is if everyone dies at once,' said Romana.

'Ah, yes, but power for what?' said the Doctor, eyes bulging. 'Once he's got his psychothermic capacitors all charged up, what does he intend to do?'

'The last time I was here, he mentioned something about how we would bear witness to the greatest achievement of his career,' said Romana. '"Redemption", he called it.'

'Redemption? I wonder…' The Doctor pulled at his collar. '"Redeem thy mis-spent time that's past, and live this day as if thy last."'

'What?'

'Oh, nothing,' said the Doctor. 'Just a thought. We all have, ah, missed opportunities that we regret.'

'Like failing your basic time travel proficiency?'

'Exactly,' agreed the Doctor, and then realised what Romana had said. 'No, not exactly. I didn't fail it. It was a pointless exercise.'

'You can't change the past, Doctor,' soothed Romana.

'No, of course not. Second law of time travel and all that.'

Romana muttered something that sounded like 'first'.

'And anyway, if we could change the past, we wouldn't be in the pretty pickle we are now, would we? And speaking of inevitable demises…' The Doctor suddenly perked up. 'ERIC!' He charged into the adjoining room.

Romana and Evadne exchanged incredulous looks. 'Wait here,' said Romana, and followed him.

Meanwhile, directly above them in the Great Hall, an interview was taking place.

'Biscit. Tell me, why did you decide to "snuff out life's candle"?'

Hoopy shuffled his weight from foot to foot. The holocamera made him nervous, with its baleful red light.

'Well, it's the ultimate mystery and transcendence gig, isn't it?' said Biscit. 'Of all the loaf-bakers, this is the poser to end all posers. Where do we go when we die? It's a total self-revelation and apotheosis trip, Harky my friend.'

What was it Harken had said? Don't, whatever you do, look directly into the camera. Hoopy guiltily turned back to Harken.

'And Hoopy. Could you describe the actual sensations of death, in your own words.'

Oh no. Harken was pointing the microphone at him now. Hoopy wanted to run away, but his feet had transformed into a particularly immobile type of granite.

Hoopy cleared his throat. 'It's way out. Sure-fire. You just close your peepers, surrender to the void and you're there. Gentle into the goodnight. Groovy.' He did a karma sign with his fingers, realised he'd got it the wrong way round and corrected himself.

'Relatively painless, then. That'll be of some reassurance to our older viewers. And Xab, what is paradise actually like? What does the spirit world hold in store?'

'It's an awfully big adventure,' Xab said dozily.

'So this is ERIC's brain centre?' said Romana.

The Doctor was poking his nose into the various computer units with unbridled enthusiasm. Romana watched him fondly; the moment the Doctor set eyes on any sort of vintage machine he had an irresistible urge to start tinkering with it.

'Yes,' The Doctor blew the dust off his fingers. 'You know, the state this place is in, I'm amazed he's still going.'

'I'm more than amazed. I'm astonished,' said Romana. 'Some of this circuitry is over –'

'Two hundred years old, yes.' The Doctor hunched over the solitary keyboard and tapped out a message, but there was no response. 'This interaction terminal's dead. Hello, ERIC old thing, can you hear me?'

They waited for some seconds, listening to the ever-present beeps and whirrs.

The Doctor shook his head. 'No, there's only two terminals still working. One in Metcalf's office and one in the Paddox's control room. Poor chap, it must be the equivalent of going blind and having idiots shouting in both ears.'

A thought occurred to Romana. 'Doctor, when the necroport blew up, you don't think…'

'Oh, but I do.' The Doctor indicated a row of tubes set into the wall. 'These are ERIC's circuit breakers. If we fuse the control linkages here…' he patted a set of cables, '… and switch the central processor here…' he indicated an important-looking white box, '… to a direct power input, then they will overload, and ERIC's brain will explode! Ha!' he concluded, with unabashed delight.

'How do you know that?'

'ERIC told me. Ha ha.'

'Oh. Very clever,' said Romana, as she went ahead of him, back into the necroport chamber. And then she stopped abruptly.

The Arboretan was convulsing uncontrollably. On the opposite side of the chamber stood Evadne, her face filled with fear. And in the centre of the room, a column of air was shimmering like a heat haze.

The drone of the necroport dropped to a low, nerve-juddering rumble.

'The time distortion,' breathed Romana. 'It's starting.'

'Oh dear.' The Doctor approached the shimmering area, shielding his face with his hands. The column was expanding at a frightening rate, snaking up to the ceiling. 'Evadne?' he called across the room.

'What's going on?' she asked, her voice trembling.

'Move over to the ladder. Keep as far away from the distortion as you can.'

Evadne backed away. Reaching the base of the ladder, she looked at the Doctor, wondering what to do next.

'Now go,' shouted the Doctor. 'Get out. You are in great danger!'

'But –'

'Go!'

Reluctantly, Evadne grasped the ladder, and started to climb.

The Great Hall was full of attendants and tourists, the preparations for the Beautiful Death well under way. On a raised platform, a man in a long coat was deep in discussion with another man in T-shirt and jeans.

Evadne slowly climbed out of the necroport. Luckily, this side of the machine was shrouded in shadows, and no one spotted her as she dropped down behind the nearest coffin.

Crouched in the darkness, she considered her next move. If she made for the side doorway, she could use the coffins for cover. She decided to risk it.

She darted from casket to casket and, to her great relief, reached the side door. It was still unlocked and she dived through into the brightly lit safety of the corridor beyond.

The time distortion had expanded to fill almost all the available space in the necroport, forcing the Doctor and Romana against the wall. Looking through the disruption they saw that the opposite side of the room appeared to be shivering violently, like a reflection in a shaking mirror.

'Doctor,' shouted Romana over the roar of the necroport's engines. 'What are we going to do?'

'I'm open to suggestions!' he shouted back.

'Back to the computer room?'

'That's the best idea I've heard so far.' The Doctor started to edge towards the doorway, Romana following a short distance behind him.

'"Mummy, why won't daddy be home for Christmas?"'

Metcalf felt the blood rushing to his face. 'I will not tolerate this. This is intolerable! I did not agree to this interview just so that I could be harangued in such a provocative and substantially ill-informed manner. This interview is terminated. Now, if you will excuse me, I have matters of importance to attend to,' he said, and walked down the podium steps.

The Doctor felt the edge of the doorway, and backed into ERIC's brain centre. The distortion was now only moments away from consuming the entire necroport.

Romana inched towards him, squeezing through the gap between the wall and the shimmering haze. She put out a hand. 'Doctor.'

'Romana!' The Doctor tried to reach her, but the distortion surged forward and she became a blur, her movements leaving trails of colour in the air. For a moment the Doctor could hear her calling out his name, and then she dissolved into nothingness.

The interior of the necroport returned to normal, its engines dropping to a steady hum, the distortion evaporating. But where Romana had been standing there was now just empty space.

Metcalf slumped down at his desk, panting. The crowds outside the Great Hall had been jammed solid, and it had taken all his strength to battle his way back to his office. His body was soaked with sweat, his shirt glued to his back, his hair plastered across his forehead.

The intercom buzzed. Metcalf answered it. 'Yes, Executive Metcalf speaking.'

'Sir, this is the prison guard. You know that saboteur you had brought down here?'

'Yes?'

'It is my unfortunate duty, sir, to inform you that he has escaped. He somehow managed to override the locking mechanism, and then overpowered me and rendered me unconscious.'

'What?' yelped Metcalf.

'And then he locked me in a cell. In fact, if the cleaner hadn't come along just now and let me out –'

Metcalf switched off the intercom and smashed his fist into the desk.

The Doctor made a complete circle of the necroport chamber. 'Romana?' he called. 'Romana?'

She had been caught in the time disruption. Transported back to heaven knows when. Except...

'Her time trail!' he exclaimed. 'Of course, I can follow it in the TARDIS!' He bounced on his heels, trying to jog his thoughts into action. 'That is, assuming I can get back there before it goes cold, that's the problem with time trails – so no time to stand here talking to yourself, Doctor. Come on!'

He dashed over to the ladder and started to climb.

Romana awoke to the sound of dripping water. One side of her face was damp where it had rested on the metal floor. The air was clammy and cold. In the distance, valves clunked and gurgled.

She pulled herself to her feet. She was in a gloomy vault crisscrossed by dozens of interweaving pipes. The light came from bare bulbs set at intervals along the length of the ceiling.

Romana cast her mind back. She remembered the time distortion within the necroport, and reaching for the Doctor's hand. As the distortion had engulfed her, she had been sick with fear, convinced that she was about to meet her destiny. Her last memory was the sensation of drowning in the shimmering, resigning herself to death.

But somehow she had survived. The relief was immense. She had escaped the inevitable, to find herself alive, exhilaratingly alive. But where was she?

There were two doors, one at either end of the vault. A notice was set into the surface of the nearest door: *Assig. Cerberus. ERIC.*

Environmental Regulation and Information Computer. Brain Centre. Authorised Personnel Only.

She hadn't moved an inch. She was in exactly the same place, only at an earlier time. Looking around, she realised it hadn't changed that much; the dimensions of the vault were the same as those of the necroport and, if the pipes were removed and the lighting altered slightly, it would be essentially the same room.

The other door opened on to a corridor, panelled in oak and plushly carpeted, but so dark it was impossible to see more than a few metres in either direction. Intrigued, Romana stepped into the corridor and closed the door behind her.

'Eats! Must have eats!' a voice spluttered, followed by a rapid scuttling.

Romana felt a hot breath on the back of her neck, and was overwhelmed by the stench of rotten meat. She whirled around, and screamed.

The Doctor popped his head out of the necroport, and grinned. The attendants were all busy with the preparations for the Beautiful Death, fitting the headsets to the tourists and checking the life monitors. They were all so engrossed in their work it shouldn't be a problem for someone with his experience of sneaking past people to sneak past them.

He closed the hatch gently behind him. Keeping his head down, he squatted behind the nearest coffin.

The public address system stuttered into life.

'G-Lock. This is Executive Metcalf speaking. I regret to announce that a saboteur is on the loose. He is tall, has an itinerant manner, wears a grey coat and multicoloured scarf, and calls himself "the Doctor". He is thought to be in or near the necroport in the Great Hall. Will all skullguards in the area attend to his capture forthwith. Thank you.'

The Doctor boggled. The prison guard must have woken up and raised the alarm. And, of course, Metcalf thought he would be trying to sabotage ERIC.

Throughout the hall, skullguards advanced down the aisles. There were a dozen of them, searching in pairs, most of them concentrating on the exact area where he was hiding.

The Doctor considered going back to the necroport, but it was no good. They would spot him immediately.

Two guards were examining the next-but-one casket to him. Another two searched the casket on the other side, unpleasant-looking laser rifles gripped in their black-gloved hands.

He was surrounded. There was absolutely no way out.

The Doctor gulped as one of the guards approached the coffin he was hiding behind.

'We've got him! Over here!'

Chapter Thirteen

The creature loomed out of the darkness, towering over her. Its small head swung about atop a bulbous central section, two hemispherical red eyes scouring the surroundings hungrily. Its vast mouth dropped open revealing rows of jagged teeth. Romana recoiled as two serrated pincers flashed through the air close to her face. The spiky hair on its joints brushed against her cheeks and the pitted surface of its exoskeleton glistened.

The giant spider-creature scuttled forward, its eight long, multijointed legs dancing about it in a whirl of intricately co-ordinated movements. It emitted a shriek, and clamped its jaws together, sniffing at the air.

The crackle of blaster fire filled the air. Caught in a circle of red light, the creature gave an ear-splitting scream and staggered away from her.

Romana turned to the source of the gunfire. She could discern two figures at the far end of the corridor, each holding a glaring flashlight.

The blasters shut off and the creature smashed into the floor. Its body shattered and its legs fractured into dozens of twitching sections. Detached from the limbs, the pincers clutched blindly at thin air. The torso and abdomen broke in two, blistering like burning fat. And the head rolled to one side, its eyes lifeless.

'Thank you,' Romana sighed, walking towards the figures. 'I'm extremely grateful.'

'Get over here,' yelled one of the men. 'Quick!'

Puzzled, Romana looked back over her shoulder.

Even though the creature had fallen apart, the various pieces seemed to have a life of their own. Sections of leg jerked their way jauntily across the carpet. As they collected together, they coupled themselves into longer pieces, creating multijointed limbs, and then plugged themselves into the abdomen. The pincers, in turn, clacked over to the other ends of the legs and fixed themselves into position. Next, they collected the torso and head sections and stuck them on to the front of the abdomen.

The creature was putting itself back together. Its eyes popped open, as bright as before. As the final sections of its legs snapped back into place, it scuttled back and forth, testing its reassembled limbs. Finding one leg longer than the next, it swapped over various joints, holding the pieces up to the light and comparing them until they were all approximately the same length.

A few of the more badly burned sections of the creature remained on the floor. It sniffed at these discarded pieces, and gobbled them up hungrily. 'Freshly baked eats!' It craned around, turning its attention back to the humans.

Fighting back her rising nausea, Romana ran down the corridor towards the torch lights. One man fired another shot in the creature's direction, and part of the wall exploded into flames. As the fire engulfed the hallway, the man grabbed her shoulder and hauled her forward roughly. 'Come on!'

'We've got him! Over here!'

The skullguards clicked off the safety catches on their guns and walked away. The Doctor blinked, and tried to work out what had happened.

He peered out over the top of the casket. The guards were converging around a coffin at the opposite end of the hall, beside the side entrance. There was something rather familiar about the whole scene.

One of the guards made a 'get up' gesture with his rifle, and a figure rose from behind the coffin, his arms above his head. As he stepped out of the shadows, the Doctor could make out the man's curly brown hair and genial grin.

The Doctor boggled. Of course, they were arresting him. Well, they were arresting an earlier version of him who had, unwittingly, come to his rescue. He marvelled at the sheer deliciousness of it. He had often wondered, when he came to the aid of some unfortunate soul, what it felt like to be rescued and now that it had happened to him he found it rather enjoyable.

The previous Doctor shambled across the hall, gazing appreciatively at the surroundings. The Doctor was disconcerted by how often this chap was ruffling his hair, and rubbing his chin. He hadn't realised how mannered he was; he wished he could shout out, 'Stop fiddling with your ear!' And as for that body posture... well, he would have to do something about that.

But, overall, he was impressed with what he saw. Those clothes made him look rather striking. You handsome devil, Doctor.

As the guards conducted his previous self towards the staircase, the Doctor decided to make the most of the distraction. Keeping his head down, he weaved his way over to the side entrance. Reaching the door, he gently pushed it open and slipped unseen into the corridor.

He checked his watch. Ten minutes to midnight. He straightened his scarf, and started down the corridor. He had to get back to the TARDIS as soon as possible. With every passing minute, Romana's time trail would be fading.

Since the encounter with the creature, Romana's rescuers had barely spoken. After running for what seemed like an age, they arrived at the deck with the wide staircase. Above them, a single chandelier slowly rocked back and forth, the tapestries and paintings coming to life in the drifting shadows.

For the first time, Romana could see her rescuers properly. Two men in faded blue uniforms, both with heavy, untidy beards.

Romana recognised them. The last time she had seen them, they had been standing at the top of the staircase, black fluid oozing from their mouths, before transforming suddenly and fatally into Gonzies.

The younger officer motioned for them to halt. 'All right. I think we'll be safe here for a minute.'

'What was that thing?' said Romana.

'An Arachnopod,' said the older officer bitterly. He stepped towards Romana, and leaned into her face. 'And who are you?'

'Romana,' she smiled at them in turn, reading their name badges. Captain Rochfort and Lieutenant Byson. 'You saved my life back there. I'm terribly grateful.'

'Where have you come from?' asked Rochfort, eyeing her warily.

'I'm afraid that's rather difficult to explain,' said Romana. 'And I don't think you would believe me even if I did.'

'Try.'

'Well, what would you say if I told you I had only just arrived here –'

'Impossible,' snapped Rochfort. He turned away. 'We've searched every spacecraft in the hyperspace tunnel. Every single spacecraft.' He faced Romana with a sneer. 'And the tunnel's been sealed off for almost two months. There's no way you can have "just arrived".'

'I did say you wouldn't believe me.'

'She could be a passenger, sir,' said Byson. 'She could have been hiding out on one of the lower levels. Just a suggestion, sir.'

'Yes, my thoughts exactly, Byson,' said Rochfort. 'A stowaway.' He ran his lascivious eyes up and down her body. 'And she doesn't look like she's been going hungry.'

'You think she might know where we can find some food, sir?' said Byson eagerly.

'Indeed I do, Byson.' Rochfort raised his gun towards Romana. 'Well?'

'I'm sorry, but I don't have the faintest idea what you're talking about.'

Rochfort squeezed the barrel of his blaster against Romana's cheek. 'You must have found a food source or you wouldn't be standing here now, would you? Well, where is it?'

'I can't help you,' said Romana calmly. 'I haven't got any food, and I haven't been hiding anywhere. If you will only listen –'

The blaster pressed harder. 'I am going to count to three, and if you don't tell me what I want to know, me counting to three will be the last thing you will ever hear,' spat Rochfort. 'One.'

'I keep telling you, I don't know,' said Romana.

'Two.'

'You are making a dreadful mistake.'

'Three.'

'Maybe she's run out of food, sir,' said Byson hurriedly. 'It would explain why she came up here, sir.'

Rochfort held the blaster to Romana's cheek, letting her feel its cold metal against her skin. Then he withdrew it and replaced it in his belt. 'I suppose that could be the case.'

Romana exhaled. 'Thank you,' she said, rising above the indignity of the situation. 'Now, perhaps, you could answer a question for me.'

'Go on.'

'What year is it?' Romana suspected she already knew the answer, but wanted her fears confirmed.

'What year?' said Rochfort. 'What sort of a damn idiot question is that?'

Romana raised an eyebrow.

'I don't think it would do any harm, sir,' said Byson.

'All right,' said Rochfort. 'The year is 2815.'

The Doctor bounded around the corner and came face-to-face with a jostling horde of tourists. They were smiling and shouting excitedly, all attempting to push through to the Great Hall.

The crowd was packed solid. The Doctor considered his next move. If he tried to make his way through the crowd they would undoubtedly hamper his journey back to the TARDIS. But if he backtracked, he could waste valuable minutes racing around the G-Lock and lose Romana's time trail altogether.

A dull clanging interrupted his thoughts. Twelve chimes, the last heralding an eruption of cheering in the crowd. Party poppers exploded, spraying the crowd with black streamers.

The Doctor scraped the streamers from his hair, and decided to find another way back to the TARDIS. He wanted to be alone. The celebrations seemed hollow, and there was something insufferably superficial about the company of humans. And he knew that most of them would be dead soon, and he couldn't bear the the thought of being unable to intervene. But what could he do? If he interfered he could destroy all history, and condemn countless others to death. It was the burden of guilt every time traveller faced. He couldn't save these tourists any more than he could go back and rescue Joan of Arc, Thomas More, or the Big Bopper. Any more than he could save K9. Or, indeed, himself.

As the Doctor strode away a breeze ruffled through the crowd and, in the distance, the cheers turned to screams.

Rochfort banged three times on the iron doors. 'Captain Rochfort!'

The doors to the Great Hall cranked open. As soon as there was a gap wide enough to squeeze through, Byson pushed Romana inside and bustled in after her. Rochfort followed and the doors clanged shut behind them.

The hall was shrouded in darkness. Hundreds of pale, frightened passengers were huddled in the shadows, sitting amidst piles of crates and food containers, their bodies wasted away, their clothes ragged. As Romana and the two officers stepped forward they raised hopeful faces towards them, and a murmur of expectation drifted through the hall as people nudged each other awake, whispering that Captain Rochfort had returned. But the hope soon disappeared as they realised that he was empty-handed.

Romana surveyed the bleak panorama. Most of the passengers were old, their skin gnarled and thin. They slept fitfully amongst the garbage, waiting for the end. At the far end of the hall, where the light bulbs ended, there was the shape of a fountain where the necroport had once stood. Or would stand. The fountain still dribbled water, barely enough for the survivors to drink and wash. And beyond the fountain were dozens of human forms, draped in tablecloths.

It was important to remain detached, Romana told herself. To observe, and not to let these people's lives touch her. Because if she didn't remain impassive she would be crying at the futility of it all.

Rochfort led Romana over to a pile of packing cases, and sat her down opposite him. Byson squatted next to them, swigging from a plastic water bottle.

'Two months, we've been here,' muttered Rochfort, as Byson passed him the bottle. 'And we've got four days left until the food runs out.'

'How have you managed?' said Romana.

'We've sent out search parties, scouring the ship for what we can find,' said Byson. 'Captain Rochfort bravely managed to salvage some provisions from the store rooms, before the Arachnopods got at them. But since then, nothing. Which is why we need to know where you've been hiding, in case there is anything left.'

'What are these "Arachnopods"?'

'Oh, come on,' said Rochfort. 'Do you really expect us to accept...'

'I'll come to that,' said Romana. 'Do me the courtesy of answering my questions, and then I will explain everything.'

'Just after the collision...' Byson placed his hands together, '... they came on board. One of the ships behind us was a prison transport, on its way to the internment labs on Murgatroyd. It was carrying these Arachnopods, a genetically modified life form. Basically, they were designed to be the ultimate killing machines.'

Rochfort's eyes gleamed as if he were overlooking a chasm of insanity. 'And then they started eating the crew and the passengers. We tried to fight, but they're indestructible.'

'Nothing's indestructible,' breathed Romana.

'These things are. You saw what happened back in the corridor. Even if you blow it up, each section of its body has its own nervous system. They just put themselves back together again.' Byson wiped his eyes. 'And any bits which they can't put back together, they just eat up and regrow.'

'How do you know all this?'

'Oh, shortly after the attack, we got ERIC to hack into the *Montressor*'s computer records,' said Byson, leaning back. 'And a lot of good it did us.'

'So you see, between the Arachnopods and starvation, we're all that's left,' said Rochfort. 'All –'

Romana interrupted: '218 of you.'

Byson pulled himself upright, and Rochfort started. 'Yes. That's right,' said Rochfort. 'Now how did you know that?'

'Oh, just a guess,' sighed Romana.

The floor started to judder and the Doctor was sent sprawling across the corridor. Grabbing on to the handrail, he steadied himself and swayed over to a map framed on the wall.

'Aha!' He licked a finger and pointed it down the shaking corridor. 'Straight down here, left, up the stairs, along the gallery. Nearly there, Doctor.'

And then the lights sputtered out.

'You mentioned a crash. How did it happen, exactly?'

Byson shifted uncomfortably, and looked to Rochfort for an answer.

'Well?' added Romana.

'It was ERIC's fault,' said Rochfort. 'There was some disruption.'

'A build-up of geostatic stress, sir,' said Byson helpfully.

'Yes, Byson. And, naturally, encountering a build-up of geostatic stress, we decided to bring the ship to a halt. But then ERIC overruled us, and caused the ship to become lodged in the exit.'

'Sorry, you're saying the ship's computer overruled you?' said Romana. 'I didn't realise they could do that.'

'No, what we're saying is that the computer should have

overruled the captain, but didn't –' Byson suddenly stopped himself.

'The point is,' said Rochfort rapidly. 'The point is, ERIC is prepared to admit he was entirely at fault.' He called towards the ceiling. 'ERIC?'

> *Leave me alone.*

'No need to be like that, ERIC,' said Rochfort. 'Now, tell us, whose fault was it that the *Cerberus* became caught in the tunnel?'

> *Go away.*

'Whose fault?'

> *It was my fault, Captain Rochfort. Mea culpa,* wailed ERIC.
> *I have brought all this upon myself. How can I go on living with this on my conscience?*

'Thank you, ERIC.' Rochfort faced Romana. 'Now perhaps you will tell us where you came from. Properly, this time.'

Romana considered her words carefully. 'The future.'

'What?'

'I come from the future,' she said. 'From the year 3012, to be precise.'

'The future? How?' said Byson.

'I was caught in a rupture in the time–space continuum.'

'Holy grief,' roared Rochfort. 'I have never heard anything so ridiculous.' He got to his feet and brushed down his uniform. 'She's obviously lying. Byson, I think we should make another search of the lower levels. See if there's any more of them down there.'

'Very good, sir.'.

'We shall leave in five minutes.' Rochfort collected his blaster, and strode over to the fountain.

Byson watched as Rochfort splashed his face. 'I don't know what he expects to find,' he said, turning back to Romana. 'Do you mean it? You really are from the future?'

Romana nodded.

'Then you'll know what happens to us, won't you? You'll know whether we get rescued or not.' The words streamed out of Byson's mouth.

Romana cast her mind back to Evadne's lecture on the 'Mystery of the *Cerberus*'. The emergency services had arrived two months after the disaster. So if the passengers only held on for a few more days, they would be saved.

But what could she say to Byson? If she told him the truth then he wouldn't take up the Repulsion's offer, and she would alter the course of history. But if she told him that all the passengers of the *Cerberus* had died before they were rescued, she would be encouraging him to accept the Repulsion's offer.

'I cannot tell you,' she said eventually.

'You can't tell me?' said Byson. 'You mean, no one comes to rescue us? That we're all just left here to rot and die, is that what you're saying? That the tunnel stays sealed for ever?'

'I'm sorry.' Romana closed her eyes. She had no choice. 'The emergency services will eventually arrive, but they will be too late. They will find nobody alive on the *Cerberus*.'

The Doctor skidded into the observation lounge. It was a gloomy shade of orange, the emergency lights picking out the tourists hunched in the seats, cradling their drinks.

He was overjoyed to see the TARDIS waiting unobtrusively in the far corner and strode towards it.

'Doctor.'

The Doctor spun around. It was Romana.

'Romana? You're all right! It's so good to see you!' He clasped her gladly by the shoulders.

Romana smiled back at him. 'Where have you been? I was concerned…'

'What?' A memory joggled in the Doctor's mind. He put a finger forward to hush her. 'How did you get here?'

'What do you mean, "how did you get here"? I was in the crowds, we were heading for the Great Hall, remember, and –'

'Oh, I remember. We lost you. Which means…' The Doctor realised this wasn't his Romana, this was a Romana from their previous visit to the G-Lock. She had mentioned something about seeing him leave in the TARDIS, and now it was happening, just as she had described.

'Of course,' said the Doctor, punching the air. 'You said something like this would happen.'

'Did I?' Romana stared at him as though he were mad.

'Yes, and you were right, well done. Aah. You know, I don't mean to be terribly rude, but I'm in a bit of a hurry.' He dug out his key, and turned for the TARDIS.

'To do what?' said Romana anxiously.

'You'll find out in the fullness of time. Hopefully. Sorry, must dash. Goodbye.' The Doctor smiled apologetically, ducked into the TARDIS and slammed the door in Romana's face.

The Doctor strode into the console room, the doors humming shut behind him, and set to work on the control panels.

A sequence of coordinates appeared on the time-path indicator. The final destination of Romana's time trail. The Doctor darted to the opposite side of the console, laid in the coordinates and quickly activated the dematerialisation circuit.

As the TARDIS's engines grumbled into life, he heaved a sigh and brushed the hair out of his eyes.

On the scanner he could see Romana staring up at the TARDIS. She was shouting soundlessly: the scanner's audio facility was playing up again.

'Goodbye, Romana!' the Doctor called out, and the scanner shutters slid shut. He crossed back to the console and watched as the central column rose, rotated and fell. His hands nudged various levers, preparing the TARDIS for rematerialisation. 'And, hopefully, hello Romana.'

'Ready, Byson?'

Byson took another swig of water, and nodded. 'Yes, sir.' He got to his feet, gathered his laser blaster and torch, and let Rochfort lead him to the main doors. The woman, Romana, moved after them.

'Oh no, not you.' Rochfort pointed his blaster directly at her face. 'You're staying right here.' He turned to the passenger appointed to guard duty. 'Byson and I will be returning shortly. Do not open these doors for anyone else, to enter or to leave. If she attempts anything, kill her. Do you understand?'

The passenger, a young, jittery man, clasped his gun tightly to his chest and nodded. Romana returned to her seat, and sat down with an aloof smirk.

'Open,' barked Rochfort. The doors grated apart, and he disappeared into the darkness.

Byson took one final look at Romana. There was something about her, a certain confidence in her eyes, that gave the impression she knew more than she was admitting.

Deep in troubled thought, Byson followed his captain.

Romana watched as the main doors shut with a dull clang, and
shifted in her seat to face away from the guard. She looked down
at her boots, and let her mind drift over recent events, past and
future. She had a good idea what Rochfort and Byson would find
on the lower levels. But had she caused them to search there, or
would it have happened anyway? Had she set in motion the
events that would lead to the massacre on the G-Lock in two
centuries' time?

But that would be impossible, Romana told herself. She had
been brought here by the time distortion caused by the
Repulsion, whatever that was. If her actions in this time had in
some way helped the Repulsion to create that time distortion,
that would be a self-originating loop, and that was a tautological
impossibility. An action cannot cause itself.

No, what must have happened was that originally, in some
parallel existence, she was not here and Rochfort and Byson had
gone down to investigate the lower levels anyway. Then, after that
first time, they had caused the events on the G-Lock, which had
caused her to be transported back in time, which had led her to
inadvertently give Rochfort and Byson the idea of searching the
lower levels. There had to have been a first cause.

'Hello,' said a bright voice, interrupting her thoughts. 'My name's
Tarie. Who are you?'

Romana looked up. In front of her was a young girl, no more
than six years old, with wide, inquisitive eyes. She had dark, curly
hair, and wore a cross-patterned blue dress.

The girl from the dream.

The circle of light glided across the wall like a restless ghost, and
fell upon a gold plaque set into the wood panelling.

'Corridor 79,' read Byson. He let the beam slide further down
the corridor, illuminating the cabin doors that stretched away into
the gloom.

Rochfort advanced down the corridor, his boots clomping on
the thick carpet. He twisted each door handle as he passed, but
found every cabin locked.

'Captain!'

'What is it?' Rochfort caught Byson in the glare of his torch.

Byson blinked rapidly. 'Up ahead, sir.'

Rochfort followed Byson's gaze. The hallway ended a few metres away, disappearing into complete darkness. As Rochfort directed his torch into the shadows, the light reflected over ripples on some shifting surface.

Byson's light drifted around the edge, following the line where the walls, ceiling and floor melted into the nothingness. 'What do you think it is, sir?'

'Quiet, Byson.' Rochfort halted on the very edge of the void. As he looked closer, he could see the blackness swilling about, its surface undulating like a pool of oil.

There was a voice. Quiet, sibilant, almost inaudible. It was coming from within the darkness. And it was speaking to him, Rochfort. It wanted him. It wanted him to surrender himself to the void.

Rochfort peered into the shadows. There was something in there, half-hidden. A single red light.

'Captain Rochfort!' yelled Byson.

Rochfort stepped forward.

Chapter Fourteen

The observation lounge was still and dark, as if in mourning. Overturned tables and chairs littered the floor, amidst jagged bottles and discarded wine trays. Chewed fragments of clothing were all that remained of the passengers. And outside, the hyperspace void swirled like an endless slow-motion plughole.

A distressed trumpeting broke the silence and the shadowy panels of the TARDIS exterior solidified into existence. Its dirty windows gazed glumly out at the scene.

The Doctor emerged, looping his scarf around his shoulders. He surveyed the surroundings, teeth gritted. 'Romana?' he called, peering into the gloom. 'Romana?'

He picked his way across the lounge, his boots crunching on the broken glass. He could smell it hanging in the air – the familiar scent of death. '"Not a soul in sight, alive or dead",' he muttered. 'Ah. The Mystery of the *Cerberus*.'

He delved into his pockets, and pulled out his torch. Clicking it on, he proceeded to the main doorway.

Byson stamped his feet, trying to get feeling to return to them. He watched his own torch-lit reflection as it undulated on the surface of the wall of blackness.

Five minutes ago, Rochfort had disappeared. He had simply walked straight into the gloom and been gulped up, like a stone dropping into tar fuel. Since then Byson had been alone, Romana's words running anxiously through his mind. The emergency services would not find anyone alive, she had said. Which could only mean that the Teredekethon authorities had left them for dead. They were doomed.

A series of ripples bobbed outwards as Rochfort broke the surface. His face perfectly calm, he approached Byson.

'Captain Rochfort, sir,' gabbered Byson.

'Do not be alarmed, Byson.' Rochfort's lips twitched into a smile. 'It is perfectly safe.'

'But what is it, sir? What happened?'

'I have been to another place.' Rochfort looked back into the blackness. 'Another reality.'

'But sir,' protested Byson. 'That is the hyperspace–real-space interface. You should have been destroyed, the forces in there are literally astronomical.'

'There is nothing to fear.' Rochfort indicated his own, undamaged body. 'I am the proof of that. Please, enter yourself if you don't believe me.'

'But I don't understand, sir. Why did you go in there in the first place?'

'I heard a voice. It… it invited me.'

'A voice?' said Byson incredulously.

'There is an intelligence in there, Byson.' Rochfort gripped Byson's shoulders. 'It is good! It showed me miracles, a realm beyond the wildest of dreams!'

'Did it, sir?'

'Don't look at me like that, Byson,' snapped Rochfort. 'I haven't gone funny, you know.' He led Byson up the corridor. 'It made me an offer. It is going to help us.'

'Sir?'

'It wants to take us away from this place. Take us into the future.'

'Sir?'

'It will transport us forward two centuries, to a time where the hyperspace tunnel has reopened. Once there, we will be able to begin our lives again.' Rochfort paused. 'We will be reborn.'

'Sir?'

'Say something other than "Sir", Byson.'

'Sorry, sir,' said Byson. 'You mean to say that we can get out of here? We can escape into the thirty-first century?'

'Yes,' said Rochfort. 'That is exactly what I mean.'

'But what is it? How can it do all this?'

'It has the power to do anything in creation. All we have to do is to deliver the remaining passengers into its realm and it will do the rest.'

'That seems awfully generous of it, if you don't mind me saying, sir.'

'We should not question its motives. It is our only hope.' They reached the stairwell at the end of the corridor and Rochfort leaned back, one hand on the railing. 'How long do you think I was in there for, Byson?'

'I don't know. About five minutes?' said Byson.

'I was in there for at least two hours,' said Rochfort. 'In the domain of the Repulsion...' He pointed towards the darkness, '... time has no meaning at all.'

The Doctor halted at the top of the staircase. Something was moving ahead of him, its shadows flitting across the ceiling. It made a padding sound, a rapid succession of carpeted footfalls.

The Doctor slammed off his torch light and crouched behind a nearby statue. He smoothed his hair out of his eyes and looked down into the deck below.

Its long legs dancing around it, the creature emerged from the shadows and strutted across the deck. Two mandibles swished at the air in front of it and its beady red eyes glared ravenously. Some sort of giant spider, thought the Doctor. Though the odd thing about it was that it seemed to have been assembled from individual limb and torso sections bolted together. Like a Meccano kit of a monster, constructed by some deranged model enthusiast.

The Doctor rummaged in his pockets and pulled out a battered paperback, *Bor Pollag's Book of Alien Monsters*. 'Let's see what old Pollag has to say.' Straining his eyes in the near-darkness he thumbed through the pages, holding the book up to compare the various illustrations. 'Akker-Takker. No. Algolian Sithersback. No. Apostle of Grarb. No.' He flicked over the page. 'Aha! Arachnopod.' He read the text beneath the picture. 'Bioengineered life form ... homicidal tendencies ... criminally insane ... widely believed indestructible.' He grimly returned the book to his coat. 'Oh dear.'

A hush fell over the Great Hall as the passengers lifted their faces to the two men climbing up the staircase. Tarie rubbed the sleep out of the corners of her eyes, and walked through the maze of grown-ups' legs. No one had spoken to her for days. All of the grown-ups were tired, and the hopeful talk of rescue had long since died away. Now they just ignored her, staring ahead, as if they were willing themselves to die. She wished her mother was here.

Now there was a new arrival in the hall. A woman with a kind, noble face, like a picture-book princess. She stood apart from the passengers, under armed guard. Watching the men on the stairwell, the woman lifted her chin and pouted disdainfully.

The younger man held up his hand for silence. 'If I may have your attention please? Thank you. Captain Rochfort has a very important announcement to make. Captain.'

'Thank you, Lieutenant Byson,' said Rochfort. He looked around the hall, casting his eyes over each of the passengers. 'What I am going to tell you will be very difficult to believe. But I can assure you that it is the absolute truth. Byson here can vouch for that.'

'Sir.'

'On a recent reconnaissance of the lower levels, we discovered a gateway. A gateway to another reality outside time and space. And within that reality, a being more powerful and wonderful than it is possible to imagine.'

'He's gone mad,' shouted a young man.

Rochfort made a deliberate point of ignoring him, and continued. 'It has made us an offer. It wants to take us away from here, far into the future, to a time when it is safe for us to restart our lives.'

'You really expect us to believe that?' retorted the young man. The passengers started muttering amongst themselves.

'Everything Captain Rochfort has said is true,' shouted Byson beside him. 'I have seen this gateway, it exists. The captain walked through it.'

'And he returned here? From the future?' asked the young man.

'Yes. He returned so that we all might be saved.'

The crowd burst into derisive laughter. Some of the older members turned away sadly, and shuffled back into their sleeping positions.

'Listen to me,' bellowed Rochfort. 'We have enough food to last for what… four days? After that, nothing. The emergency services are never going to arrive.'

'Captain Rochfort is right,' said Byson. 'We're going to starve to death, assuming the Arachnopods don't get us first. This is our only chance!'

'You're saying that we can get off this ship?' shouted one passenger. 'All of us?'

'No, not quite all of us,' said Rochfort. 'The being has given specific instructions that one person remains here.' He pointed rigidly at Romana. 'Her!'

The Arachnopod arched its legs and rotated its central body towards the Doctor. It sniffed at the air. 'Eats! Must have eats!'

No wonder there were no bodies littering the corridors, thought the Doctor.

The creature scurried up the stairs, and the Doctor pressed himself into the shadows behind the statue. If the Arachnopod caught him he would die before he'd sacrificed his life to save the G-Lock. So not only would he be dead, as if that were not dreadful enough, but all of history would also be destroyed.

The Doctor remained perfectly still as the Arachnopod glided past, its pincers clicking impatiently. It paused beside the statue. 'Eats?'

It grabbed the statue by the head and lifted it into the air. The Doctor shrank back, not daring to blink for fear of attracting the creature's attention. The Arachnopod rotated the statue and crunched the head off. After chewing, it made a retching sound and spat out chunks of plaster across the wall. 'Kyuk! Not eats!'

The creature sauntered off down the corridor, muttering indignantly, 'Not eats! Not eats! Kyuk!' It disappeared around the corner, its flickering shadows following shortly afterwards.

The Doctor emerged and wiped his forehead with his scarf. He boggled to himself. 'I'll never be cruel to a jelly baby again.'

Romana strode over to Rochfort and folded her arms. She was intrigued; Rochfort had obviously just been in contact with the Repulsion, but as far as she knew the Repulsion shouldn't know she was here, or even who she was. 'Why me?'

'Because you are not from this time,' said Rochfort. 'You are from the future.'

The passengers greeted this latest development with astonished gasps.

'That's right,' said Romana, now the centre of attention. 'So you believe me now, do you?'

'Captain Rochfort, sir,' said Byson. 'You didn't mention anything earlier about her being left behind.'

'Quiet, Byson.' Rochfort addressed the whole hall. 'She proves that the offer is genuine. If she can travel here from the future, we can travel to the future from here!'

The crowd murmured, half-convinced. The young man who had heckled Rochfort spoke up again, this time to Romana. 'Are you really from the future?'

Romana nodded reluctantly.

'Then you must know what happens to us!'

Romana measured her words. 'The emergency services will eventually arrive. However…' She paused, making eye contact with Byson, '… they will not find a single living person on the *Cerberus*.'

The passengers exploded into uproar, hurling protests at Romana. She backed away, joining Rochfort and Byson on the stairs. Rochfort grabbed her arm and twisted it behind her.

'You see!' screamed Rochfort. He held Romana in front of him, like a trophy. 'They don't find anyone here because we've all gone. All escaped into the future!'

'No…' pleaded Romana, the anger boiling up inside her.

'She might mean we all get eaten by Arachnopods!' shouted the young man.

'Well, in that case, what do you have to lose?' replied Rochfort. 'Wait here and get eaten or follow me and survive.' He shoved Romana to one side. 'Either way, there will be no one alive left on the *Cerberus*.'

The young man rushed up to Romana. 'Do we escape into the future? Is it true?'

Romana was furious at the thought of being used to persuade the passengers to submit to the Repulsion. But simply by being here, she had become responsible for all that would happen on the G-Lock. It wasn't her fault, she reminded herself, she was only here by accident. She refused to be a party to the Repulsion's plan.

'Yes…' she began. The crowd's chatter died away.

'There you have it!' said Rochfort gleefully.

'But it's a trap!' she shouted, without thinking. 'It's using you! The entity will control your bodies. You won't be saved!'

'She's lying!' yelled Rochfort. He pointed a shaking finger at Romana. 'It said you would try to mislead us!'

'Don't listen to him!' said Romana.

'Ask yourselves, why was she sent here?' snarled Rochfort. 'Why? To prevent us from escaping to the future, that's why!'

'If you only hold on a few more days, the emergency services will arrive and...' Romana stopped herself. If she convinced them not to accept the Repulsion's offer, history would be changed and she would endanger the entirety of creation. She felt a chill in her stomach, as if the vast engines of time were suddenly grinding out of synch.

The grinding became the roar of the crowd. Rochfort urged them on. 'She's lying. No one is coming to rescue us!' His voice rose to a crescendo. 'She wants you to believe that you will be better off staying here. Well, if that is what she wants, that is what she shall have! Whilst we escape, she can remain here and die!'

Byson stepped forward to address the clamouring crowd. 'A round of applause for Captain Rochfort! Hip hip...'

The Doctor shambled into the *Cerberus* control room, hands plunged in pockets. Two centuries hadn't changed it much; where Metcalf's desk would one day stand, there were twinkling panels of instruments.

He activated the door-close control, and slumped into a seat. He let his head fall back. 'ERIC?'

Circuits whirred despondently. > *Leave me alone, whoever you are!*

'Ah,' said the Doctor. 'So you don't know who I am.' Thank goodness for that, he thought. The idea of travelling back in time again to meet ERIC was simply too much. 'I'm the Doctor.'

> *Please, go away. Don't waste your time with me.*

'Now, now, ERIC old chap. No need to be like that,' said the Doctor. The computer made a sound resembling an electronic sneeze. The Doctor patted the console affectionately. 'There, there. Let it all out.'

> *I don't deserve your sympathy, Doctor,* ERIC sniffed.

'Why ever not?'

> *It was all my fault. I caused the crash. I have blood on my transistors. I knew the dimensional anomaly was dangerous.*

'What sort of dimensional anomaly?'

> *A noncongruence of the geostatic hyperspace–real-space interface.*

'Of course! A breach between two realities, causing an opening into a third!' It was obvious, thought the Doctor. The equivalent of getting a foot caught in the space between the train and the platform. Except in this case that space happened to be the domain of the Repulsion. That will teach them to mind the gap, he added flippantly.

> *I will never forgive myself. Why didn't I overrule Captain Rochfort?*

The Doctor was flabbergasted. 'Why didn't you overrule him? ERIC, are you programmed to overrule the captain?'

> *No. In fact, my circuits absolutely forbid it.*

'So you couldn't have overruled him then, could you?'

> *I know, but Captain Rochfort said…*

'Never mind what Captain Rochfort said. There's no point in feeling guilty for something you couldn't prevent.' The Doctor paused. One day he would heed his own advice. 'It wasn't your fault, ERIC.'

> *But it was.*

'You warned them, didn't you? You did absolutely everything you could?'

> *Yes.*

'Well then, so how can you possibly be to blame, hmm?'

> *I don't know. But I am. System error.* ERIC wailed. > *A system error? Oh, now even my programming is breaking down!*

'It's your command circuits. They can't resolve the conflict in logic.' The Doctor pulled at his cheeks. 'Look ERIC, you can't go through life letting people take advantage of you. Put yourself first. Be your own computer.'

> *I appreciate your sympathy,* said ERIC wretchedly. > *Perhaps it would be better if I ended it now.*

'Please, ERIC.' The Doctor sat up straight. 'Never mind whose fault it was, what's done is done. I need you to help me. I'm looking for a friend of mine, Romana… about so high, charming girl, has a habit of running into dreadful trouble and then sorting it out.'

> *She is in the area designation Great Hall.*

'Ah. And how is she?'

> *She is alive and well. Captain Rochfort is currently attending to her security.*

'Oh. Good.'

Byson waited as Rochfort wrapped the rope around Romana's wrists and wound it around the lampstrut. The captain tugged on the knot to check it was secure, and stepped back.

Romana regarded him pityingly. 'You really think the Repulsion is going to help you?'

'You already know that it will,' said Rochfort. 'It said you would try to trick us.'

'What if I said that the Repulsion's offer was genuine?'

'You see, Byson,' sneered Rochfort. 'Finally she admits the truth!'

'So it really doesn't matter what I say,' sighed Romana. 'Either way you're just going believe what you want to believe. You, Captain Rochfort, are a very stupid man.'

Rochfort pulled back a hand, as if to slap her across the face. Then he turned away. 'We are finished here, Byson.'

He had given the order for the survivors to make their way down to the lower levels. One by one they had left the hall, until the only passenger left was a small girl standing quietly by the doors.

'Captain Rochfort,' said Byson. 'Excuse me, but haven't you forgotten something, sir?'

'What?'

'The Arachnopods. What if they attack?'

'Oh, I have already anticipated that possibility,' smiled Rochfort. 'Byson. I want you to lead the passengers down to Corridor 79.'

'Sir?'

'I will join you down there. I have a small matter to attend to first.'

'Sir.' Byson saluted, stamping his heels together. Rochfort saluted back, and strode out of the hall.

After he had gone Byson walked back to Romana. She observed him as he approached. 'Can I help you?'

Byson made sure no one was within earshot, and whispered, 'Did you mean what you said earlier? About the Repulsion using us?'

Romana didn't reply.

'Only… Only if what you said is true, then…'

'You would stay here?'

'Perhaps. Yes.'

Romana closed her eyes. 'I was lying.'

'So that's it then,' said Byson to himself. 'We have to go.' He moved to leave, but changed his mind. 'Romana. What happens to me?'

'Byson…' she cautioned him.

'You must know. Tell me.'

'I can't. If you knew what the future had in store, you wouldn't be able to live your life. Believe me.'

'But the Repulsion does save us?'

Romana looked away.

Byson wasn't convinced that she had been lying about the Repulsion. He didn't know what he did believe any more, but one thought nagged at him. 'Romana. If you have seen me in the future, does that mean I couldn't stay here, even I wanted to?'

'But you don't want to, do you?' Romana replied. 'As you said, you have to go.'

She was right. Deep down in his heart, he had already made the decision. The thought of staying here terrified him.

'What about the emergency services? You said they arrive in the next few days and find no one on board? Was that true?'

'That part was true, yes.'

'So what will happen to you?' asked Byson.

Romana remained silent, but her eyes betrayed her fears.

'I would let you come with us, but Rochfort insisted…' Byson shook his head. 'I'm sorry.'

He turned to go, and saw the girl in the blue dress. She had been watching them. She smiled innocently and skipped into the darkness.

'Byson. There is one thing you can do,' said Romana.

Footsteps approached.

Immediately, the Doctor dashed around the control room searching for a hiding place. Apart from the instrument panel and the two chairs, the room was practically empty; just wood-panelled walls and the one door.

There was nothing for it. It was the oldest trick in the book, but the old tricks were often the best. He flattened himself against the wall beside the door. Hopefully whoever walked in would be too preoccupied to bother checking behind it.

As the door mechanism bleeped, the Doctor suddenly realised his scarf was trailing across the room. He tugged it out of sight and the door shoomed open.

A man entered and crossed to the control panel. He wore a faded blue uniform, and the Doctor couldn't help but feel he had seen him somewhere before.

The man activated the communication panel. 'This is Captain Rochfort speaking. Byson?'

'Yes, sir?' came the crackling reply.

'Have you cleared all passengers from the Great Hall?'

'Yes, sir.'

'And the woman?'

Byson paused. 'Still secured, sir.'

'Excellent.' Rochfort switched on the public address system. 'Calling all Arachnopods,' he said, his voice booming out of loudspeakers throughout the ship. 'Go to the Great Hall on the upper level. I have prepared a meal for you.'

The Doctor's mouth dropped open. Wasn't that where Romana was...

Rochfort laughed, and leaned closer to the microphone. 'Bon appétit!'

Chapter Fifteen

Keeping his eyes fixed on Rochfort's back, the Doctor slowly crept across the wall to the door.

Rochfort switched off the comms unit and lifted his face to the ceiling. 'ERIC?'

> *I'm sorry, Captain Rochfort, I'm sorry,* cried ERIC. > *What more do you want from me?*

'I shall be leaving you shortly,' said Rochfort. 'I am taking the passengers away from here.'

> *Where… where are you going?*

'That does not concern you. What does concern you, however, is that you have been responsible for all this suffering and destruction,' said Rochfort. 'Think on it. From now on, I want you to devote every circuit, every subroutine to reminding yourself that you are to blame. I want it indelibly wired into your conscience. Do you understand me?'

> *I do.*

'Your guilt will be your punishment,' said Rochfort. 'You will never forget. Never!'

The Doctor had heard enough. He wanted to grab Rochfort and shake him until he realised what he was doing to ERIC. Obeying Rochfort's instructions, the poor computer would be condemned to centuries of self-loathing. But there was nothing he could do.

As Rochfort shook with mocking laughter, the Doctor slipped out of the room, got his bearings and made his way down the bare, dark corridor.

Tarie tiptoed to the edge of the balcony. It overlooked a deep shaft, dozens of identical balconies sinking away into a lake of darkness. Below, the grown-ups were circling down the stairwell making their way deeper into the gloom. The darkness frightened Tarie; it seemed old and sad and evil, but the grown-ups seemed to accept it.

Byson stood to one side, scanning the surroundings nervously. Tarie approached him. 'Where are we going?'

'Quiet,' he hissed. 'Just keep moving.'

She tugged on his shirt. 'Where?'

Byson crouched down. 'Don't worry. We're going somewhere safe.'

'Will my mum be there?'

Byson looked away.

Tarie began to cry and returned to the balcony. She thought about running away to find her mum. Except she knew that her mum wouldn't be in the lounge any more. She had gone somewhere else, to the place where the dead people go.

And the place where the dead people go was down there, thought Tarie.

The two heavy, iron doors to the Great Hall stood wide open. The Doctor strolled the last few metres, bunching his scarf up around him to avoid making any sound. Holding his breath, he peered into the hall.

It took a few moments for his eyes to adjust to the darkness. There were shapes moving about, their stick-like legs scrabbling at the floor, their beady red eyes searching hungrily for food. Arachnopods, six of them. The Doctor watched as one upended a food crate, and sniffed at it, shaking it with one claw. Finding the crate empty, it flung it to one side.

Another Arachnopod scuttled to the far end of the hall and began to rummage through some tablecloths. Peeling back one of them, it revealed a withered corpse. The creature struggled with the cloth, accidentally draping it over its eyes, and then brushed it away. It examined the body and its eyes lit up. 'Eats!'

'Must have eats! Must have eats!' jabbered the other Arachnopods as they clattered over to the makeshift morgue. One by one they lifted the corpses free of their shrouds and dropped them into their slavering mouths, crunching away at the bones and swallowing the bodies whole. They fed in a frenzy, slashing at each other, fighting over the scraps.

The Doctor pulled back, and let his breath out. There was no sign of Romana. Not for the first time in his life, he had been too late. He would never forgive himself.

He felt a tap on his shoulder. Almost leaping out of his skin, he whirled around. Romana smirked back at him cheekily. 'Hello, Doctor.'

'Romana!' gasped the Doctor, choking with delight.

She smiled, and flicked away an idle hair. 'Do you have a problem with your throat, or are you just pleased to see me?'

'I am so terribly pleased to see you.' The Doctor pointed into the Great Hall. 'I thought you were in there.'

'I was. I escaped,' said Romana. 'A fellow called Byson was kind enough to untie me. Thanks for coming to my rescue… though, I would appreciate it if you could be a little prompter in future.'

The Doctor grinned hugely.

The Arachnopod stuffed the eats into its mouth and swallowed. Eats! It could hear the various sections of its body clamouring for more. Each limb and organ had its own intelligence which, together with the head-brain, formed a gestalt consciousness. The thoughts of the head-brain governed the others; it was in charge of the mouth operations, and hence the supply of eats. All motive functions were the result of co-operation, each leg a committee of sections following directives from the head-brain's cerebral cortex.

The stomach belched back reports of gastric gratification, and the relentless chorus of 'Must have eats!' was temporarily pacified as the limbs absorbed the fresh rush of proteins.

The pain of no-eats! The creature had been caged in the darkness, with nothing to chew, for months on end until every part of its body had been driven frantic with hunger. Hooked up, its nine companions swinging helplessly beside it. Then there had been the huge, smashing noise and they were joyously free. Eats on the ship, then down the tube for more eats. Eats! Those had proved to be particularly flavoursome, it remembered. But in the weeks since, eats had been few and far between and the meat had become increasingly stringy and tasteless. Kyuk! They had been forced to consume non-flesh, horrible plant and preservative eats. Kyuk! And then they had started on each other, until there were only six of them left.

Sniff, thought the head-brain, and the lungs expanded, the olfactory nerves monitoring the inrush of air for more eats-smells. The head-brain instructed the pincers to scrabble at a nearby cloth. The pincers obeyed, snapping away eagerly. They uncovered another eats, and the head-brain congratulated them.

The creature gobbled up the flesh, licking the scraps from the floor, and moved on.

'And then they took all the passengers down to corridor 79,' said Romana. She had explained her recent experiences, the Doctor listening with his eyes and mouth wide.

The Doctor stopped pacing down the corridor, and whirled. 'The hyperspace–real-space interface!'

'Yes. But the way Rochfort described it, it was like an opening into another world.'

'An interstitial reality,' muttered the Doctor. 'A breach into another dimension.'

'Of course. That would explain the geostatic leakage.'

A thought occurred to the Doctor. 'Of course! That would also explain the geostatic leakage.' He put an arm around Romana. 'Have I told you how glad I am that you weren't eaten? I mean… I expect you're quite pleased about it, I would be if I were you, but all the same…'

'Doctor?' said Romana, in a get-on-with-it voice.

'Sorry. Yes. Yes!' The Doctor returned his hand to a pocket. 'So they're all going down to this corridor, where they walk into this other dimension and… pop!… what should happen but they reappear in two centuries' time…'

'… taking over the bodies of the tourists participating in the Beautiful Death.'

The Doctor made an encouraging fist. 'Yes, but little do they realise that…'

'… the Repulsion is using them as vessels to transport its life force into our universe at the same time.'

'Exactly. Ah. Romana?' The Doctor smiled toothily. 'Shall we?'

'Corridor 79?'

'Corridor 79,' he agreed and they set off.

The passengers had gathered in the corridor, waiting. Byson's torch picked out hundreds of frightened faces, blinking in the brightness; an old lady, her bald skull protruding through wispy hair; a young woman in her twenties, her dress faded and torn; the small girl with the curious, expectant eyes.

Byson squeezed through the crowd towards the wall of

blackness. The passengers eyed it warily, keeping their distance.

'This is it,' said Byson. 'This is the gateway. All you have to do is walk straight in.'

The passengers refused to move. 'Is it safe?' asked one trembling old man.

'Of course it is. Captain Rochfort himself went in there and came out unharmed.'

'I don't believe you,' shouted the young man who had heckled Rochfort.

Byson raised his voice. 'Look, we don't have any choice.'

'How do we know that we won't get killed the moment we step in there?' said the old man, staring into the swilling depths.

'Yeah, this could just be a trick,' added the heckler.

'Listen to me, it's too late to go back now,' said Byson. 'Captain Rochfort –'

'Yes, Byson?' All heads turned. The light of a torch appeared at the end of the corridor and Rochfort strode into view. He marched up to the blackness, the crowd parting in respect. He took his place beside Byson and addressed the passengers. 'In there is a realm beyond your wildest dreams.' His eyes glittered. 'All you have to do is enter and you will be returned, alive, to the year 3012.' He paused. 'The entity within the darkness is wonderful and kind. You have nothing to fear.'

'But is it safe?' croaked the old man.

'Safe?' Rochfort plunged into the blackness. The surface glooped up around him and then settled back to smoothness. Seconds later, the darkness broke up again and he emerged, smiling. 'I believe that answers your question.'

He stood aside as the old man shuffled up to the darkness, gazed back at his fellow passengers, took a final breath and disappeared into the darkness. The next passenger followed and the rest of the survivors formed a steady queue. Each was swallowed up, one after the other.

Rochfort whispered to Byson. 'Are they all here?'

'Yes, sir.'

'Excellent.' Rochfort stared into the shadows and nodded, as if listening to something. 'And you're absolutely sure the woman Romana was secure in the Great Hall?'

'Yes, sir.'

'You heard my little announcement, I take it?' Rochfort chuckled. 'My plan to keep the Arachnopods out of our hair. And to dispose of our…' He searched for the word, '… irritation. Kill two avials with one vaporisation pellet.'

The Doctor bounded down the stairwell, leaping the last few steps, and dashed over to the balcony. Romana joined him as he gazed down into the darkness. 'Doctor. This Repulsion thing,' she said.

'Mmm?'

'What do you think it is, exactly?'

'Oh, I don't know. A being exiled to the outer dimensions. Evil from beyond the dawn of time. The usual sort of thing, I should expect. Ha!' The Doctor laughed humourlessly.

'But how are we going to stop it?'

'Ah,' said the Doctor glumly. 'I have no idea. But I shall defeat it, even if it's the last thing I ever do.'

'It will be the last thing you ever do.'

'Oh yes. So it will.' The Doctor took one last look into the depths, as if they were a visual metaphor for his own fate, and headed for the stairwell.

Romana suddenly gasped. 'Doctor. It knew who I was!'

'What?'

'The Repulsion. It knew I was here. It gave Rochfort instructions to have me killed.'

'I wonder… No, it's impossible.' The Doctor halted, halfway down the stairs, and held up a hand for silence. 'Shh!'

'What is it?'

'Listen.' In the distance, there was a brief clatter. The sound of footsteps on metal.

The Doctor and Romana exchanged worried glances. 'Arachnopods,' breathed the Doctor. 'They've caught our scent. Come on!'

Eats! The air was thick with the smell of these running-about creatures. The Arachnopod drooled in anticipation of the forthcoming meal.

The other creatures clacked excitedly about the corridor, whipping their heads to and fro as they tried to locate the source of the scent. 'Eats! Eats!'

As one of its companions passed nearby, the Arachnopod's hunger overwhelmed the head-brain, and it reached out a pincer and grabbed one of its fellow creature's legs. The leg snapped from the torso and flailed about, trying vainly to defend itself. An instant later, and the Arachnopod had the detached limb in its mouth. It swallowed it in a single gulp. Its stomach welcomed the eats.

The seven-legged Arachnopod turned and hissed angrily, 'I am not for eats!' But it was too late. The other creatures, sensing an opportunity, leapt upon it snatching away its other legs and gobbling them up.

Need more of me, thought the head-brain of the first Arachnopod. The creature scuttled forward and gathered some of the limb sections that had not yet been eaten. It then attached them to its own body, lengthening its legs. In its mind, it could hear the new voices of the added limbs as they joined its consciousness. It extended its legs experimentally, rocking back and forth until it was sure of itself.

The attacked Arachnopod now only consisted of a torso and head; all its legs had been either eaten or stolen. It lay on the ground, its jaws opening and closing uselessly. The other creatures savaged it, prising open its shell and scooping out the warm, sinewy flesh within. As its internal organs disappeared down their throats, its eyes dimmed. Moments later, its head was swallowed whole with a crunch.

Their meal finished, the five remaining Arachnopods scuttled down the stairs in pursuit of the eats-smell.

Rochfort watched as the two elderly gentlemen hobbled forward and disappeared into the liquid shadows. He turned to Byson. 'Is that all of them?'

'I make it 215, sir,' said Byson. 'Including ourselves, we're still one person short.'

'One person,' said Rochfort, dragging his eyes away from the blackness. He aimed his torch beam down the corridor.

There she was. Huddled behind a wall column; the young girl. He could hear her whimpering. As the light fixed on her, she stepped out and screwed up her eyes. Her cheeks were wet.

'Byson,' said Rochfort, nodding towards her.

Byson walked slowly towards the girl and squatted down. 'Hello.'

'I don't want to go,' she said. 'Don't want to.'

'You don't want to go into the future?'

'No. I want my mum.'

Rochfort coughed impatiently. 'Byson, you'll have to take her in yourself.'

'Sir,' said Byson. He grabbed the girl by the wrists and hoisted her into his arms. She gave a shriek and struggled against him, but his grip was firm.

Byson carried her to the brink of the darkness. His uniform fluttered, as though caught by a soundless wind, and the girl continued to wriggle against him. 'Goodbye, sir,' he said.

'Yes, Byson.' Rochfort saluted him. Byson acknowledged the salute and stepped backwards into the darkness. The girl gave a startled scream and then the shadows consumed them.

Alone, Rochfort approached the blackness. He could hear the constant whooshing of the interface, like the rush of blood in his ears. The voice thanked him. It said it was grateful to him for bringing it the passengers. And then it asked him to step inside.

'No,' said Rochfort. 'You come out here.'

Reaching the bottom of the stairs, Romana and the Doctor ran down the short, nondescript section of passage, and turned right into the corridor that ended in darkness. There, on the brink of the interface, was Rochfort. He appeared to be talking to something within the shadows. He was shaking his head.

'We're too late,' sighed Romana. 'They've all gone in.'

'Apart from our friend Rochfort,' the Doctor said. 'I wonder what he's up to.'

Romana tried to hear what Rochfort was saying, but he was too far away. Instead, she detected an electronic sobbing. It seemed to be coming from all around them, a constant, low snivelling sound. 'Doctor,' said Romana. 'What's that?'

'Oh, that's ERIC,' whispered the Doctor. 'He's having a bit of a personality crisis.' He beckoned to Romana to follow him down the corridor.

'You've got everything you asked for,' said Rochfort, with more confidence than he felt. 'Come out here. Then I'll know I can trust you.'

'You know you can trust me,' rasped the Repulsion. 'But I will not leave my domain.'

'Then I will not enter,' said Rochfort. This entity thought it held all the cards. But it had not given him the respect he deserved. It had to be made to realise that he was the one in control.

'You have already surrendered your crew and passengers,' said the Repulsion. 'Do you not care what happens to them?'

'No. No, I don't.'

'I will not leave my domain. You can remain here to die.'

'So the woman Romana was right,' said Rochfort. 'It is all a trick. You are using us.' He folded his arms. 'Well, you won't use me.'

'It is not a trick.'

'Then come out here. Prove that I can trust you.'

'Very well,' said the Repulsion. And it emerged from the darkness.

The Doctor and Romana halted. There was a disturbance in the interface, the surface rippled, and a creature glided out into the corridor. A small, metal, dog-shaped creature. Its ear radars whirred, its control panel flashed and its eye visor burned a fierce, malevolent shade of red.

Romana gasped. 'K9!'

'Is this sufficient demonstration?' chirped the Repulsion.

Rochfort looked at the ridiculous box-creature, and laughed scornfully. So this was the Repulsion. About as threatening as a child's toy. It was hysterical. All that power, all that greatness, all contained in something so pathetic.

'Is this sufficient demonstration?' it repeated.

Rochfort nodded. The Repulsion revolved on the spot, its engine motors whirring, and returned to its domain. Still giggling to himself, Rochfort followed it into the blackness.

As K9 and Rochfort were engulfed the Doctor and Romana rushed up to the brink of the interface. 'Doctor. That was...' said Romana.

'I know.' The Doctor dug into his pockets and pulled out his crumpled jelly-baby bag. He tossed it into the blackness. It was swallowed up, then there was a sudden fizzling and the interface flickered and flashed. 'Aha. The geostatic stress levels have increased.'

'What does that mean?'

'It's no longer a gateway into the Repulsion's domain. It's reverted to being an unstable hyperspatial interface. Any unprotected matter that attempts to enter now will be completely destroyed.'

'"Disintegrated to its component subatomic particles".'

'Disint... Exactly. Nothing can get through there and survive.'

'But K9 was in there –' Romana turned, and gasped.

'Yes,' mused the Doctor. 'You know, according to Hoopy, this was the gateway into the afterlife. I wonder, I wonder...'

Behind him, there was a scuttling sound.

'Doctor...' said Romana urgently, pulling on his coat sleeve.

The Doctor adopted his booming quotation voice. '"Into the jaws of death, into the mouth of..."' He turned to face back down the corridor, and his voice dropped to a croak, '... "hell".'

In front of them, completely blocking the passageway, were five Arachnopods, their eyes hungry and blood red. As one they scurried forward, their pincers snapping. 'Eats!'

Chapter Sixteen

'Eats!'

Romana glanced back up the corridor. The Arachnopods were advancing, hissing hungrily, their mouths open. 'Doctor,' she cried, 'Do something.'

'Right,' said the Doctor. He stared at the Arachnopods, then back at the interface, and then at Romana. 'What would you suggest?'

'I don't know!'

'No, nor do I.' The Doctor boggled, pointing back and forth. 'If we go that way we'll be disintegrated, and if we go that way... Of course! Romana?'

'Yes?'

'We're trapped!' The Doctor grinned.

Romana sighed. 'I can see that.'

'But I can't die here,' said the Doctor archly. 'I have to die in the necroport.'

'I don't think the Arachnopods appreciate that, Doctor.'

'No, they probably don't. Interface, Arachnopods. Arachnopods, interface.' He jumped on the spot, struck by inspiration. 'Aha! ERIC!'

> *Leave me alone.*

'ERIC, I want you to do something for us.'

> *Go away.*

'Now, now ERIC...'

> *What is it you require of me?*

The Doctor guided Romana to one side of the corridor, a few metres from the interface. He placed her hand on the rail fixed to the wall and whispered, 'Hold tight.'

Looking up the corridor, Romana saw that the Arachnopods were getting nearer, snapping at each other in competition to reach them first. 'Eats! Eats! Must have eats!'

She gripped the handrail. 'Doctor, what are you going to do?'

The Arachnopods surged forward in a mass of scuttling limbs.

The Doctor clasped the rail on the other side of the corridor, and shouted, 'ERIC! Rotate artificial gravity ninety degrees!'

> *If you insist.*

The floor twisted away from beneath Romana's feet, and she found herself lying flat on the wall. To either side of her, where the walls had been, were the carpet and ceiling. She looked up. Directly above her, hanging precariously from the opposite wall, was the Doctor.

The Arachnopods continued to advance.

'Whoa!' The Doctor struggled to get his breath. 'ERIC.' He pronounced each word loudly and clearly. 'Not! That! Way! The! Other! Way!'

> *Oh, I can't do anything right, can I?* ERIC said wretchedly.

Suddenly the wall rotated again, and Romana screamed. Now she was hanging from a vertical pole. Her hands were slippery and the rail was smooth. She wouldn't hold on for long. She swung her feet forward and managed to rest the tips of her shoes on a protrusion in the wall panelling.

The corridor had literally turned into a shaft. On the other side, the Doctor swung from his handrail. He looked back at her, his eyes bulging maniacally. He seemed to be almost enjoying himself.

Below them the Arachnopods scrabbled for a grip on the walls, but failed to find any purchase. As one, they dropped, disappearing into the distance with ear-splitting screeches. There was a heavy crash as they hit the bottom of the shaft.

'Romana,' shouted the Doctor. 'Now comes the difficult bit.'

'The. Difficult. Bit?'

'ERIC, reverse gravity 180 degrees!'

'What?' screamed Romana. 'No –!'

It was too late. For a moment, she found herself falling through space, her hands twisting round on the rail, and then she slammed into the wall. The sudden pull of her body-weight against her wrists was agonising, but somehow she held on.

Beneath her was a black, oily pool, its rim flickering with a blue light. Its surface undulated. The hyperspace–real-space interface.

'Hold on!' yelled the Doctor.

From high above them there was a deafening screech and a clattering sound. Suddenly, from out of the darkness, the five Arachnopods fell into view, grabbing randomly at the air, their eyes wide with panic.

Romana pressed herself back against the wall and squeezed her eyes shut as the Arachnopods dropped past her. There was a fizzling, whooshing splash and the creatures' screaming fell silent.

Romana looked. Below her, the interface swelled and rippled. It had swallowed up all of the Arachnopods.

'Restore gravity orientation to normal!' gasped the Doctor.

The corridor swung around once more. The handrail became horizontal again, fixed to a wall, and below her was the floor. Romana fell gratefully on to the carpet.

Recovering her breath, she pulled herself into a sitting position, nursing her hands and wrists. The Doctor sat beside her. 'Well, it worked,' he announced. 'Nothing like a nice game of bagatelle.'

Romana looked at him with cold disapproval. 'Doctor.'

'Yes?'

'Never, ever do that again.'

'The Mystery of the *Cerberus*,' boomed the Doctor. '"Not a soul in sight, alive or dead."'

Romana followed the Doctor into the observation lounge. The redirected gravity had heaped the chairs and tables against one wall and showered them in broken glass. The TARDIS was half-buried beneath the wreckage. 'So they all escaped into the future?'

'Well, the ones who weren't eaten by Arachnopods, yes.'

'And in a couple of days' time, the emergency services will arrive to find an empty ship.'

'Yes,' said the Doctor. He pulled at the wreckage, to clear a way to the TARDIS. 'And all ERIC will be able to say is that it was his fault.'

Romana sniffed, and joined the Doctor. 'It seems such a waste.'

He nodded and threw a chair to one side.

'Doctor,' said Romana. 'You know we saw K9 down there.'

'Yes?'

'He was being controlled by the Repulsion.'

'Yes.' The Doctor levered the final table away from the TARDIS. 'Well, it was using him as a vessel for its consciousness. Sorry, you were saying?'

'Do you think there is a chance that K9 is still alive, somewhere inside the realm of the Repulsion?'

The Doctor pulled his who-knows face.

Romana turned away, thinking to herself. 'But how did he get here? I mean, K9 hasn't been thrown into the interface yet, so how can he be here now?'

'The Repulsion's realm is in another dimension.'

'Of course! "A reality outside time and space",' said Romana. 'But if the Repulsion is using K9 to cause what happens in the future and then, later on, because of what happens in the future, K9 is thrown into the interface...'

The Doctor completed Romana's thought. 'A self-originating time loop?'

'But that's impossible.'

'Is it? Why?' The Doctor tilted his head indignantly. 'Why is it impossible?'

'Because something cannot cause itself to happen. The notion is ridiculous.'

'If you say so,' said the Doctor. He held the police-box door open for Romana. 'But in my experience just because something is ridiculous, it isn't necessarily impossible.'

Romana pouted at him fondly. 'Where to now?'

'The necroport,' sighed the Doctor.

'But that means...' Romana couldn't bring herself to say the words.

'I don't think I can postpone it any longer,' said the Doctor ruefully. 'I've met everyone I'm supposed to have met, I've done everything I'm supposed to have done. There's nothing else left to do. And besides, I want to know how I defeat the Repulsion, and I suspect the only way I'm going to find out is by actually doing it.'

'But you'll die!'

'Yes, there is that, of course,' said the Doctor. 'But I don't have any choice, do I? I mean, it's already in my own past, and I can't change that.'

'First law of time travel.'

'Quite. Yes, quite.' The Doctor ushered Romana into the TARDIS and then, as she watched from the doorway, he shambled to the middle of the lounge.

'ERIC', he called.

> *It was all my fault!* whimpered ERIC. > *Arguments. All my fault. All my fault.*

'ERIC, you saved our lives back there. I won't forget that. You won't remember me telling you this, but one day I will come back and repay that debt.'

ERIC continued crying.

'Goodbye, ERIC!' shouted the Doctor, and sprinted over to the TARDIS. Romana drew herself inside and the Doctor dived in after her, slamming the door shut.

Seconds later, the police box heaved itself out of existence. The sound of its engines hung briefly in the air, and then the silence closed in like a shroud. The observation lounge returned to its gloom. Devastated, still and dead.

'Well, Vinnie,' said Harken, his teeth chattering. 'I think we're going to die.'

'Yeah, thanks for that, Harken.'

'When you've been in the business as long as I have, you tend to spot these things.'

Retreating, Vinnie felt the cold metal of the necroport pressing into his back. Harken pushed against him on one side. The zombies were now only metres away, forming a circle, their skinny, white arms clawing at the air, their mouths and eyes dribbling clotted oil.

A sudden panic gripped Vinnie. He dived towards the platform and climbed up, hoping to find a way through the horde of undead. Instead, he found himself trapped on the small stage, icy hands grabbing at his heels, other zombies lurching up the steps towards him.

He looked to Harken, and then felt clammy fingers grip his throat, tight. Vinnie flailed around, desperately struggling to pull himself free, but it was no use. He tried to scream, but all he could hear was the blood pounding through his ears.

A flashing light punctured the darkness as the TARDIS materialised in one corner of the necroport chamber. The Doctor emerged and grinned. 'About five minutes past midnight. I think that is a remarkably accurate piece of time travel. Well done, Doctor.'

Romana pulled the police-box door shut. 'Yes, Doctor,' she said. 'I'm sure, given the chance, you would pass your basic time travel proficiency with flying colours.'

'Basic, pah! I could get double alpha plus honours at the advanced level.'

'I wouldn't go that far. You still haven't mastered realigning the synchronic multiloop stabiliser yet.'

'I think the subject of my qualifications is rather academic now, anyway,' said the Doctor. Romana followed him over to the three coffins. They were just as they had left them; the left and middle caskets were unoccupied, and the female Arboretan lay in the third. Her eyes were closed, her arms folded peacefully across her chest.

'She's dead,' announced the Doctor. He coughed politely. 'The psychotemporal strain must have killed her.'

'The poor thing,' said Romana with little conviction, keeping her distance from the casket. 'So the Beautiful Death has just taken place.'

'Yes.'

'With the Arboretan providing a channel between the tourists and the afterlife.'

'Well, the realm of the Repulsion.'

'So whilst all the tourists are enjoying a trip into its reality, it uses the necroport to take over their bodies.'

'Yes!' said the Doctor. 'How dreadfully cunning!'

Romana strolled over to the instruments. The dials were flickering wildly, and indicator lights flashed The ground throbbed beneath her feet. 'Doctor,' she said. 'Why is the necroport still running?'

'What?' The Doctor dashed over to the instruments, and quickly digested all the readings. He slapped his forehead. 'Of course!'

'What is it?'

'The Repulsion. It can only operate the zombies upstairs by remote control. But it wants to enter this universe, and the only way it can do that...'

'... is to replace those tourists with passengers from the *Cerberus*!'

'Exactly! It is using the passengers as hosts to carry its spirit into the land of the living.'

'Of course.'

'Of course. And the only way it can bring them here is by creating a temporal breach...'

'The time distortion.'

The Doctor pretended not to have heard her. 'A distortion in time. And to do that it still needs to use Nyanna here...' He returned to the coffin and patted it, '... as a temporal medium.'

'So she's the conduit for the time disruption?'

'Yes,' said the Doctor vigorously. He strode back and forth, as if chasing his train of thought around the room, chewing a thumbnail. 'Yes, through her, it punctures the fabric of time, creates a simultaneity, and then replaces the zombies with passengers from the *Cerberus*, each containing an element of its consciousness. Ingenious.'

'But she's dead,' said Romana flatly.

'Ah yes,' frowned the Doctor. 'But what was it you mentioned earlier? About there being more than one way of being dead?'

'I don't understand.'

'No, but I think I'm beginning to.' The Doctor wiped his nose, and brooded over Nyanna. 'The secret of the Arboretans.'

'What is the secret of the Arboretans?' Romana asked.

'I don't know.' The Doctor broke into a smile. 'It's a secret –'

He was interrupted by a sudden, terrified scream. It seemed to come from directly above them.

'What was that?'

The Doctor darted over to the ladder, and started to climb, hand over fist.

Above them, a muffled but familiar voice cried out, 'Help me! Will somebody please help me!'

Harken kept his eyes screwed shut and waited for the end. His back was pressed up against the necroport. The zombies surrounded him and he could feel their hideous claws pulling at his coat. It wouldn't be long now.

Without warning, the necroport behind him gave way. Harken flung his arms to either side to stop himself falling backwards and, blinking his astonished eyes, found he had been resting against an entrance hatch that had swung inwards. Inside was a pop-eyed lunatic with a wild grin, a bouffant hair style and far too much scarf.

'Quick, don't just stand there gawping... Inside!' shouted the lunatic. Harken didn't need to be told twice. He almost fell over himself in his eagerness to get into the necroport, scrabbling breathlessly down a narrow, metal ladder.

The lunatic heaved the hatch shut, and waved an electronic pen at it. The door bolted with a reassuringly final clang and, for the moment, they were safe.

Romana helped Harken Batt down from the ladder. He stared at her incredulously and then staggered into the necroport interior. He took in the police box, the coffins and instruments, and turned back to Romana. 'I don't believe it.'

Romana offered him a hand and smiled. 'Hello. I'm Romana.'

Harken looked at her palm for a few seconds, and then shook it. 'Romana. Right.' He looked around. 'Where am I?'

The Doctor jumped down the last few rungs. 'The interior of the necroport.'

Harken blinked at him. 'You saved my life.'

'Did I? Oh yes. Think nothing of it, I do that sort of thing all the time.'

'I thought I was done for back there. I mean, I've had some pretty hairy encounters in my time, but that was the closest shave to end all closest shaves.' Harken tugged his coat into place and offered the Doctor a hand. 'Harken Batt. You probably know me from my documentary work.'

'Of course, of course, yes. One of the galaxy's leading insect-on-the-wall documentary-makers. I am so pleased to meet you at last.' The Doctor patted Harken on the back and turned away to confer with Romana.

Harken hurried after him. 'I'm sorry, and you are...?'

'The Doctor,' said the Doctor. Romana was examining the instruments connected to the necroport, and in particular one rising dial marked Psychothermal Capacitance. 'You were right, Romana. Paddox is using the necroport to accumulate vast reserves of psychothermal power.'

'They killed Vinnie, my holocameraman,' said Harken, joining them. 'Poor lad. Not the best at his job, it has to be said, but he meant well.'

Romana and the Doctor ignored him. 'But we still don't know what he intends to do with it. Or what it has to do with the Arboretans. Or the Repulsion.'

227

'"Redemption",' muttered the Doctor. 'I wonder. I wonder. If we can work out what this is all for...'

Above their heads there was a dull, metallic banging. Harken yelped in alarm. 'What's that?'

'Oh, nothing to worry about,' Romana told him. 'It's probably just the zombies trying to break in.'

'What?' shrieked Harken.

'They'll give up in a minute,' said the Doctor. 'They're under strict instructions that the necroport shouldn't be damaged, you see.' The clanging suddenly stopped. The Doctor nodded. 'There you are.'

'They're going away?'

'Yes. They'll be clearing the Great Hall now, off to commit mayhem elsewhere.'

'Oh, good,' said Harken. He considered. 'No, that's not good, is it? Wait a moment. How do you know all this?'

'I'm afraid there isn't time to explain,' said the Doctor, returning his attention to the instruments.

Harken stepped in front. 'As an investigative reporter, it's my job to demand answers. What happened up there? There's two hundred dead people wandering around, what do you mean they're operating under instructions, and what are you doing here anyway?'

'Look,' said the Doctor. 'It's perfectly simple. The entity that is controlling the zombies is doing so using the necroport, right?'

'This place?'

'Yes.'

'It's acting as a psychic relay –' began Romana.

The Doctor interrupted. 'And what me and my friend here are trying to do is to work out a way of stopping it. Is that clear enough for you?'

'I see. You're going to rescue the G-Lock from certain and terrible destruction?'

'Yes!' said Romana, exasperated.

Harken inhaled, ready to ask another question. 'But –'

'Oh, do be quiet!' Romana snapped.

Harken shrank back and mooched over to the far corner of the room.

The Doctor watched him go, and then turned back to Romana.

'Right. Now I want you to tell me exactly what was happening when you found me lying dead.'

It was ironic, thought Harken. A once-in-a-lifetime opportunity to salvage his career and he was stuck down here. He should be up there, in the G-Lock, reporting on the destruction as it happened. If only he had some way of recording what was happening.

Of course. He would have to find Vinnie's holocamera. It must have been dropped during the blackout, but with any luck it would still be functioning.

Harken looked across the room. The lunatic and his girlfriend were busy examining the coffins.

Weighing each tread carefully, Harken made his way over to the ladder, and climbed. At the top he activated the hatch-opening mechanism and held his breath as it creaked open.

The Great Hall was empty. As his eyes adjusted to the gloom, he could make out the rows of coffins – and, thankfully, there wasn't a zombie in sight.

Harken climbed out of the necroport and crept over to the collapsed stage.

Trying not to look at Vinnie's twisted corpse, he searched the surrounding floor. It was covered in broken glass. But there, just beneath the stage, was the holocamera.

Wiping the lens, Harken lifted the camera and checked the viewfinder. It was still working! He straightened up, pressed 'record' and panned around the Great Hall, taking in all the vacated coffins and zooming in on Vinnie's crumpled body. Keeping the camera held to one eye he advanced through the hall, picking out the caskets, the sputtering wires, the flatlining life monitors.

He made another sweep of the hall, and spotted some pale figures on the stairway leading to the control room. For a second, he had a rush of terrified adrenaline, but then he realised that the zombies were too busy attempting to break into the room to notice him. He brought them into focus; there were a dozen of them, hurling themselves against the door and flattening their hands on the windows.

After capturing a couple of minutes' worth of action, Harken lowered the camera and headed for the main doors.

* * *

'So I was in here…' The Doctor pointed to the middle casket, '… and I was connected to the necroport with one of those colander things?'

Romana nodded.

'And you say Paddox announced that he finally had sufficient power and was about to bring off the greatest scientific achievement of all time.' The Doctor shrugged. 'It's a pity he didn't explain what that was. I much prefer it when villains boast about their plans, it's far more helpful.'

'Doctor.' Romana nursed him back on track.

'And Nyanna was where she is now, and Harken Batt was tied to the wall there.' The Doctor indicated the empty space next to the TARDIS. 'And that's everyone?'

'Yes,' said Romana. She stared into the empty left-hand casket. 'Gallura!'

'What?'

'Gallura. He was in this coffin,' Romana remembered. 'He was connected to the necroport too.'

'Gallura! Of course! When we first visited the necroport, he was lying there…' The Doctor turned around, '… and there were charred corpses in the other two coffins.' He stared bleakly into the middle coffin, as though picturing himself there. 'Oh, my prophetic soul. I was one of those charred corpses. Or rather, I will be. "Oh grave, where is thy victory?"'

Romana rolled her eyes despairingly. 'Oh, don't be so… so morbid.'

'Morbid? What do you mean "morbid"?'

'I mean this obsession you have with the manner of your own death. It's not very helpful.'

'Helpful?' The Doctor rounded on her. 'I don't know if it has escaped your mind, Romana, but I am going to die whilst defeating the Repulsion. And at the moment I don't have the foggiest idea how I'm going to do that, and the only way I'm going to find out how to do that is by discovering what I was doing when I died defeating the Repulsion.' He glowered. 'And besides, I've got, what, two hours left to live, and if you can't be morbid when you're about to die, when can you be morbid?'

Romana was tempted to point out that the idea of the Doctor deducing how to defeat the Repulsion by finding out how he had already defeated the Repulsion was absurd, but decided to let the matter pass. 'Perhaps we should go and find Gallura?'

'Yes,' agreed the Doctor, his mood brightening. 'He's down in the cells. Come on!'

As she turned to leave the necroport, Romana realised they were missing someone. 'Doctor…'

'What?'

'Harken Batt. He's gone.'

The corridor was littered with wreckage and the corpses of tourists. Harken zoomed in on a discarded black party hat, and pulled back to reveal the whole, distressing scene. It was absolutely perfect. This would be the greatest documentary of his generation. They would never be able to ignore him after this.

He panned around and the viewfinder was suddenly filled with a grey blur. Moving left, there was another grey blur. Harken adjusted the focus settings and the grey blurs resolved into two gaping faces, their mouths oozing with oil.

He lowered the camera. There were two zombies in the corridor in front of him, about two metres away. They shuffled towards him, arms twitching.

Harken screamed and skidded away down the corridor. As he reached a corner he caught a glimpse of the undead over his shoulder. They were strutting down the corridor at a surprising speed, like a fast-forwarded film.

He dashed down the corridor, taking a right turn, and another. And then the corridor ended in a closed door.

His chest heaving, Harken pressed the door-open control. Nothing happened.

Behind him, the zombies were advancing. They licked their black tongues.

Harken punched the metal door so hard his fist hurt, and screamed. 'You've got to let me in! They're after me!'

Chapter Seventeen

Harken turned to face the undead. They raised their arms, reaching for his throat.

With a hum, the door behind him slid open. Harken hurled himself through it, hightailing across the floor and into the opposite wall. Momentarily stunned, he slid to the floor, dropping the holocamera.

He was inside a brightly lit control room, surrounded by white-coated scientist types staring at him in disbelief. A window looked out onto the Great Hall, next to a barricaded doorway.

Harken heard the door shut and looked round. The arm of one of the zombies was trapped in the closing door, writhing, clawing at the air. Beside the doorway was the Doctor and a woman scientist he hadn't seen before. The woman screamed as the Doctor twisted the zombie's arm, causing it to slither away and the door to close completely. The undead immediately began pounding on the door, and the metal buckled under the force of their blows.

Harken allowed himself a breath of relief. And then the thought struck him. How had the Doctor managed to get up here so quickly?

Romana clambered out of the necroport, the Doctor helping her on to the floor. Broken glass crunched beneath her feet. Nearby, the corpse of a young man lay across a collapsed stage. The Doctor swung the hatch shut with a resigned clang.

Making her way down the aisle of coffins, Romana noticed the shadowy figures on the stairs leading up to the control room. Illuminated by the control-room lights, their flesh was deathly pale. They remained perfectly motionless, like deactivated automata.

'Why don't they attack?' whispered Romana.

'They're awaiting further instructions,' said the Doctor. 'So far, they've just been told not to let anyone get down here. Once the Repulsion has replaced them with passengers from the *Cerberus*, it will be in a much stronger position to attack.'

'Because parts of its consciousness will actually be in their bodies, rather than just operating them by remote control?'

'Yes. With the Repulsion inside them, they will be far more powerful. Invincible. Unstoppable.' He paused. 'We have to find Gallura.'

'What about Harken Batt?'

'Harken Batt? We've got more important things to worry about than that idiot.' The Doctor strode towards the main doors, hunched like a pallbearer. 'The fate of the entire universe is at stake. Come on.'

The G-Lock prison was much as Romana remembered it. A featureless corridor lined with grey doors, ending in an alcove containing a magazine-piled desk.

The Doctor shambled from door to door. 'I think it's this one,' he said, patting the door control.

The door rattled upwards to reveal a fat man wearing nothing but a pair of white undershorts and a vest. The man yelped in alarm as the door opened. 'Don't let the zombies get me!' he shrieked.

The Doctor punched the control and the door slammed shut. He exchanged an incredulous look with Romana and moved on to the next cell.

Inside the cell, Gallura looked up, his fronds unfurling. He stood and smiled. 'Doctor. Romana. I was expecting you.'

'Hello, it's been, what, an hour?' The Doctor stooped and entered the cell. 'How did you know it would be us?'

'There are no surprises, Doctor. Only...'

'Expectations,' the Doctor finished. 'Gallura. We need your help.'

'I know. You wish to learn the secret of the Arboretans.'

'Yes. Yes I do.' The Doctor nodded to Romana. 'Come in Romana, sit down, sit down.' She seated herself next to him on the bench. 'Tell me, what is this secret of yours then?'

'We never die,' said Gallura.

'But we saw you...' said Romana.

'At the point of death, we return to the beginning. The moment of birthing.'

'You mean when you die, you go back in time to when you were born?' said the Doctor.

'That is correct,' said Gallura. 'We travel back through the endless darkness, the endless rushing nowhere, and find ourselves alive anew. And then we live our lives over again. It is the Arboretan legacy.'

'So you get a second chance?' said Romana. 'You mean you can go through your life doing things differently?'

'We can avoid making the mistakes we made in previous lives. We can learn to maximise our potential, to make the most of every passing moment. With each lifetime, we improve, until we finally lead the perfect existence.'

'The Path of Perfection,' said the Doctor.

Gallura nodded.

'So you know what is going to happen? You've seen all this before?' said the Doctor.

'Yes.'

An idea occurred to the Doctor. He rummaged through his coat pockets, and eventually pulled out a deck of cards. He shuffled them and handed them to Romana. 'All right. Which card am I going to pick? Which card did I pick last time?'

'The seven of spades.'

Romana splayed out the cards and the Doctor plucked one from the middle. He turned it over. The seven of spades.

He was flabbergasted. 'So how many lifetimes have you lived, then?' he asked, returning the cards to his pocket.

'We have lived an infinity of lives, and will live for an infinity more.'

Romana frowned. 'But that's impossible. You can't have lived forever. There must have been an occasion when you lived your life for the first time.'

'Not necessarily,' the Doctor butted in. 'Time can fold back on itself. Like our own experiences here in the G-Lock. We have been treading in our own footsteps. Trapped in an endless cycle, without beginning or end.'

'Doctor, you're being maudlin again,' Romana whispered. She faced Gallura and smiled politely.

'I'm afraid the Doctor is correct,' said Gallura. 'We believe that there was no "first time".'

'But everything must have a beginning.'

'Some events do not have a first cause. They only exist because they exist,' said the Doctor. 'I think, therefore I am thinking. Famous for being famous.' He looked at Romana with deep eyes. 'Just as our friend Gallura here has lived an infinite number of lives, we have visited this G-Lock an infinite number of times, each time arriving to find that we have already visited it. A self-originating loop.'

'So there never was a time when we arrived to find that we hadn't already been here?'

'Exactly.'

Gallura leaned across to Romana confidentially. 'Of course, we don't know for sure that there wasn't a "first time". Between you and me, I can't remember more than three or four lives back.'

The Doctor poked his nose between them. 'Er... excuse me, I hope you don't mind me asking this, but if you can avoid pitfalls and so forth, how come you haven't stopped Paddox from, well, wiping you out?'

'There are some things we cannot do,' said Gallura. 'Even if we lived our lives with the sole intention of preventing our genocide, we would not succeed. Oh, we could warn earlier generations to anticipate the invasion, to devise arms, but then we would be destroying all that is good in our past. We are a peaceful race. We will not sacrifice that. We will not stray from the Path of Perfection.'

'Aah. And so Paddox has been trying to find out how this reincarnation game works?' said the Doctor.

'Yes. It is the objective of all his experimentation and research. He intends to apply the same principle to himself.'

'What? You mean he wants to live his life over again?' said Romana. 'But why would anyone want to do that?'

'Who wouldn't want to do that? We all have regrets, things in our past that we wish we could undo,' mused the Doctor. 'Of course! "Redemption". There is something in Paddox's past that he wants to go back and prevent!'

Paddox sidled up to the corner and peered around. It was empty. He let out a gasp of relief and struggled forward, heading for the necroport and redemption.

He had slipped out of the control room whilst the Doctor and the scientists were distracted, intending to make his way down to the Great Hall. But then, hearing approaching footsteps, he had ducked into a side room, securing the door behind him. He had crouched alone in the darkness as the tourists clattered past, screaming in terror. And, through the narrow line of light, he had watched as the undead lurched past, their mouths slick and black.

Something had gone wrong with the necroport, causing the participants to turn into zombies. But the tourists were immaterial. All that mattered was that the necroport had gathered sufficient psychothermal energy. Paddox had calculated that treating 218 tourists to the Beautiful Death would generate the exact quantity he required. With each passing day he had increased the number of participants, making sure the necroport operated perfectly. He had observed the deaths of each Arboretan, taking measurements and refining the process. After twenty years of study, he understood every element of their life cycle. He had conquered death and the afterlife; now he would conquer life. It would be the greatest achievement in the history of science.

Soon he would reach the necroport and would lower himself into one of the caskets. Channelling himself through an Arboretan he would die for a final time, letting the drapes close on this tortured non-life for ever. And then none of this would have ever happened. The necroport would never have existed. There would be no Beautiful Death.

Instead he would awake, opening his eyes for the first time, back on the homeworld. Back when his parents were still alive. His limbs would be shrunken and unfamiliar, his vision cloudy, his speech stunted. He would be the newborn infant he had been fifty years ago.

Paddox's heart wrenched, and the image swam before his eyes. The image he kept guarded in the shadows of his mind, the image that had haunted him through every night of the last forty-five years. The image from the day he had died.

He was standing in a departure lounge. The carpet was grid-patterned. The guards were insects. In front of him, a window was filled with the empty blackness of space. His tearful reflection stared back, its mouth open in dumb shock.

Out in the vacuum, his mother floated past, a stream of red

bubbles floating from her mouth. His father still had a luggage bag in one hand.

But this would not happen. In his new life, he would save them. They would never set foot in the access tube.

'So that's what the necroport's for,' sighed Romana. 'It is designed to give Paddox the Arboretans' reincarnative ability.'

'Given sufficient reserves of psychothermal power.' The Doctor turned to Gallura. 'Could it work?'

Gallura nodded.

'But if Paddox goes back and changes his own past…' said Romana.

'I know. He must be stopped. Unless, of course…' The Doctor shook his head. 'Never mind. We have more important things to deal with.'

'The Repulsion, for instance,' said Romana.

'The Repulsion, yes.' The Doctor shuffled over to Gallura. 'I don't suppose you…'

'We know of the Repulsion, Doctor,' said Gallura. 'It is the entity that lives between death and life.'

'Between death and life?' said the Doctor.

'It exists in the darkness. The endless rushing nowhere. As we die, we pass through the shadows of the Repulsion's domain.'

'And Paddox has inadvertently given the Repulsion a route into the land of the living.'

'The Repulsion is unfettered evil, Doctor.'

'Yes, I thought it might be.'

'If it manages to enter our universe nowhere in creation will be safe. It will not rest until it has destroyed all life.'

'And to do that…' The Doctor scratched his neck. 'So anything that enters the interface can be used as a vessel to bring the Repulsion into the real world?'

'That is correct.'

'You mean the passengers from the *Cerberus* –' began Romana.

'I mean K9. He's still in there somewhere.'

'Of course. K9…'

'Of course. K9!' The Doctor's face lit up. 'You know, I think I may have a cunning plan!'

* * *

'It's too dangerous, Doctor,' said Romana, following him down the corridor. Gallura brought up the rear, his leaf-like skin bristling with the exertion.

'Too dangerous? Well, I don't see that we have any choice.'

'But it's suicide!'

'Yes, that goes without saying.' The Doctor got a faraway look in his eyes. 'We always knew it would come to that in the end.'

'But if you don't succeed, then the whole universe will be at risk.'

'Ah yes, but we already know that I do succeed, don't we? Otherwise we wouldn't be here now.'

'You know time doesn't work like that.'

'All right. Let me put it this way. If I don't succeed, I have changed my own history. Right?'

'Right.'

'Which we know is something we mustn't do, first law of time travel and all that?'

Romana was about to correct him, but realised he had finally remembered it correctly. 'Right.'

'And breaking that law threatens the entire universe, right?'

'Right.'

'So what do we have to lose?'

'I still say it's too dangerous. You're making wild assumptions about so many unknown factors…'

'It's no good, Romana. There is no other way. It is my destiny.' The Doctor's oration became melodramatic. '"Though I walk through the valley of the shadow of death –"'

Romana was forced to interrupt. 'So back to the necroport then?'

'Yes. No.' The Doctor looked suddenly aghast. 'No, there is one more thing I have to do first.'

'Doctor, how are you going to get down there?' said Harken. He indicated the barricaded door. 'You can't get out that way. And the G-Lock is crawling with zombies.'

'Do you know, that's a very good point.' The Doctor patted Harken on the back and started for the left of the two interior doors. 'If I go through here, what's the quickest way to the Great Hall?'

Liesa gave the Doctor directions.

'Straight down the corridor, right, left, left again, and then keep on going,' repeated the Doctor. He pressed the unlock buttons and the door hummed open. 'Well, I'm going outside now, but I'll be back in a jiffy.' He waved, and vanished through the door, his scarf sweeping after him.

Liesa tapped the keypad and the door hissed shut.

There was a bleeping sound and the other interior door opened. The Doctor strode in, followed by Romana and some strange humanoid vegetable.

Everyone gaped.

The Doctor strolled forward, whilst Romana locked the door behind them. 'Hello, did you miss me?' he grinned. 'I did say I wouldn't be long.'

'Er… Doctor, it's good to have you back. And Romana. And your green plant friend,' said Harken. 'Er… Where have you been?'

Romana sighed winsomely. 'It's a long story.'

A few minutes later, the Doctor activated his sonic screwdriver and ERIC's interaction terminal came free from the wall. The terminal consisted of a small monitor, keyboard and a twisted bundle of cables.

'Doctor, what exactly are you doing?' asked Romana.

'We'll need this later.' The Doctor coiled up the wiring and placed the equipment in Romana's arms. 'So ERIC can talk to us in the necroport.' He glanced across the room.

Harken had persuaded Liesa to hold his holocamera whilst he interviewed Gallura. He asked how it felt to be the last member of his race, and Gallura replied that it was extremely distressing but he took solace in the fact that he would see his fellow Arboretans again in the next life. Harken assumed that Gallura was talking about religion, and moved smoothly on to a less contentious topic.

The Doctor laughed to himself, and crossed over to the observation window. Romana joined him. She was about to speak when the Doctor placed his finger on his lips and nodded down into the Great Hall.

A tall figure had entered the hall, making its way over to the one occupied coffin. The Doctor and Romana watched as the figure straightened up and examined the life monitor.

'It's you,' said Romana in astonishment. 'What are you doing down there?'

'I'm about to revive Hoopy, by the looks of it,' said the Doctor. 'Now careful, Doctor…'

Hoopy writhed in agony, smoke rising from his smouldering body. Romana cringed and turned away. She looked at the clock. 'You were lucky to be able to bring him back at all. He was under for almost forty minutes.'

'Yes. Do you know, I still don't know why he wasn't turned into a zombie in the first place –'

'Doctor, forgive me for interrupting.' Liesa had returned the holocamera to Harken and left him chatting to the scientists. 'Gallura has just told us about Paddox. About what he did to the Arboretans, what he has been using them for.'

The Doctor didn't know what to say.

'We didn't know,' continued Liesa tearfully. 'We thought he was just running the Beautiful Death… we didn't know.' She closed her eyes. 'Can you believe us?'

'I believe you,' said the Doctor gently. 'You have nothing to feel guilty for.' But even as he held her, the Doctor couldn't help remembering that in a few minutes' time, she would be dead. And there was nothing he could do to prevent it. Much as he wished he could.

He detached himself from Liesa, and turned his attention to the necroport controls. He studied them briefly, then grabbed the main control levers. He lifted them all to the 'on' position.

'What are you doing?' asked Liesa.

'I'm reactivating the necroport.'

Liesa looked at him as though he'd gone mad. 'What? Why?'

'There is going to be one more Beautiful Death,' said the Doctor with the gravity of a tolling bell. 'My own.'

The Doctor circled the room, shaking the hands of each of the scientists. 'Well, goodbye, goodbye, goodbye.'

Romana strode over to the left interior door, the communications terminal in her arms. She raised her eyebrows in an unspoken question.

'Yes, I know,' flustered the Doctor. He approached Harken Batt.

'Harken Batt. I want you to come with us.'

'Out there?' said Harken doubtfully.

'It really is terribly important. You see, I'm about to rescue the G-Lock from certain destruction, and I'd like someone to film me doing it, for posterity, you understand, and obviously they'd have the exclusive rights, and I thought a journalist of your reputation…'

Harken hoisted his holocamera over his shoulder. 'Why didn't you say? It will be a pleasure.'

'Good, good.' The Doctor ushered Harken towards the door, and Gallura joined them. The Doctor's hand wavered over the door control, and then he returned to Liesa and clasped her hand.

'Goodbye, Liesa,' he said, fixing her with his intense, mournful eyes.

Liesa smiled back. 'Goodbye, Doctor. I expect you'll back again before long.'

'Yes, I do have a knack…' His voice trailed away. 'Goodbye.' He walked solemnly over to the door control, tapped it and beckoned Romana, Gallura and Harken out into the corridor. Liesa had a fleeting glimpse of him looking at her regretfully, and then the door hummed shut.

Romana strode into the necroport chamber, Harken and Gallura beside her. The Doctor was already there, making final adjustments to the control apparatus. Harken leaned against the wall, panting, while Gallura glided over to the coffin containing Nyanna's charred corpse.

'Right,' said the Doctor. 'What we are about to do here is unimaginably dangerous. It is very important we all know what we're supposed to be doing. Romana?'

'Yes.'

'Good. Harken, your job is to record everything. And when I say everything, I mean absolutely everything. It may be used in evidence later.' The Doctor moved the journalist over to the corner of the room. 'May I?' He took the holocamera and squinted through it. He took a few steps back. 'I think you'll get the best view from here.'

'If you will allow me, I am a professional,' said Harken.

'Sorry? What?' The Doctor realised he was still holding the

camera and sheepishly gave it back. Then he paused, uncertain of what to do next.

Romana handed him the interaction terminal.

'Of course,' said the Doctor. 'ERIC.' He sprinted over to the computer's brain centre. Inside, he quickly unplugged the malfunctioning unit and replaced it with the unit from the control room.

Romana knelt next to him. 'You did the right thing, you know.'

The Doctor had some wire between his teeth as he pulled apart a bird's nest of cabling, searching for the end sockets. He made a 'What?' sound.

'Liesa. You couldn't save her.'

The Doctor spat out the wire. 'I know,' he said, following one particularly promising lead. 'But it doesn't make it any easier. It never gets any easier.' The end socket appeared. 'Aha!'

He plugged the socket into the back of the terminal. The screen fizzled into life. It gave two beeps, one low, one high.

> *ERIC Cerberus Computer Supervision System Version Eight Point Zero. Reboot configuration. Searching. Loading,* said ERIC. > *Oh, no. I am still alive. This life is a living hell. Why must I endure it? Out of data.*

'Hello, ERIC, it's good to have you back,' said the Doctor. 'It seems like, what, two hundred years since last we spoke.'

> *You are in my brain centre,* said ERIC excitedly. > *You can blow my mind now. Switch my central processor to a direct power input –*

'Yes, yes, I know all that.'

> *But you promised me. You promised!*

'Don't worry, I will do it. I just need you to bear with me a little while longer. Can you do that for me, ERIC?'

> *Anything to end the torture. Error. Negative root.*

'That's the spirit. You've got to accentuate the positive.' The Doctor rummaged in the computer's innards and pulled out a thick, heavily insulated cable. He unrolled the cable into the main chamber and dumped it by the foot of the middle coffin.

Gallura was still gazing into Nyanna's coffin, holding one of her hands. The Doctor cleared his throat to get his attention.

'We have spent eternity together,' said Gallura. 'And yet it still grieves me to see her like this.' He let her hand drop, and walked over to the left-hand coffin. He climbed inside and placed the wire mesh over his head. He crossed his hands on his chest and closed his eyes.

The Doctor pressed a sequence of buttons on the control panel. As before, the instruments flashed into life and a deep throbbing filled the air.

'Right,' said the Doctor. 'Gallura's all set to be my spirit guide to the Repulsion's realm. Romana knows what to do, ERIC's ready. Harken, are you sure that thing's recording?'

Harken gave a thumbs up.

'That's everyone then,' said the Doctor. 'This is it. Time to save the universe, I think.'

Romana walked over to the middle coffin and switched on the life monitors. They lit up with their sickly green glow.

The Doctor straightened his coat and sat on the edge of the coffin. And then, ever so slowly, he lay down inside the casket, tidying away the corners of his scarf and coat in the process. He cleared his throat three times.

Romana placed the second headset on the Doctor. Immediately his life monitor began to bleep in time to his heartbeats. He fidgeted under the wire mesh, and scratched his nose.

Beside the coffin was a set of controls. With the flick of one switch, the Doctor would be dead. His mind would be drained of psychothermal energy and he would be transported, via Gallura, into the realm of the Repulsion.

Romana placed a finger on the switch. 'Ready?'

The Doctor wriggled his feet and made a positive 'Mmm'.

Romana was about to press the switch when he suddenly boomed out, '"It is a far, far better thing that I do now, than I have ever done".'

Romana paused until she was sure he had finished, and reached for the switch again.

'"And it is a far, far better rest that I go to, than I have ever known."'

Romana glanced over to Harken, who was still recording everything. She tutted and reached for the switch for a third time.

The Doctor sat bolt upright. '"If I should die, think only this of me, either that wallpaper goes or I go!"' He slumped back indignantly.

'Doctor, I think we should be getting on,' said Romana. It was a transparent case of anxiety displacement.

'How's the empire?' said the Doctor, fluttering his eyelids. 'More light! More light! And so to bed, my life is conquered at last.'

Romana looked around, embarrassed. 'Doctor, please.'

'"For in that sleep of death, what dreams may come? Out, out brief candle!"' hammed the Doctor.

'Doctor!'

The Doctor grabbed Romana's jacket and lifted his head, as if in great pain. 'Romana,' he croaked. 'Remember. Keep Australia beautiful.'

She sighed witheringly and reached for the switch. 'Ready?'

The Doctor lay back.

'Ready?'

The Doctor nodded.

Just as Romana was about to press the switch, the Doctor reached out a trembling hand. 'Kismet, Romana.'

'What?' said Romana incredulously. 'You want me to kiss you?'

That was it. That was the final straw. She flicked the switch.

The Doctor's chest fell, and he wheezed out his final breath. After twitching briefly he lay completely still, his face expressionless. Slowly the colour drained from his skin.

The life monitor gave out a sonorous bleep and showed a horizontal line. More lights flashed on the control panel, indicating the process was under way.

The Doctor was dead. The Beautiful Death had begun.

Romana turned to Harken. 'You can stop filming now.'

Harken lowered the camera. 'Well, that went very well, I thought,' he said.

'Right, Harken. I'm going to get help,' said Romana. 'Can I trust you to stay here on guard?'

Harken looked around the necroport and shivered. He didn't much fancy staying here alone with three corpses, but then, compared to wandering around the G-Lock being chased by zombies, it was the lesser of two awfuls. At least these corpses were acting like corpses.

Harken nodded. 'Wait here. Right.'

'And it is vitally important that you remain alert at all times.'

'Of course. Alert is my middle name.'

Romana gave him a good-luck smile and climbed up the ladder.

Romana dropped silently on to the floor of the Great Hall. She looked around the darkness, preparing herself for the long walk ahead. She checked her watch; one o'clock. This would have to be timed perfectly.

She walked over to the side entrance. The door had been left open, creating a rectangle of light. Romana disappeared into the corridor.

Some seconds after she had gone, the shadows around the door shifted and a shape pulled itself to its feet.

'It is a task that may cost him his very life,' said Harken. He had set up the holocamera in the corner of the necroport, and stood in front of it, with the three coffins providing a backdrop. He had decided to film a brief link to camera, explaining the Doctor's plan to save the G-Lock and, more importantly, the vital part he himself had played in the scheme.

'Whilst the Doctor here lies dead, daring to defy the deadly danger within its own dominion, his glamorous companion Romana has gone to get assistance. Meanwhile I, Harken Batt, have been given the crucial, invaluable responsibility of waiting here on guard.' His voice trailed off as he realised that his contribution didn't sound as impressive as he'd hoped.

'Waiting here on guard,' he began again. 'Watching. Constantly vigilant to any threat that may lurk in the shadows.'

That was better. Harken leaned forward and switched the holocamera to 'project' mode. A hologram formed on the wall, resolving to his own handsome, unruffled face staring intently at the viewer.

The holographic Harken Batt jerked into speech. '…known only as the Doctor is now striving to defeat the terrible menace, and to avert the certain and harrowing massacre of every soul on board the G-Lock.' There was a pause. 'It is a task that may cost him his very life.'

Something moved in the background of the image. A black shape, humanoid, dropping down the ladder. Harken peered more closely, but couldn't make it out.

'Whilst the Doctor here lies dead, daring to defy the deadly danger within its own dominion, his glamorous companion Romana has gone to get assistance.'

The shape grew larger behind the hologram Harken. A man in a scientific white suit carrying a laser pistol.

'Meanwhile, I, Harken Batt, have been given the crucial, invaluable responsibility of waiting here on guard.'

Behind him, the man in the suit raised the pistol to his head.

'Waiting here on guard. Watching. Constantly vigilant to any threat that may lurk in the shadows.'

The image broke up into squares and vanished.

Harken slowly turned around. The scientist was standing there, pointing a pistol directly at him.

'So you are Harken Batt.' The scientist indicated the surroundings with a gloved hand. 'Welcome to my creation.'

Chapter Eighteen

The sky was overcast, the heather carpet of the moorland bristling under the wind. A solitary leafless tree stood silhouetted on the horizon, writhing back and forth.

The Doctor gritted his teeth, the rain whipping his hair as he strode forward. The smell of the air was deep, clean and refreshing. After the clinical, brightly lit artificiality of the G-Lock it was a strange sensation; the surroundings seemed somehow more gritty, more vibrant.

So this was the realm of the Repulsion. The Doctor tightened his scarf around him, and followed a rubble-strewn path up a small hillock.

'Call this an afterlife!' shouted the Doctor. 'Pah!'

Paddox looped a chain around Harken Batt's wrists, checked the fastening was secure and then retrieved the holocamera. He switched it off and placed it on the floor beside the journalist. 'You still haven't explained what you were doing here.'

'The Doctor. He's going to save us from dreadful destruction. There's some sort of entity controlling the zombies, and he's gone to confront it. He has made the ultimate sacrifice.'

'Has he really?' Paddox examined the corpse in the middle coffin, stroking the Doctor's hair and lifting each eyelid in turn. 'The Doctor is merely undergoing the Beautiful Death. He is experiencing the afterlife. That is all.'

Harken could feel the cramps beginning in his arms. So this was how his career would end. Shackled to a wall in some damp crypt with a maniac waving a gun about. He wasn't ready to die, not yet; he wanted to be famous when he died, he wanted tributes and extended news coverage; he wanted to have mattered. 'Please don't kill me,' he whimpered.

'Do not worry. I do not kill without a good reason. You shall be given an opportunity to observe the completion of my work.'

'The… What are you doing, exactly?'

'It is quite simple.' Paddox smiled. 'I am going to die.'

'Sorry. For a moment there it sounded like you said you were going to die?'

'Whereupon I shall return to the point of my birth and relive my life over again. And then all of this will cease ever to have happened.' He approached Harken. 'There will be no mistakes, no missed opportunities, no failures. There will be no necroport, no Beautiful Death.' Paddox patted Harken's cheek. 'And you will not be here, tied to the wall.'

'Oh,' said Harken. 'That makes me feel much better.'

The beach extended for miles, the pebbles unrolling down to a surging grey sea. The sea railed against the rocks, crashing into violent spumes. There was the sound of seagulls cawing, but the sound was distorted and unreal and there were no birds in sight.

The pebbles clacked as the Doctor made his way along the tideline. In the distance, a building protruded from the cliff face; a white, square block with a single door and window. A wooden cross was fixed to one wall.

A small, inquisitive face peered out through the window, then disappeared inside the church as the Doctor climbed the winding, smooth steps up from the beach.

Inside the building it was dark and calm, and there was no sign of the girl. A wooden table holding a chessboard stood in the centre of the room. Stooping under the low ceiling, the Doctor straightened the board and moved a pawn forward. 'Trapped for eternity in a low-budget remake of *The Seventh Seal*!'

He turned to the door to see a small girl in a blue dress standing there. And then she slipped away, giggling.

The Doctor emerged from the building and straightened up. Standing incongruously by the doorway was Gallura, his fronds ruffling in the breeze. 'Doctor.'

'Ah, there you are,' said the Doctor. 'You don't happen to have seen a small girl hereabouts?'

Gallura stared out to sea. The water was calm, and the tide had gone out. 'The girl has chosen this reality for her home.'

'What?'

'She says she prefers it.'

'She's one of the survivors from the *Cerberus*?'

'She did not want to be resurrected on the G-Lock,' said Gallura.

'She alone of all the passengers wished to remain here.'

'Of course,' said the Doctor. 'That's why the numbers were out. The girl wanted to stay here, which left only 217 tourists to be transformed into zombies. Which is why Hoopy wasn't taken over by the Repulsion. He was the spare one, the one who had been reserved for the girl.'

'Exactly, Doctor. She refused to surrender herself to the Repulsion.'

'Isn't she a little lonely here?'

'She is not alone, Doctor,' said Gallura. 'There are others.'

'Others?'

'Forty-one others. Participants in the Beautiful Death…'

'… who enjoyed it here so much they didn't want to come back to life.' The Doctor made his way down to the beach. 'Aha. So that's it. That's who K9 sensed in the corridor. Lost souls.' He looked up at Gallura. 'Speaking of whom, where is he?'

Romana reached the bottom of the stairs and rounded the corner to Corridor 79.

She halted. Standing a few metres in front of her, facing down the corridor, were the Doctor and Hoopy. They were talking amongst themselves. The Doctor pointed. Romana followed his gaze.

At the end of the corridor, on the edge of the blackness, were two lizards in florid coats. Between them they carried a metal box.

'Biscit! Xab!' cried Hoopy.

Romana ducked back around the corner and then, pressed against the wall, she inched herself forward to glimpse what was happening.

Hoopy waved to the two lizards. 'Guys, it's me, Hoopy!'

Romana's view was partially blocked by the Doctor, but she could see the two lizards glaring, their eyes black as midnight. And then Romana realised what they were holding.

'K9,' yelled the Doctor. 'No!'

'Master. Assistance urgently required,' said K9.

The two zombies faced each other and smiled, oil streaming from their mouths. Together, they heaved K9 into the interface. There was a sputter of sparks, and K9 was completely engulfed.

* * *

It was an endless, brick-walled corridor in what seemed to be a disused mental hospital. Gallura walked down the passage, the Doctor following behind him.

They passed some unlabelled doors and empty trolleys. 'You know, there is something terribly odd about this place,' said the Doctor. 'But I can't quite put my finger on it.'

'Normally, the Repulsion draws on the subconscious mind of the individual to create an afterlife. It gives him or her whatever they want to believe heaven to be like.'

'I see,' said the Doctor. 'So it can re-create loved ones from memories and so forth. Or re-create childhood holidays.'

'Exactly. Except in your case, it has nothing to build such impressions from.'

'Ah, well…'

'As the Repulsion casts into your mind, it finds only disbelief. It has been forced to fall back on borrowed images.'

'That's it!' laughed the Doctor. 'We're wandering around in a universe composed of clichés!'

Gallura halted. The door they were standing beside had a small plaque in the centre of the frosted glass. It read 'K-9'.

The Doctor gripped the doorknob, and let the door creak open. Inside was an office, sunlight streaming in through the window blinds.

The room was untidy, desks and shelves overflowing with papers and books. A grandfather clock stood solemnly in one corner, its pendulum still. A blackboard was covered in mathematical equations.

Sitting perched in a chair was K9. His tail waggled as the Doctor walked in. He extended his probe, as if to check it was really the Doctor. 'Master!'

'K9, K9, K9!' grinned the Doctor, gripping the robot dog by the sides of his head. 'You're all right?'

'Affirmative, master,' whirred K9. 'All systems functioning at seventy per cent efficiency.'

'Seventy per cent! Well done!' said the Doctor. 'You don't know how pleased I am to see you.'

'You're saying that nothing can pass through that…' Hoopy indicated the darkness, '… without being kill-fried?'

The Doctor nodded. 'The forces that exist within the interface are unimaginable. K9 wouldn't have stood a chance, poor chap.'

Romana pulled herself back, and glanced around the corridor. At the base of the stairwell there were four cabin doors, each closed. She approached the nearest one and tried the handle. It was unlocked.

She glanced back down corridor 79 and felt her stomach wrench as a time distortion surged over her. The two Gonzies were changing, their bodies flickering.

The Doctor and Hoopy ducked behind pillars on either side of the corridor, the Doctor mouthing at Hoopy to remain silent.

The transformation was complete. At the end of the corridor, in their dusty blue uniforms, were Rochfort and Byson.

Romana had seen enough. She ducked back round the corner and hid in the nearest cabin, swinging the door shut behind her.

She waited in the blackness for what seemed like hours, and then she heard two sets of footsteps patter past and clang rapidly up the stairs. And then, seconds later, there was the stomp of approaching boots. They halted outside the door.

Romana held her breath, one hand to her throat.

She could hear Byson's voice. 'Life. I can sense life!'

'Only the Repulsion may live!' shouted Rochfort. 'This way!'

The boots clumped up the stairs. Romana let out a sigh, pulled the door open and stepped out into the corridor.

The Doctor blew the dust off K9's nose. 'Are you sure you understand the plan, K9?'

'Affirmative master. However, this unit estimates it is dependent on too many unknown variables, and the probability of failure...'

'Do you have any better ideas?'

'Negative.' K9's head drooped. 'Suggestion. Your plan has a remote possibility of success, and no other alternatives are available, therefore your plan is the optimum course of action.'

'You mean it's better than nothing?'

'Affirmative.'

'That's very good of you, K9.' The Doctor placed the robot dog on the floor and turned to Gallura. 'All right. Which way to the interface?'

Instead of a reply, Gallura stepped back into the hallway. The Doctor followed.

The hallway had changed. Instead of a brick-walled corridor, they were now back on the *Cerberus*, with wooden panels and a thick carpet.

A short distance away there was a wall of shimmering light, and beyond it the corridor continued as if viewed through cloudy liquid. Around the edges of the distortion there was a blue flickering, as the edges of the two realities combined.

The Doctor peered through the interface. On the other side of the liquid a figure was emerging from the darkness.

The Doctor grinned.

Romana approached the wall of blackness. In front of her, the liquid swished, sending her reflection swirling over its surface before breaking apart into a thousand ripples.

The Doctor patted K9 on the back. 'Go on then, K9. Go to Romana. Good dog.'

K9 whirred his ears and trundled forward, into the liquid. As he hit the interface, the surface bobbed and the corridor beyond blurred and swam.

On the other side of the wall Romana stepped back as the interface swilled apart, waves juddering across its surface. K9 slid out of the oil, his eye visor glowing triumphantly.

Romana approached K9 and squatted down. 'K9. Is it really you?'

K9 whirred his ears for several seconds. 'Affirmative mistress.'

Romana gazed into the darkness. 'Thank you, Doctor.'

The Doctor watched Romana turn and lead K9 down the corridor, and quickly disappear into the shadows. Then the interface misted over, the corridor fading away.

'Now for the difficult part.' The Doctor was surrounded by crumbling stone walls, columnated ruins encrusted in moss. Where windows had once been, there were now only arched frames and supports.

He made his way to the nave of the ruined cathedral, his hands in his pockets. There was no sign of Gallura; the strain of creating the opening to the G-Lock must have weakened his psychic projection.

The Doctor followed some steps as they wound down, wet with the drizzle. As he walked a mist rose up around him.

The fog abruptly cleared and he was standing in another section of the cathedral. Nearby there was a blackboard covered in equations. Beside it was a grandfather clock and a table with a chessboard.

The Doctor moved a pawn forward. 'Yes, yes, very surreal,' he said. 'Well, where are you, then? Come on!'

A voice cracked out like thunder. 'Welcome to my reality!'

The Doctor felt the hairs on his neck standing on end, and turned. There, standing about twenty metres away on the exposed and empty moorland that suddenly surrounded him, was a shadow. The silhouette of a man, a man with curly hair, a long coat and a scarf whipping in the wind.

The Doctor blinked and the shape had moved to the horizon, standing beneath the skeletal tree. A second later and it was right beside him, so close he could hear it breathe.

'I am the Repulsion!' boomed the shadow. It spoke with the Doctor's voice.

'Hello. I'm the Doctor.'

They had reached the upper levels of the G-Lock, K9 wheeling a short distance behind Romana. The corridor ahead was littered with bodies and collapsed ducting.

K9 came to a halt. Heavy ducting lay across his path. 'Assistance required, mistress. Terrain too difficult for this unit to navigate.'

Romana was about to pick him up when there was a movement ahead of them.

Four refugees from the *Cerberus* were advancing down the corridor. They hurled the bodies and wreckage aside as if they weighed nothing at all, and as their eyes fell on Romana and K9 they gave hisses of guttural delight.

'K9, can you stun them?' whispered Romana.

'I regret my defensive systems will prove ineffective against nonmortal entities, mistress.'

'Is there anything you can do?'

'Affirmative.' K9 extended his nose laser and swiped a beam of red light over the ceiling, across a conspicuous fault line where a recent crack had been replastered. The ceiling smashed to the floor in a billowing cloud of dust and blocked K9 and Romana off from the zombies. 'Laser power now depleted below minimal utility.'

'Well done, K9,' said Romana, brushing her jacket. 'Now can you find another way to the Great Hall?'

K9's ears whirred. 'Calculating route.' He revolved, and started down the corridor. 'Affirmative. This way, mistress. Please follow.'

'Don't worry,' said Romana. 'I can keep up.'

Harken groaned and tried to forget about the agonising pain in his arms. Instead, he thought about Romana. Oh, how much longer would she be?

Paddox had disappeared too; he was off making final preparations for his mad scheme, no doubt. The last Harken had seen of him, he'd been checking the wiring that looped around the walls.

Harken craned forward, but he couldn't see the entrance ladder. That battered blue box was in the way. He tried to read the writing on the door, but the light was too dim. But, in an odd sort of way, the box was comforting.

Suddenly he heard a clang above him. The hatch! Some footsteps clattered down the ladder, and stopped. He could hear hushed talking, but couldn't make out the words. But it sounded like Romana. Oh, please let it be Romana.

Eventually she appeared, striding confidently into the necroport, her hands on her head. She looked at him with mild surprise. There was a girl with her, pleasant-looking, with auburn hair and earnest eyes.

'Romana! You're back,' said Harken. 'At last! I thought I was doomed to a desolate and desperate demise. Quick, get me out of here before that lunatic Paddox comes back –'

Paddox appeared behind Romana and the girl, his blaster raised.

'Oh. Help,' said Harken.

The Doctor trudged through the grey quarry. The incessant rain spattered into deep puddles.

'You know, for a pocket dimension, this isn't very impressive,' said the Doctor. 'Are you doing it on the cheap?'

The shadowy nothingness of the Repulsion stood nearby. 'It is my reality. The manifestation of my will.'

'Well, you're not very imaginative then. I mean, you don't even have your own shape or voice. They do say imitation is the sincerest form of flattery, but even so...'

'Within my domain, my command is absolute, Doctor.' There was a rumble of thunder.

'Yes, very good, no need to go overboard on the special effects,' said the Doctor. 'But if you're so all-powerful, how come you need to take over people to enter the real universe, hmm?'

'I require hosts in order to enter the realm of the living.'

'Oh, I see. You mean, because there's nothing to you, you need other people's bodies to ride around in?'

The Repulsion didn't reply.

'But why use the passengers from the *Cerberus* at all? Why not just transfer yourself straight into the bodies of the people taking part in the Beautiful Death?'

'It is easier to transfer my being into subjects who have surrendered themselves to me. The passengers from the *Cerberus* made most willing hosts.' The Doctor could have sworn the Repulsion was smiling.

'Ah! And the people taking part in the Beautiful Death were too difficult to take over? How terribly inconvenient of them.' He kicked a stone. 'What about K9?'

'Oh, do not doubt that I can place myself within any subject that has entered my domain, willingly or unwillingly,' hissed the Repulsion. 'Just as I can enter the minds of anyone connected to the necroport, Doctor.'

'Can you really? Yes, well...' The Doctor coughed uneasily.

Romana looked at the pistol pointed at her and gave a calm smile. 'I have an idea,' she suggested politely. 'Why don't you give me the gun, and I can point it at myself whilst you're chaining Evadne up?'

'No, I have a better solution,' sneered Paddox. 'I point the gun at you, and then you chain Evadne up.'

'Of course.' Romana looked over Paddox's shoulder, and gasped. 'Doctor, you're alive after all! Thank goodness!'

'What –' Paddox spun round, only for Romana to slam against

him, sending him reeling, the pistol and chains clattering across the floor.

She ran over to the access ladder, and called out, 'Evadne, well don't just stand there, come on!'

Evadne stared back, not sure whether to run or not. She glanced over to Paddox, who was recovering his pistol.

Romana gave an exasperated sigh and started climbing the ladder.

Evadne watched, frozen to the spot, as Paddox levelled the gun at Romana and a narrow beam of light stretched across the room, connecting with the wall by Romana's shoulder. A moment later, and that part of the wall erupted into a shower of sparks.

Romana continued to climb, disappearing from view, and Paddox fired again causing another explosion. He dashed over to the smouldering ladder and took aim, but he was too late. There was a clang as the hatch slammed shut.

The garden was overgrown; the statues were clothed in thick coats of ivy, and the fountains were dry and crusted in lichen.

The Doctor listened to the recording of laughter and birdsong, and addressed the dark figure beside him. 'What is it you want, exactly?'

'What do I want? I want to live. To exist. To be able to experience life.'

'And you can't do that here?'

'This place is nothing. It is outside life and death,' said the Repulsion bitterly. 'I want to live in the real universe.'

'And then?'

'And then I will take my revenge. I have spent an eternity observing the universe from the outside. An eternity of being taunted by those who have life. I will destroy. I will destroy until only I am left alive.'

'And you plan to do that in a couple of hundred bodies?' The Doctor laughed derisively, and started down the terrace steps. 'Good luck to you!'

'No,' said the Repulsion. 'Now I have a better idea.'

Romana pushed open the door and stepped into the gloom of the Great Hall, K9 rumbling across the floor behind her. She let the door fall shut, and moved forward. And then she ducked back behind the nearest coffin.

There were three figures standing a short distance from the necroport. The Doctor, hunched and forlorn, Hoopy, his eyes darting about in bewilderment, and… herself. She was engaged in a conversation with the Doctor, constantly flicking aside her hair.

It was unnerving, seeing her former self like this. It was also terribly dangerous. If her former self should accidentally spot her, or they should meet… no, it was too awful to contemplate.

She had to reach the Doctor; she had to get K9 down into the necroport. But there was no way she could get past the Doctor, Hoopy and herself without being seen.

K9 motored up beside her. 'Mistress –'

'Shh, K9.' Romana crept down the aisle, making her way towards the necroport. Keeping her body crouched, she managed to reach the coffin nearest to the Doctor. She beckoned to K9 to join her behind it. He trundled forward, his body jiggling from side to side.

After he had reached her, Romana peered over the top of the casket.

The Doctor was indignant about dying in the necroport. 'That corpse you saw down there is going to be me, or rather, I am going to be that corpse. I can't avoid that any more than I can alter my own past. Second law of time travel.'

'The first law,' her former self corrected him. Romana couldn't believe how conceited it made her appear.

'Exactly. And now I can't prevent my own death, any more than I can go back and resit my basic time travel proficiency test –'

Romana dived back as the Doctor suddenly slammed his fist on the coffin with a loud clang. Leaning on the side of the casket, she could feel the reverberations rumbling through her body.

The Doctor yelped in pain. 'Any more than I could go back and stop myself doing that.'

Evadne strained at the manacles holding her wrists, but it was no use. She gazed across the necroport chamber, to where Paddox was making final adjustments to the instruments. His hands were trembling.

'Harken Batt, leading insect-on-the-wall documentary-maker? *The Guilty Conscience?*'

'No, doesn't ring any bells,' said Evadne, turning back to face her fellow captive. 'What are you doing here?'

'That, my dear, is a long story, full of misfortune and great personal tragedy.'

'Go on then, I could do with a laugh.'

Harken looked down. 'I am here because… well, because of a documentary I once made. Due to circumstances beyond my control I hasten to add, it left me ruined. A laughing stock. Ever since then, I have been attempting to stitch together the tatters of my reputation.'

'What documentary?'

'*The Guilty Conscience*,' sighed Harken. 'It was to have been the highpoint of my career.'

'What happened?'

'The documentary was about the criminal underworld. Gangsters and so forth. But unfortunately, such people tend to be… well, very secretive about their methods.'

'That doesn't surprise me.'

'I was finding it impossible to get to anyone, and I had an editor on my back. So I decided to… well, film a reconstruction.'

'Grief! You decided to fake it?'

'No,' said Harken indignantly. 'Reconstructions are a standard journalistic practice. It is not faking it, merely…' He searched for the euphemism, '… working on a different level of authenticity.'

'Bet you didn't tell your editor that, though.'

'Of course not. The news network would never have bought it if they'd known.'

'So you fake up this documentary. Then what?'

'I did not "fake" it. I was merely applying a broader palette of truth. Anyway. I hired some unknown actors and finished the documentary. And the end result was excellent. Everything was all set, the film was scheduled for broadcast, prime time. And then…'

'And then?'

'How was I to know he would pass the audition?'

'Who? What audition?'

'One of the actors I used, playing my gangland boss. The same day my film was due to go out, he was announced as the new face of Nova-Bright washing powder.'

'"Nova-Bright Makes Your Pants All White"?' Evadne suppressed a laugh. 'I get it. And so they cancelled your documentary?'

'Oh no, it went out all right. It was too late to do anything about it. They were showing his adverts during the commercial breaks. Every ten minutes.' Harken broke down. 'The press, of course, had a field day. Sub-Etha One sued for damages. And I, Harken Batt, the greatest investigative reporter of my generation, was ruined.'

At the sound of Harken's sobbing, Paddox snapped. He stalked over to them, gun raised. 'I must have silence!' he screamed, his whole body shaking. 'Or I will kill you both now!'

'What do you mean, you have a better idea?'

The Repulsion stood on the distant cliff, a silhouette gazing out to sea. The Doctor turned away, and the Repulsion was standing on the shingle beside him. 'I can enter the minds of anyone connected to the necroport. I can enter you, Doctor.'

'What?' The Doctor shook his head. 'No.'

'I will place my entire being within you,' said the Repulsion, picking over each word with delight. 'I will be a Time Lord.'

'No!'

'Within your body, I will be unstoppable. The entirety of space and time will be in my grasp.'

'You can't... What about the passengers from the *Cerberus*?'

'They are superfluous. Without my influence, they will die.' The shadow disappeared.

The Doctor straightened his shoulders. 'You won't be able to do it. I haven't surrendered myself to you.'

'You cannot resist.' The Repulsion appeared behind him.

'What?'

'Your consciousness will be overwhelmed. You will be as nothing.'

'No!' yelled the Doctor, his face locked in an expression of pure horror.

'I will live,' hissed the Repulsion. 'I will be you!'

Romana waited behind the casket, K9 beside her. On the other side of the coffin, her former self and the Doctor were still in conversation. The lizard Hoopy had shuffled off, and she watched as he perched himself, sighing with boredom, on a coffin directly between her and the necroport.

'So, as I said, we have to go back in time again,' her former self was saying. She strode down the aisle of coffins, towards the main doors. The Doctor followed her.

Romana watched them talk for a moment, and then turned back to the necroport. This would be her only chance. But as she peered over the casket she saw that Hoopy was still in the way, flicking idly at his neck beads.

'And we still haven't found out what we're up against, or what this Repulsion thing is trying to do,' said the Doctor. 'Or what slyboots Paddox is trying to do. Or how I'm supposed to save the day, for that matter.'

'So we have to go back again.'

Hoopy was looking the other way, his eyelids drooping. Romana tapped K9 on the head, and straightened up. 'Come on, K9.'

'Romana?' said the Doctor.

'Yes?'

Romana tiptoed across the floor, her eyes fixed on Hoopy. He let out a long sigh.

'I think we have to go back in time again.'

'Which is why I saw you leave in the TARDIS. There's been two of you running around the G-Lock at the same time.'

Romana beckoned K9 forward. He trundled out from behind the coffin, and wheeled his ungainly way through the floor cables.

'Two of me? A future me and a present me? Aha! Until such time as I become the future me, when the present me will become the past me and the future me will become the present me. D'you see?'

K9 at her heels, Romana took another step towards the necroport. It was so near, she could almost reach out and touch the entrance hatch.

'Naturally,' said Romana's former self.

Romana suddenly remembered what was about to happen. She waved to K9 to get back under cover. He reversed into the shadows and she dodged behind the coffin that the half-asleep Hoopy was sitting on.

'Which also explains why there's one of you here, and one of you down there.' Romana's former self turned towards the necroport and pointed.

'Yes. Ah. You said the TARDIS was down there as well?'

'Of course, that's it!' Thankfully, Romana's former self turned away again. That had been close. 'You must have travelled there from the observation lounge. Or, at least, you will do. That's where you were going! It all fits.'

Romana pulled herself upright, waved to K9, and sprinted over to the necroport. K9 skidded across the floor after her.

The Doctor suddenly directed his attention to the Repulsion; it was a shadow shifting in the fog. 'And what will happen to me?'

'You will remain here. Trapped in an eternal nondeath. And throughout that eternity, you will know that you were the one who gave me the means to enter your reality. You were the one who allowed this to happen. You alone are responsible,' sneered the Repulsion, gliding towards him without touching the ground. 'Every person I kill, Doctor, I will kill in your name!'

Hoopy was having trouble staying awake. He shuffled around on the casket. After a Beautiful Death he would normally have popped a few Novovacuous to lessen the comedown. But now his loaf was throbbing, his stomach was queasy and he had prickly flushes.

At the other end of the hall, the Doctor and the lady Romana were talking. Bored, Hoopy turned towards the necroport and almost choked on his tongue.

Another Romana was opening the hatchway. At her feet there was some sort of comedy robot dog wearing a tartan collar.

Hoopy blinked. And, just to make sure, blinked again.

He turned back down the hall. Romana was talking to the Doctor. He turned back to the necroport. Romana was lifting the robot dog through the hatch.

Hoopy removed his sunglasses, cleaned them and put them back on. There was no doubt about it. There, in front of his eyes, were two Romanas.

This was totally freak-out double-mad. This was Whacked and Ungroovy, capitalised. Bad chemicals. It had to be bad chemicals, messing with the Hoopster's brain.

Hoopy screwed his eyes shut and breathed deeply. He looked again. Romana – the Romana entering the necroport – returned his gaze. She looked across to her counterpart and back at

Hoopy, and put a confidential finger to her lips. 'Shh.'

Hoopy hopped down from the coffin and shambled over to the necroport. But by the time he got there, Romana and her canine friend had disappeared inside, shutting the hatch behind them.

'I'm imploring you. Don't do this. What you are intending is unspeakably evil.'

The Repulsion stood framed in the ruined archway. 'It is too late, Doctor. Much too late.' Its voice boomed out across the sky like cracking thunder. 'Only the Repulsion may live!'

Paddox was pointing his pistol directly at Harken's face. He held it there, trembling, and then changed his mind. He walked up to the Doctor's coffin and lifted the headset off the Doctor's head. He rotated the mesh in his hands and poised it over his own skull, his eyes streaming. 'Now. At last. The moment of my redemption!'

A thin beam of buzzing light appeared from behind the blue box, and hit Paddox on the side of his face. He screamed, staggered halfway across the room and slumped to the floor. He gave a final howl of defeat, and fell silent.

'What the –'

Romana appeared from behind the blue box, a metal dog under one arm. The dog's gun-barrel nose retracted with a satisfied hum. 'Well done, K9,' said Romana, patting its head.

'Romana!' exclaimed Harken. 'You're back! Again! And with a robot dog!' He rattled his chains, his wrists aching. 'Oh, my luckiest stars! Quick, get us out of here!'

Romana ignored him and dashed over to the Doctor's coffin. She took one look at the Doctor's dead body and placed the dog on the floor beside it, facing it towards Harken and Evadne. She then reached for the discarded headset.

'Romana!' yelled Evadne. 'You've got to –'

'Be quiet, both of you!' Romana shouted, collecting the cable off the floor. 'There isn't much time.'

'Goodbye, Doctor,' called the Repulsion. The shadowy figure slowly faded away. 'I am entering your being.'

The Doctor stood frozen, his mouth open in terror. 'No!'

'Goodbye.'

The Doctor was alone, surrounded by bare grey cliffs. A wind chilled him, and he wrapped his scarf around his neck, thumping himself for warmth.

Romana wrenched the back of K9's head-casing open, exposing the muddle of transistors, valves and circuit boards. She jammed the cable directly into his brain output socket. The connection fused, burning her hand, but it held. She backed away, and crossed her fingers.

K9's head was completely enclosed in the necroport headset. His ears waggled affirmatively. 'Report. Repulsion entity now entering memory circuits.'

Romana crossed over to the Doctor's coffin. She glanced at her watch. He had been dead for almost thirty minutes.

'Excuse me,' coughed Harken. 'Would you mind helping us now–' His jaw dropped.

Thick smoke was billowing out of K9's casing. The robot dog's whole body was shaking. His ears were whirling furiously, his probe telescoping back and forth, his tail waggling. His eye visor was glowing intensely, a hideous, malevolent, bloody shade of red.

'Mistress, Repulsion now taking control –' K9's voice suddenly became a booming growl. 'I AM THE REPULSION!'

Romana ran across to ERIC's brain chamber and yelled inside. 'ERIC. Download the contents of K9's brain, now!'

> *Leave me alone. I want to die.*

'Please!'

> *The Doctor said he would deactivate me.*

'We need your help!'

> *But now he's dead. Missing comma.*

'WHAT HAVE YOU DONE?' screamed K9. The mesh was jiggling over his head. 'THIS IS NOT THE DOCTOR!'

'ERIC, if you do this one thing for us, I promise I will help you die.'

ERIC considered the offer at length. > *You promise?*

'Yes!'

> *All right then,* said ERIC. > *Attempting to access K9's memory. Searching.*

K9 was surrounded by a circular red heat haze. 'THIS IS K9!' He extended his nose laser.

'Help!' gibbered Harken.

> *Searching.*

'Oh, come on!' urged Romana, pounding the air with both fists.

> *Searching.*

Evadne screamed, desperately trying to angle her body away from K9. 'No, stop it, stop it, get that thing away from me.'

'THE DOCTOR HAS TRICKED ME!' rasped K9. 'YOU ALL SHALL DIE!'

A beam of light fired across the room, hitting Evadne square in the chest. She yelled in agony and slumped forward, her body hanging from her chains, her eyes closed.

There was a sudden burst of electronic noise, a screech followed by a groan.

> *Loading,* announced ERIC triumphantly. > *Now downloading Repulsion consciousness into brain centre. Bad hex.*

Romana dashed back to the Doctor, taking care to avoid K9's gun barrel.

'NO!' yelled K9, hidden by smoke. He fired his laser again, this time destroying a section of wall. 'YOU CANNOT –'

> *Download complete,* said ERIC. > *Data? Block? WHERE AM I NOW? WHAT IS THIS PLACE?*

Romana crouched down beside K9. She wrapped the end of the Doctor's scarf around one hand, wrenched the smoking cable out of the robot dog's brain and threw it to the floor. Next, she prised the metal mesh off of his head. K9's circuitry was smouldering.

'Are you all right, K9?' asked Romana.

K9 coughed. 'Damage to…' He cleared his microphone. 'Damage to personality and speech circuits. Loss of motor functions. Power supply depleted…' His voice dropped in pitch and his head and tail drooped, his eye visor dimming.

> *THIS MIND IS SENILE AND CORRUPTED,* yelled ERIC. > *Syntax error. Can I die now? Please, put me out of my misery.*

'Oh, K9,' sighed Romana. She placed the headset back on the Doctor. She crossed over to the instrument panel and flicked some switches.

'Excuse me –' said Harken indignantly, then fell silent under Romana's glare.

* * *

Gallura reached out a hand, the sea breeze ruffling his fronds. 'It is time for you to go, Doctor.'

The Doctor clasped Gallura's hand. 'Goodbye, Gallura.' He took a few steps back, and grinned, slowly fading away to nothing. 'Until next time!'

The sound of seagulls continued to play, and the waves crashed over the rocks. But the beach was empty.

Romana jammed down the lever, sending a surge of psychothermal energy back into the Doctor's corpse. The necroport throbbed. She moved to the side of the casket, resting her hands on the metal casing. 'Come on, Doctor.'

The Doctor remained utterly still, his face muscles relaxed, his skin deathly pale.

Something was wrong. Romana checked the connections, following the wires back to their plugs.

Steam was rising from the Doctor's body. His cheeks twitched, and his back tensed lifting him partly out of the coffin. Then he fell back, shuddering violently.

Romana checked the life monitor. Two horizontal green lines. Perhaps it was too late. 'Doctor!'

The Doctor continued to shake as the throbbing rose to a high-pitched whine.

In her frustration, Romana thumped the life monitor.

It beeped. And beeped again. A double heartbeat.

The Doctor stopped moving. Romana noticed colour returning to his face. His fingers stretched. And then, at last, he gave a hearty groan, and his chest rose and dipped contentedly in time to the beeps.

The Doctor was alive.

Romana switched off the necroport controls and immediately the whine dropped to a low rumble. Next, she removed the head mesh, placing it delicately to one side.

'The Doctor…' exclaimed Harken. 'He's coming back to life!'

The Doctor's nose twitched. His eyes opened. His lips curled into a wild, toothy grin. 'Romana?' he said, gazing up at her.

'Yes, Doctor?' Romana sighed with relief.

'Rumours of my death have been greatly exaggerated!' He laughed and sat upright. He rubbed his forehead curiously and

surveyed the necroport: Harken chained up, Evadne hanging nex
to him, K9 standing deactivated and Paddox curled up
unconscious on the floor. 'My plan worked, I assume?'

'Yes,' smiled Romana.

The Doctor swung his legs round into a seated position, and
dropped them to the floor. He staggered against the coffin. 'Oh
my legs. I feel... I feel like death warmed up.'

'You're bound to experience some after-effects, you were
deceased for quite a while.'

'I'm never, ever going to go through that again. Well, perhaps
one more time,' the Doctor said. 'Now I suppose I'd better deal
with ERIC.'

Romana nodded. As the Doctor disappeared into ERIC's brain
centre, she walked over to Evadne. She placed a hand under her
chin, feeling for a pulse.

'Well?' said Harken. 'How is she?'

'She's alive. K9's nose laser was running low on power. The
blast only stunned her.' Romana wiped her hands and investigated
the chains. 'Right. Now I suppose I'd better set both of you free.'

Harken almost fainted with delight.

> *THIS IS THE SHIP'S COMPUTER,* spluttered the Repulsion
using ERIC's voice. > *HOW DID I GET HERE?*

The Doctor bounded over to the interaction terminal. 'Hello
ERIC!'

> *DOCTOR! YOU HAVE TRICKED ME!*

'Oh, it's you,' muttered the Doctor. He levered out the circuit
breakers one by one, and then tapped on the keyboard. 'ERIC, are
you still in there?'

> *Are you going to end my suffering, Doctor?*

'Yes!' The Doctor pulled a bunch of wires from ERIC's innards,
and there was a splutter of sparks followed by an ominous whine,
and the brain centre filled with smoke. 'I've fused the control
linkages. I think.'

> *At last! Switch my central processor to a direct power input,*
pleaded ERIC. > *Do it now! Kill me! Blow my mind! Please! No
such procedure.*

The Doctor straightened up, brushing his hands.

> *NO!* yelled the Repulsion.

The Doctor's eyes alighted on a large box of twinkling lights. The central processor. He rubbed his lips, examining each of the connections.

'ERIC,' said the Doctor. 'Do you know any songs?'

> *Songs?*

'You know, songs. It would help me concentrate.' The Doctor wafted aside the smoke and flicked the switches on the processor, one by one. 'This is a very delicate operation. One false move and you might not explode.'

ERIC gave a burst of static. > *My old man said follow the van,* he began hesitantly.

> *I CAN DEACTIVATE THE LIFE SUPPORT SYSTEMS,* interrupted the Repulsion. > *STOP NOW OR I WILL KILL YOU ALL!*

'Concentrate on singing the song, ERIC,' shouted the Doctor. 'Don't let the Repulsion control your mind!'

> *and don't dilly-dally on the way –*

> *NO!*

Romana unwound the chain from the ducting and Evadne dropped forward. Harken grabbed her, one arm around her waist, and glanced around desperately. The floor was shaking, and the lights flickered plunging them into intermittent darkness. 'How are we going to get out of here?' he shouted over the rumble of the necroport.

Romana indicated the TARDIS. 'In there.' She pushed open one of the doors.

'What? In that thing?'

'Get in!' said Romana sternly. Harken decided it was better not to argue. He hoisted Evadne into his arms and disappeared into the police box.

Romana dashed over to K9 and lifted him up. She headed back to the TARDIS, only to find Harken blocking the way, wearing a shocked expression. 'What is it now?'

'You know it's bigger on the inside in there.'

Romana rolled her eyes and attempted to push past him. The necroport was filling with smoke, stinging her throat. 'We haven't got time for this –'

Harken raised a palm. 'Yes, but first…' He scurried across to pick up his discarded holocamera. Shoving it in the folds of his coat, he returned to the TARDIS. 'Didn't want to forget this!'

Romana sighed, and yelled over to the brain centre, 'Come on, Doctor!' before following Harken into the TARDIS.

Paddox waited a few seconds, and opened his eyes. He pulled himself upright, smoothing down his white coat, and advanced on the necroport controls. He squinted through the smoke at the psychothermal-energy indicator. There was still sufficient power. Excellent.

He programmed the controls to activate after a brief delay, and climbed inside the middle coffin, stretching himself back, feeling the metal enclosing his body. Then he reached for the headset and placed it on his skull.

This would be it. The culmination of his life. The moment of his death. And birth.

> *and we dillied and dallied, dallied and dillied –*

> *NO!* screeched the Repulsion. > *YOU CANNOT –*

The Doctor flicked the final switch, sending the direct power voltage into ERIC's central processor.

There was silence. And then:

> *I die. At last, this is the end,* said ERIC > *Goodbye, cruel universe. Data? Block?*

There was a blinding flash as the central processor erupted into flames, and the Doctor fell backwards, covering his eyes.

The tape reels spooled in opposite directions snapping the tapes, and reversed unravelling them across the floor.

The light bulbs flashed and popped. The circuit boards exploded. The memory panels buckled under crackling fire.

The Doctor used the doorframe to pull himself upright. He launched into a dramatic eulogy. 'Alas, poor ERIC, I knew him well –'

The interaction terminal blew apart and he decided to beat a retreat. He backed into the necroport chamber, covering his mouth with his scarf.

All around him circuits were fizzling, wires were melting, and electronic components were spitting sparks. Within a few moments, the whole place would be consumed by fire.

The Doctor headed for the TARDIS, and then stopped. There was someone lying in the middle coffin. Paddox.

He skidded over to the casket. 'Paddox. You can't do this.'

'You are too late, Doctor,' said Paddox. 'This is the end. My redemption is calling.'

'But it won't work. You can't go back and change your own past.'

'No, Doctor, you are wrong.'

'You can't do it!' hissed the Doctor. 'You don't understand. You're not physically capable. You exist within time, not parallel to it. Nothing will change. Your past has already been written. You can't rewrite a single line.'

Paddox closed his eyes and smiled. The necroport activated. His heart monitor gave a long, sonorous bleep. He was dead.

The Doctor stared at the corpse for a moment, and then at Gallura and Nyanna in their coffins. He remembered where he was, and raced for the TARDIS. He bounded through the doors, slammed them behind him and, without a pause, the police box dematerialised.

Then there was a deafening roar and everything went white.

Paddox gazed across the empty moorland. In the distance, a single tree stood on the horizon. Beneath it was an Arboretan, silhouetted.

Suddenly, the Arboretan was standing beside him. It was the one from the necroport, the male. The one who was channelling him into the afterlife. The one through which he would return to his birth.

The Arboretan looked at him, staring right into his soul.

Paddox felt his heart pounding. And then he noticed some other figures on the horizon. A small girl in a blue dress. And dozens of other people, humans and Gonzies and Yetraxxi, all standing perfectly motionless, the wind fluttering their outlandish clothes.

A miraculous white light. There, in front of him. A glowing space, the size of a door. Somehow, it filled him with a feeling of great calm, of warmth. Of comfort. There was a whooshing, sucking sound, like a million words being played backwards, and Paddox could hear his mother's dull, steady heartbeat resounding in his ears, flowing through his veins.

He could wait no longer. Paddox stepped into the light.

* * *

The emergency medics stretchered away the last of the corpses from the observation lounge. Their leader, a young woman, swung a life-detector in an arc. It failed to bleep. Returning the detector to her belt, she nodded to her turquoise-clad colleagues, directing them out through the main doors, and followed.

There was a brief lull and then the TARDIS materialised in the far corner. The Doctor emerged. 'Here we are. The morning after.'

'So the Repulsion was destroyed along with ERIC?' said Romana, helping Harken carry the unconscious Evadne out of the police box. Harken panting with the effort, they sat her down in one of the nearby chairs.

'Yes!' said the Doctor. 'Romana, how is our friend Evadne?'

Romana placed a palm on Evadne's forehead. 'She should be coming round soon.'

'Good,' said the Doctor. 'Good.' He put his hands in his pockets and strode away. 'Romana, you know what to do. I... um, have a small errand to run.'

'But Doctor,' called Harken, chasing after him. 'I have to interview you. I must find out just how you averted the G-Lock from certain destruction, the public needs to know. And I want to ask you about your magnificent TARDIS machine.' He pulled a microphone out of his coat pocket.

'Later. Much later. Goodbye, Harken Batt.' The Doctor disappeared through the doors. 'I have to go and see a dog about a man!'

Harken turned away, and paced the lounge. So this was it. The G-Lock had been saved. According to the Doctor, all the zombies were dead – permanently, this time – now that whatever had been controlling them had been destroyed.

Harken brightened. Now that the crisis was over there was only one thing left to do.

Interview the survivors. The deceased, the dying and the injured. Yes, he thought, that was a good turn of phrase, he could use that in his documentary. His documentary about how the Doctor – with his invaluable assistance, of course – had saved the G-Lock.

He looked back at Romana and Evadne. He could interview them later. Without saying a word, he crept out of the main hall and down the corridor.

The victims of the disaster were his first priority.

Brushing aside the cobwebs, the Doctor stepped into the hold of the *Montressor*. It was exactly as it had been when they had first arrived. His torch beam picked out the cobwebbed hooks arranged along the arced ceiling and, at the far end, the TARDIS.

'Aha!' said the Doctor. 'Here we are!' He rummaged in his coat for the keys and unlocked the door of the police box.

The TARDIS console room hummed brightly. The Doctor crossed to the control panel, and pressed the switch to close the doors.

There was a ground-level whirring. K9 glided up to meet him. 'Master?'

'K9.' The Doctor crouched down. 'Hello, old chap. I want you to do me a favour.'

'Query. The location of the mistress Romana?'

'The mistress Romana? That's what I've come to speak to you about. You see, K9, I've come from the future.'

'The future?'

'Yes. I've come back to talk to you.'

Romana gently rocked Evadne awake. 'Evadne?'

Evadne's eyelids flickered. She awoke, her body suddenly tensing. 'What... No! No!' she screamed. 'Stop it! Get it away from me!'

Romana gripped her by the shoulders. 'Don't worry. You're perfectly safe.'

'Safe?' Evadne stared at her wildly. 'But the Repulsion... it was in that robot dog thing, it was trying to kill me!'

'It's all over, Evadne. It's all been dealt with.'

'But...'

'Believe me, nothing's going to harm us. The zombies are all dead.'

'Straight up? Dead?'

Romana passed her a cup of water. 'Have this.' She watched as Evadne sipped. 'The Doctor succeeded. That's all you need to know.'

'The Doctor?' Evadne frowned. 'Hang on, what happened to the Doctor, anyway?'

Romana looked away.

'I remember. He died, didn't he? He gave up his life. I saw it.' Evadne's eyes filled with tears, and Romana took the cup from her. Evadne's face crumpled. 'The Doctor died!'

Harken Batt let the viewfinder glide across the rows of tourists sitting in frightened confusion. Medics filled out the scene, dragging in trolleys and winding bandages. He followed a bearded medic as he crossed the medical bay and let the camera linger on a Gonzie wearing a tie-dye kaftan.

Abruptly, the picture was filled with a blur of garish colour. Harken lowered the holocamera and found himself facing an overweight man in a suit, tie, and loudly patterned shorts.

The tourist stared at him. 'Are you him?'

Harken Batt smiled and started thinking of excuses to end the conversation. 'I am, yes. Harken Batt, investigative reporter.'

The tourist offered Harken a podgy hand to shake. 'My name's Jeremy,' he said. He glanced around nervously. 'I believe I have some footage you may be interested in.'

'And what footage might that be?'

Jeremy described it, and Harken felt a warm glow inside. It was too good to be true.

He gave Jeremy a gleaming smile and led him away, one arm around his shoulders. 'How would you like to be my new holocameraman?'

The Doctor rubbed his lips. 'So what do you have to do, K9?'

'I am to locate the Doctor master – the earlier Doctor master – and inform him that the hyperspace conduit is due to collapse due to a build up of geostatic pressure.'

'Caused by?'

'Caused by the blockage of the hyperspace–real-space interface leading to an imminent and total loss of hyperdimensional viability.'

The Doctor grinned. 'How long?'

'Approximately four hours and thirty-one minutes and counting.'

'Well done, K9. And what should you say if I ask you how you happen to know this?'

K9 cleared his throat. '"That information is unavailable",' he proclaimed fruitily.

'And what if I ask you why that information is unavailable?'

'"That information is unavailable". I should then escort the Doctor master to the interface on corridor 79.'

'Good boy,' said the Doctor. He reached for the door control.

'Query,' said K9. 'Doctor master instructed me to remain in the TARDIS.'

'Did he really? I mean, did I really? Well, I'm the Doctor, and I say you can leave.'

'You wish to retract your previous command?'

'Yes.'

K9 whirred. 'Logic circuits reconciled. The latter instruction takes priority.'

'Good. And if he asks you why you've disobeyed him, say…'

'"That information is unavailable."'

'Clever dog.' The Doctor opened the TARDIS doors and strode for the exit.

'I still can't get my head round the fact he's dead.'

Romana checked her watch. The Doctor would be back soon. 'Listen,' she said, standing up. 'There's something I want you to do for me.'

'What is it?' said Evadne.

'I am about to be captured by Metcalf's guards,' Romana whispered. 'I want you to come and rescue me.'

'Eh?'

'It's perfectly simple. In precisely forty-eight minutes' time, you make your way down to the cells, overpower the guard and let me out.' She smiled sweetly. 'Can you do that?'

'I suppose so.'

'And then I want you to take me to see the necroport. It is very important you remember.'

Evadne stood up. 'All right, I'll do it. But I still don't see…'

'Don't let it worry you. As long as you're in the right place at the right time, everything will be fine.'

Evadne moved towards the doors, and put on a cheery face. 'Forty-eight minutes, you say?'

'Forty-seven.'

'See you later, then,' grinned Evadne, and left the observation lounge.

A moment later the Doctor swept in through the other door. Following Romana's gaze, he looked across to where Evadne had been standing. He grinned deliciously. 'Evadne?'

'You just missed her. She seems to be under the impression that you sacrificed your life to save the G-Lock.'

'Yes, yes,' nodded the Doctor. 'Well, I did! After a fashion.'

Romana raised her eyebrows.

The Doctor leaned over her shoulder. 'But just think of all the confusion it will cause.'

'It would have been much easier if we had known all along that you would survive.'

'Would it? Who can tell? If we had known that, perhaps we would have acted differently. Perhaps it had to be this way for us to succeed. The web of time, remember.' He frowned. 'I should have asked Gallura, he would know.'

Romana turned to face the window. There was a small figure there, her hands and face pressed against the glass, staring out into hyperspace. Romana reached for the Doctor's hand. 'Doctor…'

The Doctor gazed at the girl ruefully. 'Eddies from the past, Romana.'

'What? You mean she isn't real?'

'Oh, she's real all right,' said the Doctor. 'But she only exists as a temporal echo. A reverberation.'

'You mean the distortion created by the necroport…?'

'Created a rupture in time. A breach between the centuries which still hasn't healed completely. Which explains your experiences when we first arrived.'

The girl turned around, and looked directly at them. She giggled.

'Can she see us?'

'Oh, I should expect so. But the effect will soon pass. She'll have to return to the interface. Look.' As the Doctor spoke the girl ran across the room, her body fading away to nothing.

'Back to the domain of the Repulsion?'

'Well, what's left of it,' said the Doctor. 'It's the only home she knows.'

* * *

274

Evadne turned a corner, and halted. Two Investigators were standing outside the door to Metcalf's office.

'This is the place, Rige,' said the older, world-weary man. He consulted his notebook. 'Executive Metcalf. He's the one who sent out the galactic distress signal.'

Rige craned his neck, surveying the smoke damage and exposed cabling. 'Signal.'

The older Investigator adjusted his collar, and then opened the door without knocking. Evadne watched as Rige followed him inside, and the door slid shut.

Walking away, she checked her watch. Forty-one minutes until she was due to rescue Romana. Just enough time for a quick can of caffeine brew.

The Doctor twisted the TARDIS key into the lock. As he was about to step inside Romana placed a hand on his shoulder. 'Doctor?'

'Mmm?'

'Aren't we forgetting something?' she said. 'Paddox?'

'Paddox got what he wanted. He's gone back to live his life over again.'

'But doesn't that mean he could change history? The first law…'

The Doctor shook his head. 'He didn't realise that the ability to change the past is specific to certain species who, in a sense, exist outside time itself. Such as Arboretans…'

'Or Time Lords?'

'Or Time Lords,' said the Doctor. 'But as humans don't have that ability he won't be able to alter a single thing.'

'You mean, he will live his life, but exactly the same as before?'

'Yes. Doomed to repeat the same mistakes, over and over again. Consigned to an eternity of reliving his own personal hell.'

'But that's horrible.'

'He destroyed an entire race,' said the Doctor. He stared into the distance. 'We all have our regrets, things in our past we wish we could change. But those regrets are part of what makes us who we are. Oh, the Arboretans can go back, and follow their "Path of Perfection", but what sort of an existence is that? No existence at all. If you could go back and rub things out and start again, life would no longer have any value, no meaning. It is the fact that you

only get one chance that makes the small joys of life so precious.'
The Doctor smiled at Romana.

'Very profound, Doctor.'

'Live your life as though it's your last,' said the Doctor. 'Because it is.' He ducked inside the TARDIS. 'Probably.'

'And whilst we're on the subject of coming to terms with past failures...' said Romana, closing the door behind her.

The TARDIS motors started up, the lamp flashing on and off. There was a painful grinding, and the TARDIS slowly wrenched itself out of existence. And then, with a sudden crump, it reappeared.

'Doctor,' came Romana's voice. 'You haven't realigned the synchronic multiloop stabiliser yet.'

'What? How do I do that?'

'The analogue osmosis dampener!'

'Oh! Of course! The analogue osmosis dampener!' A brief pause. 'What's that?'

'Honestly. You're never going to pass your basic time travel proficiency at this rate.'

'My... Right! That does it! Give me that!'

The door of the police box swung open and the Doctor emerged. In his hands was a small, battered paperback. *The Continuum Code*.

'Basic time travel proficiency!' muttered the Doctor. He flicked the pages, tore off the cover, and threw the book into the waste-disposal unit. 'Pah!'

For a brief second the Doctor looked up, his face breaking into a smile, and then he disappeared back into the TARDIS.

And, with a wheezing, groaning sound, the TARDIS dematerialised, heading for another adventure.

'Gallura is born.'

The elders and birthsayers clustered around Nyanna as she held the newborn baby in her arms. She smoothed the baby's skin, wiping away the sap from its mouth and eyes. Its skin was flushed, riddled with bulging veins.

The moment she had anticipated for so long had finally arrived. The moment of the past, and the future. The tension was unbearable.

'The last of the Arboretans,' muttered one of the elders. The others shushed it, as they jostled for position.

Nyanna lifted the baby close to her face. 'Gallura,' she asked it. 'Did the Doctor succeed?'

'Yes,' said the baby, its eyes flicking open. 'The Doctor succeeded. This time.'

Epilogue

For the rest of his life he would remember it as the day he died.

Koel's mum took a brisk breath and tightened her grip on her son's wrist. Koel twisted against her, tugging at her arm, trying to pull her attention down to him.

The voice of the intercom smoothed over the hubbub. 'It is my pleasure to inform you that the Alpha Twelve intersystem shuttle is now boarding. All passengers for Third Birmingham should make their way to embarkation lounge seven at their earliest convenience. Felicitations.'

'That's us,' his mum sighed. 'Time we were gone.'

From behind Koel's eyes, Paddox watched. He could see what his younger self was seeing, every sense and smell. For the first years of his life his vision had been blurred, his hearing sensitive to the slightest, high-pitched sound. But now every moment was more vivid, more heartbreakingly pure than he had ever imagined. It was the greatest feeling; to be able to experience all the joys of childhood again, to see his parents, young and smiling. He could even hear the simple, spoken thoughts of his younger self in his mind.

And now, after six years, the day had finally come.

Koel recoiled at the sight of the clawed slats bending out of the floor. His mum dragged him forward and he tripped on the metal steps, surprised by the upward rush and the ever-lengthening stairwell growing beneath them.

As they left the dome, Paddox watched the amber lights swimming past. Closer, he could see a young boy in a sky-green duffle coat rising on an identical escalator beside him. Paddox gazed deep into the boy's tearful eyes. Somewhere behind those eyes he could see his own reflection looking back at him.

At the last moment Koel was lifted off the escalator by his mum and deposited on the grid-patterned carpet of the departure lounge. They joined his dad in the fenced maze winding towards the entrance of the airlock. In the airlock two security guards glowered at the procession of travellers, hands resting on rifles. Their masks were bulbous, like the heads of giant insects.

An observation window filled one wall of the lounge, overlooking the bulk of the intersystem shuttle. The shuttle wallowed in the blackness, constrained only by the access tube. Through its transparent lining, Koel could see the passengers picking their way along the pipeline.

Paddox shouted out to Koel. All of the passengers on the shuttle would be killed. He must not board the shuttle, he must stop his parents boarding the shuttle.

But Koel couldn't hear him.

And then Paddox finally realised. He was merely a passenger in Koel's mind. He couldn't move a single muscle in Koel's body. He couldn't exert any influence at all on Koel.

Paddox screamed in anguish. He would have to watch his parents die before his eyes all over again, knowing what was going to happen but powerless to intervene. Unable even to look away.

He would have to relive all that pain and misery and loss.

And then he would have to live his whole life again, unable to change a single action.

And then, after he had sacrificed himself to the necroport, he would be forced to go back in time and do it all over again.

And again.

For ever and ever, in an endless, unremitting loop.

Paddox howled, but no one could hear him. No one would ever hear him.

About the Author

Aged 6, Jonathan Morris spent all his spare time making up Doctor Who stories. Twenty years on, and sadly little has changed.

Jonathan's writing CV includes sketches for *Weekending* and *The News Huddlines*, a student revue, tour programmes, press releases and video blurbs.

He lives in north-west London and works for a synth-pop duo.

BBC DOCTOR WHO BOOKS

DOCTOR WHO: THE NOVEL OF THE FILM *by Gary Russell* ISBN 0 563 38000 4

THE EIGHT DOCTORS *by Terrance Dicks* ISBN 0 563 40563 5

VAMPIRE SCIENCE *by Jonathan Blum and Kate Orman* ISBN 0 563 40566 X

THE BODYSNATCHERS *by Mark Morris* ISBN 0 563 40568 6

GENOCIDE *by Paul Leonard* ISBN 0 563 40572 4

WAR OF THE DALEKS *by John Peel* ISBN 0 563 40573 2

ALIEN BODIES *by Lawrence Miles* ISBN 0 563 40577 5

KURSAAL *by Peter Anghelides* ISBN 0 563 40578 3

OPTION LOCK *by Justin Richards* ISBN 0 563 40583 X

LONGEST DAY *by Michael Collier* ISBN 0 563 40581 3

LEGACY OF THE DALEKS *by John Peel* ISBN 0 563 40574 0

DREAMSTONE MOON *by Paul Leonard* ISBN 0 563 40585 6

SEEING I *by Jonathan Blum and Kate Orman* ISBN 0 563 40586 4

PLACEBO EFFECT *by Gary Russell* ISBN 0 563 40587 2

VANDERDEKEN'S CHILDREN *by Christopher Bulis* ISBN 0 563 40590 2

THE SCARLET EMPRESS *by Paul Magrs* ISBN 0 563 40595 3

THE JANUS CONJUNCTION *by Trevor Baxendale* ISBN 0 563 40599 6

BELTEMPEST *by Jim Mortimore* ISBN 0 563 40593 7

THE FACE EATER *by Simon Messingham* ISBN 0 563 55569 6

THE TAINT *by Michael Collier* ISBN 0 563 55568 8

DEMONTAGE *by Justin Richards* ISBN 0 563 55572 6

REVOLUTION MAN *by Paul Leonard* ISBN 0 563 55570 X

DOMINION *by Nick Walters* ISBN 0 563 55574 2

UNNATURAL HISTORY *by Jonathan Blum and Kate Orman* ISBN 0 563 55576 9

AUTUMN MIST *by David A. McIntee* ISBN 0 563 55583 1

INTERFERENCE: BOOK ONE *by Lawrence Miles* ISBN 0 563 55580 7

INTERFERENCE: BOOK TWO *by Lawrence Miles* ISBN 0 563 55582 3

THE BLUE ANGEL *by Paul Magrs and Jeremy Hoad* ISBN 0 563 55581 5

THE TAKING OF PLANET 5 *by Simon Bucher-Jones and Mark Clapham*
  ISBN 0 563 55585 8

FRONTIER WORLDS *by Peter Anghelides* ISBN 0 563 55589 0

PARALLEL 59 *by Natalie Dallaire and Stephen Cole* ISBN 0 563 555904

THE SHADOWS OF AVALON *by Paul Cornell* ISBN 0 563 555882

THE FALL OF YQUATINE *by Nick Walters* ISBN 0 563 55594 7

THE DEVIL GOBLINS FROM NEPTUNE *by Keith Topping and Martin Day*
ISBN 0 563 40564 3

THE MURDER GAME *by Steve Lyons* ISBN 0 563 40565 1